ACCESS
DENIED

Bailey switched on the computer and fed in his personal code. The words ACCESS DENIED flashed across the screen. For a moment he wondered if somehow the access code had been tampered with by a professional hacker. But even if the code had been altered, he could press the "9" button which would automatically cancel the whole program.

Bailey pressed each key carefully then immediately put his finger lightly on the "9," just in case he did need to use it. ACCESS DENIED. The door sealed behind him and the ten-second countdown began flashing on the screen. He pressed the "9" frantically. Someone had overridden it. He kicked over the chair and ran to the door, banging furiously on it. But the whole room was soundproofed. Nobody could hear him. He looked round at the screen again. The countdown finished and the word ACTIVATE began flashing across the screen. A jet of nerve gas streamed from the nozzle of the canister built into the wall directly above the door. He stumbled away and fell to the floor . . .

ALISTAIR MacLEAN'S
TIME OF THE ASSASSINS

ALASTAIR MacNEILL

HarperPaperbacks
A Division of HarperCollins*Publishers*

This is a work of fiction. The characters, incidents, and dialogues are products of the author's imagination and are not to be construed as real. Any resemblance to actual events or persons, living or dead, is entirely coincidental.

HarperPaperbacks *A Division of* HarperCollins*Publishers*
10 East 53rd Street, New York, N.Y. 10022

A hardcover edition of this book was published in 1991 in Great Britain by HarperCollins*Publishers*.

Cover illustration by Danilo

First HarperPaperbacks printing: July 1993

Printed in the United States of America

HarperPaperbacks and colophon are trademarks of HarperCollins*Publishers*

10 9 8 7 6 5 4 3 2 1

PROLOGUE

On an undisclosed date in September 1979 the Secretary-General of the United Nations chaired an extraordinary meeting attended by forty-six envoys who represented virtually every country in the world. There was only one point on the agenda: the escalating tide of international crime. Criminals and terrorists were able to strike in one country then flee across its borders, secure in the knowledge that pursuit would breach the sovereignty of neighboring states. Furthermore, drafting extradition warrants (at least for those countries that had them) was both costly and time-consuming and many contained loopholes that lawyers could exploit to secure their clients' release. A solution had to be found.

It was agreed to set up an international strike force to operate under the aegis of the United Nations' Security Council. It would be known as the United Nations Anti-Crime Organization (UNACO). Its objective was to "avert, neutralize and/or apprehend individuals or groups engaged in international criminal activities"*. Each envoy then submitted a curriculum vitae of a candidate their Government considered suitable for the position of UNACO Director, and the Secretary-General made the final choice.

UNACO's clandestine existence came into being on 1 March 1980.

---

*UNACO charter, article I, paragraph 1c.

◆ CHAPTER
ONE

It was dark by the time he reached his destination. He got out of the taxi, paid the driver, then wiped the sweat from his forehead with the back of his hand. He had forgotten how humid it could get in Beirut at that time of year. He waited until the taxi had driven off before crossing the road to the Windorah, a small bar run by Dave Jenkins, an Australian who had named it after his birthplace in Queensland. Well, he assumed Jenkins still ran it. He hadn't been back to Beirut in four years. He pushed open the door and went inside. Nothing had changed. The two large propeller fans still rotated slowly above the room, the prostitutes still mingled with the foreign journalists and Jenkins was still behind the counter. Their eyes met.

Jenkins shook his head in disbelief. "Well, I'll be damned. Mike Graham. What the hell brings you back to Beirut?"

"Business," Graham answered, his eyes flickering slowly around the room.

"Lookin' for somebody?"

"Yeah."

"Russell Laidlaw?"

Graham turned back to Jenkins, his eyes narrowed. "He told you I was coming?"

Jenkins shook his head. "An educated guess, that's all. He's the only old friend of yours I know who comes in here every night. What time did he say he'd meet you?"

"Eight," Graham replied, glancing at his watch. It was seven fifty.

"That's when he usually gets here. You want a beer while you wait?"

Although Graham rarely touched alcohol, he could do with a beer in the heat. "If it's cold."

"Comin' up," Jenkins replied then bent down to open one of the fridges under the counter.

A prostitute caught Graham's eye but he shook his head before she could get off her bar stool. She gave him an indifferent look then turned her attention to another potential customer.

"One Budweiser, ice cold," Jenkins said, placing the bottle and a glass in front of Graham. He held up a hand when Graham reached for his wallet. "It's on me, Mike."

"Thanks," Graham said, forcing a quick smile.

"I was real sorry to hear about what happened to your family, Mike—"

"I'll be over there," Graham cut in sharply and indicated an empty table in the corner of the room. "Tell Russell when he gets here."

"Sure," Jenkins replied but Graham had already gone. He shrugged then turned his attention to a new customer at the other end of the counter.

Graham crossed to the table and sat down. He was thirty-eight years old with a youthfully handsome face, tousled auburn hair that hung untidily over the collar of his open-necked white shirt and a sturdy, muscular physique which he kept in shape with a daily five-kilometer run followed by a punishing workout in his own private gymnasium.

He had been with UNACO for two years and, despite his maverick tendencies, he was widely regarded by his peers as the best field operative in the organization. It hadn't always been that way. He was the first to admit that he had been psychologically screwed-up when he joined them after eleven years with the élite American anti-terrorist squad, Delta—a state of mind that had come about as a result of his last Delta mission. The mission had been to penetrate a terrorist base in Libya and eliminate all personnel, which included Salim Al-Makesh, an advisor to the Black June, a movement founded by Abu Nidal in 1976 in protest at the involvement of Syria in the Lebanese civil war, and Jean-Jacques Bernard, a senior member of the Popular Front for the Liberation of Palestine. He was about to give the order to advance when news reached him that his wife and five-year-old son had been abducted by three masked men outside their apartment in New York. The men spoke Arabic. It had been an attempt to force him to withdraw. He refused and although the base was destroyed, Al-Makesh and Bernard managed to escape. The FBI immediately launched a nation-wide hunt for his family but no trace of them was ever found.

A month later Al-Makesh was killed by Israeli commandos at his home in Damascus. Bernard went into hiding and was only heard of again when news reached the Israeli Mossad that he had been assassinated in a car-bomb attack in Beirut. The information had come from a reliable source and they had no reason to doubt it. Graham remained unconvinced. It had been too easy. Then, the previous day, he received a telephone call that vindicated his years of skepticism . . .

Laidlaw entered the bar, looked around slowly, then crossed to where Graham was sitting. Graham could hardly believe how much Laidlaw had changed since he had last seen him when they were both still with

Delta. Laidlaw had always been the unit's fitness fanatic, pushing himself to the limit to keep his lean, muscular body in shape. And he had always been so meticulous about his appearance, almost to the point of vanity. Now he was overweight with a bloated, unshaven face and his unwashed brown hair fell untidily onto his hunched shoulders.

Graham rose to his feet and shook Laidlaw's extended hand. The grip was still firm. He indicated the chair opposite and sat down again.

"I'm just going to get myself a beer. I won't be a moment," Laidlaw said, indicating the counter behind him.

Graham pushed his untouched bottle across the table. "Have this one. I don't want it."

Laidlaw picked up the bottle then pulled out the chair and sat down. "You're looking well, Mike," he said at length.

"You're not," Graham replied bluntly. "Christ, Russ, what the hell's happened to you?"

Laidlaw poured out his beer then sat back and exhaled deeply. "It's a long story, Mike. I'll tell you about it sometime." He drank a mouthful of beer then placed the glass on the table. "How was the flight from New York?"

"Fine," Graham replied brusquely then sat forward, his arms resting on the table. "Have you found out any more about Bernard?"

Laidlaw shook his head. "Nothing came of the enquiries I made this morning. I did see him, Mike. He's changed, though. The beard and long hair have gone. I had to take a long, hard look at him before I was sure. But it was him, I'd stake my life on it."

"I wouuldn't be here if I didn't believe you," Graham replied softly. "So what's our next move?"

"Barak."

Graham frowned. "Nazar Barak?"

Laidlaw nodded. "He's the best informer Delta's

ever had in Beirut. I still see him about. If anyone knows where Bernard is, then it'll be Barak."

"Why didn't you speak to him this morning?"

Laidlaw drank another mouthful of beer. "You try pinning him down at such short notice. He'll be at home tonight about nine. I have that from a reliable source."

"I'm just amazed he's still around. I thought someone would have put a bullet in his back by now."

"He knows too much. And it's all written down and stored away in some bank vault in the city."

"You're joking," Graham muttered.

"That's the story he's put around. I doubt it's true but it's certainly worked. Nobody's called his bluff."

"Yet," Graham added.

Laidlaw smiled wryly then drank the remainder of the beer. He wiped the back of his hand across his mouth then stood up. "If we get to the house early we can grab him when he arrives. It's the only way we'll get to talk to him tonight."

Graham gave Jenkins a wave then followed Laidlaw out into the street.

Barak's house turned out to be a small bungalow in West Beirut, less than a mile away from the Mar Elias Camp. It was in darkness. Laidlaw drove past it and pulled up at the end of the dirt road. He switched off the engine then reached into his pocket for his cigarettes and lit the third one since leaving the Windorah. Graham climbed from the car and instinctively ducked as a mortar exploded in the distance. When he straightened up he saw Laidlaw looking at him across the roof of the car, a faint smile on his lips.

"You get used to it," Laidlaw said, closing the door behind him.

"I don't know how you can live here," Graham said then winced as another explosion rocked the night.

"It's become a part of me. I could never leave. You only see the negative side of Beirut on the news back home. There's a lot more to it than that . . ." Laidlaw trailed off when a car suddenly came into view at the other end of the dimly lit street.

Graham looked toward Laidlaw for confirmation that it was Barak. Laidlaw shielded his eyes against the glare of the headlights, trying to distinguish the make and color of the car. A green Peugeot. He nodded then dropped his cigarette and ground it underfoot.

Barak parked in front of the house and climbed out of the car, locking the door behind him. He was a short, fat man in his early fifties with greasy black hair and thick pebble glasses. The passenger door opened and an aging prostitute got out.

"Having a party, Barak?"

Barak swung round then let out a deep sigh when Laidlaw emerged from the shadows of an oak tree on the other side of the road. "You startled me, Mr. Laidlaw," he said breathlessly in English and clamped his hand over his heart as if to emphasize the point. "What are you doing here?"

"We need to talk."

"We can talk tomorrow," Barak replied then glanced lasciviously at the prostitute. "I am busy tonight."

"You *were* busy tonight," Laidlaw corrected him. "Get rid of her."

A look of concern crossed Barak's face. "I have already paid her for tonight."

"You'll be reimbursed."

The prostitute, who didn't speak English, demanded to know what was happening.

Barak managed to pacify her then turned back to Laidlaw. "She will need money for a taxi back to the city."

"Then give it to her," Laidlaw said.

"Me?" Barak replied in horror. "Why should I pay her?"

"I've told you, you'll be reimbursed," Laidlaw snapped angrily. "Now pay her and get her out of here."

Barak pulled a roll of banknotes from his jacket pocket, reluctantly peeled off a couple and handed them to the prostitute. She snatched them from him, cursed angrily at them both, then strode off in search of a taxi.

Laidlaw waited until the prostitute was out of sight then nodded to Graham who had been standing by the tree. Barak's eyes widened in amazement as Graham approached them. He looked at Laidlaw, searching for an answer. Laidlaw said nothing.

"Still as tight as ever, Barak," Graham said, indicating the notes in Barak's hand.

Barak instinctively stuffed them back into his pocket then rubbed his hands together nervously. "What are you doing back in Beirut, Mr. Graham?"

"Let's go inside," Graham said, gesturing toward the house.

Barak led them up a narrow concrete path to the unpainted door and opened it. He beckoned them inside and immediately closed the door behind him. He showed them into the lounge and drew the threadbare curtains before switching on the light. The room was unpainted and the only furniture consisted of a lime green sofa, two wooden chairs and a three-legged coffee table which was propped up against the wall to prevent it from toppling over.

"This is very irregular," Barak said at length. "I never do business at my house. You know that, Mr. Laidlaw. Why did you come here? If anyone saw you—"

"Nobody saw us," Graham snapped.

Barak's eyes shifted from Laidlaw to Graham. "Why are you here?"

"Bernard."

Barak scratched his stubbled chin then sat on the edge of the sofa. "Jean-Jacques Bernard?"

"Yeah."

"But he is dead. He died—"

"I saw him outside the American University Hospital yesterday morning," Laidlaw cut in quickly. "He's changed his appearance but it was Bernard."

"You must have been mistaken," Barak replied, shaking his head. "Bernard is dead."

"If Russell says he saw Bernard yesterday then that's good enough for me," Graham said sharply.

Barak removed his glasses and rubbed his eyes wearily. "I knew Bernard well. Do you not think I would know if he was still alive, especially if he was living here in Beirut?"

"I didn't say he was living here," Laidlaw replied. "He could be here on business. But it was Bernard."

Graham took an envelope from his pocket and tossed it onto the sofa. "There's five-thousand dollars there, in cash. Find Bernard and I'll double it."

Barak opened the envelope and fanned the banknotes with his finger. He looked across at Graham. "Why do you want Bernard so badly?"

"That doesn't concern you. Find him and you'll get the rest of the money."

"Where are you staying?" Barak asked Graham.

"You call me if you find out anything," Laidlaw said. "Any time, day or night."

Barak nodded then pushed the envelope into his pocket. "I still say you are wasting your time. Bernard is dead."

"For his sake, I hope you're right," Graham said softly then followed Laidlaw down the hallway and out into the night.

Barak waited until Laidlaw and Graham had driven off then got into his own car and drove straight to a white,

Spanish-styled mansion on the outskirts of the city, overlooking the sea. He drew up in front of a pair of wrought-iron gates where he was immediately challenged by a bearded man wearing jeans and a faded black T-shirt. A kalashnikov AK-47 was slung over his shoulder.

"I must see Mr. Devereux right away," Barak announced through the open driver's window.

The guard eyed him contemptuously. "Is Mr. Devereux expecting you?"

"No, but it's urgent."

The guard glanced in the direction of the house. "Mr. Devereux gave specific instructions not to be disturbed."

"Tell him it's Barak—"

"I know who you are," the guard said with obvious disdain. "Come back in the morning. Maybe then Mr. Devereux will see you."

"I must see him now!" Barak retorted.

The guard unslung the kalashnikov. "I told you, Mr. Devereux isn't to be disturbed tonight."

Barak glared at the guard. "Mr. Devereux's life is in danger. If anything happens to him then I'll see to it that you're held personally responsible."

The guard wavered. "What danger?"

"I'll tell that to Mr. Devereux, when I get to see him."

The guard turned away from the car and spoke softly into a two-way radio. A minute later the gates were activated from somewhere inside the grounds.

The guard peered through the window at Barak. "Follow the road to the courtyard. Someone will be waiting there to meet you."

Barak put the Peugeot into gear and drove the hundred yards to the courtyard. He pulled up in front of the stone steps and got out of the car. Another guard frisked him expertly then led him up the steps into the house. Barak looked around the spacious hallway in awe. The three-tier Czechoslovakian crystal chandelier was the only reminder of its once resplendent grandeur. He could imagine that the walls had once been lined with an array of expensive paintings or tapestries and the wooden floorboards covered with elegant, sculpted carpeting.

"The house once belonged to a Turkish prince when the Lebanon was still a part of the Ottoman Empire," a man said, tying the belt of his white dressing-gown as he descended the stairs. He was a tall, handsome man in his late thirties with short black hair, which was already beginning to gray at the temples, and a neatly trimmed black moustache. A faint scar ran the length of his left cheek. He reached the foot of the stairs and looked around him slowly. "Some would call it beautiful," he said, still speaking Arabic. "All I see is decadence."

"I'm sorry to disturb you like this, Mr. Devereux—"

The man held up a hand to silence Barak then turned to the guard beside him and dismissed him with a curt nod of the head. He waited until he had left then ushered Barak into a small study. "I told you never to come here!"

"I had no choice," Barak replied defensively. "I had to speak to you in person."

"What is it?"

Barak shifted uneasily on his feet. "You've been recognized, Mr. Bernard."

Bernard dug his hands into the pockets of his dressing-gown and moved to the window where he stared across the lawn at the empty swimming pool. He finally turned back to Barak. "Who recognized me?"

"An American, Russell Laidlaw."

Bernard pondered the name then shook his head. "I don't know him. Who is he? A journalist?"

Barak shook his head. "He used to be with Delta. He lives here now. But he's not your problem. There was another man with him, Mike Graham. He offered me ten-thousand dollars to find you for him. This has got something to do with the murder of his family, hasn't it? Were you involved?"

Bernard ignored the questions. "Where's he staying?"

"He didn't say. I'm to contact Laidlaw if I come up with anything."

Bernard took a cigarette from the pack on the table and lit it. He exhaled thoughtfully then sat in the armchair in the corner of the room. "Tell Graham you've made some enquiries and that you've come up with something. Arrange to meet him at your house later tonight."

"My house?" Barak stammered. "I don't want to get involved—"

"You're already involved," Bernard cut in sharply. He smiled coldly. "Don't worry, I won't kill Graham there. I can't have the police finding any clues at your house. You don't have the guile to talk your way out of it."

Barak knew it would be futile to argue. "What time?" he asked with a resigned sigh.

"Midnight. That gives me plenty of time to make the necessary arrangements. But don't call him until eleven thirty. That way it will look as if you've been asking around about me."

Barak rubbed his hands together nervously. "What about the extra five-thousand dollars Graham would have paid me?"

Bernard stubbed out the cigarette and got to his feet. "Everything you do has to have a price, doesn't it?"

Barak stepped backwards, his eyes flickering between Bernard and the floor. "I have to make a living . . ."

"You make more money than most people in this town," Bernard snapped.

Barak swallowed nervously. "I think I should go now. We can discuss the money another time."

Bernard grabbed the front of Barak's shirt and

slammed him up against the wall. "You're paid a retainer every month to keep me informed on developments in and around Beirut. I don't know how you negotiate your other deals, nor do I want to, but you can be sure you're not going to get another cent out of me. Is that understood?"

Barak nodded his head vigorously and Bernard let go of his shirt. Barak dabbed his face with a dirty handkerchief, his eyes wide with fear.

"And don't even think about trying to double-cross me. You know what Hezbollah would do to you if anything were to happen to me?"

"I would never double-cross you, Mr. Bernard—"

"Devereux!" Bernard snapped angrily. "How many times must I tell you? Jean-Jacques Bernard is dead. I'm now Alain Devereux."

"I'm sorry, Mr. Devereux. It's just force of habit."

Bernard gestured toward the door. "Get out."

Barak left the room, leaving the door ajar in his haste to get out of the house.

Bernard took another cigarette from the packet and lit it. He had always known that Graham would find him again one day. It had been inevitable. But now he had the advantage, and he intended to use it . . .

"I still say I should go in with you," Laidlaw urged after he had parked the car outside Barak's house.

Graham shook his head. "We've been through this already. Barak gave specific instructions that I was to go in alone. I've got to play by his rules. He's my only chance of finding Bernard."

"It could be a trap."

"Don't you think that's crossed my mind? It's a chance I've got to take."

Laidlaw sighed deeply then nodded. "OK, but if you haven't shown your face at the window in the first couple of minutes I'm coming in after you."

"Deal," Graham replied and got out of the car.

Laidlaw watched Graham until he had disappeared into the house then touched his holstered P220 automatic as if to reassure himself. Not that he would use it. He couldn't. Not since that fateful mission in Honduras. He had tried several times at a local shooting range but he couldn't bring himself to pull the trigger. He knew it was psychological. It was why he had been forced to retire from Delta. But he couldn't tell Graham. How could he? Graham was depending on him. He wiped the sweat from his forehead, willing Graham to appear at the window. Where the hell was he?

The gunshot came from inside the house. Then silence. Laidlaw banged the steering wheel angrily with his fist. It had been a trap. Why hadn't Graham listened to him? He pushed open the door and scrambled out of the car, careful to keep out of sight of the house. He pulled the automatic from his holster but stopped short of curling his finger around the trigger. Sweating, he peered round the side of the car at the house. It was in darkness, just as it had been when they had been there earlier that evening. He would have to go round to the back. He ran, doubled-over, to the adjoining house. It, too, was in darkness. But that was to be expected. Staying alive in Beirut depended on ignoring trouble. He vaulted over the gate and hurried up the narrow driveway. An overgrown hedge divided the two properties. He found a hole in it and squeezed his way through. Barak's back door was barely ten yards away from where he was crouched. He wiped the sweat from his eyes and looked down at the automatic in his hand. But he still couldn't bring himself to touch the trigger. He cursed himself angrily. What happened if the gunman was still in the house? Could he defend himself? He was breathing heavily, but it had nothing to do with the run he had made from the car. It was fear. Delta had taught him that fear was all in the mind. It could be overcome. But that was when he could still pull a trigger.

He swallowed hard and ran to the back door, pressing himself against the wall beside it. He bit his lip as he tried to thread his finger through the trigger guard. It was almost as if an invisible hand were pressing his finger against the barrel. He couldn't do it. He gritted his teeth and tested the handle. The door was unlocked. He kicked it open and dived into the small kitchen, rolling to the safety of the old, battered fridge. He remained there for a few seconds then slowly got to his feet and moved to the door leading into the hallway. Again he pressed himself against the wall and peered cautiously into the hall. At first he couldn't see anything in the semi-darkness. But as his eyes grew accustomed to it he could make out a hand protruding from the open lounge doorway. He was about to swivel round into the hall when he heard the sound of a car starting up outside the house. He recognized the sound of the engine straight away. It was Barak's Peugeot.

He ducked into the first door down the hall. It turned out to be a bedroom. Hurrying to the window, he peered through a tear in the curtains just in time to see the Peugeot drive off, heading toward the city. There was only one person inside but he couldn't make out who it was. It could have been Barak. Or the killer. Unless Barak was the killer. He doubted that. Barak hated violence, especially if it involved guns.

He made his way carefully down the hall until he reached the lounge. Pressing himself against the wall he looked down at the body. It was Barak. He was lying face down, blood seeping from the bullet hole in his back. Laidlaw checked for a pulse. He was dead. Laidlaw stared at the body. There had only been one shot. So where was Graham?

He stood up slowly and entered the lounge. It was empty. He quickly checked the remaining rooms. They, too, were empty. He called out Graham's name but there was no reply. Graham had gone. And Barak was dead. It only left one possible explanation. Graham had been in the Peugeot. He had killed Barak. Laidlaw couldn't believe it. Why? Then a sudden thought flashed through his mind. What was it Graham had said back at the Windorah about Barak? For a moment he couldn't remember his exact words. Then they came to him.

"I thought someone would have put a bullet in his back by now . . ."

Laidlaw didn't care that Barak was dead. What did bother him was that Graham used him to get at Barak. That hurt, especially after all they had been through together.

He looked down at Barak's body again. One of the neighbors was sure to have made an anonymous call to the police, reporting the gunshot. And it would only be a matter of time before they came to investigate.

He left the way he had come. He couldn't get involved. There would be too much explaining to do.

◆ CHAPTER

TWO

New York was swathed in sunlight. Temperatures were in the high seventies and with the absence of any wind it felt sticky and humid.

On the twenty-second floor of the United Nations building, overlooking the East River, Malcolm Philpott was also feeling the heat. A fifty-six-year-old Scot with gaunt features and fine wavy hair, he had been UNACO Director since its inception in 1980. He reached for his handkerchief and dabbed his forehead again—a cold, clammy sweat that only seemed to have surfaced in the last half an hour. Was he going down with an infection? He wouldn't have been surprised. He was a workaholic and he knew his body was run down and in need of rest. But how could he rest with so much activity going on at UNACO headquarters? Especially now with Mike Graham's maverick action in Beirut.

He pushed his handkerchief back into his pocket and looked across at his deputy, Sergei Kolchinsky, a Russian in his early fifties who had become an invaluable member of the team since joining UNACO from the

KGB four years earlier. He had a brilliant tactical mind and had helped to crack some of UNACO's toughest assignments in the past.

Neither man had spoken for the last few minutes. Both were smoking, Philpott his pipe and Kolchinsky a cigarette. Three unopened files lay on Philpott's desk. Each had a name typed on its cover: Mike Graham; C.W. Whitlock; and Sabrina Carver. They made up one of the ten élite "Strike Force" teams, all top field operatives who had been siphoned off from police, military and intelligence services around the world. They were able to request anything they wanted from their administrative colleagues which they felt could aid them on any given mission. Those requests used to have to go through either Philpott or Kolchinsky, but they had recently decided to waive the routine and allow the field operatives a free hand. Now both men regretted ever having made the decision.

They had discovered that Graham had drawn three false passports, in the names of Michael Green, Miles Grant and Mark Gordon, and used one of them to fly to Beirut. He had managed to get a Beretta from a contact in Beirut which was now in the hands of the local police. It had his fingerprints on it. It had been fired once—the bullet which had killed Barak. And now Graham was missing. He was a wanted man in the Lebanon and UNACO couldn't do anything publicly without endangering their own clandestine existence. That meant Graham was on his own. Certainly for the time being . . .

"Malcolm, are you feeling alright?" Kolchinsky asked, breaking the silence. "You're looking very pale."

"I'm fine," Philpott replied tersely then reached for his cane and got to his feet. He moved to the window, walking with a pronounced limp on his left leg, the result of a shrapnel wound in the last days of the Korean War. He turned back to Kolchinsky, his eyes blazing. "I can't believe he could have been that stupid.

We've made plenty of enemies over the years, even politicians here at the UN, and this will provide them with the perfect ammunition for them to shoot UNACO down in flames. We've got to find him before the Lebanese authorities do. If he goes on trial we may as well all start looking for other jobs. UNACO will be crucified."

Kolchinsky gave a resigned nod. "What do you suggest?"

"We've got to bring C.W. and Sabrina in on the case as quickly as possible. But we can't do anything until I've spoken to Langley."

"What have the CIA to do with this?" Kolchinsky asked with a frown.

"I'm as much in the dark as you are, Sergei. I got a call from their Deputy Director, Robert Bailey, this morning. He wouldn't go into details over the phone but he said it had something to do with Bernard. He's coming over later this morning to see me."

"Do you want me to see to C.W. and Sabrina?"

"Yes, put them on a Code Red standby. I want them here by two at the latest—" Philpott stopped abruptly as a crushing pain seared through his chest, radiating out to his neck, jaw and arms. His cane fell from his grasp and he sagged forward against the wall.

Kolchinsky leaped from his chair and grabbed Philpott before he could fall to the floor. Philpott clutched his chest in agony. It felt as if it were going to burst. The pain was unbearable. His eyes watered as the pain increased. He tried to speak but he couldn't get the words out. He thought he was about to die. At that moment he would have welcomed it, an escape from the agony burning through his chest.

Kolchinsky lowered him carefully to the floor then flicked on the intercom switch on the desk. "Sarah, call an ambulance. And hurry. The Colonel's had a heart attack."

He switched off the intercom before she could reply

and hurried back to where Philpott lay. He remembered his first-aid training with the KGB—always keep the sufferer as warm and calm as possible. He took off his jacket and placed it over Philpott's chest.

"You're going to be alright, Malcolm. Sarah's calling for an ambulance."

The pain had subsided to a tightness of the chest. He suddenly felt cold but he could also feel the sweat running down the sides of his face. He had known right away what had happened. His mother had suffered two heart attacks before the third one had killed her. He knew the symptoms. A coronary thrombosis, the doctor had called it. It was strange. He felt perfectly lucid yet he couldn't speak. The words wouldn't reach his lips.

Kolchinsky noticed Philpott trying to speak and squeezed his arm reassuringly. "Don't try and say anything, Malcolm. You're going to be alright."

The door slid open and Sarah Thomas, Philpott's secretary, hurried across to where Kolchinsky was crouched. "The ambulance is on its way. It should be here in about ten minutes."

"Have you told security it's on its way?"

She nodded. "Can I do anything to help?" she whispered.

Kolchinsky shook his head. "The worst's over. He's going to be alright, don't worry." He turned toward her. "Get hold of Sabrina and C.W. Tell them I want them here by two this afternoon."

Sarah returned to the outer office. Her hands were shaking when she picked up the receiver and dialed the number of Sabrina's flat.

Sabrina wasn't in her flat. She was taking in the boutiques on Fifth Avenue. It was her second-favorite pastime. Her favorite was listening to jazz, either live at one of her regular haunts, Ali's Alley or the Village Vanguard, or sitting at home with the headphones on, listening to the likes of David Sanborn or the Yellow-jackets. Sanborn was her idol and she tried to get to as many of his live gigs as possible when he was playing in New York. Jazz had become a way of life for her.

She was dressed casually in a pair of faded Levi jeans, brown ankle boots and a baggy white T-shirt. Her shoulder-length blond hair was hidden underneath a New York Yankees baseball cap, a present from Mike Graham. She was a stunning twenty-eight-year-old with a near perfect figure, which she kept in shape with regular aerobics classes, and she had a friendly, out-going disposition. She had given up counting the number of marriage proposals she had turned down over the years. Her independence was too important to her. Moreover, any serious relationship could well jeopardize her position with UNACO. As far as her friends were concerned, she was a translator at the United Nations. None of them knew that she had been with the FBI for two years, where she had specialized in the use of firearms, before joining UNACO three years ago. She was still the only female field operative in the organization but her gutsy determination and self-confidence had won over her male colleagues who now regarded her as an equal. She could think of no greater compliment.

She paused in front of Barnes and Noble and pretended to look at the book display in the window. She was sure she was being followed. Not that she had seen anyone. It was just an instinct that came with the job. She waited a few moments then turned into East 48th Street, still pretending to look in the shop windows as she walked. She didn't increase her pace—it would only alert her pursuer. But who was it? She was more than capable of defending herself if the need arose, but what if her pursuer was someone who had recognized her from a previous UNACO assignment, someone out to blow her cover? That did frighten her.

She stopped again, this time in the doorway of a

delicatessen, and reached into her bag for her sunglasses. She slid them on. Now she could use the shop windows to look behind her without arousing any suspicions. A movement caught her eye as she stepped back out onto the pavement but before she could react a black youth shot past her on rollerskates, snatching the bag out of her hand. He dodged between the startled shoppers, none of whom made any attempt to stop him. She immediately sprinted after him. He glanced over his shoulder and grinned at her, knowing she couldn't catch up with him, but when he looked round he found himself heading straight for a display of fresh produce outside a delicatessen. He swerved sharply to the left but his leg hit the edge of the wooden stand and he fell heavily to the ground, spilling an assortment of fruit across the pavement. He scrambled to his feet and looked round nervously at Sabrina who was closing in fast on him. He set off again, his face now twisted in pain, and flung the bag to an accomplice in an alley twenty yards further on.

Sabrina ignored the fleeing youth on the rollerskates and went in pursuit of his accomplice. She followed him through a network of alleyways until he mistakenly darted into a cul-de-sac. He realized his mistake too late and when he turned back to the entrance Sabrina was already there, blocking his escape. She was breathing heavily, her hands on her hips. She met the youth's eyes. He was a Puerto Rican, no older than twenty, with long, greasy black hair and a red headband. He pulled a switchblade from his pocket and opened it inches from his leg.

"You want some?" he asked, the switchblade extended menacingly toward her.

"I don't want any trouble," she said calmly then held out her hand toward him. "Give me the bag and that will be the end of it."

The youth laughed then spat on the ground. "You want the bag, you come and get it."

Sabrina shrugged and moved toward the youth. He dropped the bag then, tightening his grip on the switchblade, he waited until she was in range before lunging at her, the blade slashing the air inches from her face. Pity to cut such a pretty face but she'd asked for it. He grinned as he came at her again.

She waited until he stabbed at her then, using her left forearm to block his wrist, she followed up by slamming the heel of her right hand against his chin and kneeing him in the groin. He cried out in agony and stumbled back against the wall. The switchblade fell from his hand as he sagged to the ground, whimpering softly, his hands clutched between his legs. She picked up the bag, checked inside to see that everything was still there, and was about to confiscate the switchblade when she heard the sound of a police siren in the distance. She couldn't be involved in a police investigation. The way in which she had dispatched her attacker would certainly make news.

She ducked into the adjoining alley. The siren was getting closer. She ran to the end of the alley and was about to scale the ten-foot wire fence when the bleeper attached to her belt suddenly shrilled into life. It was UNACO headquarters. Of all the times for them to call, she thought irritably. She switched it off then clambered over the fence, landing nimbly on her toes, and walked down another alley which brought her out onto Madison Avenue.

She called headquarters from a phone booth, spoke briefly to Sarah, then hurried to the curb to signal a taxi to take her back to her flat.

"Afternoon, François."

The maître d'hotel looked up from his reservation book and smiled warmly. "Ah, good afternoon, Mr. Whitlock. You are looking well."

"I am, thank you. Has my wife arrived yet?"

"Not yet," François replied.

"I'll be in the bar. Tell her when she arrives."

"Of course," came the cordial reply.

Whitlock had been going to Le Chantilly restaurant on East 57th Street since he had first arrived in New York in 1980. It was where he had taken a vivacious Puerto Rican paediatrician, Carmen Rodriguez, on their first date. A year later to the day he had proposed to her at the same table. They had been married now for seven years.

He hoisted himself onto one of the bar stools and nodded in greeting to the barman who was busy serving another customer. The barman smiled back and told Whitlock he would be with him shortly. Whitlock was a forty-four-year-old Kenyan with sharp, angular features softened by the neatly trimmed black moustache he had worn since leaving university in his early twenties. He was photophobic and always wore a pair of tinted glasses to protect his eyes. He had been educated in England and after graduating from Oxford had returned to Kenya where he served with the Intelligence Corps for ten years before being recruited to UNACO as one of its first field operatives. He was now the only survivor of the original team.

"What can I get you to drink, Mr. Whitlock?" the barman asked, leaning his hands on the counter in front of Whitlock.

"The usual, Rick," Whitlock replied.

The barman nodded, took a bottle of beer from the fridge and opened it. He poured the beer into a glass and placed it on a coaster in front of Whitlock.

"How are things in the world of politics, Mr. Whitlock?" he asked, referring to Whitlock's cover as a member of the Kenyan embassy at the United Nations. Carmen was the only person outside UNACO who knew about the deception.

"The usual, Rick."

The barman, sensing Whitlock wasn't in a talkative

mood, left him alone. Whitlock took a sip of beer then glanced over his shoulder at the entrance. Still no sign of Carmen. He turned the glass slowly on the coaster as he thought about her. Their marriage had nearly ended a few months back. Well, that was when it had all come to a head. But it had been simmering for a couple of years before that. It all stemmed from her desire for him to leave UNACO. She was frightened for his safety. But he had been adamant: he was staying. She had finally walked out on him and it had only been the intervention of Philpott that had brought them back together again. He had told them that Whitlock would be promoted to Deputy Director when he retired at the end of the year. Kolchinsky would take over as Director. Then, after a year, Kolchinsky would step down and Whitlock would take his place. Other than the four of them, and the Secretary-General, the only other person who knew about it was Jacques Rust, head of UNACO European operation, based in Zurich. Carmen had then thrown her full support behind him, knowing he would be out of the field by the end of the year. Whitlock knew he would miss working in the field, especially with Mike and Sabrina, but he also knew it would be a small price to pay to keep his marriage intact. And that meant everything to him . . .

"C.W.?"

Whitlock looked round sharply, startled by the voice behind him. He grinned ruefully at his wife then kissed her lightly on the lips. "How long have you been standing there?"

"A few seconds," she replied, allowing him to help her onto the adjacent bar stool.

"I'm sorry, I was miles away."

"So I noticed." She ordered a spritzer then turned back to him, her face solemn. "I've got some bad news. Rosie was arrested last night."

Whitlock stared at her in horror. Rosie was the teenage daughter of Carmen's sister, Rachel, and her German husband, Eddie Kruger.

The barman placed the spritzer in front of her. She waited until he was out of earshot before continuing. "She was caught buying drugs in Times Square. I don't know what it was. Rachel didn't say."

Whitlock sighed deeply and shook his head sadly. "I suppose I shouldn't be that surprised."

"And what exactly is that supposed to mean?" she demanded.

"Come off it, Carmen, you know damn well what I'm talking about. They've hardly been the best parents in the world, have they? Rachel had that affair with her boss and Eddie's drinking has been getting steadily worse these last couple of years—"

"She had that affair as an escape from Eddie's drinking," Carmen cut in quickly.

"That's irrelevant. Look at it from Rosie's perspective. Can't you see? This is her way of escaping from *them.*"

"Will you talk to her?"

He shook his head. "No; it's up to Eddie and Rachel to talk to her."

"Rachel asked if you would."

"Where's Eddie?"

"He went to an all-night poker game last night. She hasn't seen him since."

"Some father," Whitlock muttered.

"Talk to her, C.W. You're the only person she's ever listened to in the past."

"I'm not using UNACO to pull any strings, Carmen. Let's get that straight right from the start."

"Just talk to her," she replied softly. "Please."

"OK," he replied at length. "Where is she?"

"At home. Rachel put up the bail—"

The bleeper clipped to Whitlock's belt suddenly activated and he was quick to silence it. He shot Carmen a despairing look. "This is all I need right now. I have to answer it, Carmen."

"I know," she replied and squeezed his hand gently.

"I will talk to her, I promise you. But when I don't know. It all depends on what's come up," he said, patting the bleeper.

"Would you like to use this phone, Mr. Whitlock?" the barman asked, having heard the bleeper from the other side of the bar.

"No, but thanks anyway, Rick," Whitlock replied then turned back to Carmen. "I've suddenly lost my appetite."

"I lost mine when I heard about Rosie," Carmen replied.

"Come on then, let's go."

Sarah Thomas had been Philpott's secretary for the last five years. Her sparsely furnished office on the twenty-second floor of the United Nations building was an antechamber to the UNACO headquarters. The wall opposite the door, constructed of rows of teak slats, contained two seamless sliding doors, invisible to the naked eye, which could only be activated by miniature sonic transmitters. The door to the right led into the UNACO Command Center, a soundproofed room where teams of analysts worked around the clock to monitor the fluctuating developments in world affairs. The door to the left led into Philpott's private office.

Kolchinsky sat behind Philpott's desk, his eyes riveted on Whitlock and Sabrina. He had just broken the news to them about Philpott.

"Will he be alright?" Sabrina asked anxiously, breaking the sudden silence.

"I spoke to the doctor before I left the hospital. He's optimistic that the Colonel will make a complete recovery. They're keeping him in hospital for another few days to carry out more tests."

"Unless he discharges himself first," Whitlock said and eyed Kolchinsky knowingly. "He'll want to be back at work as soon as possible. You know the Colonel."

"I've already been in touch with the Secretary-General. He's going to see the Colonel tonight to tell him to take a month's leave after he's been discharged from hospital."

"I wish him luck," Whitlock said. "You know just how stubborn the Colonel can be when he wants to get his own way."

"I don't think he'll put up much resistance this time," Kolchinsky replied then paused to light a cigarette. "He's been overworking and he knows it. The next attack could be fatal."

They lapsed into silence again.

Whitlock got to his feet and crossed to the dispenser against the wall. "Coffee anyone?"

They both shook their heads.

"Where's Mike?" Whitlock asked, pouring himself a coffee.

"That's a good question," Kolchinsky replied gruffly. "The last I heard was that he's on the run from the authorities in Beirut."

"What?" Sabrina asked in astonishment.

"Beirut?" Whitlock said, pausing in front of the desk to look down at Kolchinsky. "Is he on assignment?"

"No, he is not," Kolchinsky boomed angrily, stressing each word in turn. "He's gone after Bernard."

"Jean-Jacques Bernard?" Sabrina said, her eyes flickering between Kolchinsky and Whitlock. "He's dead, isn't he?"

"Sit down, C.W.," Kolchinsky said, waving toward the black leather sofa where Sabrina was sitting. "I'll tell you what I know so far. And believe me, it isn't much."

Kolchinsky waited until Whitlock was seated before opening the file on the desk in front of him and outlin-

ing the sketchy details Philpott had received from their
UNACO contact in Beirut earlier that morning.

"Mike would never have shot this Barak in the
back," Sabrina said once Kolchinsky had finished.
"That's coldblooded murder. He's been set up—"

"Spare the lecture, Sabrina," Kolchinsky cut in
sharply. He placed the cigarette on the edge of the
ashtray before looking at her again. "Look, I hear what
you're saying. And if it's any consolation, I don't think
he shot Barak either. But we can't be sure until we find
him. And we have to find him, quickly."

"What if the person who murdered Barak killed
Mike as well?" Whitlock said and immediately noticed
the look of horror on Sabrina's face. He turned to her.
"It's a possibility we have to face."

"Why set Michael up to take the rap then kill him?
If the killer wanted Michael dead, why not shoot him at
Barak's house?"

Kolchinsky shook his head. "No, if Michael was set
up then it's obvious the killer wants him alive."

"What about Laidlaw?" Sabrina asked. "Have any of
our people contacted him?"

"We can't risk it," Kolchinsky replied. "The police
know he met Michael last night. They don't have any
evidence linking him to the murder but you can be sure
they'll be watching his every move. That's where you
come in."

"How?"

"You're going over there as Michael's girlfriend.
And it's imperative that you play it all above board.
Contact the police once you arrive to let them know
you're looking for him. That way you'll be able to see
Laidlaw without arousing their suspicions. I'm not
saying you'll find out anything, but you have to start
somewhere."

"Where do I come in?" Whitlock asked.

"You'll find out soon enough," Kolchinsky replied

then pressed the intercom button on the desk. "Sarah, ask Mr. Bailey to come through."

Kolchinsky used a miniature transmitter to activate the door. Moments later Sarah appeared, followed by a man in a pale gray suit. He was in his early fifties with wavy black hair and a craggy face which was scarred around the cheeks and mouth from teenage acne. He smiled quickly at Sarah when she withdrew and closed the door behind her.

Kolchinsky came round from behind the desk and the two men shook hands. He introduced Whitlock and Sabrina to Bailey who then sat down on the second black leather sofa and took a cigar from his pocket. He unwrapped the cellophane then looked across at Kolchinsky. "I was shocked to hear about Colonel Philpott. How is he?"

"He's expected to make a full recovery," Kolchinsky replied.

"That is good news. Please send him my regards when you next see him. We may not have always seen eye to eye in the past but I have great respect for him nevertheless." Bailey lit the cigar and exhaled the smoke toward the ceiling. "Have you had a chance to look through the dossier I sent you this morning?"

"I've read it," Kolchinsky said, unable to keep the disdain from his voice.

"And have you briefed your operatives?" Bailey asked, indicating Whitlock and Sabrina on the adjacent sofa.

"They've only just got here. We've been talking about the events in Beirut."

"That's understandable," Bailey said with the hint of a smile. "It's quite a mess he's got you into, isn't it?"

"You let us worry about that, Mr. Bailey," Kolchinsky replied icily. "I'll let you explain the gist of the dossier to C.W. and Sabrina. After all, it is your dirty work."

Bailey got to his feet and moved to the window. He

puffed thoughtfully on the cigar then turned back to face Whitlock and Sabrina. "What I'm about to tell you can never be repeated outside these four walls. It's one of the CIA's most closely guarded secrets and I intend to keep it that way. Any indiscretion on your part—"

"There will be no indiscretion on their part," Kolchinsky cut in angrily, his eyes blazing.

Bailey shrugged, not altogether convinced by Kolchinsky's outburst. But he let it pass. "It would never have needed to come out if Graham hadn't rushed off to Beirut to find Bernard." He paused to draw on the cigar, still loath to reveal what he had come to say. When he spoke it was in a barely audible voice as if he feared that his words would carry beyond the four walls. "Jean-Jacques Bernard works for me."

"Bernard's CIA?" Whitlock said in astonishment.

Bailey nodded.

"Was he working for you when Mike's family were kidnapped?" Sabrina demanded.

"Yes," Bailey answered then held up his hand to silence Sabrina before she could speak again. "But the kidnapping had nothing to do with him. It was carried out on the orders of Salim Al-Makesh to give himself time to flee the terrorist base before Delta destroyed it."

"And now Al-Makesh is dead. How convenient."

"You can drop the sarcasm, Sabrina," Kolchinsky said sharply, pointing a finger of warning at her.

She opened her mouth to speak, thought better of it, then slumped back angrily on the sofa and folded her arms across her chest.

"Why was Mike never told about this?" Whitlock asked, his eyes riveted on Bailey. "He's been through hell these past two years trying to come to terms with the loss of his family. Had he known the truth it might have made his loss that bit more bearable."

"Bernard told us what happened and as he and Al-Makesh were the only two survivors of the attack we couldn't say anything without endangering his cover."

"You bastard," Sabrina snarled.

Bailey inhaled sharply and glanced at Kolchinsky, fully expecting him to reprimand her again. Kolchinsky said nothing.

"What did happen to them?" Whitlock asked, breaking the tense silence.

"I don't know the details," Bailey replied with a shrug. "But I do know they were killed in retaliation for the attack on the base camp. That's all Bernard could find out from Al-Makesh."

Whitlock bit his lip pensively then looked across at Kolchinsky. "When I asked you earlier where I fitted into the assignment you said that I'd find out soon enough. There's more to this than just finding Mike before he gets to Bernard, isn't there?"

"Yes," Kolchinsky replied bluntly then took another cigarette from the packet on the desk and lit it. He indicated toward Bailey. "I'll let you explain."

"Very well," Bailey said. "Have either of you ever heard of Zimbala?"

"Sure," Whitlock answered. "It's a small country in central Africa. Borders Chad and Niger."

"You're unusually well informed," Bailey said with thinly veiled sarcasm.

"I am African," Whitlock rejoined. "Born in Kenya, but educated in England. That's where I learned about Zimbala."

"Then you'll also know that Zimbala has been a one-party state since it was granted independence by the French forty-five years ago."

"A dictatorship run by Alphonse Mobuto," Sabrina said.

"Until his death last month," Bailey said.

"That I didn't know," Whitlock said.

"Me neither," Sabrina added.

"It's hardly surprising. His death received very limited coverage outside Zimbala."

"Who's running the country now?" Whitlock asked.

"His eldest son, Jamel. He's due to arrive in New York tonight for an official three-day visit."

"So where does Bernard fit into this?" Sabrina asked exasperatedly.

"I'm coming to that. It's Jamel Mobuto's intention to bring democracy to Zimbala. That's caused a lot of resentment within certain sections of the country, especially amongst the rich who would stand to lose a great deal if Mobuto has his way. A team of four assassins, made up from the now disbanded Security Police, have vowed to kill Mobuto while he's here in America. It's a threat we've taken very seriously. I told Bernard to infiltrate the team so that he can keep us posted on their movements. He approached them with an offer to train them. Naturally they accepted, knowing how invaluable his expertise would be to them. They now trust him implicitly. He'll tip us off when he knows where and when the hit is due to take place so that it can be stopped in time. That's why Graham has to be found. If he gets to Bernard before we know the details of the hit it'll leave us totally in the dark. And if Mobuto was killed on American soil it would prove a severe embarrassment not only to us but to the President as well. After all, it's not as if we haven't been forewarned."

"And I'm to babysit Mobuto?" Whitlock concluded.

Bailey nodded. "You'll work with two of my men. He's bringing half-a-dozen bodyguards with him but they're all amateurs, made up of officers from the Zimbalan army. If anything does happen, it'll be up to the three of you to deal with it."

"You'll be in charge," Kolchinsky said, looking at Whitlock.

"The three of them will be in charge," Bailey corrected him.

"C.W. will be in overall charge," Kolchinsky retorted. "It's important to have one leader. I've read the files on your men. They may be the best bullet catchers you've got but they don't have C.W.'s experience. And if you want to take the matter further I suggest you call the President. The Secretary-General spoke to him earlier today and he agreed that C.W. should be in charge."

"I'll tell my men," Bailey said tersely.

"I'll be in touch so that we can arrange for C.W. to meet your men before Mobuto arrives tonight," Kolchinsky said then picked up the transmitter on the desk and activated the door.

Bailey left the room and Kolchinsky closed the door behind him.

"What a slimeball," Sabrina said, staring at the closed door.

Kolchinsky smiled. "He could have been sitting here instead of me."

"What do you mean?" she asked.

"You never knew my predecessor, Gronskin, did you?"

She shook her head. "He was before my time."

"Well, when he was deported back to Russia for spying the CIA suggested Bailey as a possible replacement to take over as the Colonel's number two. The KGB put my name forward. The Secretary-General initially wanted Bailey, which I suppose was understandable under the circumstances, but the Colonel threatened to resign if Bailey got the job. As Bailey said, the two of them never saw eye to eye. It would have been catastrophic if Bailey had come here. So I got the job instead."

"I never knew that," Whitlock said.

"I'm sure glad the Colonel put his foot down," Sabrina said, glancing at the door again.

Whitlock stood up and dug his hands into his pockets. He crossed to the far wall then turned to look at Kolchinsky. "I was at university with Jamel Mobuto."

"Why didn't you say something when Bailey was here?"

"Because we didn't get on," Whitlock replied.

"Why not?" Kolchinsky asked.

Whitlock sighed deeply then returned to the sofa and sat down. "He'd never set foot outside Zimbala before he came to Oxford. It must have been a bit of a culture shock for him. But instead of trying to adapt to the British way of life he rebelled against it and reverted to his African heritage. He wore African clothes, his room was an African shrine and he made no attempt to befriend any of the British students. He became a pariah although he did have an avid following amongst some of the more radical left-wing students who regarded him as something of a guru."

"Was he a Communist?" Kolchinsky asked.

"No, strangely enough. He was just very pro-African and Africa's particular way of life. He had a younger brother who went to Oxford as well and he did become a Communist. But that was after I'd gone. I don't know anything about him."

"His name's Remy," Kolchinsky said and tapped the dossier on the desk. "It's all in here. You'll both get copies of it."

"You still haven't said why you and Mobuto didn't get on," Sabrina said.

"I was born in Kenya but educated in England. To him, I was little more than a traitor. I'd sold out my race. And let's face it, I am more British than I am Kenyan. That's what he couldn't accept. So we just kept out of each other's way."

"Why did he stay if he hated it so much?" Sabrina asked.

"Because his father had sent him. If he'd gone back to Zimbala it would have brought disgrace on the family. Africans take failure far more seriously than you do here in the West." Whitlock dismissed the subject with a curt flick of his hand. "Anyway, that was a long time ago. I certainly don't hold any grudges now."

"Let's hope Mobuto feels the same way," Kolchinsky said.

"Does he know I'm going to be babysitting him when he gets to New York?"

Kolchinsky nodded. "Bailey's already briefed him on the telephone but he won't know you're in charge of the operation until he gets here. You'll have to break that to him yourself."

"I look forward to it," Whitlock said with a faint smile.

Kolchinsky handed them each a dossier which contained details of their particular assignment (to be destroyed after reading) and, in Sabrina's case, an airline ticket, maps of Beirut, written confirmation of her hotel booking, the name of her contact and a sum of money in Lebanese pounds.

She glanced at her watch and immediately got to her feet. "My flight leaves at four thirty this afternoon," she said. "I'd better get going. Send the Colonel my best wishes when you see him again, Sergei."

"I will," Kolchinsky replied and activated the door for her. "And Sabrina?"

She paused in the doorway to look round at him.

"Bring Michael back before he gets himself into any more trouble."

She nodded grimly then left the room.

Kolchinsky closed the door again. "The Colonel might not be coming back. The Secretary-General's waiting for the doctor's report before coming to a decision."

"He was due to retire at the end of the year anyway. Perhaps it's for the best if he did take an early retirement."

"Try telling that to the Colonel. It's not as if he's taking voluntary retirement. It's been forced on him by his doctor. So you can be sure he'll want to see out his time here, if only to prove a point to his doctor."

"And possibly kill himself in the process."

Kolchinsky reached for his cigarettes and lit one. "That's why the Secretary-General's delaying his decision. He'll give the Colonel every chance to prove that he's fit enough to return to work."

"And if not, I'll leave Strike Force Three and join you here."

"You don't sound very enthusiastic about it," Kolchinsky said.

"I'm not. Stuck behind a desk all day isn't my idea of fun, Sergei." Whitlock picked up the dossier. "Let me out, will you?"

"The Colonel said you were over the moon when he broke the news to you."

"How did you expect me to react? Carmen was there." Whitlock walked to the door and looked back at Kolchinsky. "Don't worry, I won't let anyone down. Especially not her."

THREE

Remy Mobuto had always lived in his brother's shadow. He had known from an early age that Jamel, as the older brother, would take over as leader of Zimbala once their father died. That had never bothered him. He had never had any aspirations to enter politics. When he followed Jamel to Oxford he immediately joined the Communist Party, more as an act of rebellion than anything else. His father's response was not only to stop sending him money but also to bar him from returning to Zimbala until he renounced his Socialist beliefs. He refused to comply and left Oxford after the first year to join the *Guardian* where he remained for seven years before taking up a post as an investigative journalist with a left-wing French newspaper. By then he had become an outspoken critic of the numerous dictators in Africa, especially his father. His father disowned him publicly and said he would never be allowed back to Zimbala in his lifetime.

He returned for his father's funeral, the first time he'd been back to Zimbala in seventeen years, and Jamel was able to persuade him to stay on as the new editor of the country's leading daily newspaper, *La Voix*.

Remy had only been in charge for a month and already he had a major scoop on his hands. It concerned the plot to overthrow his brother and form a new dictatorship; but he had discovered another side to the story, a sinister angle that would make international headlines if it were ever made public. But before he could do that, or tell Jamel, he needed proof to back up those allegations. And he was about to get it . . .

He drove down the main street of Habane, the capital of Zimbala, and turned into the basement carpark where he had arranged to meet his informant. There were only a couple of cars there at that time of the evening. He glanced at his watch. Eight fifty-seven. He had told his informant to meet him at nine o'clock. He pulled into the prearranged space, climbed out of the car, then took a pack of cigarettes from his jacket pocket and lit one.

He looked around him slowly. The silence was eerie. He took a long drag on the cigarette and looked at his watch again. Eight fifty-eight. He cursed his anxiety. There was no reason for it. But still the uncertainty lingered. He looked round again, this time taking more notice of his surroundings. Then he saw it: his informant's car, a blue Fiat. It was parked next to the wall and almost hidden from view by the red Studebaker beside it. He exhaled sharply and managed a faint smile. Typical of his informant to take such precautions.

He ground his cigarette underfoot and walked slowly toward the Fiat. He could see his informant behind the wheel. Why hadn't he shown himself? Mobuto dismissed the question; at least he was there. He reached the Fiat and leaned over to peer through the driver's window. The man's throat had been cut from ear to ear, soaking his shirt and trousers in blood. Mobuto recoiled in horror, stumbling back painfully into the Studebaker's wing mirror. He felt his stomach heave and he retched against the wall. He remained doubled over for several seconds before slowly straightening up and wiping the sweat from his forehead.

Then he heard a sound behind him. He turned, his eyes wide with fear. Two men stood behind the Studebaker. Both were dressed in blue overalls. One had blood on his sleeve. The killer? He was about to speak when he noticed a movement out of the corner of his eye. He was still turning when the cosh struck him behind the ear.

Then nothing.

Zimbala's main prison, La Tambier, was less than ten minutes' drive from the center of Habane. It took its name from the district in which it was located. It had been built when Alphonse Mobuto first came to power and quickly became known throughout the country as *La Boucherie*, the Butcher's Shop, because of the number of antigovernment dissidents who were tortured then murdered there by the feared and hated Security Police. Jamel Mobuto's first two decrees on taking office had been to free all political prisoners being held there and the immediate dismantling of the Security Police. Now, ironically, its most notorious prisoner was *Le Boucher*, Tito Ngune, the head of the Security Police for the last twenty-three years. There had been cries for his public execution but Jamel Mobuto had made it quite clear that Ngune would be tried and, if found guilty, sentenced to life imprisonment. He refused to continue the legacy of executions which had been symptomatic of his father's regime.

Ngune lay on the single mattress in the corner of his cell. He was a stocky fifty-eight-year-old with gray hair and a small goatee beard which looked as if it had been stuck on to his chin with glue. His face and body were a mass of bruises after he had been attacked at his home by a forty-strong mob who were preparing to lynch him in the remains of his once beautiful garden when the military had arrived and bundled him into the back of a police van and brought him to La Tambier.

He sat up gingerly and looked slowly around the cell. All those years of unswerving loyalty to Alphonse Mobuto and this was all it had brought him. Mobuto had always had one weakness, his family. Although he publicly renounced Remy and repealed the law making Jamel his natural successor, he had always refused to allow Ngune's men to touch them. But, unknown to Mobuto, Ngune had tried on three different occasions to have Jamel killed. Each attempt had ended in failure. He certainly had guts, Ngune had to give him that. Anyone else who had dared to criticize either Mobuto or his Government was immediately arrested and taken to La Tambier or to the now abandoned Branco prison in Kondese, the second-largest city situated in the south of the country. None of them ever left.

A jackhammer started up somewhere beyond the prison walls. It had become a familiar sound over the last couple of days. At first it had been an irritation but now he had grown strangely accustomed to it—a break from the monotonous silence that filled the prison. He had wondered what they were doing out there. Digging up the road? Or tearing down part of the prison? It was certainly feasible under Jamel Mobuto's new liberal leadership. Not that it mattered. It was all academic to him now. But it still interested him, if only to put his mind at rest. He reminded himself to ask one of the guards when they brought him his next meal . . .

Michael Sibele had known for the last two days why the gang of workmen was busy outside the main gates: repairing a burst mains pipe. He had been the guard on duty at the gate for the last week. It was his last day. Tomorrow he would return to his duties inside the prison—with mixed feelings. He had enjoyed the workmen's company but he would also be grateful to get away from the noise of the machines, especially the incessant throbbing of the jackhammers. The workmen had offered him ear plugs but his commanding officer had forbidden him to wear them. So he just had to put up with the noise. Well, only a few hours to go . . .

One of the workmen broke away from the group and approached him. Sibele knew him only as Johnny. His real name was Thomas Massenga, once Ngune's right-hand man, who had been on the run since Jamel Mobuto came to power. It was only when he got closer that Sibele saw the blood on the sleeve of his blue overall. Massenga pulled a Mini-Uzi from inside his overall and shot Sibele at pointblank range.

The bulldozer which had stood dormant for the past two days coughed into life and rumbled toward the prison gates. Two guards, who had been alerted by the gunfire, ran toward the gates. Both were armed with FN FAL semi-automatic rifles. Massenga shot them before they could fire at the bulldozer. It smashed through the gates, tearing them off their hinges as though they were made of plastic. Massenga gestured to the other six men who immediately followed him into the prison compound, each carrying a Mini-Uzi.

The skeleton staff were no match for Massenga and his team of ex-Security policemen. The fighting was over within a minute and they were able to make their way down to the cells. The two guards outside Ngune's cell threw down their weapons when challenged by Massenga. They had no option. Massenga took the keys from one of them and unlocked Ngune's cell door. He hurried over to where Ngune lay and crouched anxiously beside him, horrified at the sight of Ngune's discolored, swollen face. Immediately he ordered two of his men to carry Ngune then locked the two terrified guards in an adjoining cell. Discarding the keys, he then led the way back to the front of the prison. He glanced at his watch. They had made good time. Although the telephone wires had been cut minutes before the assault he knew the authorities would still have been alerted and were almost certainly on their way to the prison at that very moment.

A black van reversed through the shattered remains of the main gate and the back doors were thrown open. Ngune was helped into the back of the van and placed gently on a palliasse with his head resting on a pillow. Massenga closed the doors then climbed into the cab beside the driver who engaged the gears and pulled out into the road.

The plan was to change vehicles on the outskirts of Habane then continue on to Kondese where hundreds of men, mostly ex-Security policemen loyal to Ngune, were waiting to launch a crushing offensive against Jamel Mobuto's inept, and disorganized, government troops, many of whom had only joined up when the new regime was instated. And with a team of assassins awaiting Jamel Mobuto's arrival in America, it would only be a question of days before Tito Ngune was inaugurated as the new President of Zimbala.

It was a plan that couldn't fail.

The New York Police Department, which was responsible for security at John F. Kennedy Airport, had drafted in fifty men for the arrival of Jamel Mobuto's delegation in America. Fifteen snipers, each with M16 rifles (and infra-red night scopes), were positioned at strategic points overlooking the runway while another fifteen, in plainclothes, mingled freely with the crowds inside the terminal building itself. A section of runway had been cordoned off that afternoon by the remaining twenty policemen who had strict orders not to allow anyone through without an official pass. The authorities were determined not to take any chances, not with so much at stake.

Whitlock had driven to the airport a couple of hours before the delegation was due to arrive to ensure that all the security measures had been put into operation. He had been satisfied with the arrangements. He glanced at his watch. The two hours were almost up and, according to air-traffic control, the presidential plane would land on schedule.

He looked around. To his left were three NYPD police cars, parked bumper to bumper, and behind them a human chain of police officers, all armed with handguns and rifles. To his right were the four black limousines that would be used to transport the Zimbalan delegation around New York. The opaque dark windows, like the chassis, were bulletproof, and each of the drivers could activate a row of razor-sharp spikes secreted on the undercarriage if any attempt was made to overturn the car. Every eventuality had to be covered.

The official welcoming party had congregated in front of the limousines, talking amongst themselves. The Zimbalan mission was headed by their newly appointed ambassador to the UN and the White House's Chief of Protocol was the official representative from the American administration.

Whitlock's eyes flickered to the two somber-suited men standing apart from the others, Paul Brett and Jack Rogers. Bailey's men. Both had been presidential bodyguards with the Reagan administration but neither of them had ever had to draw his gun in anger. Whitlock had spent most of the afternoon with them and he'd come away with the distinct impression that they held him in little regard. Although they never said it, he knew their bitterness stemmed from the fact that he would be in charge of the operation. They would be taking orders from someone outside the CIA. Brett suddenly glanced across at him. His face remained expressionless. Rogers said something and they both laughed. Whitlock stared back at Brett. The hell he'd be intimidated by one of Bailey's flunkeys. Brett looked away.

Whitlock suddenly noticed that a member of the Zimbalan mission had been watching them. She was an attractive, light-skinned African in her late twenties in a blue suit and white blouse. The translator. The official languages of Zimbala were Swahili and French; and several of the Zimbalan delegates didn't speak English. He smiled at her. She smiled back then looked away quickly as if she had been caught doing something wrong. He suddenly thought of Rosie. He'd been so busy that afternoon that he'd completely forgotten to call her. He felt a sense of guilt but at the same time knew he could never have spoken to her anyway. He made a mental note to call her and arrange a time to meet, away from her parents.

Someone called out, breaking his train of thought. The presidential plane was making its final descent. He immediately ordered the policemen to take up their designated positions on the runway then crossed to where Brett and Rogers were standing. They glanced at him but said nothing.

The white Gulfstream One executed a perfect landing but it was only when it taxied toward them that Whitlock saw the blue, red and white Zimbalan flag painted on the side of the fuselage with the words "Air Zimbala" above it in black lettering. It was obvious that the plane had been repainted before its journey and Whitlock suddenly wondered if it had been done to erase the memories of the previous regime. He let the thought pass as the plane came to a halt less than twenty yards away from the limousines. The hatch opened and a set of steps was driven up to it. The Chief of Protocol led the way to the foot of the steps, waiting for Mobuto to appear. The first man to emerge had to duck through the opening. Whitlock judged him to be at least six foot six. He looked around him slowly then disappeared back inside the aircraft. He reappeared a moment later and Whitlock immediately recognized Mobuto when he emerged behind the bodyguard. He was a tall, handsome man who had an air of confidence about him. He was dressed in an expensive gray Dior suit and wore dark glasses. It was hard to believe he was forty-two years old. He looked ten years younger. He removed the glasses on reaching the tarmac and he shook the Chief of Protocol's extended hand. Rogers and Brett immediately flanked him at the foot of the steps and walked with him as he shook hands with each member of the Zimbalan mission in turn. His grip lingered on the translator's hand and he smiled faintly at her before turning back to the Chief of Protocol who was standing behind him. It was then that he noticed Whitlock standing discreetly in the background. He told Brett and Rogers to hold back then crossed to where Whitlock stood and held out a hand of greeting.

"It's been a long time, Clarence," Mobuto said in his faultless English.

Whitlock bit back his anger. He had never forgiven his parents for christening him Clarence Wilkins.

"Over twenty years," Whitlock replied, gripping the extended hand. "You look well, Jamel."

Mobuto inhaled sharply and glanced at the massive bodyguard who was hovering in the background. He turned back to Whitlock. "You call me President Mobuto in front of my people!"

"And you call me C.W. in front of mine," Whitlock retorted, holding Mobuto's stare.

Mobuto smiled coldly. "You haven't changed a bit. Still as insolent as ever."

"And you're still as arrogant as ever." Whitlock looked past Mobuto and gestured for Brett and Rogers to approach them. He introduced them to Mobuto then went on to explain that one of them would always be at his side for the duration of his visit.

"And you?" Mobuto asked once Whitlock had finished speaking.

"I'm in charge of security. Brett and Rogers report directly to me. As do your bodyguards."

"Very well," Mobuto replied after a moment's

thought then moved away with the Chief of Protocol, heading toward one of the limousines.

"Brett, you're taking first shift, aren't you?"

Brett nodded.

"Rogers, you'll relieve him tomorrow at seven A.M.'

"Fine," was all Rogers said.

Whitlock dismissed Rogers then he and Brett hurried after Mobuto. Brett went to the lead limousine and climbed in beside the driver. Whitlock caught up with Mobuto but remained discreetly in the background while he finished talking to the Chief of Protocol. Mobuto spoke briefly to the Zimbalan ambassador in Swahili then beckoned the tall bodyguard toward him. He introduced him to Whitlock as Masala, his personal bodyguard, then told Masala that he and the other three Zimbalan bodyguards were to liaise directly with Whitlock.

"President Mobuto and I will be in the second car," Whitlock said to Masala. "You ride up front in the third. Spread your men amongst the other two cars."

Masala nodded then went off to carry out Whitlock's instructions.

Mobuto climbed into the back of the limousine. The Zimbalan ambassador got in beside him and the driver closed the door behind them. Whitlock got into the passenger seat and the driver immediately started the engine.

Whitlock looked round at Mobuto. "I'm going to seal off the back of the car with a sheet of soundproof glass. Not only is it bulletproof but it will also give you privacy to speak to the ambassador. There's a private telephone in the compartment in front of you if you need to make any outside calls. And if you need us, just dial zero."

Mobuto nodded.

Whitlock activated the switch on the dashboard and the glass slid into place, sealing off the back and front seats of the car. He sat back and exhaled deeply. The driver glanced at him but sensed that Whitlock wasn't in the mood to talk. He switched on the radio, found a music station and followed the first limousine out of the airport onto the Grand Central Parkway, heading toward Manhattan.

The convoy, led by a police car and two police motorcycles, made its way through Long Island City, across the Queensboro Bridge into Manhattan then down First Avenue to the United Nations Plaza, the hotel where the Zimbalan delegation would stay for the duration of their three-day visit to New York. It was situated close to the United Nations headquarters as well as being only three blocks away from the African American Institute which Mobuto had requested to see at some point during his visit. And with Mobuto due to address the United Nations' General Assembly, the locale couldn't have been better.

The convoy drew to a halt in front of the hotel; Whitlock jumped out of the limousine and looked around him slowly. The press, who had been alerted by an anonymous call to Reuters the previous day by one of the assassins, were out in force, waiting and hoping to get an exclusive of an assassination, or at least an attempted assassination, for the morning papers. Whitlock shouted at the two policemen on the motorcycles to get the photographers back a few feet to give Mobuto a chance to get out of the limousine. They immediately set about the task of pushing the jostling photographers away from the limousine. Brett and Masala flanked the back door and the other three bodyguards took up positions on the other side of the car, facing the photographers. Satisfied, Whitlock nodded to Masala who opened the back door. Mobuto climbed out slowly and turned to wave at the waiting photographers. Flashbulbs popped incessantly and Whitlock found himself struggling to focus on the sea of cameras, his eyes darting about in search of anything untoward.

Suddenly one of the Zimbalan bodyguards shouted

a warning and lunged at the photographers. Whitlock knocked Mobuto to the ground in the split-second before a bullet smashed into the wall behind them. The photographers scattered in panic as the bodyguard made a grab for the gunman. A second shot rang out and the bodyguard stumbled back, clutching his stomach. The other two Zimbalan bodyguards immediately drew their snub-nosed Smith & Wesson .38s and sprinted after the fleeing gunman.

The getaway driver, in a blue Ford, laid down a burst of suppressing fire, forcing the bodyguards to dive for cover. By the time they had got to their feet the gunman had jumped through the open passenger door and the wheels shrieked in protest as the car sped away from the hotel.

Whitlock mounted one of the police motorcycles, kick-started it, then slewed it violently in an ungainly one-hundred-and-eighty-degree turn and took off after the getaway car. He unhooked the radio and called for backup, giving a description of the car and its registration number. The Ford swung sharply into East 34th Street, mounted the curb, and narrowly missed a couple of teenagers waiting to cross the road. The driver managed to regain control and turned into Second Avenue.

Suddenly he felt the car beginning to skid and in his panic trod on the brakes. The wheels locked and the car careered across the road, clipping the side of an oncoming Greyhound bus. The car overturned and ploughed into the side of a stationary delivery van. The driver was dead, his chest crushed by the steering wheel.

The gunman managed to unbuckle his safety belt and struggled to push open the passenger door. Eager hands reached out to help him as he eased himself out of the car. He wiped the blood from a gash on his forehead then waved the Walther P5 threateningly at the growing crowd of onlookers. They immediately stepped back, anxious not to alarm him.

He fired blindly at Whitlock as he turned into Second Avenue. Whitlock lost control of the motorcycle and fell heavily onto the road. The gunman looked around him wildly and the crowd parted as he darted up a narrow alleyway. Whitlock pulled himself to his feet and winced as a sharp pain shot through his left leg. He looked down at it. His trousers were ripped and the blood seeped down his leg from the gash inches above his knee. It hurt like hell but he was damned if he was going to let the gunman escape. He drew his Browning Mk2 and went after the gunman. Ignoring the pain that shot through his leg with every step, he reached the end of the alleyway. It forked off in two directions. And the gunman was nowhere to be seen. He cursed softly, knowing he'd lost him.

A bullet cracked inches above his head and he flung himself behind a row of metal dustbins, the Browning clenched tightly in his hand. The shot had come from the left fork. He couldn't see the gunman but at least he knew where he was. He could wait. The gunman fired again but the bullet was well off target. He was panicking; and panic invariably leads to mistakes. He suddenly darted out from behind a metal ladder and Whitlock aimed at his legs. He needed him alive.

A police car emerged from the other alleyway and screeched to a halt ten yards in front of Whitlock, blocking his shot. Whitlock cursed angrily and got to his feet. The policeman got out of the car, his Colt Python drawn. He shouted to Whitlock to drop his weapon. Whitlock tried to explain but the policeman's grip tightened on the revolver and he repeated the order. Whitlock snarled angrily and tossed the Browning onto the ground.

The policeman kicked it away and gestured for Whitlock to approach the police car. "I want ten fingers on the hood. Do it!"

"I'm working with you guys, for Christ's sake!" Whitlock snarled in exasperation.

"Sure, now put those fingers on the hood."

"My name's Whitlock, check with your superior. I'm head of the Zimbalan President's security team."

The policeman waited until Whitlock had put his hands on the police car then used his foot to spread his legs. "I was told to apprehend an armed black suspect in this alley. I don't see another one, do you?"

"That's because you've let him get away," Whitlock snarled but the policeman snapped at him to face the front when he tried to look round.

The policeman frisked him then reached for his handcuffs. Whitlock, sensing his moment, swung round and felled him with one punch. He tossed the Colt Python onto the front seat then locked the keys inside the police car. Retrieving his Browning he hurried over to where he had last seen the gunman. He had gone. Then he heard a noise, a metal bin being knocked over. He followed the sound and was just in time to see the gunman climbing a wire fence at the end of an adjoining alleyway. Whitlock purposely fired wide. It had the desired effect—the gunman tumbled over the top of the fence, landing painfully on his back. Whitlock scrambled to his feet but by the time he reached the fence the gunman had already crossed the twenty-yard clearing and disappeared into a derelict warehouse. Whitlock clambered over the fence and landed nimbly on his feet. He straightened up then noticed the gunman's Walther P5 lying at the edge of the clearing. He must have lost it when he fell to the ground. Whitlock doubted he would have another gun but he still approached the warehouse with professional caution.

He reached the open doors and peered in. It took his eyes a few seconds to get accustomed to the gloom then he darted inside and ducked down behind a rusty skip close to the door. He looked around slowly then carefully scanned the catwalk that criss-crossed the warehouse above him. No sign of the gunman. He slipped out from behind the skip and moved slowly across the concrete floor, the Browning gripped tightly in his hand, his eyes continually darting about him. He reached the other side of the cavernous room and paused to wipe the sweat from his eyes. Where the hell was he?

A shower of dust sprinkled his face but before he could react the gunman leaped onto him from a ledge on the wall. They both fell heavily to the ground and the Browning went spinning from Whitlock's hand. The man lashed out with a rusted chain but Whitlock managed to roll clear before it struck the ground where he had been lying. Whitlock kicked out at the man, catching him on the leg so that he overbalanced and fell against the wall. The chain clattered noisily to the ground. Whitlock sprung to his feet and caught him on the side of the head with a stinging haymaker then followed up with two brutal body punches that dropped him to his knees. The man clutched his stomach in agony then noticed the fallen Browning out of the corner of his eye. He grabbed it and turned on Whitlock who managed to deflect it before he fired. They struggled for possession of the gun. It slipped from the gunman's hand, landing at his feet. Whitlock shoved him back onto a tarpaulin in the corner of the warehouse and scooped up the Browning. He levelled it at the gunman then let his hand drop to his side. The man had been impaled on the rusted spikes of a security gate that had been discarded underneath the tarpaulin.

Whitlock swallowed back the bile in his throat and crossed to where the gunman lay, his shirt soaked in blood. He felt for a pulse then, letting the gunman's arm drop, he holstered the Browning before walking back slowly toward the doors. As he reached them he heard the first of the police sirens in the distance. He dusted off a box and sat down to wait for them.

◆　　◆　　◆

Kolchinsky was waiting in the foyer when Whitlock got back to the hotel.

"How's the leg?" were Kolchinsky's first words.

"OK," Whitlock replied with a grim smile. "It didn't need stitches. But I got a tetanus jab as a precaution. Thank for clearing everything for me with the NYPD. I had visions of being stuck in a cell all night."

Kolchinsky patted Whitlock on the shoulder. "Come on, Mobuto's waiting to see you."

"How is he?"

"Remarkably well under the circumstances," Kolchinsky replied as they walked to the lift. "You wouldn't believe someone had just tried to kill him. He's acting like it never happened."

"Acting being the operative word," Whitlock retorted as the lift door parted.

"You really don't like him, do you?"

"As a person, no. But he's obviously genuine about bringing democracy to Zimbala. And that makes all this worthwhile."

They rode the lift to the thirtieth floor and were immediately challenged by a uniformed policeman as they stepped out. They both held up their passes and were allowed through. The entire floor had been booked by the Zimbalan delegation although only ten rooms were being used. It was a security measure.

Another policeman challenged them outside Mobuto's suite and again they had to produce their passes. Kolchinsky knocked on the door. It was opened on the chain by Masala who immediately unlocked it to allow them in. They were ushered into the lounge then Masala discreetly withdrew, closing the door behind him.

Mobuto was alone. He was seated on the sofa sifting through a batch of papers he had taken from his attaché case. He looked up, removed his reading glasses, then got to his feet and indicated the second sofa.

Kolchinsky sat down and asked if Mobuto minded if he smoked.

"Please, feel free," Mobuto replied then turned to Whitlock. "You saved my life tonight. Thank you. I believe you were injured while chasing the gunman. Nothing serious, I hope?"

Whitlock shook his head. "I cut my leg when I fell off the motorbike. It's nothing. I'm sorry about your man. He's the one who really saved your life."

"He died without ever regaining consciousness. At least he was spared the pain." Mobuto folded the glasses and placed them on the coffee table in the center of the room. "Can I offer either of you a drink?"

"Nothing for me," Kolchinsky replied, shaking his head.

"Clarence?"

"Nothing, thank you." Whitlock sat down beside Kolchinsky. "Where's Brett?"

"He's next door," Mobuto replied indifferently.

"And Masala's in the other room. You've got no protection—"

"I've got half the New York police force in the corridor and bodyguards in every adjoining room," Mobuto cut in sharply. "I feel like a prisoner."

"It's important that you always have at least one bodyguard in the room with you all times," Whitlock countered.

"Even when I'm sleeping?"

"Even when you're sleeping," Whitlock shot back. "These assassins are obviously prepared to sacrifice their own lives to kill you. That means they'll go to any lengths to get you."

"What exactly are you implying?"

"What I'm saying is that even in this room you're not safe. They could come through the window—"

"We're thirty floors up, for God sake," Mobuto cut in then chuckled softly to himself. "I think you're being a little melodramatic."

"No, sir, he's not," Kolchinsky said sternly. "C.W.'s right. You must always have at least one bodyguard with you at all times. Tonight proved that."

Mobuto sat down opposite them and sighed deeply. "Very well. You are the experts."

Whitlock got to his feet. "Which room's Brett in?"

Mobuto pointed to his left. "He's next door."

Whitlock left the suite and knocked on the adjoining door. He grabbed Brett the moment he opened the door and slammed him up against the wall. "You're supposed to be next door, not sitting here on your arse watching a ball game."

Brett broke free from Whitlock's grip and stared angrily at him. "The President told me to go. What the hell was I supposed to do?"

"You were supposed to explain to him that it's your job to stay with him. You don't tell him his job and he doesn't tell you yours. You're supposed to be a professional. Start acting like one."

Brett glared furiously at Whitlock then slipped on his shoulder holster and scooped up his jacket before leaving the room. Whitlock followed him into Mobuto's suite. Brett pulled up a chair and sat discreetly in the corner.

"The President's just received a telephone call from Zimbala," Kolchinsky said. "His brother's been kidnapped."

"What happened?" Whitlock replied, looking at Mobuto.

"He went to meet an informer. An hour later the newspaper's deputy editor received an anonymous call to say that Remy had been abducted by Ngune's men. That's all the caller would say." Mobuto glanced at Whitlock. "I presume you have been briefed about the Ngune breakout?"

"Yes, sir, I have," Whitlock replied. "Has Ngune got the backing to attempt a *coup d'état*?"

"He's got men and money," Mobuto answered matter-of-factly. "The men are his ex-Security Policemen. The money comes from the wealthy Moslem community in the south of the country. Many of them built up vast fortunes under my father's regime, illegal fortunes, I hasten to add. They know that if I do bring a new democratic freedom to my country then it'll mean the confiscation of those fortunes. And as you know, greed knows no bounds. They'll go to any lengths to reinstate a dictatorship that will protect them, just as my father's regime did for forty-five years. I'm the one obstacle in their way. The people look to me as a new Messiah. I won't let them down."

"One thing puzzles me," Whitlock said at length. "Your father repealed the law making you his natural successor once he realized you'd never follow in his footsteps. So how did you manage to wrestle power from the government after his death?"

"My father *was* the government. He made the decisions, he passed the laws. His ministers were just yesmen, puppets. So, when he died, the puppets had no-one to pull their strings anymore. They panicked. And I used that panic to my benefit. But I had to act fast. Ngune was my biggest threat. He was the one man my father trusted, really trusted. Fortunately for the country, the police and the Security Police had never got on. And with the police and most of the armed forces behind me, I was able to stop Ngune from seizing power. Unfortunately I underestimated the strength of his support. But I'm determined not to cut short my visit here. That would just play straight into his hands. It would make the people think *I* was panicking. And that could lose me support." Mobuto got to his feet and moved to the sideboard to pour himself a bourbon. "Well, gentlemen, if you'll excuse me, I've got some work to finish before I go to bed."

"Of course," Kolchinsky said, getting to his feet.

Whitlock crossed to where Brett was sitting. "Don't let him out of your sight," he said softly.

"I won't," Brett replied tersely.

Whitlock said good night to Mobuto then followed Kolchinsky out into the corridor. "I wish we could have used our own people to babysit Mobuto. I'd have felt a lot happier."

Kolchinsky nodded grimly. "I know what you mean. But we're stuck with Bailey's men, I'm afraid. There's nothing I can do about it."

"I know," Whitlock replied and pushed the button for the lift.

"I'm going to drop by the hospital to update the Colonel on today's developments. Fancy coming?"

Whitlock shrugged. "Why not? Carmen won't be home yet. She works late Tuesdays." He looked at his watch. "But aren't visiting hours over?"

"The Secretary-General had a word with the hospital's administrator who reluctantly agreed to make an exception in the Colonel's case and waive the normal visiting hours. It was one of the conditions the Colonel laid down if he was to remain in hospital."

Whitlock shot Kolchinsky a knowing look then ushered him into the lift.

Kolchinsky drove the short distance to the Bellevue Hospital, conveniently situated less than two miles away from both the hotel and the United Nations building. The receptionist directed them to a private ward on the third floor.

Kolchinsky knocked lightly.

"Come in," Philpott called out.

Kolchinsky opened the door and entered. Philpott was sitting up in bed, his face hidden behind a copy of the *New York Times*.

"Just put them by the bed. I'll take them later," Philpott muttered gruffly from behind the newspaper.

"It's me, Malcolm," Kolchinsky announced.

Philpott lowered the newspaper and gave them a

wry smile. "I'm sorry, I thought it was another of those damn nurses. They've been coming and going all day." He glanced at Whitlock. "I see he managed to drag you along as well."

Whitlock smiled and pulled up a chair. "How are you feeling, sir?"

"A little weak, but otherwise fine."

Kolchinsky sat down on the second chair and handed Philpott a brown packet. "It's from the deli on 44th Street."

Philpott opened the packet and looked inside. "Grapes! I was hoping it might have been some tobacco. The doctor confiscated mine." He put the packet on the bedside table and picked up his empty pipe. "I'm dying for a smoke. C.W.—"

"I'm not fetching you any tobacco," Whitlock cut in quickly. "Get better first, then you can smoke your pipe again."

"I am better. I should have discharged myself this morning." Philpott gave a resigned sigh. "Any news of Mike?"

Kolchinsky explained the day's events, culminating in the attempted assassination of Jamel Mobuto.

"Good God," Philpott muttered when Kolchinsky had finished talking. He looked at Whitlock. "Are you alright?"

"I cut my leg when I fell off the motorbike. It's nothing serious. But my suit's a total write-off. It'll break my tailor's heart."

"At least you're alright. Any news on the assassin and his accomplice?"

"Nothing yet," Kolchinsky replied. "They weren't carrying any ID but they're almost certainly Zimbalan. Probably ex-Security policemen. I've had their photographs and prints faxed through to the police in Habane. Hopefully they'll have come up with something by tomorrow."

"And what was that you said earlier about Bernard. He's CIA?"

Kolchinsky nodded then opened the attaché case. He handed his photostat copy of Bailey's file to Philpott. "It's all in there. I'll leave it with you tonight. It certainly makes interesting reading."

"I bet it does," Philpott hissed. "Be careful of Bailey, Sergei. Tell him as little as possible. And don't trust him an inch."

"I think we all realized that when we met him," Kolchinsky said, glancing at Whitlock.

"And as for those two bullet-catchers . . ." Whitlock trailed off with a shake of his head.

"What about them?" Philpott asked.

"Let's just say I wouldn't want them protecting me," Whitlock replied. "As I said to Sergei back at the hotel, I only wish we could have used our own people to babysit Mobuto. I'd have slept better."

"I did try, C.W.," Philpott said with an apologetic shrug. "I wanted to bring in Strike Force Seven as his personal bodyguard team. That would have left you free to work with Sabrina in Beirut. But the President wanted this to be a joint operation and Bailey managed to convince him to use CIA men as bodyguards. There was nothing I could do. At least the President saw enough sense to agree to my request to put you in charge of the unit. I know you won't let me down, C.W. Just keep an eye on Bailey's goons. If President Mobuto had been killed tonight we'd have been crucified."

"We've still got three days to go, sir. They're sure to try again."

"You can count on it. And what happened to this warning Bernard was supposed to have passed on to Bailey?"

"I spoke to Bailey after the attempt on the President's life," Kolchinsky said. "He claims Bernard never contacted him. His theory is that the two men were either freelance or else they decided to try and kill the President by themselves without telling the others."

"It just dosen't ring true, does it?" Whitlock said.

"Of course it doesn't," Philpott snapped tersely. "But we're dealing with Bailey, remember?"

Kolchinsky nodded then rubbed his eyes wearily. "Well, there's nothing more we can do tonight. And I'm shattered. It's been some day."

Whitlock got to his feet. "Only three to go. Can you drop me off at the apartment on your way home, Sergei? If I get the subway I'll probably fall asleep and end up at Washington Heights."

Kolchinsky patted Whitlock's shoulder. "Of course. Come on."

Philpott watched them leave then stared at the folder Kolchinsky had left with him. He knew Bailey was up to something, but what? The thought lingered as he opened the folder and started to read its contents.

◆ CHAPTER
FOUR

Sabrina paused outside the door, knocked, and entered. The man behind the desk was in his early forties with a dark, swarthy complexion and a thick black moustache which arched over the corners of his mouth. He looked up from the document he was reading and his eyes lingered on her body before he sat back and raised his eyebrows quizzically, waiting for her to speak.

"Are you Captain Farouk?" she asked.

"That's what it says," he replied in faultless English, gesturing to the nameplate on his desk.

"If you read Arabic," Sabrina replied with a smile. "I spoke to you earlier on the phone—"

"Ah, yes," Farouk cut in and glanced down at the notepad in front of him. "Miss Cassidy, not so?"

"Sabrina Cassidy," she replied, using the name on her UNACO passport.

"Please, won't you sit down, Miss Cassidy?" Farouk said, indicating the wooden chair in front of his desk.

"Thank you," she said and sat down.

"Is this your first time in Beirut?"

"Yes," she replied truthfully. "I didn't know where to begin looking for Mike so I called the police and they put me on to you. They said you were in charge of the investigation." She feigned nervousness by fidgeting with the handbag in her lap. "But what investigation? What's happened?"

Farouk raised his hand to silence her. "There's a warrant out for the arrest of Michael Green."

The name on one of the passports Graham had drawn from UNACO stores in New York. She sat forward. "On what charge?"

"Murder."

She slumped back in the chair. "Oh, my God. Murder? I don't believe it. Sure, Mike's a bit of a rebel but he'd never kill anybody."

Farouk uncapped his pen and pulled the notepad toward him. "I'd like to ask you a few questions, Miss Cassidy?"

"Yes, of course," she replied, continuing to feign nervousness. "Anything."

"You said on the phone that he'd called you in New York. What exactly did he say?"

"All he said was that he was in trouble and that he needed some money to get out of the country. Then the line went dead."

"Do you know why he was here?"

"The first I knew he was in Beirut was when he rang me." She sighed deeply. "Mike's a loner. It's not the first time he's gone off by himself."

"And he owns a company in New York?" Farouk said, consulting his notes again.

"Whitaker Haulage," she added. "He's the boss."

"Yes, I know. We found some business cards in his hotel room." Farouk tapped thoughtfully on the notepad. "And his fellow directors don't mind him just going off by himself without letting them know where he is? What if something were to happen to the company?"

"They're used to his erratic behavior by now. And anyway, he pays their salaries. What can they say?"

"Did he have any friends that you knew of in Beirut?"

She shook her head. "None that he ever mentioned."

"Russell Laidlaw?"

She pretended to think for a moment. Then she shook her head again. "No, I can't say the name means anything to me. Is that the man who was murdered?"

"No," Farouk replied. "He was the last person to see your boyfriend here in Beirut. He used to be in the Special Forces in America, the Delta unit."

"Are you suggesting that Mike was once a member of Delta?" She shook her head in disbelief. "I don't believe it. Not for one minute."

"I'm not suggesting anything, Miss Cassidy. It's just strange that Laidlaw was with Delta and the murdered man, Barak, was an informer for Delta here in Beirut. Delta seems to be the common denominator, doesn't it?"

"Haven't you asked this man Laidlaw about Mike?"

"He claims to have met him for the first time at the Windorah; it's a bar frequented mainly by foreigners. The owner's borne out his story. So I'm back to square one."

"Can't you ask Delta?"

"I already have. They say no Michael Green has ever been with them. And it took a lot of persuasion for them to just admit that."

"How do you know Mike was involved? Did someone see him?"

"His fingerprints were on the murder weapon. I checked with Interpol and they confirmed they were his prints."

"Interpol?" she replied with surprise. "You mean he had a criminal record?"

"No, but the New York police had his prints on file."

The NYPD had Graham's fingerprints on file. They

had all UNACO operatives' fingerprints on file. It was a precaution in case any of them were injured, or killed, and weren't carrying any formal identification. But Michael Green? Then it hit her. Why hadn't she thought of it when Kolchinsky briefed them? UNACO must have given the NYPD permission to release the prints under Graham's assumed name. But why? It made no sense. They had set up their own operative. She wanted some answers and she was determined to get them when she next spoke to Kolchinsky.

"Is something wrong, Miss Cassidy?" Farouk said, noticing her frown.

She cursed herself silently for letting her guard drop. "Sorry, I was just surprised that the New York police had his fingerprints on file. I never realized he had a criminal record."

"He was once convicted of a drink-driving offense."

"I didn't know that," she said then sat forward, her eyes burrowing into Farouk. "I still don't believe Mike killed this man. It's not in his character."

"Well, unless he turns himself in we have to assume that he is the killer. And the longer he remains on the run, the worse it will become for him."

"I think he's being held against his will somewhere," she said.

"Perhaps he's already fled the country. Interpol's been alerted."

"How could he have fled the country without any money?" She shook her head. "No, it all points to him being held against his will somewhere. Mike never travels without cash and credit cards. So why call me unless he had lost them? Or had them stolen?"

"You really believe he's innocent, don't you?"

"Yes, I do." She got to her feet. "Is there anything I can do to help him?"

"It's a police matter now, Miss Cassidy." Farouk capped his pen and pointed it at her. "If he should contact you, tell him to call me. It would be in his best interests."

"I doubt he will call me," she said with a dejected shrug. "He doesn't even know I'm here."

Farouk got to his feet and came round the desk to shake her hand. "Thank you for your time, Miss Cassidy."

She nodded and walked to the door.

"Oh, Miss Cassidy?" Farouk waited until she turned to look at him. "If you're caught trying to help him escape you'll be charged with aiding and abetting a wanted criminal. Bear it in mind."

"Sure," she replied and closed the door behind her.

Laidlaw had been detained by the police only hours after Barak's murder and although they had interrogated him at regular intervals every four hours, trying to break him down, he had managed to stick to his story. He had met Graham, or Green as he had referred to him throughout the interrogation, for the first time at the Windorah. They had talked for a while then he had given Green a lift back to his hotel. He had never seen him again after that. He knew no-one had seen him at Barak's house otherwise he'd have been charged straight away.

He had been finally released after thirty-six hours. He had tried to sleep when he got home but to no avail. The voice haunted him: the voice of the policeman, Farouk. But he had never seen Farouk's face. He had asked the questions at every interrogation but always from behind the sanctuary of a powerful table lamp. Why hadn't he shown his face? Laidlaw had racked his brains over and over but he couldn't place the name. So why had he been so secretive? Laidlaw knew he could be overreacting from lack of sleep—it could have been a plan to try and break him down: a voice, no face. But still it troubled him. Who was Farouk?

He punched the pillow angrily. Forget Farouk. Just get some sleep. But he couldn't. That monotonous, grinding voice was in his head and he couldn't get rid of it. He kicked the sheet off and swung his legs onto the floor. Pushing the hair from his face he looked at the bedside clock. It had been five hours since he'd got home, and he hadn't slept in that time. All because of that damn voice. He stifled a yawn then stood up and went into the kitchen. He opened the freezer and helped himself to a cold beer and the last of the chicken drumsticks from the packet he had bought earlier in the week. He tossed the empty packet onto the overflowing bin in the corner of the room and sat down at the table. Just as he was about to open the beer the doorbell rang. He shook his head in despair then got to his feet and went to open the door.

"Russell Laidlaw?"

"That's right," Laidlaw muttered. "You're not a reporter, are you?"

"My name's Sabrina Cassidy, I'm a friend of Mike's."

"Mike?"

"Mike Graham," Sabrina retorted with a hint of irritation in her voice. "We need to talk."

"Look, come back later. I'm absolutely exhausted. I've been in police custody for the last thirty-six hours. And it's all thanks to your friend Mike."

"I think he's in trouble," she said. "Please, we need to talk."

Laidlaw rubbed his eyes wearily then pulled open the door. "What the hell. I couldn't sleep anyway."

"Thanks," she said and stepped inside.

"You'll have to forgive the mess," Laidlaw said, closing the door. "I'm not very domesticated."

She followed him into the kitchen and sat down in the chair offered to her.

"You want a beer?" he asked.

"Coffee, if you've got it."

"Somewhere," he replied and switched the kettle on before rummaging through the drawers. He found the coffee jar and put a heaped spoonful into the only clean mug he could find. "You say you're a friend of Mike's. You work with him?"

"That's right," she replied.

Laidlaw opened the beer and drank a mouthful. "And you're out here to find him? Well, I wish you luck."

"You saw him, didn't you?"

"I met him, yes—at the Windorah; it's a bar in town. We talked a bit then I gave him a lift back to his hotel. I never saw him after that."

Sabrina exhaled deeply. "How can I convince you I'm on the level?"

Laidlaw filled the cup with hot water then placed it on the table in front of her. He put the milk bottle beside the cup. "Help yourself. Look, Miss Cassidy, I met your friend—"

"Spare me the act," she cut in angrily. "You served in Delta together. It was on an operation in Libya that his family was kidnapped by Arab terrorists to try and force him to countermand the order to attack. The two men behind the kidnapping were Salim Al-Makesh and Jean-Jacques Bernard. Al-Makesh was killed by the Israelis. Bernard was thought to have been killed in a car-bomb attack a year and a half ago. Mike obviously found out Bernard was alive and came out here to get him. You were his contact. That's all we know. I've been sent here to find out what really happened and get him back to the States."

Laidlaw pulled out the chair opposite her and sat down. "Carrie gave Mike a watch as a Christmas present. What make was it?"

"Piaget. Gold-plated. And it was a birthday present. Satisfied?"

Laidlaw nodded. "Satisfied. Who's this 'we' you mentioned?"

"I can't tell you, I'm afraid."

"Undercover work in other words?"

"Something like that," she replied.

"Are you his partner?"

She nodded. "Did you tip him off about Bernard?"

"Yeah. I saw Bernard outside the American University Hospital. I knew Mike would want to know."

"And where did this Barak fit into the picture?"

"Barak had been a Delta contact for years. If anybody could find Bernard, then he could. Until Mike put a bullet in his back."

"Mike didn't kill him, you know that," she retorted sharply.

"All I know is that when I reached the house Barak was dead. Then I saw Barak's car being driven away at high speed. And Mike had gone. Put two and two together."

"It has to be a set-up. Why kill the one man capable of leading him to Bernard? It makes no sense."

"I wasn't there when he went into the house. He insisted on that. I don't know what they discussed."

"Only Mike knows that. That's why we have to find him."

"Not 'we'. You can count me out. I put myself on the line for him once already and look where it got me: thirty-six hours in jail. Interrogations every four hours. No, Miss Cassidy, if you want to find Mike, you find him by yourself."

"I don't know my way around Beirut."

"So get a guide. There's plenty of them. And they don't cost much."

"If it's money—"

"Don't insult me, Miss Cassidy," Laidlaw snapped sharply.

She raised a hand in apology. "I'm sorry. I shouldn't have said that. I need your help, Mr. Laidlaw. And so does Mike. If the police get to him first, he'll be put away for life."

"And what if he did kill Barak? What if he is guilty? You're going to help a killer flee justice."

"I don't know how well you know Mike. I think I know him pretty well. He's a damn good professional and he wouldn't jeopardize his career by putting a bullet in the back of some two-bit informer."

"Mike's changed," Laidlaw answered, staring at the beer can he was turning on the table. "I noticed that the moment we met. He used to be the most stable guy I ever knew. Nothing ever riled him. But that was before he lost his family. Now he's bitter, unpredictable: I'd even say psychotic. I don't go along with your assessment, Miss Cassidy. I think he was more than capable of shooting Barak in the back. Especially if you consider he was on the trail of the man he believes had his family abducted and almost certainly murdered. No, I don't want any more to do with Mike. He's trouble."

Sabrina pushed her chair back and stood up, her eyes blazing. "At least Mike hasn't run away from his past. What about you? Hiding away in this squalor, trying to forget what happened in Honduras." She noticed the surprise in his eyes. "Oh, I know all about you, Mr. Laidlaw. I read your file on the plane. I know why you left Delta. I don't think you're in any position to pass judgment on someone like Mike."

"Just get out," Laidlaw hissed between clenched teeth.

"My pleasure," she retorted then walked to the door where she paused to look back at him. "And don't forget, you were the one who contacted Mike in the first place. It's thanks to you that he's in this mess right now. Think about that when you open your next beer."

Laidlaw sunk his face into his hands. A moment later the front door slammed shut. He suddenly grabbed the beer can and hurled it against the wall then upturned the table, sending it crashing against the cooker. He checked himself as he was about to kick the chair out of the way then walked slowly to the bedroom and slumped onto the bed. He put his hands behind his head and closed his eyes. Within minutes he was asleep. It proved to be a disturbed, restless sleep.

"You look like death," Dave Jenkins said when Laidlaw arrived at the Windorah that evening.

"I feel like it," Laidlaw retorted, climbing onto one of the bar stools. "A beer, Dave."

"Comin' up," Jenkins replied, uncapping a Budweiser and placing it on the counter in front of Laidlaw. "Where were you last night? I was thinking about sending out the cavalry to look for you if you hadn't shown up tonight."

"It's nice to be missed," Laidlaw muttered then took a drink of beer.

"So where were you last night?"

Laidlaw shrugged. "I didn't fancy coming in. Is that such a crime?"

"If it affects my profits, yes," Jenkins said with a grin then pushed a coaster across to Laidlaw. "What do you think of the design? A batch of them came in this morning."

"What?" Laidlaw replied in amazement.

"Just look at the design." Jenkins picked up another four and handed them out to the other customers sitting at the counter.

Laidlaw glanced at it, turned it over, and was about to discard it when he saw the handwritten note scrawled across it. He looked up but Jenkins was busy discussing the logo with one of the other customers. He read the note: Go upstairs to Room 4. Knock twice. Pause. Knock twice more.

"Interesting, isn't it?" Jenkins said, deftly taking the coaster from Laidlaw's hand and discarding it unobtrusively in the bin under the counter. "But then I'm biased anyway."

Laidlaw took another mouthful of beer then got to

his feet and walked to the stairs at the end of the room. He paused, his hand on the banister. What the hell was going on? He sighed deeply then mounted the stairs and looked around him slowly. The Windorah had been a small family hotel before Jenkins bought it seven years earlier. The ten rooms were all situated on the first floor. Jenkins had decided to concentrate on the bar and closed the rooms. He converted the first two into toilets and the others were only used for customers, invariably foreign journalists who were too drunk to drive home. He never charged for the rooms and the journalists repaid him by keeping their custom at the bar.

Laidlaw stopped outside Room 4, glanced round to see that nobody was about, then knocked twice. He paused momentarily then knocked twice more. A bolt was drawn back from inside then the door opened fractionally before a hand reached out and hauled him into the room. The door closed behind him immediately.

"Mike?" Laidlaw said in amazement as Graham bolted the door.

"You took your time! Where the hell were you last night?"

"Being interrogated on a murder charge," Laidlaw snapped back. "Thirty-six hours without any sleep. And all thanks to you. You've got some explaining to do."

Graham walked to the unmade bed and sat down. "I didn't kill Barak."

"So where were you when I got to the house? And who drove off in Barak's Peugeot?"

Graham rubbed his unshaven face and looked up at Laidlaw. "All I know is that when I entered the house someone coshed me. When I woke up I was in some back alley. I still don't know where it was. And my Beretta was gone."

"The police have got it," Laidlaw said coldly. "It was the gun that killed Barak."

"I know," Graham retorted. "Why the hell do you think I've been holed up here since yesterday? When I saw my picture on the front page of the local newspaper I knew it meant trouble."

"So why did you come here?"

"I went to your house first but the cops were watching it. I also saw them putting a tap on your phone. That's why I couldn't call you. Then I thought of Dave. He's the only other guy I could trust here."

Laidlaw moved to the window and tweaked the edge of the curtains. The police car that had followed him to the Windorah was still parked across the road.

"Were you followed here?" Graham asked.

"Yeah," Laidlaw replied, letting the curtain fall back into place. "But that was to be expected. Jeez, I still don't know what to make of your story. It doesn't make sense. If Bernard did kill Barak, why not kill you as well? What would he have to gain by setting you up?"

"That question's been going round in my head ever since I woke up in that alley."

"And?"

"And nothing," Graham replied. "Like you said, it makes no sense. I'm still a threat to him alive."

"What if Bernard wasn't behind it?"

"It has to be Bernard. Hell, I wish I knew why though."

Laidlaw looked down at Graham. "The cops aren't the only ones on your tail. Your partner's in town."

Graham's eyes narrowed suspiciously. "My partner?"

"Calls herself Sabrina Cassidy. Looks like a model out of one of those Coke ads, only better."

Graham smiled faintly. "That's her. When did she get in?"

"Dunno. We didn't exactly hit it off."

"I know what you mean. I didn't get on with her either when we started working together. We'd fight like cat and dog. Hell, we still have our spats. But she's still a damn good professional all the same."

"She thinks a lot of you, you know. I made the mistake of criticizing you and she came down on me like a ton of bricks."

"She's very maternal. It can be a pain in the ass at times."

"Is that what you call it?" Laidlaw replied, an eyebrow raised quizzically.

There were two knocks on the door before Graham could muster a reply. A pause then another two knocks.

"That's Dave," Graham said. "He said he'd be up. I'll get him to find out where Sabrina's staying."

Graham unlocked the door. Jenkins entered, followed by two Arabs in jeans and open-necked shirts. Both were armed with Russian Makarova pistols.

"I'm sorry, Mike," Jenkins said, giving Graham a despairing look. "They caught me unawares. They were in the opposite room."

"Shut up!" one of the Arabs snapped in a thick English accent. "You are Mike Graham?"

Graham nodded slowly. "Who are you? Bernard's goons?"

"Captain Farouk want to see you," the Arab replied.

"That's the bastard who interrogated me," Laidlaw hissed.

"If you not come, the girl will die." The Arab took a passport from his pocket and tossed it on the bed. "Captain Farouk say you look. He serious."

Graham picked up the passport and looked at Laidlaw. "It's Sabrina's." He turned on the English-speaking Arab. "If you or this Farouk have touched her I'll tear you apart with my bare hands."

The Arab's face remained motionless. "You come. All of you."

"Farouk wants me, let the others go," Graham said.

"If you not come, the girl will die."

"It's like talking to a robot," Graham hissed then

glanced at Jenkins and Laidlaw. "We're going to have to do as he says. I'm sorry."

"What about the bar?" Jenkins asked.

"The bar closed."

"Closed?" Jenkins replied indignantly.

"It has been closed. We go out the back door. And if you are thinking about trying to fight us—"

"Yeah, we know," Graham cut in angrily.

"The girl will die," the Arab concluded.

Jenkins led the way down the stairs into the now empty bar room. He opened the hatchway at the end of the counter then turned to the English-speaking Arab. "Can I at least lock up?"

The Arab nodded then ordered his accomplice to go with Jenkins. When they returned Jenkins again led the way out into the side alley behind the bar. A black van was parked by the door. Jenkins locked the door, pocketed the keys, then his hands were tied behind his back before he was bundled into the back of the van after Graham and Laidlaw. The doors were closed, enveloping them in darkness, and locked from the outside. The two Arabs then climbed into the front and moments later the van spluttered into life and turned out of the alley.

"Mike, can you reach into my jacket pocket?" Jenkins said, nudging Graham with his elbow.

"What the hell for?"

"My keys," Jenkins replied. "There's a Swiss Army knife on the keyring. That's why I insisted on locking the bar. We can cut ourselves free."

"Good thinking, Dave, but we can't risk it."

"What do you mean?" Jenkins replied. "If we can cut ourselves free we can jump those two when they open the doors again. Three against two. We'd have a good chance of overpowering them."

"If we could be sure it would only be the two of them. What if there are others waiting for us when we do reach our destination?"

"It's worth a try, surely?" Jenkins retorted.

"It's not just that. We don't know where Sabrina is. Even if we did manage to overpower them we could be putting her life in danger. I won't take that risk."

"Great, so we're just going to sit here like trussed up chickens—"

"If you quit whining, Dave, I could tell you what I've got in mind."

"That's gratitude for you. Who took you in—"

"Dave, shut up," Laidlaw snapped then turned to Graham beside him. "Well, what's the plan?"

"We loosen our ropes. Then, once we know Sabrina's safe we can make our move. It's a long shot, I know, but there isn't much else we can do under the circumstances."

"I had the same idea," Laidlaw said. "Let's just hope Cheech and Chong up front aren't telepathic."

"We've got to chance it," Graham replied grimly.

They set about loosening the ropes just enough for them to be able to reach the knot once Graham gave the signal. Their only concern was that, in the darkness, one, or more, of the ropes had been loosened too much and it would be noticed when they emerged from the back of the van. All they could do was wait.

Twenty minutes later the van came to a halt, but the engine was kept running. They heard one of the Arabs get out and moments later a metal gate was opened and the van drove forward a few feet before stopping again, presumably to pick up the Arab. They drove another couple of hundred yards before the van came to a halt and the engine was switched off. This time both Arabs got out and the back doors were unlocked.

The English-speaking Arab ordered them to get out. Jenkins scrambled out first, followed by Graham and Laidlaw. They looked around. They were in an illuminated yard lined with a row of six red and black pantechnicons. Graham couldn't understand the writing across the side of the nearest one. It was in Arabic.

The Arabs spoke briefly together then the English-speaking one stepped back, his Makarova trained on the three men. His colleague walked behind Jenkins and tugged at the rope binding his wrists. He cursed angrily and immediately tightened it. Graham and Laidlaw remained motionless, not daring to look at each other. Laidlaw was spun round and the Arab checked his rope then he was pushed aside and Graham subjected to the same treatment. The Arab shook his head at his colleague.

"Inside," the English-speaking Arab ordered, gesturing with the pistol to the door behind him.

Graham and Laidlaw exchanged relieved glances then followed Jenkins into the white-walled corridor. They were led to a metal door. The English-speaking Arab pulled it open and indicated for them to enter. They found themselves in a cavernous room lined with scarred wooden workbenches and rows of metal hooks hanging from the ceiling. They were all on runners and could be manoeuvred the length of the room. It was spotlessly clean. The second Arab walked to a door and disappeared inside. Moments later the door opened and he emerged with Sabrina. Her hands were bound behind her back but she was otherwise unhurt. He pushed her onto a chair by the door. Graham took a step toward her but the English-speaking Arab levelled the pistol menacingly at him and ordered him to remain where he was.

"You OK?" Graham called out.

"I'm fine. I didn't realize Farouk . . ." she trailed off when she saw Graham and Laidlaw both look past her, their eyes riveted on the man who had appeared in the doorway.

"Good to see you again, Mr. Graham. It's been a long time."

Sabrina looked from Farouk to Graham, a puzzled frown on her face. "You know Farouk?"

"Farouk?" Graham snorted contemptuously. "That's Salim Al-Makesh."

"What?" Sabrina replied in amazement. "But he was killed by Israeli commandos in Damascus."

"That's obviously what they wanted us to believe," Graham said without taking his eyes of Al-Makesh. "Which only leaves one logical explanation. You're working for the Israelis now, aren't you?"

Al-Makesh stepped away from the door, his hands dug into his trouser pockets. He nodded. "It was either that or be killed. It was a question of survival."

"Now it makes sense," Laidlaw said, nodding to himself. "I couldn't understand why you never showed yourself when you were interrogating me. You knew I'd recognize you straight away."

"I wasn't sure whether you would or not," Al-Makesh replied. "I have changed my appearance considerably since I was with the Black June but it seems I made the right decision after all."

"Who killed Barak?" Graham demanded. "You or Bernard?"

"Bernard. I had nothing to do with it," Al-Makesh said. "When Barak told him you were in Beirut—"

"Barak worked for him?" Graham interceded.

"Barak worked for anyone who paid him," Al-Makesh replied with a dismissive shrug. "But he had started to drink heavily in recent months and Bernard felt he had become a liability. So when he heard you were in town he hit on a plan to get rid of both of you. He'd kill Barak and set you up as the fall guy—I believe that's the term you Americans use. He would knock you out when you went to the house, kill Barak, then dump you in an alley near the Cola Roundabout in western Beirut. All I had to do was go there and arrest you. But when I got there, you'd gone."

"Why didn't Bernard just kill me when he had the chance?" Graham asked.

"And have UNACO crawling all over Beirut?" Al-

Makesh smiled when Graham looked at him in surprise. "I have my sources, just like you. But if you were arrested for murder they would have to be very careful not to blow their cover. Any sort of publicity could have splashed UNACO across the front page of every newspaper in the world."

"I would have recognized you the moment I saw you," Graham said.

"Who would have believed you? The Israeli Mossad would have confirmed that I'd been killed in Damascus. I have a watertight cover for all those years I was with the Black June. The authorities would think you'd finally cracked under the pressure of what had happened to your family. You'd probably have ended up in an asylum."

"I could have backed him up," Laidlaw said.

"My superiors would have dismissed Graham's allegations about my past as the ramblings of a broken man. But if you'd also been able to identify me then they would certainly have initiated an investigation. For that reason you would have had to be silenced once Graham was in custody. An accident. But when Bernard's plan backfired I needed you alive in case you could lead me to Graham. Which, as it turned out, you did."

"Were the CIA in on this?" Sabrina asked.

"No," Al-Makesh replied bluntly. "And neither were the Mossad."

"The CIA?" Graham asked, staring at Sabrina. "What the hell have they got to do with this?"

"Bernard works for them," she told him.

"What?" Graham snarled.

"She's right," Al-Makesh said then gestured around him. "This all belongs to Bernard. It's a meat-processing plant, paid for with money from a CIA slush fund. He's now a legitimate businessman."

"And how did the Israelis get you into the police?" Sabrina asked.

"I was a policeman for twelve years in Jordan before I joined the Black June. It wasn't difficult for me to fit in here. So not only am I in a job I know, I'm also in a position to pass vital information back to the Israelis. It's the perfect cover."

"And now you're going to kill us to protect your cover," Laidlaw concluded.

"You know too much."

"Kill us and UNACO *will be* crawling all over Beirut," Sabrina warned him.

"I'll have to take that risk. But even if they do come they still won't find any bodies. There's a beef shipment due out tomorrow destined for Syria. You'll be going with it." Al-Makesh pointed to a wooden container in the corner of the room. "Your bodies will be put in there. The container will then be sealed and loaded onto one of the trucks in the morning. Then, once over the border, it will conveniently disappear. Who knows how long it will take before it's discovered?"

"All neatly worked out," Graham said facetiously. "You two must be very proud of yourselves."

"This is all my idea. Bernard doesn't even know you're here. We have an arrangement. I use this place if I need to get rid of someone. The blood gets washed away in the morning so there's no evidence to suggest a crime ever took place. And his foreman makes sure the containers are loaded onto the trucks and dumped over the border. No questions asked. All very amicable." Al-Makesh looked at the English-speaking Arab standing beside Graham. "Samir, you know what to do."

Graham had managed to untie his hands soon after entering the room and lashed out at Samir, catching him on the side of the face with his fist, rocking him back against the wall. The Makarova fell to the floor. Laidlaw, who had also managed to untie his hands, tackled the second Arab. Graham picked up the Makarova and shot the second Arab as he turned his pistol on Laidlaw. Laidlaw's hand was on his P220 automatic but he knew he couldn't fire it, no matter how hard he tried. Samir grabbed Graham from behind as Al-Makesh unholstered his Beretta. Graham broke the hold and swiveled Samir round as Al-Makesh fired. The bullet took Samir in the chest. Sabrina leaped from her chair and shoulder-charged Al-Makesh before he could fire again. His gun clattered noisily to the floor. Graham swung the Makarova on Al-Makesh who was still reaching for the Beretta. All the hate welled up inside him as he thought of Carrie and Mikey. He squeezed the trigger. Nothing happened. The pistol had jammed.

"Shoot him!" Graham screamed at Laidlaw who was staring at the pistol in his hand. "Russ, shoot him!"

Al-Makesh's fingers curled around the Beretta. Sabrina lunged at him. He swung the gun on her. She kicked out, catching him on the wrist. The bullet was deflected harmlessly into the ceiling. Graham tore Laidlaw's P220 automatic from his hand and shot Al-Makesh through the head. He was dead before his body hit the floor.

Graham swung round to Laidlaw and grabbed him by the front of his shirt. "What the hell were you playing at? Christ, Russ, he was about to kill us and you're standing there admiring the damn gun. What's your problem?"

Sabrina was quick to intervene and nudged Graham with her elbow. "Mike, untie me."

Graham shoved Laidlaw away from him then turned to Sabrina and untied her hands.

"Who's the other guy?" she asked, massaging her wrists.

"Dave Jenkins, he runs the Windorah, it's a bar in the city. He's been hiding me for the last couple of days."

Jenkins waited until Laidlaw had untied his hands then approached Graham who introduced him to

Sabrina. "Mike, you deliberately loosened my ropes more than you needed to. Why?"

"You're not a soldier, Dave. I didn't want to get you involved in the fighting. Also, it was a psychological move. I knew the goon would automatically check to see if our ropes were as loose as yours. That's how we were able to deceive him." Graham looked angrily at Laidlaw. "I should have left your ropes loose as well."

"You've got every right to be mad at me, Mike. I know I should have told you but . . ." he trailed off with a shrug and stared dejectedly at his feet.

"Told me what?" Graham demanded. "That you've become some kind of born-again pacifist?"

"Can we discuss this later?" Sabrina said, stepping between them. "We've got to get out of here. What if someone heard the shots?"

"Al-Makesh would have taken care of that," Graham said. "He would hardly have wanted anyone alerting the authorities, would he?"

"I guess not," Sabrina replied then gestured toward the bodies. "What about them?"

"They take our places when the meat shipment leaves for Syria tomorrow," Graham answered.

"What if they check the container?" Jenkins asked.

"They won't if it's sealed. They'll just assume it's us. Come on, let's get them in the container."

They carried the bodies in silence across the room and dumped them into the wooden container. Graham then nailed on the lid.

"Can we get out of here now?"

"Sure, Dave," Graham answered with a reassuring smile.

"We've got to talk," Sabrina said to Graham. "Alone."

"Come back to the Windorah," Jenkins offered. "You can talk there in private."

"Yeah, we'll take you up on that, Dave," Graham

said then suddenly looked despairingly at the sealed container. "Oh God, the keys for the van . . ."

"Are here," Sabrina said, jangling them behind Graham. "Well, someone had to be alert."

"What *would* I do without you?" Graham replied facetiously.

"What indeed?" she answered with a questioning glance in his direction before walking to the door.

Jenkins unlocked one of the bedrooms when they got back to the Windorah and switched on the light after he had crossed to the window to draw the curtains. "Anyone thirsty?"

"I'd love a coffee," Sabrina said, sinking into the armchair beside the window.

"Make that two," Graham added.

"Russell?"

"Beer please, Dave," Laidlaw replied.

Jenkins left the room.

"You want me to leave as well?" Laidlaw asked.

"Not until you've told me what the hell happened to make you trigger shy." Graham sat on the edge of the bed and looked up at Laidlaw. "Well?"

Laidlaw's eyes flickered toward Sabrina. She knew. She'd read his dossier. He pulled up the wooden chair from beside the bed and sat down. "Last year we went into Honduras to help the government troops suppress an attempted *coup d'état* by Communist-backed rebels. We'd been there about a week when we got news that the rebel leader and his council would be holding a meeting at a farmhouse on the outskirts of Choluteca—it's a town in the south of the country: rebel territory. We were asked to infiltrate the area and retrieve as many documents as we could from the farmhouse. But no prisoners. Why, I don't know. But those were our orders. Six of us went in. There wasn't a single guard on duty when we got there. That should have alerted us.

But, as I said, we had our orders. We launched our offensive just as the meeting was supposed to have started. Three of us went in the front, the other three through the back. We'd been told which room would be used for the meeting so we didn't have to search the whole building. We threw stun grenades into the room then went in firing." He shifted uncomfortably on the chair and wiped a bead of sweat that ran down the side of his face. "There were no rebels there. Just four missionaries and thirty-five kids. None of the kids were over ten. Orphans of the war. It only took us a few seconds to realize the mistake but by then twenty-eight kids and three of the missionaries were either dead or dying. Two of the kids and the fourth missionary died later in hospital. Five kids survived. Five out of thirty-five. The rebels blamed the massacre on the government troops and the government blamed it on the rebels. It became just another story from Central America. Nobody took much notice."

He rubbed his hands over his face. "The six of us were immediately flown back to the States to undergo psychiatric treatment. I was the worst affected. I couldn't touch a gun. Christ, I even broke out into a sweat if I saw one on TV. The other guys responded to treatment. I didn't. After six months the psychiatrists gave up on me. So I was retired. It was another six months before I was able to pick up a gun again. But I still couldn't touch the trigger. I wanted to shoot that bastard tonight, Mike. My brain told me to pull the trigger but my finger wouldn't respond. I know I should have told you earlier but I reasoned that if I did you wouldn't want me along; and you needed a guide. You wouldn't have lasted five minutes if you'd gone after Bernard by yourself. They protect their own around here."

"Yeah, I know." Graham stood up and patted Laidlaw on the shoulder. "I'm sorry, buddy. I only wish you'd told me this earlier. Like when we first met.

It would have saved a lot of unnecessary antagonism."

"I realize that now," Laidlaw replied with a shrug. "But like I said, I didn't think you'd want me along."

"I wouldn't have let you off that easily," Graham said with a halfsmile.

The door opened and Jenkins entered carrying a tray. He placed it on the bedside table.

Laidlaw took a beer, drank a mouthful, then looked at Graham. "You guys want us to leave?"

Sabrina nodded. "Please. Mike and I need to talk."

"Sure," Laidlaw said then followed Jenkins to the door.

Graham closed the door behind them then turned back to Sabrina. "You're here to take me back, aren't you?"

"Yes."

"Then you're wasting your time. I came out here to find Bernard and that's what I intend to do."

She sat down then outlined the case to him, careful not to leave anything out.

"So what you're saying is that Bernard's the only person who knows when the hit on Mobuto's going to take place?" Graham concluded once she had finished speaking.

She nodded. "And if you put a bullet into him before he can pass the information on to Bailey then Mobuto's as good as dead. It would almost certainly mean the return of a dictatorship to Zimbala; and the reinstatement of the Security Police. Could you live with that on your conscience for the rest of your life?"

Graham rubbed his hands over his face then stared thoughtfully at the carpet for some time before finally looking up at Sabrina again. "I'll make a deal with you."

"A deal?" she replied with a frown.

"You help me find Bernard—"

"Forget it!" she cut in sharply.

"Hear me out, Sabrina. If you help me find Bernard

I'll wait until he's tipped off Bailey before I kill him. If you refuse then I'll go after him regardless of what happens to Mobuto. Could *you* live with that on *your* conscience for the rest of your life?"

"I don't believe what I'm hearing," she replied. "What the hell's the matter with you, Mike? This isn't some game show where you barter with another contestant for the big prize. We're talking about a man's life here. We're talking about the future of a country."

"If Bernard gets away after tipping off Bailey he's certain to be given a new identity by the CIA. He could go anywhere he wanted and I'd never find him again. Never."

"Let it go, Mike. This vendetta's going to destroy you. You didn't kill Barak; I can vouch for that when we get back to the States. You'll catch hell for coming out here but that will be the end of it. But if you kill Bernard you'll be thrown out of UNACO. You could even be indicted for murder. Is that what you want?"

"I want Bernard, that's what I want. And if they throw me out . . ." he trailed off with a shrug. "Those are my terms, Sabrina. Take them or leave them."

"You do what you want, Mike," she snapped then got to her feet and strode to the door. "I've tried to reason with you. I should have known better. I'm going to call Sergei and tell him what's happened."

Graham grabbed her arm as she opened the door. "Help me, Sabrina. Please. I don't want anything to happen to Mobuto. But I have to go after Bernard, don't you see that? I owe it to Carrie and Mikey. I owe it to them."

She pulled her arm free and walked to the booth, lifting the receiver off the wall. She could hear Jenkins and Laidlaw talking in the bar room below her. At least they were occupied. She dialed the unlisted number, identified herself to Sarah at UNACO headquarters, and gave her the number of the phone to call back. She replaced the receiver and tapped her fingers on the dog-eared directory as she waited for it to ring. Graham appeared at the door. She glanced at him but before he could speak the phone rang. She picked up the receiver and had to identify herself again before she was patched through to Kolchinsky.

"Sabrina?"

"Speaking," she replied.

"You just caught me. I was on my way home. Any news of Michael?"

She looked across at Graham, her mind still in turmoil over his ultimatum. She knew if she helped him she would be reprimanded, perhaps even suspended. But if she refused, Mobuto's life would certainly be at risk. She had to make a choice. Then she thought of the picture Graham always carried in his wallet of Carrie and Mikey. What price justice if Bernard were allowed to go free?

"Sabrina, are you still there?" Kolchinsky barked, interrupting her thoughts.

"Sorry, Sergei, it's a bad line," she lied.

"It's very clear this end. I asked if there was any news of Michael?"

"No, not yet. Why was he set up?"

"What?" Kolchinsky replied in surprise.

"You know exactly what I'm talking about, Sergei. I spoke to the policeman in charge of the case this afternoon. He said the NYPD identified Mike by his prints. But they only know him as Graham. He traveled under the name of Green. How could they have matched the prints unless UNACO authorized it?"

"We had no choice," Kolchinsky said at length. "If the Beirut police had continued to probe who knows what they might have uncovered? We had to protect the organization."

"And what if Mike gets arrested? Will UNACO leave him to rot in some Beirut jail to protect themselves?"

"He brought this on himself. It was an unauthorized

mission." Kolchinsky sighed deeply. "No, we wouldn't leave him in some Beirut jail. We'd get him out. Somehow. But don't let it come to that, Sabrina. Find him and bring him back."

"That's easier said than done. All my enquiries have drawn a blank so far."

"I suggest a change in tactics. He's after Bernard, right? If you find Bernard first you won't have to chase after him any more. He'll come to you. And then you can intercept him before he can get to Bernard."

"And how do you suggest I find Bernard? According to Bailey's dossier, his bodyguards are Hezbollah fundamentalists. They're hardly going to take very kindly to a woman poking her nose into their affairs, are they?"

"They only act as his bodyguards in the Lebanon. He flew out of Beirut last night, destination Habane. He used the name Alain Devereux."

"Zimbala? Why?"

"I don't know. Bailey told me this morning. And he only found out from one of his operatives who had seen Bernard at Beirut Airport last night."

"So he still hasn't contacted Bailey about the hit?"

"Not a word. This is a critical stage of the operation, Sabrina. That's why you've got to stop Michael from getting to Bernard."

"I'll get the next flight out to Habane," she assured him. "Who's my contact in Zimbala?"

"We don't have anyone in Zimbala. Bailey offered to get one of his men at the embassy to liaise with you but I decided against it. I don't want the CIA interfering in our business. What they will do is leave an envelope for you in one of the lockers at the airport. It'll contain your hotel reservation, money, maps of the city—the usual. I've also asked them to leave a Beretta there for you. The key will be at the information desk. But apart from that, you're on your own."

"It won't be the first time," she muttered.

"Call me when you get there. I hope to have more on Bernard by then."

"How's the Colonel?"

"He's fine. I saw him this morning."

"Send him my regards when you next see him, will you?"

"Of course. And Sabrina, be careful."

"You can count on it." She replaced the receiver and looked round at Graham who was hovering at the door. "Bernard left for Zimbala last night."

"I got the gist of the conversation. Why the sudden change of heart? You were determined to spill the works when you went to the phone."

"What good would it have done telling Sergei I'd found you? You wouldn't have come back with me anyway. Then I'd have had to chase after you wherever you went. It would have been like something out of the *Keystone Cops*. At least this way I know where you are. And I know Bernard will be able to tip off Bailey before *you* get to him." She gave him a wry smile. "Well, that's what I'll say in my defense when I get back. I don't think it'll save me from suspension though."

"Why should you be suspended? It's not as if I gave you much choice. You did what you thought was best under the circumstances. The Colonel can't fault you for that. And what was all that about sending him your regards? Is he ill?"

"I haven't told you, have I? With all this going on, it completely slipped my mind."

"Told me what?"

They returned to the room where she explained about Philpott's heart attack and his subsequent convalescence at the Bellevue Hospital where he would remain for the next few days.

"He can be a cantankerous old fossil at times but I hope this isn't going to force him to retire. The place wouldn't be the same without him."

"It's up to his doctor to decide if he'll be fit enough

to return to work. But the signs are encouraging by all accounts." She gestured to the door. "Well, I'd better get back to the hotel and pack."

"How will I know where you're staying once you reach Zimbala? You're sure to get there first."

"We don't need to travel separately. UNACO don't have anyone in Zimbala so word can't get back to Sergei that we're working together."

"But word can get back to Bernard. Remember, he doesn't know what happened at the factory tonight. As far as he's concerned, I'm still a threat to him. And that means he's sure to have people at the airport ready to intercept me the moment I arrive there."

"What about me? If Al-Makesh knew we were with UNACO, then Bernard's sure to know it as well. And for all he knows, we could be working together to track him down."

Graham shook his head. "He'll know the real reason why you're in Beirut."

"How? Sergei said Bernard hasn't been in touch with Bailey for days, certainly not since C.W. and I were assigned to the case."

"Because Al-Makesh knew why you were in Beirut. All Bailey had to do was tell the Mossad why you were here and they would have got Al-Makesh to pass the information on to Bernard. How else do you think Al-Makesh knew we were from UNACO? Not from some informer on the street corner. From the Mossad." Graham sat on the bed and looked up at her. "Bernard will make sure you're given a free hand wherever you go. You're his guardian angel—the one person keeping me away from him. No, don't worry, you'll be perfectly safe in Zimbala."

"How are you going to get there?"

"I don't know yet. My best bet would probably be to fly into one of the neighboring states and sneak over the border at night. Which brings us back to my original question. How will I know where to contact you?"

"I'll have the use of a locker at the airport . . ." she trailed off with a despondent sigh. "Sorry, I forget. You can't go near the airport."

"Leave it there. I'll sort something out."

"What name will you be using?"

He thought for a moment. "Well, I can't use Michael Green any more. I'll use the Miles Grant passport."

"OK, I'll leave the key for the locker at the information counter." She glanced at her watch. "As I said, I'd better get back to the hotel. I still have to make all the necessary travel arrangements before I go to bed."

"See you in Zimbala."

She walked to the door then paused to look back suspiciously at him. "I've put my neck on the block for you, Mike. Don't jump the gun and go after Bernard by yourself."

"As if I would," he replied, his hands held out in a gesture of mock innocence. His face suddenly became serious. "We made a deal. I'll stick to it."

"Sure," she replied with a quick smile then left the room.

He returned to his room and pulled his holdall out from under the bed. He could hear Sabrina in the bar below talking to the two men. Then silence. He turned his attention to rounding up his clothes and packing them in the holdall.

"Knock, knock," Laidlaw said from the open doorway behind him.

"Come in, Russ," Graham said without looking round.

"So, you're off on your travels again. Where to now, or can't you say?"

"You know the drill," Graham said.

"You're going after Bernard, aren't you?"

Graham zipped up his toilet bag and put it in the holdall. "Perhaps."

"You need an extra pair of hands?"

Graham looked round sharply and was about to

shake his head when he paused to weigh up the pros and cons of the situation. He was going into the unknown. Alone. Hell, he didn't even know where he was going. He could use someone with Laidlaw's experience. He couldn't speak any foreign languages. He knew Laidlaw spoke French, one of the main languages of Zimbala. But he was now officially working on UNACO time. And Laidlaw was an outsider, an outsider who couldn't even be relied upon to fire a gun in a crisis. Some decision.

"What do you know about Zimbala?"

"Small country in Africa. Borders Chad and Niger. It used to be a dictatorship—"

"OK," Graham cut in, holding up his hands to silence Laidlaw. "I've got to rendezvous with Sabrina in Zimbala. She's flying there. I can't risk that. Bernard's sure to have his spies out looking for me. I'm going to have to fly to either Chad or Niger and slip over the border by car. But I don't speak French or Arabic so I'm going to stick out like the proverbial sore thumb. And that means attracting unnecessary attention that could get back to Bernard."

"And you want me to get you into Zimbala."

"You speak French."

"And Arabic," Laidlaw added then smiled wryly. "It'll be like old times."

"All I want you to do is get me to Habane. That's where I'm meeting Sabrina. Then I'll cut you loose." Graham immediately saw the disappointment in Laidlaw's eyes. "What if we're caught in a firefight when we find Bernard? You'd only be a liability. I don't want your death on my conscience, Russ. We've been through too much together."

Laidlaw nodded, his face grim. "I hear what you're saying, Mike. I'll get you to Habane."

"Thanks," Graham said.

"Come on, we'll sort out the flight arrangements downstairs." Laidlaw walked to the door then looked round at Graham, a faint smile touching the corners of his lips. "It won't be the first time I've had to come to your rescue and haul your ass out of trouble."

"Like hell," Graham replied good-humouredly then picked up his holdall and followed Laidlaw into the corridor, closing the door behind him.

FIVE

Whitlock drove his white BMW down the ramp into the basement carpark underneath his apartment block in Manhattan. He pulled into the reserved space beside a red Porsche Carrera, Carmen's car. He switched off the radio and glanced at his watch. It had just gone six thirty. He stifled a yawn. It had been a long day—twelve hours with Mobuto, eight of those in the United Nations building where Mobuto and his entourage had spent the day.

Mobuto's address to the General Assembly had impressed him. It had been an eloquent, impassioned speech in which he had promised to uphold the principles of democracy as the new leader of Zimbala. Yet one aspect of the speech had surprised him. Mobuto had never once referred to his father by name or attempted to make any apology for the abhorrent crimes that had been committed under his regime. It was as if he had blocked out that part of his life and was only interested in talking about the future.

The speech was well received by the delegates and a motion was carried unanimously to send a fact-finding team to Zimbala in six months' time to monitor the situation with a view to readmitting the country to the United Nations. Its original membership, instated when the United Nations was founded in 1945, had been canceled in 1956 when Alphonse Mobuto had refused to allow a delegation to visit Zimbala to investigate accounts of mass genocide under his regime. The motion had particularly pleased Mobuto who was desperate to bring Zimbala back into world affairs. Whitlock knew that the ambassadors of two Western nations had already promised state visits to Zimbala as soon as it was readmitted to the United Nations. It had been an historic day for the future of Zimbala—and it was all down to the tactful diplomacy of Jamel Mobuto. Whitlock had found his animosity toward Mobuto beginning to waver as the day progressed. He genuinely wanted to bring about change in a country where tens of thousands of its people had been tortured or murdered under his father's regime. They still treated each other with caution but each was beginning to respect the other's professionalism. And that was certainly a start.

Whitlock had wanted to remain on duty for the banquet at the United Nations that evening but Kolchinsky had told him to call it a day. He had reluctantly agreed to go home. So the first day had passed uneventfully. But it had been the easiest of the three days. The following day Mobuto intended to tour the African-American Institute on East 47th Street then go on to visit a high-school deep in the heart of Harlem. Then, on the third day, he would be a guest at a trade fair held in New Jersey. Two days of public exposure: a security team's nightmare. But that was what he was being paid for and after hearing Mobuto at the United Nations he was now more determined than ever to ensure his safety. Mobuto was a man with a mission, a Messiah, the future of Zimbala . . .

Whitlock's thoughts were jolted by a sudden rap on

the driver's window. He looked round sharply then exhaled deeply when he saw the man's face peering in at him. Joshua Marshall had been the parking-bay attendant ever since the apartment block had been opened eighteen years earlier. He had grown up in the slums of Harlem and had been a promising middleweight fighter in the late fifties before the lure of alcohol had devastated his career. He had been dry for the past twenty years.

Whitlock activated the window and clasped his hand over his chest. "You almost gave me a heart attack, Joshua."

"I thought you'd suffered one, Mr. Whitlock. You haven't moved since you parked the car."

"I was thinking, that's all." Whitlock removed the keys from the ignition and got out of the car. "How long's my wife been back?"

Joshua scratched his head thoughtfully. "About an hour. She seemed in quite a hurry."

"Oh?" Whitlock said, locking the door. "Did she say anything?"

"She didn't see me."

"Thanks, Joshua."

Joshua touched his cap then ambled off back to his hut.

Whitlock used his personal ID card to activate the lift and tapped his foot apprehensively as he waited for it to arrive. Why had Carmen been in such a hurry? She never rushed anywhere; she was always very graceful and calm. What was wrong? The lift doors parted and he smiled fleetingly at the couple who emerged then stepped inside and pressed the button for the seventh floor. He paced the lift anxiously until it stopped and the doors parted again. He strode briskly down the blue-carpeted corridor, the apartment keys already in his hand. The door opened directly onto the lounge. Carmen was standing by the window. Her sister, Rachel, sat on the couch, her hands clasped tightly together. Her eyes were red. She had been crying. He knew then that something had happened to Rosie.

"Thank God you're back," Carmen said as he closed the door behind him.

"What's wrong?" he asked, his eyes flickering between the two women. "Is it Rosie?"

Rachel bit her lip as she struggled to hold back the tears. "She's gone."

"What do you mean 'gone'?"

"She had a blazing row with Eddie and stormed out of the house," Rachel replied. "We don't know where she's gone."

Whitlock sat down. "When did this happen?"

"About two hours ago. Eddie had just got back from work when they had a row in the kitchen. She stormed out of the house. I'm beside myself with worry, C.W. She's only wearing a T-shirt and jeans. And she doesn't have any money. I'm sure she's gone back to Times Square. That's where she's been spending most of her time these last few months."

"And one of the conditions of her bail was that she wasn't to go anywhere near Times Square until her case went to court," Carmen said.

Whitlock rubbed his eyes wearily.

"Where's Eddie now?"

"He's out looking for her," Rachel replied, "but he doesn't know Times Square."

"Do you know any of her regular haunts there?" Whitlock asked.

Rachel shook her head. "Rosie never tells us anything."

Whitlock got to his feet. "Well, I'd better get over there."

"It's no use going now," Carmen told him. "You wouldn't know where Eddie was. He's phoning every twenty minutes to see if you're back."

"When did he last phone?"

"About ten minutes ago," Carmen said, glancing at her watch.

"I'll go and change," Whitlock said.

"Are you hungry?" Carmen asked. "There's a casserole in the oven. I can put some out for you before you go."

"No, I had a big lunch. I'll eat later."

"C.W.?"

Whitlock paused in the doorway to look back at Rachel.

"Bring her home. Please."

Whitlock nodded grimly and left the room.

Rosie Kruger was in the Rollercoaster, her favorite bar on West 43rd Street, less than a hundred yards away from the heart of Times Square. She had her father's pale blue eyes but her long black hair and honey complexion had been inherited from her mother. She was sixteen-years-old but with her slim, petite figure and attractive features she could have passed for twenty. Kenny Doyle, the twenty-eight-year-old barman at the Rollercoaster, knew her real age but that had never stopped him from serving her a drink. He had been a good friend to her and when she walked out on her parents she had made straight for the bar, looking for him. He understood her plight. He had run away from his home in Chicago when he was fifteen and still bore the scars from the beating he had received at the hands of his father after his parents had discovered he was gay. He had never contacted them again. As far as he was concerned, he had no parents.

Rosie felt the same way about her parents. Her father was on the brink of alcoholism, a pathetic figure who could only face life if he had a bottle in his hand. She knew he was on the verge of losing his job. Not that it really mattered to him any more. He had lost his dignity years ago. And her mother was too weak to stop his drinking. Rosie had been the one who had had to put her father to bed every night for eighteen months while her mother took refuge behind the façade of a sordid affair with her boss, a divorcee. And then it had only ended after he had decided to go back to his wife. No, it wasn't only her father who had lost his dignity.

She could remember vividly the first time she had tried dope, the day that she had found out about her mother's affair from one of her classmates. She had felt cheap and degraded, bitter. She had shared a joint with some friends in the toilet. They each had a few tokes and by the time the roach was flushed away she was already experiencing her first rush, a warm, dreamy sensation that seemed to encompass her whole being. She never wanted it to end. A week later she made her first score from a dealer in Times Square. It made putting her father to bed that bit more bearable. She had been smoking dope now for the last year, scoring whenever she had saved up enough money from her weekend job at McDonald's.

Then, the previous day, it had all gone wrong. She had met her connection in the usual place but the moment the deal was struck they were busted by three plainclothes policemen who had been watching them from an unmarked car on the opposite side of the road. They were both frisked then cuffed and taken into custody. It was the most humiliating, and frightening, night of her life. She had never been so glad to see her mother that morning. All she wanted to do was get out of the cell. It stank of vomit and urine. And for those few hours after she got home she found she could talk to her mother properly for the first time in over two years. There was even a bond of understanding between them. Then her father had come home. All he had done was scream abuse at her, accusing her of bringing shame and disgrace on the family. The double standards appalled her. It was then she knew she couldn't stay there, not with him. She knew she was violating her bail conditions by being in the Roller-coaster but whe also knew she would be perfectly safe if she kept a low profile. And she knew Kenny would look after her . . .

"What you drinking, sweetheart?"

The voice startled her but when she looked round she winced at the stale smell of alcohol on the man's breath. He was wearing a grey suit, his tie undone at the throat. She estimated he was in his early thirties.

"You're real pretty," he said and reached out his hand to touch her face.

"Back off," she snapped and jerked away.

"Hey, leave my girl alone," Doyle said from behind the counter.

The man eyed Doyle contemptuously then muttered something to himself and moved to another table and sat down.

"Thanks," she said, squeezing Doyle's hand.

"Any time," Doyle replied. "How's the bourbon?"

"I'm OK, thanks. Anyway, I haven't got—"

"How many times must I tell you? The drinks are on the house tonight."

"Why are all the best guys either married or . . . like you?"

"You're too young to be so cynical," Doyle said. "You'll meet the right guy some day."

"Then what? Take him home to meet my parents?" she replied with a look of mock horror.

Doyle chuckled then left her to serve a customer. She looked slowly around the room. It wasn't busy, not yet. But give it another hour. She was about to reach for her drink when she caught sight of the car out of the corner of her eye as it pulled up on the opposite side of the road—a white BMW, identical to the one her uncle had. She held her breath as the driver's door opened. Whitlock got out. A moment later Eddie Kruger emerged from the passenger side and closed the door behind him.

"Kenny!" Rosie hissed, beckoning the barman toward her.

"What is it?" Doyle asked.

"It's my father. And he's brought my uncle with him," she said, indicating with her head toward the BMW where Whitlock and Kruger were in conversation.

Doyle took a set of keys from his pocket, removed one, and gave it to her. "It's for the back door. You know where it is?"

"Is it that one next to the men's room?"

He nodded. "It leads into an alley behind the bar. Wait there. I'll get rid of them, don't worry. I'll send someone out to call you when they've gone."

She made her way down the corridor that led off from the bar room, continually glancing over her shoulder, half expecting to see either her father or her uncle behind her. She reached the door and unlocked it. Her hands were trembling. She pushed it open and slipped outside, closing it silently behind her. A cold wind had picked up since she had arrived at the bar and she rubbed her arms quickly before picking her way through a sea of discarded newspaper to a metal drum and ducked down behind it, her eyes riveted on the door. She knew Doyle would do his best to protect her but what if they decided to search the place anyway? Including the alley. The wind sliced through the alley and blew a sheet of old newspaper against her leg. She brushed it away then huddled closer to the wall, hugging herself against the cold. A stray mongrel appeared at the end of the alley, its body gaunt from years of neglect. It sniffed the air then made straight for the drum. It stopped abruptly when it saw Rosie, an uncertainty shadowing its haunted eyes. Then it moved closer and began to scratch frantically at the foot of the bin. A rat suddenly darted out from a hole in the side of the drum and she had to bite back the scream that rose in her throat. It scurried over to a pile of old newspapers with the mongrel in close attendance. The mongrel tore savagely at the newspapers and the rat fled further down the alley, desperate for sanctuary. Rosie lost sight of it when it disappeared behind a cardboard box and she turned her attention back to the door. She inhaled sharply when she saw the figure there. It was the man in the gray suit who had tried to pick her up earlier. He was looking at the bin but she didn't know whether he had seen her or not.

"You can come out now," he said, beckoning toward her with his finger. "They've gone."

She didn't move. Why had Kenny sent him out to tell her? Or had he? Had the man overheard her talking to Kenny? She was frightened, very frightened.

"I know you're behind the drum," he said, taking a step toward it. "I told you, they've gone. You're safe now."

She slowly got to her feet, her eyes wide with fear. The cold didn't bother her any more. He held out a hand toward her. She instinctively shrunk back against the wall, her hands clasped tightly against her chest. His smile was chilling. She opened her mouth but she couldn't speak. Her throat was dry; her lips were dry. He stopped in front of her and wrenched her hands away from her chest. She wanted to run but her legs wouldn't move. She wanted to scream but no sound came from her throat. A faint sneer of satisfaction touched the corners of his mouth. She squeezed her eyes shut as she felt his hand slip under her T-shirt.

"Leave her alone!"

The man looked round sharply at the figure who had emerged silently from inside the bar. He was wearing a pair of faded blue jeans, a white shirt and a black leather jacket. A faint scar ran the length of his left cheek.

"You'll get your ass out of here if you know what's good for you," the man snarled menacingly.

Bernard glanced at Rosie. "Go inside. The two men have gone."

"Like hell you are," the man snarled and grabbed her arm.

She raked his face with her fingernails. He cried out in pain and stumbled back against the wall. She jerked her arm free and ran to where Bernard was standing.

"Inside," Bernard ordered, indicating the door with his head.

Her eyes flickered momentarily between the two men then she pulled open the door and hurried inside.

"You're going to pay for that, you son-of-a-bitch," the man hissed through clenched teeth as he wiped the blood from his cheek with the back of his hand.

Bernard eyed the man contemptuously then dropped his cigarette and ground it underfoot. The man lunged clumsily at Bernard who ducked his wild punch and landed a vicious one of his own, catching him painfully in the kidney. The man stumbled against the wall and Bernard followed through with two more crippling kidney punches, dropping the man to his knees. He grabbed the man's hair and slammed his face against the wall. The man slumped into an unconscious heap at Bernard's feet. Bernard brushed his hands together then walked back to the door. It swung open as he was about to reach out for the handle. Doyle stood in the doorway, a baseball bat clenched tightly in his right hand.

"It's OK," Bernard reassured him. "He won't touch the girl again tonight."

Doyle peered at the crumpled figure. "Bastard. I was ready to take his head off when Rosie told me what had happened."

"You know him?"

"Never seen him before," Doyle replied then held open the door for Bernard. "Thanks for helping her. Most people around here would have just looked the other way."

"Is she your girl?" Bernard asked as they walked back to the bar room.

"Just a friend. A good friend."

The waitress who had been covering for Doyle behind the bar eyed the baseball bat questioningly when he returned.

"I didn't have to do anything," Doyle replied, placing the bat under the counter again. "This gentleman took care of the situation." He looked at Bernard. "The least I can do is buy you a drink.

"A Diet Cola if you have it," Bernard replied then eased himself onto the stool beside Rosie. "Are you alright?"

She nodded. "I don't know how I can ever thank you. If you hadn't come along when you did . . ." She trailed off as she struggled to hold back the tears.

"Would you like another drink?" he asked, indicating her empty glass.

"Please," she replied softly then looked at him for the first time since he had sat down. "I don't even know your name."

"Marc Giresse," he replied, quoting the name on his passport.

"I'm Rosie Kruger." She looked round as Doyle returned with the Diet Cola. "I was just saying, if you hadn't sent Mr. Giresse out when you did I hate to think what would have happened to me."

"I didn't send him out," Doyle replied. "I was about to come out myself."

Rosie and Doyle looked at Bernard simultaneously.

"I was at the table behind you," Bernard said to Rosie. "I saw what happened when that guy tried to pick you up. Then when he followed you down the corridor I thought I'd better make sure you were alright."

"How did you know about my father and my uncle?"

"I overheard you two talking," Bernard replied with

a sheepish grin. "It's a bad habit of mine. I tend to do it when I'm bored."

"I'm sure glad you did," Rosie replied with a smile.

Doyle's eyes flickered to the nearest table behind Rosie. It was occupied by a young couple in their early twenties. Although he didn't know them, he could have sworn they had been there for the past hour. And they were sitting on the only two chairs at the table. He looked at Bernard, frowned, then glanced round sharply when he heard someone calling him from the end of the counter.

"A drink for the lady, when you have a minute," Bernard said as Doyle turned to go.

"Sure," Doyle replied then went off to serve the customer.

"Giresse?" Rosie said thoughtfully. "Is that French?"

Bernard nodded.

"You don't sound French. You don't look it either. You're very swarthy."

"My father was French. I was born in Tarábulus."

"Where's that?" she asked.

"The Lebanon."

A sly smile touched the corners of her mouth. "You're not a terrorist, are you?"

"Sure," Bernard replied then shook his head. "You Americans never cease to amaze me. Everyone has to be neatly packaged into defined groups. If you're Russian you must be a Communist. If you're Colombian you must be a drug dealer. If you're Libyan or Lebanese you must be a terrorist."

"I was only joking," she said with a grin.

"I know. I only wish I could say the same about your politicians." Bernard took a sip of the Diet Cola then leaned his elbows on the counter. "I'm a humble businessman, that's all. Meat packaging—far less glamorous than being a terrorist, I'm afraid."

"Do you know . . . any terrorists?"

"You meet lots of different kinds of people in the Lebanon," Bernard replied then dismissed the topic with a vague flick of his hand. "Are you a runaway?"

The question caught Rosie by surprise. Normally she would have clammed up at that juncture. She made it a point to tell people as little about herself as possible. She never shared her inner thoughts with anyone, not even her friends at school who had come to regard her as something of an enigma. Yet she felt completely at ease with Bernard. It was a feeling she had never had before, not even with Kenny, and he was probably the best friend she ever had. She felt as if she could trust Bernard. And she had never trusted anyone before in her life. Part of her was frightened. It was a new experience for her to want to open up to someone, especially a man; but another part of her was relieved to have found a kindred spirit she could confide in.

"Sorry, I didn't mean to pry," Bernard said, noticing her distant expression.

"No, you weren't prying," she replied with a quick smile. "I guess I am a runaway. I left home tonight."

"It's a start," Bernard said with a smile. He held up his glass. "Welcome to the club."

"Were you also a runaway?" she asked excitedly.

He nodded.

"I knew it. A kindred spirit," she said softly to herself.

"Pardon?"

"Nothing," she said then looked up as Doyle returned with her bourbon. "Mr. Giresse was also a runaway. Small world."

"Very small," Doyle replied tersely then placed the bourbon in front of her. His eyes darted toward Bernard. There was something about the man he didn't trust. And his instincts were rarely wrong. "Where you from?"

"Beirut," Bernard replied, holding Doyle's stare. He suddenly smiled. "How much is the drink?"

"I'm paying for Rosie's drinks tonight," Doyle replied quickly.

"Please, I insist," Bernard said then took a five-dollar bill from his wallet and placed it on the counter. "Have one yourself."

"No, thank you," Doyle replied and left the note on the counter when he walked off to serve another customer.

"What's wrong with your friend?" Bernard asked, slipping the note back into his wallet.

Rosie shrugged. "He gets like this sometimes. I suppose I would, too, if I had to serve all the creeps that come in here every night."

"Thank you," Bernard retorted.

"You know what I mean," she replied then saw the smile on his face. "Stop teasing me."

His face suddenly became serious. "Have you got somewhere to stay tonight?"

She instinctively looked across at Doyle. "I was hoping Kenny could put me up for a few days until I'd sorted things out with my parents. But he can't. He's got someone staying with him. There's a couple of friends I know who might be able to give me a bed for the night. I'll try them."

"And what if they can't?"

She shrugged. "I'll find a flop house somewhere. I've got a few bucks on me. But don't tell Kenny: I told him I was broke."

"That's crazy. You can't go walking around New York by yourself at this time of night. Look, I've got a spare room. You can use it if you want."

"Thanks, but . . ." she trailed off with an awkward shrug. "I mean, I don't even know you."

"Likewise," Bernard replied. He bit his lip thoughtfully. "I'll tell you what. Call your friends and see if they can put you up for the night. If they can't you can either stay at the flat or else I'll give you some money and drop you off at a hotel."

"Why are you doing this?"

"My father raised me. I never knew my mother. He was the only family I had. He died when I was fourteen. So I ran off to Beirut to avoid being put into an orphanage. The first night there I was accosted by three men. I managed to get away but," he paused and touched the scar on his cheek, "they left me with a memento. It looks a lot better on me than it would on you. You got off lightly in the alley tonight. Don't push your luck."

She pondered his words then glanced at the pay phone in the corner of the bar. "You got any quarters?"

Bernard rifled through the change pouch in his wallet and handed her three quarters. "Is that enough?"

She nodded then climbed off her stool and crossed the room to the phone. She dialed the first number: no reply. Then she tried the second. It was answered by a man. Three's company, she said to herself and hung up. When she turned round she found Doyle standing in front of her.

"Here, take this," he said, pushing a ten-dollar bill into her hand.

"What's this for?"

"Taxi fare to my place. You can stay there tonight."

"But what about that guy?"

"He'll understand," Doyle replied.

"Have you phoned to tell him I'm coming over?"

"I tried but he's not in. He'll be at a club."

"I appreciate the offer, Kenny, but I can't stay with you guys. It wouldn't be right."

"Why not?" Doyle demanded defensively. "You can pad out on the sofa."

"It just wouldn't be right," she replied with a shrug and slipped the money back into his pocket.

"So where are you going to stay?"

"I'll find a crash pad somewhere," she said, trying to reassure him.

"I heard that Lebanese guy offer you a room at his

place. Don't go, Rosie. There's something pseudo about him."

"Yeah, what?" she demanded.

"I don't know. It's just a gut feeling, that's all."

"Oh, really?" she retorted sharply. "He's been a perfect gentleman ever since I met him. And you don't find many of them in this dive."

"He's trouble, Rosie."

She shook her head angrily. "You've been acting weird ever since he started talking to me. What's really bugging you, Kenny? Are you jealous that we're getting along so well?"

"Jealous?" Doyle replied in disbelief. "Grow up, Rosie. I'm worried about you, that's all."

"Yeah, well, don't bother. I can look after myself." She spun on her heels and walked back to where Bernard was sitting. "I'll take you up on that offer of a bed if it's still going."

"Sure," Bernard replied.

"Can we go, now?"

Bernard looked round at her. "Now? It's only eight thirty."

"Then let's go somewhere else." She glanced up at Doyle as he returned behind the bar. "This place has got distinctly chilly in the last couple of minutes."

Bernard shrugged. "You'll have to recommend somewhere. I'm a stranger in these parts."

"I know lots of places," she retorted then glared at Doyle before striding out of the bar.

Bernard watched her leave. It was beyond his wildest expectations. All he had intended to do was keep tabs on her in case he needed a hostage after the hit on Mobuto. Whitlock's niece, the perfect weapon to foil UNACO. His American contact had told him where to find her. He didn't know his name. He only knew him by his codeword, Seabird.

No, he couldn't have asked for it to have turned out better. He pushed the Diet Cola away from him and climbed off the stool. It was then that he noticed Doyle watching him. He allowed himself a faint smile of satisfaction then slipped the five-dollar bill under Rosie's glass and left the bar.

Whitlock closed the door behind Eddie and Rachel Kruger then returned to the lounge and slumped dejectedly onto the sofa.

"You did your best, C.W.," Carmen said, massaging his shoulders.

"It wasn't enough, was it?" Whitlock replied. "Between us we must have been to every bar within a mile radius of Times Square. Nothing."

"That could be a good thing in itself. If someone is shielding her then she'll probably have a bed for the night."

"God, I hope so," Whitlock said then got to his feet and moved to the balcony where he looked out over the illuminated New York skyline.

"It's almost midnight, C.W.," Carmen said from the doorway. "We've both got to be up early in the morning."

"I know," Whitlock replied but made no attempt to move away from the railing.

"You've done everything you could to find her. She's on her own now."

"I still say we should have called the police."

"We've been through this already. Eddie and Rachel decided against it. We have to respect that. She's their daughter, not ours."

"If she was our daughter she wouldn't be in this mess," Whitlock retorted.

"Wouldn't she?"

Whitlock looked round sharply at her then conceded the point with a shrug of the shoulders.

"Come on, let's go to bed."

"Take care of yourself, kid," Whitlock said softly then went inside and closed the sliding door behind him.

Robert Bailey was obsessed with security. He drove to work in a bulletproof Mercedes 500SL, changing his route daily. His personal bodyguards were always armed. His wife and two teenage daughters were ferried about by an armed chauffeur. And his house in the Georgetown suburb of Washington was a virtual fortress. Tripwires lined the top of the perimeter wall and armed dog-handlers patroled the grounds twenty-four hours a day. Closed-circuit television cameras had been installed in every room and were monitored by guards from a control center in the basement of the house—every room, that is, except his study.

It was a soundproof, windowless room at the end of the corridor on the second floor. The only access was through a sliding metal door which could only be activated by punching a code into the bellpush on the adjacent wall. He changed the combination daily. Nobody, not even his family, was allowed inside the room. It contained his personal computer, which was linked to computers at both the Pentagon and the CIA headquarters in Langley. Hundreds of secret programs that had been built up by the CIA over the years, including data sensitive enough to topple the heads of half a dozen European governments if they were ever to fall into the wrong hands. With this in mind, he had devised more security measures to thwart any would-be intruder that managed to get past the guards. The computer itself could only be activated by an access code known solely to Bailey. If the incorrect code was programmed in it would activate a canister of lethal nerve gas which was secreted in the ceiling directly above the door. Death would result in less than ten seconds. But he had provided a double failsafe mechanism for him-

self in case he accidently pressed the wrong key while
accessing the code. The nerve gas would only be released if the incorrect code was programmed *twice* into
the computer. He was, after all, only human.

After feeding in the access code he sat back and
stifled a yawn. It was already one in the morning. He
was exhausted. He had been up seventeen hours. His
wife and daughters had long since gone to bed. They
were accustomed to his irregular hours. But they all
shared his ambition to become head of the CIA within
the next five years. And he knew he had the backing of
the President and most of the powerful Republican con-
gressmen on Capitol Hill. It was only a question of
time.

He tapped another code into the computer and moments later a dossier appeared on the screen. The name
on it was Jean-Jacques Bernard. He erased all the existing data and replaced it with a single line written in
capital letters: TO BE TERMINATED AFTER THE AS-
SASSINATION OF JAMEL MOBUTO.

♦ CHAPTER
SIX

Sabrina flew out of Beirut the following morning on a Ugandan Boeing 747 bound for Kampala via Habane and Khartoum. It was barely half full. It touched down at Habane International Airport six hours later and she was one of only eight passengers to disembark. They were met on the tarmac by a friendly ground stewardess and driven the five-hundred yards to the small, ovalshaped terminal building. The interior had recently been redecorated and the pungent odor of fresh paint still hung in the air. Armed soldiers stood guard inside the building and she could feel the tension as she joined the short queue waiting to pass through passport control. The official ran his eyes the length of her body as she approached the counter then held out his hand for her passport. He wet his finger then leafed through it slowly before looking up at her.

"What is the nature of your visit to Zimbala, Miss Cassidy?" he asked in a thick English accent.

"I'm a journalist," she replied with a smile. "And this country is news at the moment."

"And how long do you intend staying in Zimbala?"

"That all depends on my editor. I would hope to be here for about a week, though."

The official stamped the passport then handed it back to her. "Your visa is valid for ten days. If you wish to stay longer, you will have to apply to have it renewed."

"Thank you," she replied, slipping the passport back into the pocket of her fawn blouson.

"Enjoy your stay in Zimbala," he said with a half-smile then beckoned the next person in line to step forward to the counter.

She collected her lightweight Vuitton suitcase then went to the information counter where she picked up the locker key that had been left there for her. The lockers were situated at the far end of the terminal. She unlocked the one corresponding to the number on the key. Inside was a black holdall. She unzipped it. It contained a Beretta, tucked into a Boyt shoulder holster, and a manila envelope. She opened the envelope and took out the fax confirming her hotel booking. The hotel was called the International. Taking a pen and notepad from her overnight bag, she wrote down the name and address for Graham then placed the sheet of paper inside the locker and closed it again. She returned to the information counter and asked the stewardess for an envelope. She put the key inside the envelope, sealed it, and wrote MILES GRANT across it then told the stewardess that a Mr. Grant would collect it later.

Picking up her suitcase, she went outside to look for a taxi. She slipped on her sunglasses then crossed to the nearest taxi which was parked directly opposite the main entrance, a white Toyota. The driver beamed at her then took her suitcase and put it carefully in the trunk.

"Where to, Missy?" he asked.

"The International," she replied.

The driver frowned momentarily then nodded. "It only called the International after the President die. It built many years now, and always called Alphonse Mobuto Hotel."

"That figures," she muttered.

The driver closed the back door behind her, got in, then climbed behind the wheel and pulled out into the road, heading for the exit.

A pale blue Cortina, which had been parked in the carpark, followed at a discreet distance. There were two men in the car. Both wore blue overalls. The driver was Gordon Gubene, a former sergeant in the Security Police who had driven the van when Ngune was sprung from jail. Thomas Massenga sat beside him in a black leather cap and dark sunglasses. He opened the glove compartment and removed a Walther P5. He had lost count of the number of assassinations he had carried out during his seventeen years with the Security Police—dozens, certainly. Men, women, children: it had never made any difference to him.

He slipped the pistol into his overall pocket then picked up the brown folder off the dashboard. It had been given to him the previous day at the airport by a man known only to him as "Columbus". Inside was a photograph of Sabrina. "Columbus" had told him that she was part of a team which had been assigned to track down the assassins before they could carry out the hit on Jamel Mobuto. She had to be stopped before she could uncover any incriminating evidence in Zimbala. He had long since memorized her face but it was the first chance he had had to compare it to her in person. It did her little justice. But he had no time for sentimentality. She was the enemy, and he would kill her once she reached her destination.

Sabrina was immediately struck by the number of blocks of flats, all of identical height and width, that lined the road into Habane. Tall, unsightly structures positioned equidistantly from each other and painted a depressing shade of gray.

"Don't you have any houses around here?" she asked finally.

"House not here," the driver answered without taking his eyes off the road. "Other side Habane. Plenty money house for rich peoples."

"But surely all that will change now that Alphonse Mobuto is dead?"

The driver shrugged. "No money to build house."

"That's why Jamel Mobuto went to America, isn't it? To get money to rebuild the country."

"Good man, Jamel Mobuto. Not bad like his father."

Sabrina just nodded, realizing she was talking way over his head. She suddenly wondered if he even knew that Jamel Mobuto was in America. Probably not.

"Where you from, missy?"

"America," she replied.

"Like Chicago?"

"Chicago's in America, yes. But I'm from New York."

"The Yankees," he said, grinning at her in the rearview mirror.

"That's right. You like baseball?"

He nodded. "We see baseball on television. And football. Chicago Bears my team."

"I've got a friend who played professional football. He was a quarterback for the New York Giants."

"Your boyfriend?" he asked excitedly.

"No, just a friend," she replied with a smile, wondering how Graham would have reacted to being called her boyfriend.

"He still play?"

She shook her head. "No, he injured his arm in Vietnam. He couldn't play again."

"Vietnam?" the driver said with a frown. "What their team called?"

She was about to explain then decided against it. It

would only lead to more misunderstanding. She fell silent.

The military presence became significantly stronger the closer they got to Habane. Apart from the road-blocks manned by soldiers armed with M16s, old M41 tanks stood menacingly on every street corner. She could sense the same tension that she had felt back at the airport. Most of the soldiers they passed were still in their teens, the uncertainty of the situation etched onto their youthful features.

They wouldn't stand a chance against the heavily armed and well-disciplined squad of ex-Security po-licemen that were reportedly amassing in the south of the country. But the reports UNACO had received were mostly hearsay from locals in and around Kondese. Much of it would be propaganda spread by Ngune and his officers. They had also received the draft of a state-ment made by a deserter who had fled to Chad. He claimed that the squad wasn't nearly as big as Western intelligence had feared and that there was a bitter inter-nal struggle amongst the officers about who would be included in Ngune's cabinet once they had seized power. The animosity was running so high that one officer had already been executed by Ngune for killing a fellow officer in an argument. UNACO were well aware that the deserter could be a plant to try and lull Jamel Mobuto into a false sense of complacency. But they knew his claims could also be genuine. All they could do was await developments. Mobuto had so far refused the offer of a United Nations peacekeeping force in Zimbala, insisting that his troops would be able to crush any uprising by Ngune and his rebels. Sabrina didn't share his optimism. It worried her.

"Hotel," the driver announced.

"What?" Sabrina replied, her thoughts interrupted.

"Hotel," the driver repeated, pointing it out.

The International was a box-shaped building painted out in white and gold. It was certainly nothing spectacular. And it was reputedly the best hotel in town. She shuddered to think what the worst was like. The driver stopped the taxi in the forecourt and a doorman immediately stepped forward and opened the back door. He doffed his cap to Sabrina when she climbed out and snapped his fingers at a porter who came hurrying over and took the suitcase from the trunk. What it lacked in appearance, it seemed to make up for in service. She used some of the money in the envelope to pay the driver.

"Thank you," he said appreciatively. "If you want to go anywhere, I take you. My name is Harris. The staff know me."

She nodded then bit her lip thoughtfully as she watched him climb back into the taxi and drive away. Had she tipped him too generously? He'd probably ripped her off anyway. She made a mental note to study the currency more closely once she got to her room.

The Cortina slowed to a crawl and as it drew abreast of the hotel Massenga took the Walther from his pocket and aimed it at Sabrina.

"Get down," a voice yelled but before Sabrina could react she was bundled roughly to the ground in the same moment as Massenga fired.

The bullet smashed into the wall. Massenga cursed angrily, unable to get in another shot at Sabrina who had rolled to safety behind one of the two concrete pillars that stood on either side of the doors. He snapped at Gubene who immediately accelerated and sped off down the road.

The doorman, who had taken sanctuary behind the other pillar, sprang to his feet and ran over to where Sabrina lay. He helped her up, his eyes wide with concern. "Are you alright?"

She rubbed her bruised elbow painfully. "I'm alright. I hope that wasn't a traditional Zimbalan welcome."

"Rebels," the doorman spat angrily. "Now they are shooting at tourists."

Sabrina's mind was in turmoil. Why had someone just tried to kill her? Who, outside UNACO, knew she was in Zimbala? The questions disturbed her but, pushing them from her mind, she turned to the man who had shouted the warning before knocking her to the ground. He was a small man in his forties with a thin face and wirerimmed glasses. She was about to thank him when the manager emerged from the hotel and hurried over to them. The doorman explained in Swahili what had happened and the manager immediately began to apologize but Sabrina held up her hand to silence him.

"It's not your fault," she said with a quick smile.

"Are you hurt?"

"No, I'm fine."

The manager ushered her into the foyer and led her across to the reception desk. "I'm sure you want to get up to your room but we need you to fill in the register first. I'm sure you understand."

She was becoming irritated by the way he was treating her like a child but she let it pass and completed the formalities.

"I'll let you know when the police arrive, Miss Cassidy," the manager said after the receptionist had handed her key to the porter.

"Don't call the police on my account. I told you, I'm fine."

"I must by law."

"Well, you know where to find me. Now, if you'll excuse me."

"Of course," the manager replied then bowed curtly before withdrawing to his office to phone the police.

She turned to the man in the wire-framed glasses and held out her hand. "Sabrina Cassidy. I owe you my life. Thank you."

"Joseph Moredi," he replied, shaking her hand

firmly. He led her away from the reception desk. "Can we talk?"

"What about?"

He glanced at the porter who was hovering beside him then turned back to Sabrina. "Not here. Can we go to your room?"

"I appreciate what you did for me, but I do feel a little shaken right now. Perhaps you could—"

"Please, Miss Cassidy," he cut in. "It is important."

"OK," she replied, seeing the intensity in his eyes.

They took the lift to the fourth floor and the porter led them to the room. It was spacious and tastefully decorated with a bathroom *en suite*. The window overlooked the main road. Sabrina tipped the porter after he had put the suitcase on the luggage stand and closed the door behind him.

"I know who tried to kill you, Miss Cassidy."

"Rebels, I believe you call them," Sabrina replied.

"His name's Massenga, Thomas Massenga. He was deputy head of the Security Police for the last five years before it was disbanded." He walked to the window then turned back to look at Sabrina. "These 'rebels', as you call them, aren't in the habit of tailing foreigners from the airport and trying to shoot them outside their hotels. Massenga took a great personal risk coming out in the open like that. I don't know who you're working for but your investigations are obviously linked to the Mobuto brothers. It's the only reason Massenga would have tried to kill you: to prevent you from stumbling on the truth."

"This is all very interesting, Mr. Moredi—"

"Miss Cassidy, your life's in danger," he snapped angrily then held up his hands apologetically. "I'm sorry, I didn't mean to shout at you like that. I can appreciate your wanting to keep your cover intact. And I know what's going through your mind right now. You're thinking that I could be working in league with Massenga and the shooting outside the hotel was all staged to try and get you into my confidence. Believe me, it wasn't. But I don't expect you to take my word for that. Jamel Mobuto will vouch for me. We were at Oxford together. I'm sure your organization can contact him in New York. Tell him to set a question that only the real Joseph Moredi would be able to answer. Then call me at this number." He took a business card from his pocket and placed it on the dresser. "We can help each other, Miss Cassidy. Please, call me."

She waited until he had left the room then crossed to the dresser and picked up the card. Joseph Moredi, deputy editor of *La Voix*, Remy Mobuto's newspaper. If he was who he claimed to be then he could prove to be a valuable contact for them in Zimbala. There was only one way to find out. She sat down on the edge of the bed and dialed UNACO headquarters in New York.

Massenga climbed out of the car after Gubene had parked it in the garage of the safe house and slammed the door angrily behind him. Gubene waited until he had stalked out of the garage before getting out of the car himself and locking the driver's door. Moments later he heard Massenga unlocking the front door and he winced as it hammered against the wall. Then silence. He exhaled deeply then closed the garage door and walked down the narrow path. He pushed open the front door gingerly with his fingers and entered. He found Massenga perched on the edge of the sofa in the lounge, his hand resting lightly on the telephone.

"You want a drink?" Gubene asked apprehensively, gesturing toward the cabinet in the corner of the room.

Massenga shook his head then looked down at the telephone. "What am I supposed to tell him?"

"The truth," Gubene replied then crossed to the drinks cabinet and poured himself a Scotch.

"That we failed?" Massenga said then slumped back on the sofa. "He'll crucify us, you know that."

"You couldn't have anticipated what happened. She'd be dead now if that man hadn't intervened when he did. It wasn't your fault."

"You want to tell that to Ngune?"

"You're the only one with his number," Gubene said with a shrug then left the room, closing the door quietly behind him.

Massenga dialed the number he had memorized. Ngune answered it immediately at the other end. Massenga told him what had happened at the hotel.

"So she's still alive?" Ngune concluded once Massenga had finished.

"Yes, sir," Massenga muttered.

"And who was this knight in shining armor?" Ngune asked sarcastically as he struggled to control his temper.

"I didn't get a good look at him, sir," Massenga replied. "It all happened so quickly."

"You disappoint me, Thomas. I thought you were the one person I could rely on to carry out an order."

"I couldn't have anticipated his intervention, sir," Massenga replied defensively, remembering Gubene's words.

"I want results, not excuses!" Ngune snarled angrily. "And if you can't get them for me, I'll find someone who can. Do I make myself clear?"

"Yes, sir."

"Find out the identity of the man. Then call me."

"Do you want him killed?"

"If it's not asking too much," Ngune retorted facetiously.

"I'll see to it, sir."

"I hope so, Thomas. If I have to send someone else to Habane it could seriously jeopardize your chances of becoming the new head of the Security Police once we're in power. Remember that."

"Yes, sir, I realize . . ." Massenga trailed off when he heard the dialing tone. He replaced the receiver then crossed to the drinks cabinet and poured himself a Scotch. He had a feeling it was going to be a long night.

Sabrina was studying a map of the city when there was a knock at the door. She picked up the Beretta off the bedside table and peered through the spyhole. It was the man with the wire-framed glasses. She opened the door.

"Inside," she said, beckoning him into the room.

He entered and she closed the door behind him. His smile faltered when he saw the Beretta in her hand. "You won't need that, I assure you."

"Not if you're really Joseph Moredi. But I don't know that yet, do I?"

He swallowed nervously and nodded hesitantly. "Did you speak to Jamel Mobuto?"

"Not personally. I had one of my colleagues do it."

"And did he set a question for me?"

She nodded.

"Could we get on with it?" he said anxiously, his eyes darting toward the gun aimed at his stomach.

"While you were at Oxford you once went to a rugby match together. Who was playing?"

"I've never been to a rugby match in my life. We once went to a *football* match together. Arsenal was the home team. Who were they playing?" he mused thoughtfully. "They weren't from London. Black and white striped shirts." He suddenly snapped his fingers together and pointed at Sabrina. "Newcastle."

Sabrina lowered the gun. "I'm glad you got that right."

"Not half as glad as I am," Moredi said, indicating the gun in her hand. "But why did you say rugby . . ." he trailed off with a knowing smile. "Of course, a trick question."

"An added precaution," she replied then indicated

the armchair in the corner of the room. "Please, won't you sit down, Mr. Moredi."

"Thank you," he said and eased himself into the armchair.

She replaced the Beretta on the table and sat on the bed. "One thing still puzzles me. How did Massenga know I would be on that plane?"

"He was obviously tipped off, but by whom I couldn't say." He shrugged. "Was I right about your investigation being linked to the Mobuto brothers?"

"Yes, but I can't go into details."

"I appreciate that." Moredi suddenly sat forward, his arms resting on his knees. "Jamel and Remy Mobuto have been friends of mine for over twenty years. And now they're both in danger. I'll do anything I can to help them, anything."

"You said earlier that Massenga tried to kill me to prevent me from stumbling on the truth. What exactly did you mean by 'the truth'?"

"I only know part of it. Remy's the only one who knows the whole truth. And he was kidnapped earlier today."

"By Massenga?"

"By him, or on his orders. Massenga's been Ngune's right-hand man for the past five years. An anonymous caller telephoned me at the newspaper to say that the rebels were holding Remy."

"Do you have any idea where he's being held?"

"I have it on good authority from one of my more reliable sources that he's being held at the Branco prison in Kondese, in the south of the country, a couple of hours drive from here."

"How much did Remy Mobuto tell you before he was kidnapped?"

"Only that he was onto a story about a plot to assassinate his brother. It was something big, or so he claimed. It involved Ngune, Massenga and a third man, the man who would pull the trigger."

"Did he mention a name?"

Moredi shook his head. "He knew who it was but he wouldn't tell me. Not until he had the proof he needed to publish the story. Remy was like that. He always played his cards close to his chest. He went to a rendezvous with an informant who had that proof. That's when he was abducted."

"And the informant?"

"Blood was found in his car but there was no sign of him."

"So Remy is the key to this whole affair?"

Moredi nodded. "Not only does he know who will pull the trigger, he also knows where and when the assassination will take place."

"Does the name Bernard mean anything to you?" Sabrina asked.

Moredi bit his lip thoughtfully then shook his head. "No, I can't say it does. Who is he?"

"That I can't tell you," Sabrina replied apologetically. "At least not for the moment."

"I understand."

Sabrina bit her lip thoughtfully. "Why don't the army check out this Branco prison to see if Remy Mobuto is being held there?"

"Kondese is rebel country. The army won't go there. They're waiting up here, in the north, for Ngune to make his first move."

"So it's a stalemate."

"At the moment, yes. But Jamel intends to get his generals round the table for talks when he gets back from America. He wants to crush Ngune and his rebels before they set out for Habane. That's certainly one of the reasons why Ngune wants Jamel dead. He believes it would throw the army into disarray."

"Would it?"

"Yes," Moredi replied bluntly. "But then the army's already in disarray. Many of the soldiers had friends and relatives in the Security Police. Now they're on opposite sides. But will the army try and stop Ngune's men if they do march on Habane? Or will they join them? Nobody really knows the answer. That's what makes it all so uncertain. Zimbala's a powder keg waiting to explode. All it needs is a single spark to set it off. That's why Jamel wants to stop Ngune in his tracks. If Ngune does march on Habane, then the sparks will fly. And whoever does win will have inherited a country bathed in the blood of innocent people. Jamel doesn't want that. He saw enough bloodshed under his father's regime."

"I still don't see why Massenga tried to kill me this afternoon. If Remy Mobuto is the only person who knows what's going on, then how can I be a threat to them? They've got him. They're holding the aces, not me."

"They obviously think you're out here to find him. That could ruin everything for them."

Sabrina propped a pillow against the wall and leaned back against it. "How long have you had Massenga under surveillance?"

"How did you know that?"

"Why else would you have been at the hotel when he tried to kill me?"

Moredi smiled. "You're very astute. I don't know how long he's been in Habane. An informant contacted us two days ago and said he'd seen Massenga. We checked out the story and I've had a team of reporters watching him ever since. He won't know he's being watched."

"Why don't you tell the police about Massenga?"

"Two reasons. Firstly, if they did arrest Massenga it could put Remy's life in danger. And secondly, there are policemen who are sympathetic to Ngune. They would tip him off and Massenga would be pulled out. This way he could still lead us to Remy. I know it's a long shot but we've got to take it." Moredi paused to wet his lips. "I've been watching him ever since he went to the airport this afternoon. Actually, it's the second time he's been to the airport in the last two days. He met someone there yesterday off a flight from Beirut. Around noon. They spoke for about an hour. Then the man flew out again. I couldn't find out his name. Only that he'd taken a Pan Am flight to New York via Morocco and Bermuda."

"Describe him."

"He was pretty distinctive: tall, good-looking, black hair, black moustache."

"And a scar," Sabrina added, tracing her finger down her left cheek.

"Yes," Moredi replied in surprise. "How did you know?"

Sabrina swung her legs off the bed. "I've got to make an urgent phone call. In private."

"Oh, of course," Moredi said, getting to his feet. "I'll go down to the bar and get a beer. Would you like anything?"

"A Diet Cola."

Moredi left the room.

Sabrina rang Kolchinsky at UNACO headquarters and briefed him on what Moredi had told her.

"So Bernard met Massenga in Habane," Kolchinsky said once she had finished. "I don't see anything suspicious in that. He is supposed to be working with them, remember? It's part of his cover."

"That may be, Sergei, but it seems a bit of a coincidence that Massenga tries to kill me the day after he meets Bernard."

"You're reading too much into this meeting, Sabrina."

"It would certainly explain the attempt on my life this afternoon. How else would Massenga know I was due in Zimbala?"

"It's a possibility, I agree," Kolchinsky conceded.

"And what about this third man that Remy Mobuto mentioned? It has to be Bernard."

"Why does it *have* to be Bernard?" Kolchinsky retorted. "What do the CIA have to gain by assassinating Mobuto?"

"Who says it's on CIA orders? He could have made a private deal with Ngune to kill Mobuto."

"And double-cross Bailey? He wouldn't live long enough to spend the money."

"Put yourself in Bernard's shoes, Sergei. Bailey's sure to have promised him a new identity once this is all over. But Bernard's no fool. He knows the CIA will never use him again. So what's he got to lose by contracting himself to Ngune?"

There was a pause while Kolchinsky pondered her words. "So you're suggesting that Bailey would have him killed rather than give him a new identity?"

"He knows too much."

"But you don't have a shred of evidence to back up this elaborate theory of yours."

"Remy Mobuto has the evidence. I'm convinced of that now."

"Remy Mobuto has been kidnapped."

"And he's being held in Kondese."

"Don't even think of it, Sabrina!" Kolchinsky snapped sharply. "You've been assigned to find Michael, not to poke about in rebel country looking for Remy Mobuto. Stay away from Kondese. That's an order!"

"Yes, Sergei," Sabrina muttered through clenched teeth.

"I think it would be better if you caught the next available flight back to the States. After all, if Moredi's right, then Bernard's here now. And Michael's sure to be close behind him."

"I'll make the necessary arrangements."

There was a knock at the door.

"I've got to go, Sergei. Moredi's back. I'll call you if there are any new developments before I leave. Otherwise I'll see you back in New York."

"Fine. Goodbye, Sabrina."

She replaced the receiver then crossed to the door and peered through the spyhole. It was Moredi. She opened the door.

"Finished?" he asked.

"Sure," she replied and stood aside to let him in.

He handed her a can of Diet Cola. "What happens now?"

"Nothing," she replied, opening the can. "At least not until I've heard from my partner."

"Where is your partner?"

"I haven't the faintest idea," she replied then moved to the window and looked down into the street. "But he'd better contact me soon. We're running out of time. Fast."

"Not another roadblock," Graham said tersely, seeing the army patrol ahead of them. "This is the third one in as many miles."

"It is the airport road. They're obviously taking no chances," Laidlaw replied, bringing the white Toyota to a halt behind a rusty blue Fiat.

Graham looked out of the passenger window and counted eight vehicles ahead of them. He threw up his arms in despair. All they could do was wait.

It had been Laidlaw's idea that they both dress as priests. He had borrowed the costumes from a friend, who ran a small theater in West Beirut, on the pretext of needing them for a fancy-dress party the following evening. They had changed into the costumes before leaving for the airport that morning where they had caught a direct flight to N'djamena, the capital of Chad. Laidlaw had hired the car at N'djamena Airport and they had driven the eighty miles to the Chadian-Zimbalan border where the Zimbalan authorities had issued them with ten-day visas, like Sabrina. They were stopped regularly by army patrols on the main highway into Habane but each time they were waved on when the soldiers realized they were priests. And, judging by the size of the military presence around them, they assumed that this would be the last road-block before the airport.

The Fiat was waved through and Laidlaw drove up to the boom gate and cut the engine. An armed soldier approached the car and peered through the driver's window.

"Passport," the soldier said in a thick English accent.

"I speak your language," Laidlaw replied in Swahili and handed the passports to him.

The soldier was surprised to hear his native tongue and smiled at Laidlaw before opening the passports to compare the photographs with the two men in the car. "What is your business at the airport, Father?"

"We are meeting a friend," Laidlaw replied then glanced at his watch. "His flight is due in twenty-five minutes."

The soldier closed the passports and gave them back to Laidlaw. "Thank you, Father."

"Thank you, my son," Laidlaw replied.

The soldier was about to give the order to raise the boom gate when he saw his commanding officer standing at the entrance of the small Nissen hut at the side of the road. He immediately snapped to attention.

The colonel, a dark-skinned African in his early forties, told him to stand easy then crossed to the Toyota and looked through the passenger window. "Your passports," he said to Graham.

"Father Grant doesn't speak Swahili," Laidlaw said with an apologetic smile. "He's only been out here a few days."

The colonel took the passports from Laidlaw and leafed through them slowly. "Get out of the car, both of you," he said, suddenly switching to English.

"What's the problem?" Laidlaw asked suspiciously.

"Just get out of the car," the colonel repeated.

They did as they were told and the colonel walked round to the driver's side and took the keys from the ignition. He beckoned two soldiers toward him and gave the keys to one of them. He spoke to them quickly in Swahili and they immediately hurried round to the back of the car.

"And what do you hope to find in the trunk?" Laidlaw said, sticking to English.

The colonel ignored the question and watched as the boot was opened. One of the soldiers immediately called out to him. He walked to the back of the car then looked round at Laidlaw and beckoned him forward with his finger. Laidlaw's eyes widened in horror when he looked inside the boot. Two AK-47 assault rifles and a hand grenade lay beside their holdalls.

"We know nothing about these," Laidlaw said, looking to Graham for support.

"They weren't here when we hired the car," Graham snapped.

"You're both under arrest," the colonel said then gestured toward a jeep parked at the side of the road. "Get in."

"This is outrageous," Graham said. "We demand to see your superior."

"I am the most senior officer on duty," the colonel retorted then barked out an order and five soldiers immediately unshouldered their M16s and aimed them at Laidlaw and Graham. "You have a choice. Either you get in quietly or you'll be handcuffed and thrown in. It's your choice."

Laidlaw looked helplessly at Graham. Graham bit back his anger and clambered into the back of the jeep. Laidlaw glanced at the soldiers then reluctantly followed him. Their holdalls were tossed into the back after them. The two soldiers who had discovered the weapons got into the back seat and covered Graham and Laidlaw with their M16s. The Colonel ordered a soldier to move the Toyota to the side of the road then climbed into the front of the jeep and told the driver to go to the airport. The boom gate was raised and the jeep sped down the highway toward the airport terminal. The Colonel pointed to a slip road and the driver nodded before indicating and turning the jeep off the main road.

"This isn't the way to the airport!" Laidlaw shouted above the noise of the jeep's engine.

The colonel glanced at him but said nothing.

"Where on earth are we going?" Graham snarled but an M16 was pressed into his stomach when he leaned toward the nearest soldier.

The driver slowed down as he approached a stationary white Isuzu van then swung off the road and pulled up behind it.

Graham's mind was racing. What was happening? Were they about to be executed and their bodies taken away in the back of the van? But why? And where had the weapons come from? Had they been planted by the soldiers? None of it made any sense. He was about to try and signal Laidlaw for them to tackle the two armed guards when the van's passenger door swung open and Sabrina got out. Moredi climbed out of the driver's side and they walked to the jeep.

"Is nothing sacred any more?" Sabrina said with a smile as she eyed Graham's outfit.

Graham jumped nimbly from the back of the jeep. "What the hell's going on?"

"I'll tell you, later," she replied then gestured to Moredi and introduced him to Graham and Laidlaw.

Moredi shook hands with them then spoke briefly to the colonel who immediately ordered his troops into the jeep and the driver did a U-turn and headed back toward the highway.

Moredi led the colonel over to the others. "This is Colonel David Tambese, one of the few soldiers I would trust with my life. He was at Sandhurst when Jamel Mobuto and I were at Oxford together."

"No hard feelings, I hope," Tambese said, shaking Graham's hand.

"Not if you tell me what's going on," Graham retorted.

Tambese glanced at Sabrina who nodded. "When Joseph told me you were going to pick up a message from the information desk at the airport, he asked me to check the area for any signs of Ngune's men. There are at least four of them in the terminal. We had to stop you before you got there."

"Why didn't you just arrest them?" Laidlaw asked.

Tambese shot a glance at Laidlaw. "It's almost certainly a suicide squad. Any attempt to approach them would result in a bloodbath. They would open fire indiscriminately. And who knows how many innocent people would have been killed? It's a new form of terror Ngune has introduced in the last couple of days. We've already had to deal with two suicide squads in the city center. Fourteen innocent people have been killed in those two incidents alone. We'll wait for them to leave then ambush the car. It's the only way to deal with them."

"How do you know they were waiting for me?"

"We don't," Tambese answered. "But after the attempt on Miss Cassidy's life we couldn't take any chances—"

"What happened?" Graham cut in quickly.

"I'll brief you later," she replied.

"How did you know when we'd get here?" Graham asked Sabrina.

"I didn't. I just knew you had to come to the airport sooner or later. I gave Colonel Tambese a photograph of you to make sure he'd stop you before you reached the airport. It's the one I took to Beirut with me in case I needed it when I approached the Lebanese police."

"The three men in the jeep are trusted soldiers of mine," Tambese continued. "Most of the others at the roadblock are new recruits. We still don't know where their true sympathies lie. I had to make your arrest look realistic. Arresting foreigners for no apparent reason isn't exactly part of the plan for the new Zimbala. That's why we planted the AK-47s and the grenade. Word is sure to get back to Ngune that you've been arrested."

"Which means Ngune will think you're in custody, at least for the time being," Moredi added.

"Why do I get the feeling this is leading up to something?" Graham said, his eyes flickering between Moredi and Sabrina.

"It is," Sabrina said. "We're going to Kondese to find Remy Mobuto."

Graham took Sabrina to one side. "And what about Bernard? You remember our agreement."

"You don't have to whisper," Sabrina said. "They know about Bernard."

"What's so important about Remy Mobuto?" Graham asked.

"He knows where and when the hit on his brother will take place. That's why he was abducted."

"So where does Bernard fit into this?"

"Ngune and his deputy, Massenga, are obviously the two brains behind this whole operation. But, according to Remy Mobuto, there is a third man, the assassin. And from what Joseph's told me, it has to be Bernard. I think all this talk of a hit squad made up of ex-Security policemen was just a red herring to throw the authorities off the scent."

"But you've got no proof that this third man is Bernard?"

"No, it's just a hunch. And there's only one person who does know the truth."

"Remy Mobuto," Graham concluded.

"We have to find him, Mike. Quickly."

"How far is Kondese from here?"

"It's a good two-hour drive," Moredi told him.

"So what are we waiting for?" Graham said then picked up his holdall and walked to the van.

◆ CHAPTER

SEVEN

"Morning."

"Morning," Rosie replied, rubbing her eyes wearily as she emerged from the bedroom.

"Sleep well?" Bernard asked.

"Great, thanks. I haven't slept that well in ages."

"That's good." Bernard slipped on his leather jacket. "I have to rush. There's food in the fridge. Help yourself. I've left twenty dollars on the kitchen table. Buy something for dinner."

"Do you have special food?" she asked hesitantly.

"Halal, you mean? No, I'm not a Muslim. I'm supposed to be Catholic but I renounced the faith after my father died. Get anything, pizzas, burgers, whatever you like."

"What time will you be back?"

"You know what these business meetings are like. They can go on for ever. I hope to be back by six." Bernard opened the front door then looked back at her. "The money's for food, not dope. If the police catch you near another dealer they'll throw the book at you."

"I know," she replied.

"I'll score us some dope, OK?"

"OK," she replied with a grin. "Marc?"

"Yes?"

"Thanks for everything."

Bernard winked at her then left the flat and closed the door behind him.

Rosie fixed herself breakfast then changed out of the baggy white T-shirt Bernard had lent her into her jeans and the light blue shirt he had left out for her. She rolled up the sleeves then went back into the kitchen to make herself another cup of coffee. She sat down at the table and held the cup in both hands as she thought about the previous evening.

He had taken her to a steakhouse after they had left the Rollercoaster and ordered her the biggest T-bone steak she had ever seen. She had been ravenous, not having eaten properly for thirty-six hours, and managed to clear the plate and still have room for an icecream. Then, after scoring from a dealer outside Bryant Park, he had taken her back to the flat. They had talked for hours. Well, she had. He had listened patiently as she bared her soul. It was like unloading a great burden from her shoulders. She had felt completely relaxed in his company. He reminded her of C.W. Two gentlemen. C.W. was the only other person she could talk to in times of trouble. She knew C.W. would have chastised her for going off with a strange man. But it wasn't as if she did it all the time. In fact, it was the first time it had ever happened. And she wouldn't have done it if she had felt the slightest doubt about him. And her instincts had been proved right. She wondered if C.W. would understand? She would phone him. He could pass a message on to her parents . . .

Her thoughts were interrupted by the buzz of the doorbell. Her initial reaction was that Marc had come back for something. He'd probably forgotten his keys. Her mother did it all the time. She put the cup down on the table and was about to get up when another thought struck her. It could also be the police. What if they had traced her to the flat? But how? And anyway, the flat was in Murray Hill, nowhere near Times Square. She wasn't violating her parole conditions. What about last night? She had been in Times Square. Had they received a tip-off? Who from? Kenny? But he didn't know where she was.

The doorbell rang again. She stood up and walked to the front door. She opened it on the chain.

"Rosie?" a voice called out.

"Kenny?" she replied, peering through the narrow aperture at him.

"Can I come in, or are we going to talk like this?"

She unhooked the chain and opened the door. "How did you know I was here?"

"I had you followed from the Rollercoaster," Doyle replied and immediately pushed his hands against the door when Rosie tried to slam it in his face. "I did it because I was worried about you."

"So you had someone spy on me," she snapped, still trying to force the door closed. "Go away, Kenny. Go away and leave me alone."

"Rosie, I just want to talk to you. Please."

"No!" she screamed. "Go away."

"You carry on yelling like that and one of the neighbors will call the police. Is that what you want?"

She stopped pushing on the door. "OK, say what you've come to say then get out. I can't believe you're acting like this, Kenny. We used to be friends."

"We still are."

"Think again," she snapped back.

"Rosie, there's something about this guy that isn't right."

"You're not starting that again?"

"I'm worried about you, for Christ's sake. The guy saved your butt last night, granted. But there was no need for you to throw yourself at him like you did."

"Throw myself at him?" she retorted in amazement.

"That's exactly what you did, and you know it. You couldn't take your eyes off him. You live in a fantasy world, you know that?" Doyle shook his head slowly. "Open your eyes, Rosie. This is the real world. You're shacking up with—"

Rosie slapped him across the face. "I'm not shacking up with him! He hasn't touched me since we met."

Doyle dabbed the corner of his mouth with the back of his hand. His lip was bleeding. "I've tried my best. You just won't come out of your fantasy world, will you? But you'll learn. And it'll be the hard way. I'll see you around. Take care of yourself."

Rosie watched Doyle disappear into the lift then wiped a tear from her cheek. Why had she hit him? She had never hit anyone before in her life. And he was her best friend. She knew he was only trying to protect her. He had always been the big brother she never had. But why couldn't he understand that she needed her own freedom, a freedom to pick and choose her own friends? She so wanted him to like Marc. But now she knew that would never happen. He would be there for her when Marc was gone. He was always there for her. That's what made him so special. Then they could talk again. But until then she would stay away from the Rollercoaster, far away.

She closed the door and went back to the kitchen where she finished her coffee. After washing up she went through to the lounge and picked up the newspaper Bernard had been reading. The front page carried the story about the attempted assassination of Jamel Mobuto outside the United Nations Plaza. She didn't bother reading it. She wasn't interested in politics. She paged through the newspaper, found nothing of interest, and tossed it onto the coffee table in the middle of the room. She glanced at her watch. Nine fifty-five. She wasn't going to sit around the flat all day. Hell, there wasn't even a television set. She went back to the kitchen and was about to pocket the twenty dollars when she thought better of it and left it on the table. She would only use it for food. She turned out her pockets. She had six dollars and a few cents. It would be enough for a sandwich at lunchtime. She stuffed the money back into her pocket then picked up the spare key from the table in the hall and left the flat.

Doyle watched Rosie leave the building from the seclusion of a doorway on the opposite side of the street. He waited until she had disappeared from sight then crossed the road and mounted the steps leading up to the glass doors. He glanced around quickly then entered the foyer. It was deserted. He took the lift to the third floor and walked the short distance to the flat. He looked around again and, satisfied he was alone, removed a credit card from his wallet and slipped it carefully between the door and the jamb. He eased it against the lock and prised it back gently until he felt the door give under his sustained pressure.

After a quick perusal he pushed open the door and slipped inside, closing it silently behind him. He looked into the room nearest the front door, the lounge. The second door led into a bedroom. The bed was unmade. The T-shirt Rosie had been wearing the previous night lay crumpled in the corner.

He tried the adjoining door. It also led into a bedroom. The bed had been made with military precision. He moved to the wardrobe and tried the door. It was unlocked. He opened it. The clothes had been ironed then folded with meticulous care before being stacked neatly on the shelves. He unhooked the second door and opened it. Two pairs of jeans hung beside a pair of black flannels and a grey chintz jacket. He crouched down and unzipped the gray holdall at the bottom of the wardrobe. It was empty. He was about to zip it up when he noticed the black attaché case pushed up against the back of the wardrobe.

He pushed the holdall to one side then removed the attaché case and placed it carefully on the floor. Wiping the sweat from his forehead he glanced furtively over his shoulder like a naughty schoolboy about to light up a cigarette behind the toilets. He wiped his clammy hands on his shirt then tried the catches. They wouldn't move—a combination lock. He tilted the case to get a closer look at the digits. They were all at zero.

"One-nine-six-seven."

Doyle looked round, startled by the voice behind him. Bernard stood in the doorway, a Desert Eagle automatic in his hand.

"Please, carry on," Bernard said, indicating the attaché case with the pistol. "The combination's one-nine-six-seven, the year the PFLP was founded."

"What?" Doyle said, his eyes riveted on the pistol.

"You've never heard of the PFLP?"

Doyle swallowed nervously and shook his head.

"The Popular Front for the Liberation of Palestine."

"You're a terrorist!" Doyle spat the words out.

"I prefer 'revolutionary'. But not any more. I work freelance now."

"How did you know I was here?" Doyle stammered.

Bernard indicated the transmitter attached to his belt. "You activated it the moment you opened the wardrobe." He noticed the uncertainty in Doyle's eyes. "I was in the adjoining flat, working. The two flats are connected by a door built into the lounge wall. That's why you never heard me come in. Actually, I thought it was Rosie snooping around."

"What are you going to do with her?"

"Nothing," Bernard replied casually then gestured to the case again with the pistol. "You still haven't opened it. I thought you'd be curious to know what's inside."

Doyle's hands were trembling as he lined up the

digits. He placed his thumbs on the catches then paused to glance up at Bernard. His breathing was ragged and the sweat now ran freely down his face.

"It's not booby-trapped if that's what you're worried about," Bernard said. "Do you think I would be standing here if it was?"

Doyle wiped the back of his hand across his forehead then unlocked the case. He eased the lid open. Inside were the specially designed segments of a rifle and telescopic sight-attachment which were sunk into the contours of a foam base. "A gun. I should have guessed."

"A Galil sniping rifle to be exact. They may be the enemy, but the Israelis still make the best weapons in the world. So, is your curiosity satisfied now, gay boy?"

The taunt stung Doyle into action. He lunged at Bernard who sidestepped his wild punch and landed a vicious rabbit punch of his own at the base of Doyle's neck. Doyle stumbled and threw his hands up to protect his face as he fell heavily against the wall. Bernard took a silencer from his pocket and screwed it onto the muzzle of the pistol. He looked down at Doyle who was on his knees, his head bowed, his fingers gingerly massaging his neck.

"Hey, gay boy?" Bernard said, prodding Doyle with his foot.

Doyle looked up slowly. Bernard smiled coldly and shot him through the head.

Kolchinsky was reading through a dossier when the intercom buzzed. "C.W."'s here, Mr. Kolchinsky."

"Send him through, Sarah," Kolchinsky replied and used the sonic transmitter to activate the door.

"Morning, Sergei," Whitlock said, entering the room.

Kolchinsky glanced at his watch. "Afternoon, actually. It's a minute after twelve."

Whitlock shrugged. "I won't quibble about a minute."

"Sit down," Kolchinsky said, indicating the nearest of the black leather sofas. "I thought you were supposed to be accompanying the President to the African-American Institute this morning?"

"The tour was canceled." Whitlock sat down. "He's been in conference all morning. Suits me fine. The less he sees of New York the better."

"What about his trip to Harlem this afternoon?"

"Still on, unfortunately. It's scheduled for two o'-clock. That's why I thought I'd pop over and see you while I had the chance. Anything on the two assassins?"

"Not a thing. I've been on the phone to the Zimbalan authorities again this morning. It seems the Security Police shredded a lot of documents before Jamel Mobuto outlawed the organization. A lot of personnel files were also destroyed. They've promised to get back to me the moment they come up with anything." Kolchinsky pushed a folder across the desk. "This came in this morning from the lab at the Test Center. It's the report on the shooting outside the United Nations Plaza. It's routine stuff mainly. But there was something that caught my eye—second page, third paragraph. See what you think."

Whitlock opened the folder and read the relevant paragraph then looked up at Kolchinsky. "I see what you mean. Although the gunman was only thirty yards from Mobuto, he fired almost three feet wide of his target. Are they sure about their calculations?"

"They had half-a-dozen press photographs to choose from when it came to pinpointing Mobuto's position outside the hotel."

Whitlock closed the folder and replaced it on the desk. "So the gunman either missed deliberately or else he was a lousy shot."

"It doesn't make sense," Whitlock said thoughtfully.

"Any assassin worth his salt wouldn't have missed by three feet. Not from that distance."

Kolchinsky explained briefly what Sabrina had said earlier about a "third man".

"If Bernard is this mysterious third man, why not just use him to assassinate Mobuto?" Whitlock said. "Why go to all the trouble of assembling a team of Security policemen . . ." he trailed off and looked quizzically at Kolchinsky. "Decoys?"

"That had crossed my mind. But decoys for what? We know that Bernard wasn't even in the country when the attempt was made on the President's life. He was in Beirut."

Whitlock stood up and walked to the window. He chewed his lip thoughtfully then turned back to Kolchinsky. "What if this third man *was* there the other night when the attempt was made on Mobuto's life?"

"As backup?"

"As the assassin. The gunman in the crowd was just the decoy."

Kolchinsky tapped the folder. "The bullet dug out of the wall came from a nine-millimeter parabellum. It's the same gun discarded by the gunman."

"Exactly," Whitlock said, nodding. "He purposely fired wide. That would tie in with the report."

"So why didn't this third man shoot Mobuto?"

"Obviously he didn't have a clear shot." Whitlock moved to the desk and looked down at Kolchinsky. "I know it's a wild hunch, Sergei, but it makes sense, don't you see that? The decoy draws our attention to himself by firing blindly and in doing so gives the real assassin the chance to shoot Mobuto in the ensuing confusion. But, as I said, the assassin obviously didn't have a clear shot. And he's only got one shot in that situation."

"So if this theory of yours is right, why didn't the first gunman also try to shoot Mobuto? Why purposely fire wide?"

"Because they want Mobuto dead. Who would be

more reliable? The man in the crowd, armed only with a handgun, or the sniper overlooking the target area? What if the first gunman had only wounded him? They'd never have got near him in hospital. He'd have been guarded better than Fort Knox."

"If your theory is right, then Bernard can't be this third man."

"Why?" Whitlock countered.

"I've told you, he was in Beirut two days ago."

"We only have Bailey's word for that. You said that Bernard was spotted at the airport by a CIA operative. Bernard could easily have bribed him to say that. What if he's been here all the time?"

Kolchinsky stared at the folder thoughtfully then looked up at Whitlock. "If you're right, the next attempt has to be this afternoon. It's the only time the President will be out in the open."

"My thoughts exactly. I want to draft in more police snipers to cover the area around the school."

"How many?"

Whitlock visualized the plan of the area in his head. "A dozen to be on the safe side."

Kolchinsky made a note on his desk pad. "I'll arrange it with the Commissioner."

"Well, I'd better get over to the hotel. Call me when you've spoken to the Commissioner."

Kolchinsky nodded then activated the door for Whitlock. He closed it behind him then reached for the telephone.

"Hello?" Bernard said, answering the telephone after the first ring.

"This is Seabird," a voice said.

"Columbus," Bernard replied, quoting his codename.

"Whitlock's stumbled on the truth," Seabird told

him. "Abort Plan A. Don't go to Harlem this afternoon."

"What about Sibele and Kolwezi?"

"Send them in as if nothing's wrong. They're expendable. It'll also convince Whitlock he was right."

"Leaving Plan B."

"Right," Seabird agreed.

"What about the rifle?"

"I'll have someone drop by later and pick it up. Don't worry, we won't have any problems getting it past the security guards."

Bernard replaced the receiver and smiled to himself. The hit on Mobuto was now down to him. He liked it that way.

Rogers was sitting by the door of Mobuto's suite reading a magazine when the lift doors opened and Whitlock emerged into the corridor. The two uniformed policemen by the lift checked Whitlock's ID disc then let him pass.

Rogers discarded the magazine onto the coffee table beside him and got to his feet. "They're still in conference," he said when Whitlock reached him.

Whitlock glanced irritably at his watch. "What's he playing at? He knows he's got to give an address at the school in an hour. The press are already crawling all over the foyer, waiting for him to appear."

"Hoping for blood this time," Rogers muttered cynically.

"No doubt," Whitlock agreed. "If he'd been ready a half an hour ago we could have avoided them."

The door suddenly opened and the towering figure of Masala appeared. "The President will be ready to leave in five minutes."

Whitlock waited until the Zimbalan ambassador and his entourage had left before entering the suite. "Can I have a word with the President?" he asked Masala.

"The President is dressing," came the sharp reply.

"Is there a problem?" Mobuto asked from the doorway of his bedroom.

"There could be, sir," Whitlock replied.

"Then you'd better come in," Mobuto said then disappeared back into the bedroom.

Mobuto was putting on a red silk tie in front of the mirror when Whitlock entered the room. "And what seems to be the problem?"

Whitlock bit back his anger at Mobuto's sarcastic tone. "We agreed that you would be ready half an hour ago to avoid the press."

"The conference lasted longer than I anticipated," Mobuto replied, glancing toward Whitlock's reflection in the mirror.

"Well, the press are here in force now. We'll have to smuggle you out through the back of the hotel."

Mobuto finished knotting his tie then turned to face Whitlock. "Perhaps you'd like to put a paper bag over my head as well just in case someone should see me."

"None of this would be necessary if we had left on time," Whitlock retorted, unable to hold back his anger any longer.

"You sound just like my father. Everything he did had to be done with military precision. He lived by the clock. He never knew the word flexibility." Mobuto held up his hand before Whitlock could reply. "Let's get something straight, Clarence. I intend to leave here through the front of the hotel. And if there is an assassin in the crowd, then let's hope you're as quick on your toes as you were the other night. But I will not bow to their terror by sneaking out through back doors. Is that understood?"

Whitlock nodded.

Mobuto put on his jacket and slipped a carnation into his button hole. "I'm ready. Shall we go?"

The bleeper attached to Whitlock's belt went off before he could reply. He silenced it and immediately

went into the lounge where a special scrambler telephone had been installed. He rang UNACO headquarters and gave Sarah his identity number. She
immediately patched him through to Kolchinsky.

"Bailey's just called," Kolchinsky told him.
"Bernard's been in touch."

"Finally," Whitlock replied. "Did he say where the
hit would take place?"

"At the school."

"Where at the school?"

"There's no definite plan, but Bernard told the gunman to make the hit outside the building."

"Which would tie up with a second assassin."

"Perhaps," Kolchinsky replied. "It's a two-man
team, like before, one wheelman, one assassin. The
getaway car will be a red Buick, registration number
472 ENG."

"That certainly helps," Whitlock said, jotting down
the number.

"I got a bad feeling about this, C.W. Be careful."

"You can count on it," Whitlock replied.

"Keep me advised."

"Will do," Whitlock said then replaced the receiver.

"Well?" Mobuto inquired.

Whitlock recounted what Kolchinsky had said on
the telephone.

"At least now we know where we stand," Mobuto
said once Whitlock had finished speaking.

"I hope you're right," Whitlock replied softly then
followed Mobuto to the door.

The Mercedes carrying the President was hemmed in
between two police cars while a second Mercedes
brought up the rear of the convoy. Whitlock sat in the
front of the presidential car, his mind racing. Had he
anticipated every possibility when he had organized
the security arrangements at the school that morning?

Was there a weak link? He had gone over the plans of the area with the head of the SWAT team. Had they overlooked anything? If something happened to Mobuto now they had been warned that another attempt was to be made on his life, heads would definitely roll, starting with his. He had radioed through to the SWAT team before they set out for Harlem, warning them to be on the lookout for the red Buick. He had also given them strict instructions not to open fire unless it was absolutely necessary. A prisoner to question would be invaluable to a case that was crying out for answers, and there was far more chance of the gunman being killed than the getaway driver. Then there was Bernard. Where did he fit into the jigsaw? Was he the third man? And if he was, was he working for Bailey or had he double-crossed the CIA? Was he working for Ngune? So many questions and he didn't have an answer for any of them. That worried him. And like Kolchinsky, he had a bad feeling about Mobuto's visit to Harlem . . .

"Are you married, Clarence?" Mobuto asked from the back seat. "I suddenly realized I don't know anything about you since you left Oxford."

Whitlock wished Mobuto would stop calling him Clarence. But there was nothing he could do about it. Mobuto had already reported him to Kolchinsky for calling him Jamel at the airport. Kolchinsky had hauled him into the office the next day and told him to bite his tongue. Mobuto was a guest in the country, and an important one at that. Kolchinsky had also pointed out that it wasn't as if he were insulting him. He was only calling him by his name. Whitlock knew he was right. Clarence indeed!

"Yes, I've been married for seven years. Actually, my wife works in Harlem."

"Really? What does she do?"

"She's a paediatrician."

"How interesting," Mobuto said without sounding particularly convincing. "Do you have any children?"

"No."

The silence descended again.

"We're in Harlem now," Whitlock said as the Mercedes followed the police car into Lenox Avenue.

Mobuto peered through the dark glass window. "It seems so bleak and depressing."

"It is, believe me. Poverty's rife because unemployment's so high. So youngsters turn to drugs, crime and prostitution to make ends meet. It's hard to believe this is America, land of the free."

"I'd like to speak to some of the people," Mobuto said, the pained expression etched on his face. "Driver, pull over."

The driver shot Whitlock a nervous glance but Whitlock shook his head.

"We're not stopping, not until we reach the school."

"Why not?" Mobuto demanded. "These are your people as well, Clarence."

"We may be black, sir, but we don't belong here. They don't like outsiders. And can you blame them, looking around at all the squalor? This is what a succession of American governments have done for them. It makes me bitter when I come into Harlem. But they don't want my sympathy. They don't want anybody's sympathy. They just want to be left alone to try and sort out their own problems." Whitlock glanced at Mobuto in the rear-view mirror. "Don't think it was easy getting you into Harlem; it wasn't. The government had to negotiate with community leaders to let the convoy enter. We're driving through some gang's turf right now. We're violating their space. If our visit hadn't been sanctioned by the community leaders the convoy would certainly have come under attack by now."

"But surely the police cars would deter them?"

A faint smile touched the driver's lips.

"The gangs don't fear the police," Whitlock said. "If

anything, it's the other way round. You may have noticed that all the uniformed policemen in the convoy are black. They're all based here in Harlem. The people know them."

Mobuto fell silent.

The large crowd of onlookers which had congregated outside the school was being kept away from the main gates by a cordon of policemen. Some were genuinely interested in the man, others attracted by the media hype that had surrounded his visit since the attempt on his life two days earlier. The schoolchildren, who lined the approach road to the school, had been issued with small replicas of the Zimbalan flag and they began to wave them on cue the moment the cavalcade came into sight.

Mobuto smiled and waved as the car passed them. Whitlock ignored the children. His eyes were on the surrounding buildings. He could see the SWAT snipers on the roofs, their faces shaded from the overhead sun by their black peaked caps. He had given instructions that all buildings be searched and guarded within a seven-hundred-yard radius of the school. He knew it had already caused a lot of resentment amongst the occupants, especially as the SWAT team was predominantly white, but there was nothing he could do about it. His first duty was to protect Mobuto.

The Mercedes followed the police car through the wrought-iron gates and pulled up behind it two hundred yards further on in front of the main portico where the principal and a deputation of community leaders were standing. Whitlock slipped in his earpiece, which kept him in touch with the leader of the SWAT team, then got out of the car and waited until Rogers and Masala had joined him from the second Mercedes before opening the door for Mobuto.

The principal stepped forward as Mobuto climbed from the car and extended his hand in greeting. He welcomed Mobuto to the school then set about introducing him to the five community leaders who had been chosen to meet him. Whitlock and Rogers exchanged anxious glances. Why couldn't the introductions be made inside? Mobuto was a prime target on the portico. Whitlock slid on his sunglasses and scanned the roof of the adjacent building. It was guarded by two of the SWAT team. He felt the sweat run down the side of his face. Bernard had said the attempt would be made outside the school. That was why he had already persuaded Mobuto not to get out and greet the crowd. It would be tempting fate. Which left the sniper—if, in fact, there even was one. And if Bernard were the sniper, why had he tipped off Bailey about the hit? None of it made any sense. But it wasn't the time to be speculating about Bernard's involvement.

He looked around once more then turned back to Mobuto who was being introduced to the last of the community leaders. He nodded to Masala who took up his position at the door, waiting to lead the deputation into the corridor, then spoke briefly to the uniformed policemen who had formed a cordon around the portico, reiterating the point he had made several times earlier at the briefing that nobody was to get past them once Mobuto was inside the building. He also told them to keep in touch with the other uniformed officers in and around the school building and to contact him if anything untoward happened, no matter how trivial. He was desperate to apprehend the assassin, or assassins, without a shot being fired. It would make amends for the lapse of security outside the hotel. Rogers touched him on the arm. They were ready to go inside. Whitlock had been uncertain about Rogers's presence in the hall. He would be the only white face there. It had finally been decided that he would watch the door leading off from the back of the stage. He would be hidden from view by the heavy red curtains that bordered the stage on three sides. Whitlock looked around one last time then followed Mobuto into the building.

♦   ♦   ♦

Walter Sibele had been with the Zimbalan Security Police for eight years before it was disbanded by Jamel Mobuto, so he had jumped at the chance to join the four-man team selected to go to America to assassinate Mobuto. Massenga had told them not to view it as a revenge mission. It must be approached clinically and professionally. They had been training together for a week at a farmhouse on the outskirts of Kondese when Massenga had suddenly arrived unexpectedly with a man none of them had ever seen before. Massenga introduced him only as "Columbus". There was to be a change of plan. Columbus was the new team leader, and he would kill Mobuto. They were to listen to him and obey his every instruction. They didn't question Massenga's orders but there was a feeling of resentment against this newcomer. He had yet to prove himself. On the second day he had thrown down the gauntlet. If any of them could beat him on the firing range, then they would not only become the new leader, but they would also win the job of killing Mobuto. It was a challenge they had readily accepted. None of them had come close to matching his shooting ability, either with handguns or rifles. That was to be the turning point. By the time the four of them had flown out to America there was nothing they wouldn't do for him.

And now that the other two were dead, it was up to Kolwezi and himself to prove themselves to Columbus, even if it meant they would be killed in the process. They were ready for that—as long as Mobuto died with them. Then Ngune could take power and they would become the martyrs that had helped to create a new generation of power in Zimbala. And if they survived, Ngune would decorate them publicly for their bravery. Whatever the outcome, Mobuto had to die . . .

Sibele had been searched when he entered the

building and the number on his invitation had been checked against a list. It had been bought legitimately from a tout in St Nicholas Park. There had only been five hundred tickets printed and, on Mobuto's specific instructions, three hundred and fifty of those were to be sold to the public. All the money would go to help the children of Harlem. Had all the tickets gone to the wealthy black socialites of New York, as had initially been the plan, then he could never have got into the building. It was ironic that Mobuto had orchestrated his own death. The gun, a Beretta, had been smuggled into the building a week ago by a janitor who had been handsomely rewarded for his trouble. He had waited until the toilets had been searched by the police then taped the gun under the cistern for Sibele to collect minutes later. He had tucked the Beretta into the belt at the back of his trousers then taken his seat early to ensure that he was close to the stage. He had been sitting there for over an hour but he knew Mobuto had arrived at the school: it would only be a matter of minutes before he entered the hall . . .

The double doors at the back of the hall were thrust open and the menacing figure of Masala entered. There were some anxious whispers from the audience but the appearance of the principal behind him seemed to calm the situation. Most of the audience recognized Mobuto immediately from the exposure he had received on national television and they watched him walk down the aisle with the rest of the delegation and climb the stairs leading onto the stage. The principal gestured to the chair nearest the podium and Mobuto smiled briefly before sitting down. The community leaders took their seats, leaving the chair next to Mobuto vacant for the principal. Whitlock and Masala sat at the rear. Whitlock glanced toward the wings. Rogers gave him a thumbs up then peered through the curtains at the audience before turning and moving back to the door.

The principal moved to the podium. He looked out

across the sea of faces then cleared his throat. "May I straight away welcome you all here today. I had a speech all prepared to introduce our guest to you but, thanks to the efficiency of the American press, I doubt there's anyone here who doesn't know the entire life history of Mr. Mobuto by now."

There was a ripple of laughter. Mobuto remained impassive as he stared at the floor.

"Mr. Mobuto has graciously agreed to answer any questions you may have after he has finished his speech. So without further delay, please give a warm Harlem welcome to the new President of Zimbala, Jamel Mobuto."

That was Sibele's cue. As the applause echoed around the room he drew the Beretta and sprung to his feet. The woman beside him screamed. Masala knocked the principal out of the way and felled Mobuto, shoving him to safety behind the podium before Sibele could get off a shot. Women and children began screaming as chairs were kicked aside in the stampede for the back doors. Whitlock drew his Browning but couldn't shoot at Sibele for fear of hitting someone in the audience. Sibele looked toward the gallery which had been closed for renovations. There was no sign of Columbus. Where was he? He said he would be there. Something must have gone wrong. Sibele turned back toward the stage. He was on his own. Whitlock had reached the edge of the stage when Sibele swung the Beretta on him and fired. The bullet hit Whitlock in the arm. The Browning spun from his hand. Sibele ran toward the stairs leading onto the stage. Rogers swung out from behind the curtain and fired twice as Sibele reached the top of the stairs. The bullets took Sibele in the chest, punching him off the stage. He crashed into the front row of chairs, scattering them across the floor. Rogers leaped off the stage and kicked the gun away from Sibele's outstretched hand. He pressed his Smith & Wesson into Sibele's neck and felt for a pulse.

"Well?" Whitlock asked from the edge of the stage, his hand clutched over his arm.

"Dead," Rogers replied then frowned anxiously. "Are you OK?"

Whitlock nodded and hurried over to where Mobuto lay. "Sir, are you alright?"

"I'm fine." Mobuto got to his feet and winced as he looked at Whitlock's blood-soaked sleeve. "You're losing a lot of blood. You need to get to a hospital."

"The bullet went straight through. It looks a lot worse than it is."

The principal and the community leaders ventured out from behind the curtains and looked from Sibele's body to Whitlock's injured arm.

"How did he get in here with that gun?" the principal demanded. "I thought the police had searched everybody who came in here today."

"They did," Whitlock replied. "It was obviously an inside job."

Two uniformed policemen appeared at the back of the hall, alerted by the sound of gunfire.

"Call an ambulance," Rogers shouted to them. "And close those doors. The press aren't to get in here under any circumstances until the body's been removed."

"Yes, sir," one of the policemen said and closed the doors behind them.

Whitlock used his handkerchief as a tourniquet then glanced out across the now deserted hall before focussing his attention on the gallery. Why had Sibele looked up there? Was that where the sniper should have been? But the door leading into the gallery was being guarded by a uniformed policeman. Had that put the sniper off?

"You also saw it," Masala said behind him.

Whitlock nodded.

There was a knock at the door and a breathless policeman entered the hall. He glanced at Sibele's body then looked up at Whitlock. "We've been trying to reach you but you weren't replying."

Whitlock instinctively looked down at the receiver on his belt. The wire connected to the earpiece had been ripped from the socket, probably when he fell. He looked up at the policeman. "What is it?"

"The SWAT team have cornered the getaway driver a couple of blocks from here. They're awaiting your instructions."

Whitlock turned to Rogers. "Get over there right away. We need him alive. Make sure the SWAT team know that. If they are forced to shoot, tell them to maim, not kill."

"I'm on my way," Rogers said and jumped nimbly off the stage.

"Wait, I'm going with you," Masala said and looked to Mobuto for his consent.

"Go on. And remember what Mr. Whitlock said. Don't kill him."

Masala nodded and followed Rogers from the hall. They were immediately besieged by the press but neither man said anything as they shoved their way through the extended microphones. Rogers told the uniformed police on the portico to get the press out of the building then walked with Masala to the main gates where an even larger crowd had gathered after word had spread through the neighborhood of the shooting. A member of the SWAT team was waiting for them.

"What's the situation?" Rogers asked.

"We spotted him in a sidestreet. The description of the car and the registration number match the bulletin you sent through to us earlier. The street's been cordoned off but we haven't approached the car. He's just sitting there."

"Let's go," Rogers said.

The three men ran the hundred yards to where a crowd of onlookers had gathered around the mouth of the sidestreet. A police car was parked at an angle to the road, making it impossible for the Buick to get out without ramming it. Another police car was similarly positioned at the other end of the street. Half-a-dozen members of the SWAT team were positioned on the roofs overlooking the street, their rifles trained on the car. The lieutenant in charge of the SWAT team was waiting for them. Rogers told him what Whitlock had said and he immediately passed the instructions on to his men.

"What do you suggest we do?" the lieutenant asked.

"I'll try and speak to him," Rogers replied.

"The car could be booby-trapped," said the lieutenant.

Rogers shrugged. "I've got to take that chance. The longer we make him sweat it out, the more chance there is of him cracking. We need him alive, remember?"

The lieutenant nodded.

Rogers stepped out in front of the police car and took off his jacket. He carefully unholstered his Smith & Wesson, held it up for Kolwezi to see, then handed it to Masala.

"Are you crazy?" the lieutenant said in amazement. "He could gun you down."

"If he does, don't kill him, disable him."

The lieutenant sighed deeply then stepped back and spoke into his radio, telling his men that Rogers would be going in unarmed. Rogers walked slowly toward the Buick, his arms held out away from his body. He reached the front of the Buick and indicated for Kolwezi to open the driver's window. Kolwezi wiped the sweat from his face with his hand then wound down the window. He levelled the Walther at Rogers and ordered him to approach to within five feet of the window. Rogers complied. He looked up at the nearest of the SWAT snipers on the roof above them. He was at least fifty yards away from the car—out of earshot.

"We can talk—they can't hear us," Rogers told him in Arabic. "Sibele's dead."

"And Mobuto?"

"No."

"What about Columbus?"

"He couldn't get into the building," Rogers lied. "It was too well guarded. But there was no way to get a message to Sibele before he went into the hall. He didn't stand a chance."

"Twice we have failed," Kolwezi said bitterly. "Mobuto lives a charmed life, just as he did when his father was in power."

"Don't worry, your deaths won't be in vain. Mobuto will die tomorrow."

"Columbus?"

Rogers nodded then glanced across at Masala and the lieutenant. "I'm supposed to be trying to persuade you to surrender."

"Go now, my friend."

Rogers turned sharply on his heel and began to walk back toward the police car.

Kolwezi calmly pressed the barrel of the gun against the roof of his mouth and pulled the trigger.

Carmen had left her receptionist to lock up and rushed over to the hospital after Whitlock had rung to tell her that he was there. Although his arm was heavily bandaged he had assured her that it wasn't a serious wound. He knew the lie would at least put her mind at rest. It did hurt like hell, though. The doctor had given him a prescription for sleeping tablets which they had picked up on the way back to the apartment. He had eaten a light dinner then retired to bed early, determined to be back at work the following morning.

She was busy washing up when the telephone rang. She wiped her hands on the dish towel and answered the extension in the kitchen.

"Carmen?"

"Rosie?" Carmen countered in surprise.

"Yeah," Rosie replied.

She had dropped the "aunt" and "uncle" routine at

their insistence. Uncle Clarence! Whitlock had hated it. Now she just called him C.W.

"Rosie, where are you?" Carmen asked anxiously. "Your parents are going out of their minds with worry. You must call your mother—"

"No," Rosie cut in firmly. "That's why I called you. Tell her I'm fine. I'll call her in a few days."

"Where are you staying?"

"With a friend."

"Why not come and stay with us for a while?" Carmen suggested. "You don't have to see your parents until you want to. But at least they'll know you're safe."

"Well . . . ," Rosie replied. "I'll call you tomorrow at work and we'll sort something out."

"Is that a promise?"

"Sure. My money's run out. I'll call you, OK?"

"OK."

The line went dead. Carmen replaced the receiver then looked in on her husband, wondering if he had heard the telephone. He was fast asleep. She smiled then closed the bedroom door and returned to the kitchen to finish washing the dishes.

Rosie picked up a pizza from the pizzeria near the callbox then went back to the apartment. She opened the door and saw Bernard's leather jacket on the chair in the hall. He was listening to the news on the radio in the lounge.

"When did you get in?" she asked from the doorway.

"About twenty minutes ago," Bernard replied with a smile.

"How was your day?"

"Don't ask," he said then got to his feet and pointed to the box in her hand. "What's the pizza?"

"Ham and mushroom. Is that OK?"

"Great. I'm starving." Bernard made room for the box on the coffee table. "And how was your day?"

"I went out soon after you left this morning," she said, opening the box. "I only got back now."

"Where did you go?" Bernard asked.

"I took the subway to Fifth Avenue. I spent the day windowshopping. Not much else to do there with five bucks in your pocket."

Bernard smiled then helped himself to a slice of pizza.

"I rang my aunt just before I got the pizza."

"Your aunt?" Bernard asked suspiciously, the pizza slice hovering inches from his mouth.

"Carmen. She suggested I go and stay with them from tomorrow. I reckon it might be a good idea. It's not that I don't appreciate what you've done for me. I really do. But she is family. I only wish my parents were as liberal as my aunt and uncle."

"And you're going to move in with them tomorrow?"

"Yeah, I think so. We've always got on great. Is there something wrong?"

"No, I think it's a good idea. And anyway, I'm heading back to Beirut in a couple of days." Bernard's mind was racing: Carmen, Whitlock's wife. If Rosie moved in with them he could kiss his hostage goodbye. It only complicated matters. Why couldn't she have called them the next day? By then he would know if he needed her. He would have to play it by ear. It was the only way.

The doorbell rang.

Bernard frowned. Was it the courier for the rifle? He wasn't expecting him for another couple of hours, and he wasn't expecting anyone else. He wiped his hands on a paper napkin then got to his feet and answered the door. Two uniformed police officers stood in front of him.

"Good evening, sir," one said, touching his cap. "Are you Marc Giresse?"

Bernard nodded slowly. "Yes. What's the problem, officer?"

"May we come in?"

"Yes, of course," Bernard replied, opening the door for them.

"I'm Officer Deacon," the spokesman said once they were inside. "And this is Officer Cummings."

Bernard noted that their badges were genuine. "You still haven't told me what the problem is."

Deacon was about to speak when Rosie appeared from the lounge. He glanced toward her. "Are you Rosie Kruger?"

She glanced at Bernard, her eyes wide and fearful. "Yes," she stammered.

"Do you know a Kenneth Doyle?"

"Yes," she answered. A look of concern suddenly crossed her face. "Has something happened to him?"

"I was hoping one of you could answer that." Deacon took a sheet of folded paper from his pocket and held it up. "Mr. Doyle left this note with a friend. In it he said he was coming round here this morning to see you, Miss Kruger. He also said that if this friend hadn't heard from him by four o'clock this afternoon he was to go to the police with the note. It all sounds a little sinister, doesn't it?"

"Officer, there must be a logical explanation," Bernard said, fighting the anxiety that throbbed in the pit of his stomach.

"Did you know Miss Kruger was sixteen years old, Mr. Giresse? Or that she was a runaway?"

"Yes, I knew that," Bernard replied. "She told me. That was one of the reasons I gave her a bed for the night. She's too young to be on the streets at night."

"Whose bed?" Cummings asked, looking from Bernard to Rosie.

"You bastard!" Rosie snarled. "Marc's never touched me."

"Cool it, Rosie," Bernard said, holding up his hands.

"Did Mr. Doyle come round this morning?" Deacon asked Rosie.

She nodded. "He had this thing about Marc. He didn't trust him. He wanted me to leave the apartment. I told him to go away. Marc's been fantastic to me ever since I came here."

"And did he go away?" Cummings asked.

"Yes."

"Did he return?" Cummings continued.

"I don't know. I left soon after him and I only got back a few minutes ago."

"Did you see him?" Deacon asked Bernard.

"I've been out all day, officer," Bernard replied. "I'm sorry I can't be more helpful but I only met him once, and that was at the Rollercoaster where he worked."

"Have you tried the Rollercoaster?"

"We've tried all his usual haunts, Miss Kruger. He just seems to have vanished. And that's very unlike him, according to his friends."

"That's true," Rosie said. "Kenny loves company. I've never known him to be alone."

"You say he didn't trust Mr. Giresse," Cummings said. "Why?"

"Kenny was very protective toward me. He was like a big brother. He was always wary of any new friends I made, especially if they were men. I don't know why he didn't trust Marc. He just kept saying that there was something about him that wasn't right."

"You'd both better come down to the precinct with us," Deacon said.

"Are you booking us?" Bernard demanded.

"No," Deacon replied. "We'd like to question you further."

"It's OK," Bernard said to Rosie. "As I said, there's

sure to be a logical explanation to all this. Get your coat."

"I don't have one with me," she replied.

"Use mine," Bernard said, gesturing toward the chair. He turned to Deacon. "Can I get a jacket from the bedroom?"

Deacon nodded then followed Bernard into the bedroom. He stood by the door. Bernard opened the wardrobe and unhooked the gray jacket then slipped his hand under the pile of shirts and curled his fingers around the Desert Eagle. It still had the silencer attached. His first thought was to shoot Deacon on the turn, but that would alert Cummings. He had to get them together. He removed the automatic from under the bottom shirt and slipped the jacket over his hand to hide it. He closed the wardrobe then walked across to Deacon. Cummings was now in sight, standing by the front door. But Rosie was in the way of a clear shot. He cursed. What if Cummings opened the door before Rosie moved? Any gunplay outside the flat would certainly compromise his cover. His mind was still racing when Cummings reached for the handle. Bernard had to play his hand, even if Rosie were caught in the crossfire. Keeping his cover intact far outweighed her usefulness as a hostage. He raised the gun underneath the jacket and shot Deacon through the head. Rosie screamed as Deacon stumbled back against the wall before slumping face forward onto the carpet. Cummings instinctively pushed her aside and was still reaching for his holstered Colt Python when Bernard shot him. He was slammed back against the door and the surprise was still mirrored in his eyes when he slid, lifelessly, to the floor. Bernard discarded the jacket and aimed the automatic at Rosie who was crouched against the wall, her hands clutched together tightly under her chin. She looked up slowly at him, the terror plain on her face.

"Please, don't kill me," she whimpered, shaking her head slowly.

"I'm not going to kill you. You're too valuable to me."

Bernard kept the gun trained on her as he checked to see that both policemen were dead. Satisfied, he ordered her to stand up. She slowly got to her feet, petrified.

"You should have listened to your friend Kenny, shouldn't you?"

"What have you done to him?" she asked, already fearing the worst.

"He came back to the flat after you had gone. I think he fancied himself as a bit of a detective. But he was in way over his head. Pity, he meant well."

"You killed him, didn't you?"

"Yeah," he replied with an indifferent shrug.

She fought back the tears. Why hadn't she listened to Kenny? He had been right all along. She had been living in a fantasy world. And now suddenly she had been pitched headlong into the world of reality. She desperately wanted to crawl back into her old world where she knew she would be safe. But she knew that couldn't happen. Never again. Then came the damning realization that she had been partly responsible for Kenny's death. If she had listened to him he would still be alive. And in that moment of truth her fear turned to anger. She lunged at Bernard, almost wishing he would pull the trigger. He sidestepped her clawing hands and she saw the gun out of the corner of her eye as he swung it down onto the back of her head. Then everything went black.

◆ CHAPTER
EIGHT

Sabrina gazed up at the myriad stars that speckled the night sky like a panoply of diamonds on a velvet background and could almost believe there was a heaven. What else could lie beyond such beauty? Although she had been raised a Catholic she had never really considered herself very religious and now only attended mass once a year with her parents at Christmas, and that was only to appease them. She smiled to herself. Why did the subject of religion always seem to crop up when she was on assignment? A sub-conscious attempt to avoid eternal perdition? She pushed the thought from her mind and concentrated instead on their plans.

It had been decided that the five of them would travel to Kondese alone. Tambese had told them that any attempt to take reinforcements would only alert the rebels. Sabrina had spoken privately to Graham about the decision to take Moredi and Laidlaw with them. Moredi knew the layout of Branco prison, having once been a prisoner there, and Laidlaw's speciality at Delta had been his ability to plan the best way in, or out, of a compound. Both would be invaluable but neither would be part of the assault team. Satisfied, Sabrina had let the matter drop.

Tambese had then collected an assortment of weaponry from the barracks before chartering a Cessna from a private firm in the city. Not only would it be quicker by air, they would also avoid the rebel roadblocks which had been set up on all the approach roads into Kondese. Moredi had arranged for them to land at a farm on the outskirts of Kondese which belonged to Matthew Okoye, a personal friend of the Mobutos. He was one of the wealthiest businessmen in the country and Ngune had wisely given strict instructions for him to be left alone when the rebels had set up camp in and around Kondese. He knew the value of keeping on the right side of the likes of Okoye. They were the future of Zimbala, irrespective of who was in power.

It had taken them a little over an hour to reach the private airstrip and after Tambese had landed the Cessna they were driven to the farm. Okoye and his wife had discreetly withdrawn after dinner, leaving them in the spacious lounge to discuss the operation. But there wasn't anything they could do until the plans of the prison compound were delivered to the farm. So Sabrina had gone out onto the porch for a breath of fresh air.

The door opened behind her.

She looked round and smiled at Graham when he emerged onto the porch. "It's so peaceful out here. Look at the sky—not a cloud in sight, just stars as far as the eye can see. And you can even make out the lights of Kondese in the distance. Isn't it beautiful?"

"Yeah. It's at times like this that you can see where Keats got his inspiration for 'The Secret Rose', or Hopkins for 'The Starlight Night'."

"You never cease to amaze me, Mike Graham," she said, shaking her head in astonishment. "I never realized you read poetry."

He smiled then sat on the step beside her. "I grew up

with it. My mother has volumes of the stuff, all beauti-
fully bound in leather—Keats, Wordsworth, Browning,
Shelley, the lot. Every Friday night her parents would
come round for a meal and afterwards I would have to
read to them from one of the volumes. That went on
until I was in my teens."

"Do you still read poetry?"

"Only when I visit my mother at the retirement
home in Santa Monica. She's still got all the volumes on
a shelf in her room. Her eyesight's going so I always
read her favorite poems to her."

"That's the first time you've ever really spoken
about your childhood, do you know that?"

"Now you know why," he said with a wry grin.
"Imagine a ten-year-old in a suit and tie reading Gray's
'Elegy in a Country Churchyard' to his grandparents.
But she meant well, and that's what counts."

Sabrina chuckled. "I only wish I'd been there to see
it."

"You don't," Graham retorted. "She'd have got you
reading as well."

"I know you think the world of your mother. But
you never talk much about your father. I don't mean to
pry, but is there a reason for that?"

"I was never close to my father. We didn't have
anything in common, that's why. He never once took
me to see the Giants or the Yankees play. I had to go
with other kids' fathers until I was old enough to go by
myself. It was really embarrassing. I started playing
football at the age of eleven. He never once came to
watch me play, never. My mother wasn't interested in
football either, but I can't ever remember her missing a
game when I played in the New York area."

"Didn't he even go and watch you when you played
for the Giants?"

"He died seven months before I joined them. I doubt
he'd have come though. Why break the habit of a
lifetime?"

The bitterness wasn't lost on her and she decided against pursuing the subject. But she was still amazed at his openness. A year ago he would have clammed up at the mere mention of his past. Was he beginning to break down those barriers he had built around himself since he had lost his family? Or was it the thought that he was finally going to get a showdown with the man he blamed for their murder? And what would happen if he did come face to face with Bernard? Would he kill him? Or would he hand him over to the authorities? She knew she couldn't answer that question. Or perhaps she just didn't want to . . .

"You guys look cozy down there," said Laidlaw from the doorway.

"What the hell's that supposed to mean?" Graham demanded, scrambling to his feet.

"Just kidding," Laidlaw said, winking at Sabrina.

Sabrina shook her head slowly to herself. What a jerk. But then he didn't know Graham like she did. Any suggestion of any impropriety between them immediately put Graham on his guard. Some things hadn't changed.

"What do you want?" Graham snapped.

"Hey, chill out, man. I said I was only kidding." Laidlaw looked from Sabrina to Graham. "Look, I don't give a damn if you guys have got something going—"

Graham grabbed Laidlaw by the shirt and shoved him up against the wall. "We work together, period. Understood?"

Laidlaw pulled free and smoothed down his shirt. "The plans are here," he said tersely then yanked open the door and disappeared back into the house.

"Why can't a man and woman work together without there always being some sort of sexual overtone attached to it?"

Sabrina nodded tight-lipped then followed Graham into the house.

Laidlaw walked up to Graham. "I'm sorry, Mike. I was out of order."

"Forget it," Graham replied then crossed to where Tambese and Moredi were sitting on the sofa, the plans spread out across the table in front of them.

"Sit down," Tambese invited, gesturing to the second sofa which they had positioned on the other side of the table.

Graham waited until they were all seated then looked past Sabrina at Laidlaw. "What do you think?"

Laidlaw turned the plan around then looked up at Moredi. "You say the perimeter fence is electrified?"

Moredi nodded. "I don't know the voltage but it is lethal. A prisoner died trying to escape over it when I was being held there."

"Escape was impossible," Tambese told them. "I heard stories of prisoners who had just arrived at the prison breaking free from the guards and throwing themselves against the fence to avoid being interrogated. That's how much the people feared the Security Police."

"Where's the current controlled from?" Laidlaw asked.

Tambese tapped a square in the center of the building. "That's the control room. But it's situated underground. It only has one approach route which is protected by a metal grill. The door itself is made of reinforced steel and can only be activated from inside the control room itself. It's impregnable."

"David was one of the officers who liberated Branco after the death of Alphonse Mobuto," Moredi told them.

"Was that the first time you had ever been inside the prison?" Sabrina asked.

Tambese nodded. "The army and the regular police were never allowed into Branco when it was run by the Security Police."

"Wasn't the fence deactivated when the prison was liberated?" Graham asked.

"It was," Tambese agreed. "But it wouldn't have been very difficult to rig it up again."

"So you're not sure whether it has been reactivated?" Sabrina said to Tambese.

"It has, according to our sources here in Kondese," Tambese replied.

"Couldn't you instigate a power cut?" Graham asked.

Tambese shook his head. "It wouldn't work, even if we could get into the power station. There's an emergency generator inside the compound."

"What about the entrance?" Laidlaw asked without taking his eyes off the plans.

"One main gate—there," Moredi replied, pointing it out.

"Operated from the control room," Tambese added. "There are also two watchtowers overlooking the gate. Each is manned by an armed guard. We wouldn't get within a hundred yards of the main gate without been seen."

"What's it made of?" Laidlaw asked.

"Reinforced steel."

Laidlaw chewed his lip thoughtfully as he continued to study the diagram.

"How many of Ngune's men are inside the prison compound?" Graham asked Tambese.

"We think about twenty-five."

"What about the remainder of his troops?" Sabrina asked.

"I wish I knew," Tambese replied with a sigh. "I really do. There are pockets of them in and around Kondese manning roadblocks and patroling the city center. The resistance movement has been scouting the area ever since the rebels took Kondese but so far they've come up with nothing. It's uncanny. There must be a garrison around here somewhere but we just can't find it."

"What if it's a bluff and Ngune doesn't have the manpower he claims to have?"

"That had crossed our minds, Mr. Graham. But what use are tanks and aircraft without men? And we know he has both."

"Why not destroy them?" Sabrina asked in surprise.

"Because they're in Chad. If our troops crossed the border into Chad we'd be certain to cause an international incident. And that's the last thing we need now that we're on the verge of being allowed back into the United Nations. We've lodged a formal protest with the Chadian government but they claim the tanks and planes are part of their own arsenal—which, in effect, they are. But we know from reliable sources inside the Chadian army that Ngune has struck a deal with their Government to use some of their tanks and planes in the event of an attempted *coup d'état*, but only if Ngune provides the men. So at the moment, it's a stalemate."

"Couldn't the garrison be in Chad?" Sabrina asked.

Tambese shook his head. "No, we've checked. And anyway, the Chadian government's too smart for that. If they were giving a safe haven to Ngune's men it would provide us with the proof we need to discredit them."

"That's it!" Laidlaw suddenly blurted out. "The sewers."

"What?" Sabrina said, turning to Laidlaw in surprise.

"That's how we get into the compound—through the sewers. There, that's the manhole," Laidlaw said, pointing it out on the diagram.

"It'll be locked," Graham said.

"So we cut through it with an oxyacetylene torch," Laidlaw replied.

"The guards would see the flame from the watchtower," Graham shot back.

Laidlaw smiled victoriously. "No they wouldn't. According to the scale of this plan, the manhole cover can't be more than a couple of yards behind the staff quarters. The guards won't be able to see it from the watchtowers."

"And what about the men in the staff quarters?" Sabrina asked.

"If we go in at about three tomorrow morning they'll be asleep." Laidlaw looked at Tambese. "You're sure the only guards on duty then will be the two in the watchtower? There won't be any guards patroling the grounds?"

Tambese shook his head. "There's no need. The watchtowers overlook the grounds."

"OK, so let's say we do cut through the manhole cover," Graham said, staring at the diagram. "How do we get from the staff quarters to the cell block?"

"The guards will have to be neutralized first. All we'd need for that is a sniper rifle and a silencer." Laidlaw looked across at Tambese again. "Could you get them?"

"There's no need," Sabrina said to Tambese. "We can use the Uzis you brought from Habane. They've got silencers."

"It's too risky," Laidlaw replied. "Those watchtowers are a good two-hundred yards away from the staff quarters. If we don't kill the guards with the first bullet, that would almost certainly compromise the operation. That's why we need a rifle with a telescopic-sight-attachment. It has to be a first-time kill."

"I'll arrange to get them," Tambese said.

"OK, so the guards have been neutralized," Graham said. "Then what?"

"Then we cross to the cell block and find Remy Mobuto," Laidlaw replied matter-of-factly.

Graham ran his fingers through his hair, a puzzled expression on his face. "Surely the two buildings are sectioned off from each other by a fence or a wall?"

"Not according to this," Laidlaw replied, pointing to the two rectangles in the diagram.

"It isn't San Quentin, Mr. Graham," Moredi said softly then sat back and clasped his hands in his lap. "There isn't a canteen where the prisoners can eat their meals. And there isn't an exercise yard where prisoners can walk about and stretch their legs. There are no rights at Branco. That's the first thing I learned when I got there.

"I was held there for eight weeks. And like all political prisoners at Branco, my hands and feet were manacled and I was put in a dark cell, four foot by eight foot, and the only time I ever left it was when I was taken down the corridor to a windowless room where my interrogators were waiting to torture me. And every night a spotlight in the corner of the cell would be switched on and I would be told to stand to attention. That happened almost every hour. And when I was too exhausted to get to my feet any more, one of them would come into the cell and beat me. If I was lucky, he would use a whip or a baton; if not, he used a club studded with sharpened nails or a length of barbed wire. And, of course, I was helpless to defend myself because my hands and feet were in chains. They didn't even provide a bucket for sanitary purposes, so you lay in your own excrement. Then, once every few days, when the smell became too much even for the guards to endure, they would come round with a hosepipe and spray down the cells." Moredi suddenly smiled sadly at Graham. "So you see now why there was no need to put up a fence or a wall between the two buildings. We weren't going anywhere."

Graham nodded grimly but said nothing. Any words would have been hollow after what Moredi had told them.

"I can give you a rough layout of the cell block but I won't go back in there again," Moredi said, wringing his hands together, "not after what I went through."

"We understand," Sabrina said gently.

"Are we going with Mr. Laidlaw's plan then?" Tambese asked after a lengthy silence.

"It's worth a try," Graham replied. "But we can't go in there blind. We'll have to check it out first."

"Agreed," Laidlaw replied then looked at Tambese again. "Can you get a copy of the plans of the sewers for the area around the prison?"

"Not without arousing suspicion," Tambese answered. "I only managed to get a plan of Branco because I remembered there was one at our headquarters in Habane. Plans for the sewers will be kept at the city hall, and that's closed."

"We need the plans," Laidlaw said, looking at each face in turn. "We can't do anything without them."

"Which only leaves one option," Graham concluded. "Break into the city hall and get them."

"We'd never get past the roadblocks," Sabrina said.

"Added to which there's a curfew in the city from six at night to six in the morning," Moredi told them.

"That only leaves us with one alternative. We'll have to bring in the resistance movement. I'll call Matthew Okoye. Excuse me," Tambese said then got to his feet and walked to the door.

"Surely you can contact the resistance movement without involving Okoye?" Graham called out after him.

"Not really. He's their leader," Tambese replied then left the room.

Simon Nhlapo scrambled behind the wheel of the ambulance and started the engine as his partner, Joe Vuli, jumped into the passenger seat beside him. He switched on the siren then sped down the driveway and swung the ambulance out into the deserted street. He had been a paramedic for eighteen years at the Kondese National Hospital. Well, that was its new name. It had been the Margaret Mobuto Hospital, named after Alphonse Mobuto's wife who had died four years after it was opened in 1972. But Jamel Mobuto had ordered the name to be changed within days of his father's death—just as the Alphonse Mobuto Hotel became the Habane National Hotel.

Nhlapo wasn't a political man but, like many of the Swahilis in and around Kondese, he saw a future for Zimbala under Jamel Mobuto. That's why he couldn't understand why the government had let Ngune and his butchers take control of Kondese. He remembered well the days when Kondese was alive with activity at night. Now the streets were deserted, save for the patroling gangs of Ngune's vigilantes who toured the city center in search of anyone foolish enough to violate the curfew. Punishment was immediate execution. Even the police force had been disbanded by Massenga and now the only vehicles seen on the road after the curfew were those belonging to the besiegers, and they had to have special passes affixed to their windscreens—and, of course, the ambulances.

There had been an initial fear at the hospital that Ngune would install his own puppet doctors but he had assured the administrator that he had no intention of interfering with the running of the hospital, as long as the staff abided by his rules. Many did, out of fear; but others, like Vuli and himself, had joined the resistance movement as soon as the Security Police overran Kondese. It was the first time he had ever been involved in an underground movement. But he felt the time had come to make a stand against the brutality of Ngune and his Security Police. If Ngune seized power the country would again be in the hands of a corrupt dictator. Nothing would have changed. He had to be stopped. But Nhlapo also knew the penalty if he was ever caught as a resistance fighter. That had been spelled out clearly at their first rally. He would be taken to Branco where they would torture then execute him. Dozens had already died at the hands of Ngune's men since they returned to Kondese. It was as if they had never left. The rumors that the army were preparing to move in to liberate the city had been rife for the last three weeks. But so far, nothing. And the people of Kondese were becoming desperate . . .

He trod on the brake pedal as they reached the first of the numerous roadblocks that lined the city streets. It consisted of a sheet of rolled barbed wire that lay the width of the road. Four men stood beside it, all in jeans and T-shirts, and all armed with kalashnikov assault rifles. One of the men approached the driver's side of the ambulance, the kalashnikov clenched tightly in his right hand.

"Where are you going?" he demanded.

"There's been an accident on the M3," Nhlapo replied. "A car went off the road."

The man nodded, having already received word of the call-out by the controller at the hospital. The ambulance was searched for any weapons or contraband that the crew may be trying to smuggle past the roadblock but nothing was found.

Satisfied, the man returned to the driver's window. "You'll be given a free passage through to the last roadblock on the outskirts of the city."

"I know the drill by now," Nhlapo retorted tersely.

The man nodded to his colleagues and the barricade was pulled back until there was just enough room for the ambulance to get through. Nhlapo engaged the gears and sped off. They passed another four roadblocks, each time being waved through by an armed guard. They were stopped, as expected, at the last one on the edge of the city. Again the ambulance was searched before being allowed to continue.

Nhlapo drove the short distance to join the M3. It was eerie and deserted. The resistance movement had shot out most of the lights to give them the cover they had needed to launch a series of lightning strikes on rebel patrols in the area. The gutted remains of rebel vehicles on the side of the road were testament to the success of the mission. Over thirty rebels had been killed in the ambushes before Ngune pulled his men back to within the confines of the city. He had immediately reinforced the roadblocks on the edge of the city with both men and weapons to repel any attempt by the resistance movement to retake Kondese, but a succession of arrests and summary executions in the last fortnight had left the resistance movement disjointed and demoralized. They couldn't launch an offensive on Kondese without the backing of the government forces. And they seemed determined to wait for Ngune to make the first move . . .

Vuli pointed to a figure in the distance who was frantically waving a white handkerchief to attract their attention. Nhlapo switched off the siren as he neared the man then pulled over onto the side of the road, bringing the ambulance to a halt a few feet in front of him.

"Did you call the hospital?" Nhlapo asked after he had jumped out of the ambulance.

"Yes," Tambese replied, pocketing the handkerchief.

"This is such a treacherous stretch of road," Nhlapo said.

"Especially at night," Tambese added.

"Or in the rain," Vuli said, completing the password they had agreed with Okoye when he had called them earlier at the hospital. They didn't know Tambese's name and he didn't know theirs. It was a precaution in case any of them were arrested by the Security Police. That way the damage would be minimal.

"What's the plan?" Nhlapo asked.

"You get us past the roadblocks. That's all you need to know."

"How many are you?"

"Three," Tambese replied then put two fingers in his mouth and whistled loudly.

Laidlaw was the first to appear. He was carrying a doctor's black bag which Okoye's wife had lent him. She had a surgery in the city. Vuli gasped in shock when Graham and Sabrina emerged from the undergrowth behind him. Okoye's wife had spent over an hour making them up to look as though they had been involved in a car crash. Their faces and clothes were splattered with sheep's blood and both had discolored "bruises" on their faces which she had carefully shaded with an eyebrow pencil.

"It's make-up," Tambese reassured Vuli and Nhlapo.

"It's very realistic," said Vuli.

"That's the general idea," Tambese told him. "We have to get them through the roadblocks."

Graham crossed to where Laidlaw was standing. "You know what to do?"

Laidlaw bit back his anger and nodded. "Take the car back to the farmhouse and wait for your call. I still say I could be of some use—"

"No!" Graham cut in quickly. "We've been through this before, Russ. I need someone I can trust at the farmhouse to call New York in case something should go wrong."

"Moredi's there," Laidlaw shot back.

"He doesn't know Sabrina and I work for UNACO. You do. If you haven't heard from us by daybreak, call the number I gave you."

"And speak to a guy called C.W. Yeah, I know."

"Ready, Mr. Graham?" Tambese asked.

Graham nodded.

Laidlaw handed the doctor's bag to Tambese then looked back at Graham. "You watch yourself, you hear?"

"Yeah," Graham muttered then walked over to the ambulance.

"What about this?" Sabrina asked, indicating the holdall she was carrying. It contained the three Berettas, three silenced Uzis, the spare ammunition clips and the holsters that Tambese had drawn from the barracks in Habane. Okoye had made the necessary arrangements to have the sniper rifle, silencer and blowtorch left for them near the city hall by a member of the resistance movement.

Graham looked at Tambese. "Well, where do we put it?"

"We can't put it in the ambulance like that," Tambese replied. "They'd be sure to see it."

"What do you suggest?" Sabrina asked.

Tambese clambered into the back of the ambulance. "Pass me the holdall."

Sabrina handed it to him. He unzipped it and tipped the contents out onto one of the stretcher beds. Then, pulling back the top sheets on both stretcher beds, he carefully laid the weapons, holsters and clips down the center of the two mattresses before remaking the beds again.

"So we'll be lying on them?" Graham said.

Tambese nodded.

"It's the first place they'll look," Graham shot back.

"Had you been locals, yes," Tambese replied. "But you're foreigners. And you're posing as journalists. Those things can make a lot of difference right now."

Graham scrambled into the back of the ambulance and sat on one of the beds. "Why should they make a difference?"

"Because I'll tell the rebels that you were attacked by government troops outside Kondese. They're sure to see the potential of a major publicity coup if they were to get you the best possible medical care. And that would mean giving the ambulance a free passage to the hospital. It would be too good an opportunity for them to miss."

"And if they don't fall for it?" Graham asked.

"Then we're in trouble," Tambese replied, reaching out a hand to help Sabrina into the back of the ambulance. He told Vuli in Swahili to leave all the talking to him. He also told him to knock on the glass partition when they neared the first of the roadblocks. Vuli nodded then closed the back doors and climbed back into the cab.

Nhlapo started up the engine then wiped a drop of sweat from his face. "God help us if they find those guns."

Vuli glanced at Nhlapo and shook his head slowly. "Not even He could help us then."

Nhlapo swallowed nervously and did a U-turn before heading back toward Kondese.

Vuli rapped loudly on the glass partition when the roadblock came into view. Nhlapo instinctively touched the brake pedal when one of the rebels stepped out into the road to wave down the ambulance. Vuli patted Nhlapo's arm reassuringly then reached for the clipboard on the dashboard. It contained details of the "accident" which Vuli had copied down, almost word for word, from the summary Tambese had compiled before leaving the farmhouse. Ngune had insisted that the ambulance service make a report of any incident that took them beyond the roadblocks on the edge of the city. That was considered no-man's land by the rebels. It was certainly a major victory for the resistance movement. And it was only the beginning, Vuli told himself . . .

The ambulance stopped a few feet in front of the convoluted tangle of barbed wire spread across the road. A battle-scarred M41 Walker Bulldog tank stood in the shadows beside a looted corner shop. A man wearing a faded Adidas T-shirt sat on the turret, a kalashnikov rifle beside him. Vuli also noticed the front portion of a Ferret armored car which was partially hidden up a sidestreet. He knew from a former soldier who was now with the resistance movement that both vehicles were obsolete, and there was a feeling that the M41s dotted about the city didn't have the necessary parts to be used in conflict. They were merely a bluff. But they were all well guarded and all attempts by the resistance movement to capture one had ended in failure.

The man who had flagged down the ambulance rapped on the passenger window, disturbing Vuli's thoughts. Vuli opened the window.

"Out, both of you," the man ordered.

Vuli and Nhlapo climbed out and another rebel immediately set about checking for any weapons that may have been picked up when the ambulance was out of their jurisdiction.

"Report!" The man clicked his fingers and held out his hand toward Vuli. "Give it to me."

Vuli handed the clipboard to the man.

"Americans?" the man said, looking up at Vuli.

Vuli nodded. "Journalists."

"Open the back," the man ordered.

Nhlapo walked round to the back of the ambulance and opened the doors. He had to check his surprise. Graham had an oxygen mask over his face and Sabrina, who lay with head lolled to one side, had a drip attached to her arm with a strip of plaster.

The man looked from Graham to Sabrina then met Tambese's cold stare. "Who are you?"

"Dr. Moka," Tambese retorted. "I live close to where their car left the road. I was the first on the scene."

"They are Americans?"

"Journalists. Both from New York."

"Are their injuries serious?"

Tambese nodded grimly. "They were shot at by a government patrol. One of the bullets struck the woman. She was driving. She told me that much before she lost consciousness. It seems as if he struck his head on the windscreen when the car hit the tree. He's badly concussed. They both need urgent medical attention at the hospital."

"After we have searched the ambulance," came the sharp reply as if the man felt his authority was being undermined in front of his colleagues.

"The woman is haemorrhaging," Tambese snapped and indicated the bag of blood connected to the drip. "She could die if she doesn't undergo surgery within the next hour. And if she does you can be sure I'll hold you personally responsible. Your Colonel Ngune would be crucified by the international press. I doubt he'd thank you for it, do you?"

A look of fear had spread across the man's face at the mention of Ngune. He looked at Sabrina then spoke in a whispered tone to his colleagues who were congregated around the back of the ambulance.

"What's the problem?" Tambese thundered. "I need to get this woman to the hospital now!"

The man's eyes flickered around the inside of the ambulance then he snatched the clipboard from Vuli's hand and signed the accident report. Tambese sighed deeply. That was the clearance they needed.

"How many more roadblocks will we have to stop at before we reach the hospital?" Tambese asked, glancing at the man.

"You won't be stopped again," came the reply.

"Thank you," Tambese said. "That might just make the difference between life and death for this woman."

The man told Vuli to close the doors. Tambese slumped back in his chair as the doors slammed shut and wiped his hands over his face. Neither Sabrina nor Graham moved even though they had heard the doors close. The ambulance started up and the siren was switched on again as soon as it pulled away from the roadblock.

"We're clear," Tambese said.

Graham immediately sat up and pulled the oxygen

mask from his face. He winced as he massaged his spine. "Jesus, my back's killing me."

Sabrina peeled the plaster off her arm and grinned at Tambese. "I don't know what you said to him, but you sure sounded mad as hell."

"My mother died in the back of an ambulance," Tambese said after a thoughtful pause. "I guess I was just reliving those emotions."

"I'm sorry," Sabrina said apologetically.

"It was a long time ago," Tambese replied.

"Have we got free passage into the city?" Graham asked, breaking the sudden silence.

"Clear all the way," Tambese replied then wagged a finger at them. "I told you they would fall for it."

"What did you say to them?" Sabrina asked.

Tambese translated the gist of the conversation.

"Using Ngune's name seems to have done the trick," Graham said when Tambese had finished.

"It certainly helped. His minions are terrified of him."

"I can believe it," Sabrina said grimly.

Vuli pulled back the glass partition and gave them a thumbs-up. "Where do you want to be dropped off?" he asked Tambese in Swahili.

"Go to the hospital," Tambese told him. "We'll take it from there."

Vuli nodded then closed the partition again.

"What about the ambulance men?" Sabrina asked. "Won't Ngune take it out on them?"

"They'll go to ground after this. The resistance movement will have them smuggled out of Kondese."

The ambulance slowed down and Tambese peered through the glass partition, his hands cupped on either side of his face.

"What is it?" Graham asked anxiously.

"We're nearing the hospital," Tambese replied without looking round at him.

"Thank God for that. What now?"

"Get ready," Tambese answered then pulled open the glass partition again. "Go round the back," he said to Nhlapo in Swahili. "I'll tell you when to stop."

Nhlapo nodded as he swung the ambulance into the driveway. He switched off the siren. Graham and Sabrina discarded their blood-splattered clothes to reveal black jumpsuits. After tugging a black woollen hat over her head, Sabrina took a tube of camouflage cream from her pocket and squeezed a little onto her palm then tossed the tube to Graham. He rubbed the cream over his face and hands then offered the tube to Tambese who grinned good-humouredly and waved him away. Graham shrugged, poker-faced, and dropped it onto the bed.

Tambese stripped off to his black jumpsuit then peered through the partition again, watching for the line of refuse bins that Okoye had told him to use as a landmark to disembark. He knocked on the glass when they came into view and told Nhlapo to pull over. Graham handed out the weapons then divided the clips into three piles on the bed. They loaded their weapons and slipped the spare clips into the pouches on their belts. After holstering his Beretta Tambese knocked lightly on the partition. Nhlapo peered out of the driver's window and gave Vuli the thumbs-up sign. Vuli looked about furtively to make sure there wasn't anyone about then opened one of the doors and gestured to them to get out. Tambese ushered Graham and Sabrina out of the ambulance then jumped nimbly to the ground and Vuli immediately closed the back door again.

"Get rid of the clothes and wipe the ambulance down for fingerprints," Tambese said to Vuli.

"No need, we're going to torch it anyway," Vuli replied. "Those were our orders."

"Well, thanks for your help."

"Good luck," Vuli said with a quick smile then

looked around again. "Go on, a porter could come out here at any time."

Tambese hauled himself over the low wall where Graham and Sabrina were already waiting for him. "The city hall's a couple of hundred yards down the road," he whispered. He looked the length of the deserted street then turned back to them. "Ready?"

They both nodded then followed Tambese down the embankment to the pavement where he paused to listen for any approaching vehicles. Silence. He led them across the road then they ran, doubled over, to the nearest doorway. The city hall, which spanned the length of the adjacent block, was an ugly, oblong-shaped building dating back to the early nineteenth century when the country was still part of the French empire. Tambese was about to break cover again when they heard the sound of an approaching engine. They ducked into the doorway and lay flat on their stomachs, their Uzis held at the ready. A black Toyota pickup drove past with two men in the front and a third in the back, his arms resting on the top of the cab. A Sterling sub-machine gun was slung over his shoulder. He held a wine bottle in his hand. The truck continued to the end of the road where the driver idled the engine for a few seconds while he decided which turn-off to take. Then he accelerated sharply and the tires shrieked in protest as the truck pulled away and disappeared up a sidestreet.

Tambese scrambled to his feet and scanned the street before giving Graham and Sabrina a thumbs-up sign. They sprinted the hundred yards to the front of the city hall and were still trying to catch their breath when they heard the sound of an engine in the distance. Tambese pointed to a cluster of shrubs against the side of the building and they ducked down behind them only seconds before the truck came back into view.

The man in the back shouted something to the driver who pulled the jeep over and stopped in front of the city hall. The man got out and threw the empty wine bottle into the gutter. The driver shouted angrily at him as glass splinters peppered the side of the truck. The man grinned at the driver and held up his middle finger contemptuously then walked unsteadily toward the bushes.

Sabrina instinctively shrunk further away from the approaching figure and backed into someone's arm. Then she noticed that Graham, who was the closest to her, was crouched with both arms folded across his chest, cradling his Uzi. It hadn't been his arm. She turned her head very slowly, very reluctantly, and looked to see whose it was. A body was entangled in the bushes behind her. The face, which had been shot away at close range, was seething with hundreds of writhing, squirming maggots. She felt a scream rise in her throat but Graham clamped his hand roughly over her mouth before any noise could escape from her lips. He had seen the body when she backed into it and had anticipated her reaction. The man, who was urinating onto a nearby bush, didn't hear her muffled cry above his uneven whistling. When he finished he returned to the truck, still whistling to himself. The driver immediately started up the engine and pulled away from the curb. Within seconds silence returned to the deserted street.

"You OK?" Graham asked, putting a hand lightly on her arm.

Sabrina nodded guiltily.

Tambese led them a short distance away from the body. It had been decided that he and Sabrina would break into the building while Graham checked the area for the nearest manhole cover. They would meet up again outside in twenty minutes' time.

"Down!" Sabrina said sharply as a pair of headlights swept into the street.

They ducked out of sight and moments later a jeep came into view. It sped past the city hall and shot through a red light before disappearing up a sidestreet.

"Is that all they do?" Graham asked, tentatively getting to his feet again.

Tambese nodded. "It's very effective, as you've seen. You don't know when they're likely to appear. And if they're hunting resistance fighters, they'll drive without their lights on. But that won't happen around here. The resistance movement confine their attacks to the outlying areas of the city." He looked at Sabrina. "Ready?"

"Ready," she replied.

"Synchronize watches," Tambese said. He waited until the second hand reached the twelve on his watch. "Ten forty-two."

"Check," Graham said.

"Check," Sabrina added.

"Twenty minutes," Tambese said to Graham then disappeared round the side of the building.

Sabrina followed him and they kept low as they passed a succession of windows overlooking the spacious garden. The grass was now ankle-high and the beds riddled with weeds.

Tambese stopped beside a steel ladder which was bolted against the side of the building. He crouched down and looked behind a nearby bush for the holdall Okoye had said would be left there by the resistance movement. He unzipped it and checked the contents: a portable oxyacetylene blowpipe, insulated gloves, a canister of carbon dioxide, a De Lisle carbine, a torch and a length of coiled rope. He handed the torch to Sabrina then slung the rope over one shoulder, the Uzi over the other, and climbed up onto the flat roof. He surveyed the surrounding streets then beckoned to Sabrina who shouldered her Uzi and climbed to the top of the ladder where Tambese was waiting for her. She ignored his outstretched hand and jumped nimbly onto the roof.

"There's the skylight," she said, pointing to the glass window in the center of the roof.

Tambese crossed to it and, cupping his hands on either side of his face, peered through the glass.

"Well?" Sabrina prompted behind him.

"Matthew was right: it is some kind of a storeroom. There must be thousands of files down there."

"What's the distance to the floor?"

"It's a drop of about thirty feet," Tambese replied then removed the rope from his shoulder. "This is forty foot. Well, I hope it is."

"So do I," Sabrina said and indicated the flagpole behind them. "We'll need the extra few feet to tie it to that."

Tambese unwound the rope and secured one end to the flagpole. He pulled sharply on the rope to test the strength of the pole. It was anchored firmly into the concrete. He looked around slowly. The streets were still deserted. He crouched down beside the skylight again. "It shouldn't take me long to open it."

Sabrina hooked her fingers under the frame and lifted it up.

"It was open?" Tambese said in amazement.

She held up a nail file. "The wood's rotted over the years. It wasn't very difficult to release the catch."

Tambese smiled then pulled back the skylight and dropped the rope through the opening. It fell to within a couple of feet of the floor. He held the rope out toward her. She slung her Uzi over her shoulder then abseiled down, landing silently on the floor below. Tambese followed and had almost reached the floor when he noticed that Sarbina was holding out her hand toward him. The gesture wasn't lost on him. And he knew she was right. She deserved to be treated as an equal, not as a woman in a man's world. He held up his hand to concede the point. She moved to the door and opened it fractionally. The corridor was deserted. She gave him a thumbs-up then turned back to watch the corridor through the crack in the door.

He pulled Okoye's map from his pocket and used it to get his bearings. He was surrounded by rows of shelves, all ladened with dusty, dog-eared files. They didn't interest him. What did were the dozens of drawers that lined the walls. They contained the blueprints of every structure ever built in and around Kondese in the last twenty years. Okoye's contact had said the blueprints for the city sewers would be stored under section 350–400. Tambese went to the nearest row of drawers to get his bearings and it came as a great relief to discover that each drawer was numbered in multiples of ten, and not in single units as he had feared. He quickly found the section he wanted and pulled open the drawer marked 350. The blueprints, which were rolled up and secured with elastic bands, lay in neat rows, and each had a white label attached to it, identifying it by number. He cursed under his breath. Without a code, he would have to unroll each one individually. When he took the first one out he noticed a sheet of paper stuck to the bottom of the drawer. He pushed aside the blueprints lying on top and found it contained the index to identify the numbers. He ran his fingers down the list then replaced the blueprint and closed the drawer. It wasn't in there.

"Someone's coming!" Sabrina hissed.

Tambese looked round sharply at her and gestured for her to close the door. She did as he said then took up a position at the side of the door, waiting. He unslung his Uzi and trained it on the door. He was certain they hadn't been seen from the street, and Okoye's contact had said that the alarms had been cut by the Security Police when they took control of the building, so how had they been detected? He quickly reassured himself that the guard's appearance could have nothing to do with them. What if he were going to another room? It was a long corridor.

Suddenly the door handle was pushed down from the outside. The door was locked, as it had been when they got there. Sabrina stiffened, the Uzi held inches from her face. She curled her finger around the trigger when she heard the sound of keys jangling outside the door. Moments later a key was pushed into the lock and the door opened slowly. But nobody entered. Then there was a distinctive metallic click above them followed by an order in Swahili for them to drop their weapons. Tambese shook his head at Sabrina when he saw her hands tighten on the Uzi. He turned slowly and looked up at the skylight. A man stood a couple of feet away from the window, the kalashnikov assault rifle in his hand trained on Tambese. He repeated his order. Tambese dropped the Uzi. A second man entered the room and quickly disarmed Sabrina.

"I could have taken him," she hissed to Tambese.

"So could I, but at what price? The other one would have opened fire. And even if we had managed to take him out as well the gunfire would have alerted every patrol in the area. The last thing we need is a gunfight in the middle of the city center."

Sabrina remained silent. She knew he was right. She prayed that Graham had seen the man climb up onto the roof. At that moment he was their only chance. Tambese purposely spoke to the guard on the roof, hoping Graham would hear the voice. The guard grinned and pointed to the wall by the door.

"There's an infra-red sensor embedded in the wall by the door," Tambese translated for Sabrina. "That's how they detected us."

"Okoye said nothing about any sensors," Sabrina whispered back.

"They were put in when the Security Police got here. It was one way of cutting down on guards."

The guard behind Tambese told him to be quiet. He looked up at his colleague and as they spoke Tambese's face became increasingly grim.

"What is it?" Sabrina hissed out of the corner of her mouth.

"They're deciding what to do with us. The one up there says we're curfew-breakers and should be shot now. The one behind us wants to call Branco and tell Ngune."

Again Tambese was told to be quiet. The guard pulled the hat off Sabrina's head, spilling her hair onto her shoulders. He shouted something to his colleague and the two men laughed.

"What did they say?" she asked Tambese who had got to his feet again.

"You don't want to know," he replied.

The butt of the kalashnikov slammed into Tambese's back again as punishment for speaking to her. He stumbled and fell to the floor. The guard aimed the kalashnikov at him, his finger curled around the trigger. Sabrina lashed out with her foot, catching him on the wrist. The kalashnikov spun from his hand. The guard above them swung his gun on Sabrina's back. Tambese knew he could never reach the Uzis before the guard pulled the trigger. He lunged at Sabrina and knocked her to the ground. The guard on the roof opened his mouth and a trickle of blood seeped down his chin then he fell through the skylight, landing with a deafening thud on the wooden floor. There were two bullet holes in his back. Tambese and the remaining guard both made a grab for the fallen kalashnikov. The guard got to it first. He lashed out with the butt and caught Tambese on the side of the face. Tambese reeled backwards like a groggy boxer who had been rocked by a punishing right hook. The guard swung the kalashnikov on Sabrina who was still reaching for her Uzi. Then he saw a movement above him. He was still raising the kalashnikov when Graham shot him twice in the chest. The bullets punched him back against the wall and he slid lifelessly to the floor.

Graham crouched at the edge of the skylight. "You guys OK down there?"

Sabrina retrieved the Uzis then looked up at Graham. "What kept you?"

"That's gratitude for you," Graham retorted.

"Did you find the manhole?" Tambese asked, gingerly rubbing his cheek.

"Yeah, with great difficulty. The nearest is a couple of streets away. That's what took me so long. That, and dodging half a dozen patrols. You got the plans yet?"

"Not yet," Tambese replied. "But it won't take me long."

Sabrina piled her hair up on her head and pulled the hat back onto her head. She shouldered her Uzi then climbed up to the roof. Tambese rifled through the remaining drawers until he found the blueprint. He stuffed it down the front of his shirt then he, too, climbed back up to the roof. Graham pulled up the rope and Sabrina closed the window over the skylight.

"How long before they'll be missed?" Sabrina asked, looking through the window at the bodies below them.

"The next shift comes on at six in the morning. We'll be long gone before then."

Graham untied the rope from the flagpole then looped it over his shoulder and followed Tambese and Sabrina down the ladder.

"How far is the prison from here?" Sabrina asked once they had reached the ground.

"About three miles, due east," Tambese replied then pulled the blueprint out from under his shirt and put it in the holdall. "We'll look at it when we get to the sewers. At least there we won't be constantly on the lookout for rebel patrols." He took the rope from Graham and replaced it in the holdall. "Ready?"

Graham nodded then broke cover and sprinted a hundred yards to the safety of a low hedge at the bottom of the garden. He scanned the length of the deserted street then gestured for them to follow. They ran

to the hedge and crouched down beside him. Graham
was about to get to his feet when he heard the sound of
an approaching car engine. They lay flat on the ground
until it faded into the distance. Graham got to his haunches again and peered over the hedge. He nodded and
ran to the gate, wincing as it creaked open. Then he
beckoned them forward and led them across the road,
up a narrow alley linking the two adjoining streets. He
held up his hand as they reached the end of the alley
and peered cautiously the length of the second street. It
was deserted. He pointed to the manhole cover in the
road fifty yards away from where they stood.

Tambese put the holdall on the ground and flexed
his hand where the straps had dug into his flesh. He
was about to pick it up again when Sabrina tugged his
sleeve and tapped her chest with her finger. She picked
it up. It *was* heavy. But then it would be, she reminded
herself. Inside were the oxyacetylene tanks. Graham
looked round at them then slipped out into the street,
careful to keep close to the buildings in case they
needed the cover of a doorway.

They were twenty yards from the manhole when the
man emerged from the shadows of an alley on the other
side of the street. Tambese immediately recognized him
as the same man who had urinated in the bushes at the
city hall. He had another bottle of liquor in his hand. It
fell from his fingers the moment he saw them and he
was still reaching for his shouldered kalashnikov when
Tambese shot him. Graham sprinted over to him and
felt for a pulse. He looked up and shook his head.

"I thought you said they never patroled on foot,"
Sabrina said to Tambese once they had crossed to the
body.

"They don't," Tambese replied grimly.

"Which means his buddies will be back for him,"
Graham concluded.

"We've got to hide the body," Sabrina said, looking
around for a suitable place.

Graham snapped his fingers. "The sewer."

"I'll get the cover," Tambese said, already running toward the manhole.

Graham wiped the sweat from his forehead then anxiously looked the length of the street, knowing the jeep could return at any time or another patrol could appear. He hooked his hands under the man's arms and Sabrina grabbed his legs and they carried him over to where Tambese was struggling to prize open the cover.

"Hurry up!" Graham hissed.

"I'm doing my best," came the sharp riposte.

Graham laid the body on the ground and crouched down beside Tambese. Between them, they managed to lift the cover and lay it silently on the road. Sabrina dragged the body to the edge of the opening and Graham helped her tip it into the sewer. It struck the water with a loud splash. Then silence. Tambese peered into the darkness. There was a set of rungs embedded in the wall leading down to the sewer. He eased himself through the opening and descended to a ledge. The stench was awful. Graham went next.

Sabrina was about to follow when she remembered the holdall. She hurried over to the mouth of the alley but as she picked it up she heard the sound of an engine approaching at speed. She knew she would never reach the manhole in time and, looking across at Graham, gestured for him to pull the cover back over the opening. He hauled it into place seconds before the truck turned into the street.

Sabrina melted into the darkness of the alley, the holdall in one hand, the Uzi in the other. She ducked behind a row of metal drums and clamped her hand over her face to block out the putrefying smell of the rubbish that surrounded her. The truck pulled up in front of the alley and the driver shouted the dead man's name. The second man, in the passenger seat, pointed to the broken bottle then threw up his arms in despair and climbed out of the truck. The driver tossed him a torch and Sabrina crouched down as the beam cut through the darkness. It hit the drum in front of her, casting a shadowy light on the ground in front of her.

Then she saw it: a large, bloated black rat gnawing at a piece of stale bread that lay inches away from her foot. She inhaled sharply, not daring to move as the beam continued to play across the drums. It reminded her vividly of the incident when, as a child, she had been inadvertently locked in a cellar and for the next two hours all she had heard in the darkness was the incessant scurrying of the rats around her. It had left her with a deep-rooted fear of all rodents which had almost killed her while on assignment in Yugoslavia. She had broken cover after discovering that a box she and Graham were crouched behind was infested with rats. Graham had saved her life by tackling her a split-second before a bullet would have hit her.

The man finally switched off the torch and walked back to the truck. He spoke briefly to the driver and climbed back into the passenger seat. The driver cursed angrily then started the engine and drove off. Sabrina waited until the engine had faded into the distance before getting to her feet. The sudden movement startled the rat and it disappeared through a hole in the wall behind her. She was sweating. Rats still frightened her, but at least now she was able to control her emotions. And that discipline had certainly saved her life. She picked up the holdall and moved cautiously to the entrance of the alley. The street was deserted. She hurried over to the manhole and knocked on the cover. It was pushed back and Graham's head appeared above the level of the road.

"You OK?" he asked anxiously.

She nodded and handed the holdall to him. He passed it on to Tambese then pressed himself against the wall to let Sabrina climb down to the ledge. She took the torch from the holdall and switched it on. The first object the beam picked out was a dead rat floating in the water.

"There's a lot of them down here," Tambese said behind her.

"I can live with that," she replied nonchalantly.

Graham smiled to himself then pulled the cover back into place.

◆ CHAPTER
NINE

Carmen looked up in surprise when Whitlock entered the lounge. "What are you doing up, C.W.? Those sleeping tablets were supposed to have knocked you out until morning."

"I never took them," Whitlock replied, easing himself into his favorite armchair.

"I don't believe it," she retorted then closed the book she was reading and placed it on the table beside her. "You need rest. Why else do you think I asked the doctor to prescribe you such a strong sedative?"

"I'm on standby, Carmen. What if there were an emergency? What use would I be laid out cold until morning?"

She shook her head in desperation. "Your arm's in a sling, for God's sake. What use would you be anyway? I know this might come as something of a shock to you, but UNACO can function without you. Now, please, take those tablets and go to bed."

"Stop fussing, Carmen, I'm OK," he retorted then inhaled sharply through clenched teeth when he bumped his arm against the chair.

"So I see." She got to her feet. "OK, if you won't listen to me as your wife, then will you at least listen to me as a doctor?"

"I'm not one of your kid patients," he said irritably.

"No, you're not! At least they have the sense to listen to me when I tell them to take their medicine." She snatched the book off the table and disappeared into the kitchen.

He crossed to the drinks cabinet and poured himself a small whiskey before returning to the armchair. He had certainly been tempted to take the sleeping pills, if only to escape from the guilt he felt inside, a guilt that stemmed from deceit. It had started when Sabrina rang him from Zimbala to get Mobuto to vouch for Joseph Moredi. Then she had called him again to get a clearance on Colonel David Tambese. He had secretly obtained the necessary information from a computer file in the command center. In return for his help, she had confided to him that she and Graham were working together to find Remy Mobuto. But Kolchinsky had forbidden her to go near Kondese. It had to be their secret.

Whitlock had been caught in two minds. She was acting in direct violation of an order. And that could lead to her being suspended. Moreover, he would be part of it if he kept the information to himself. But they were his partners, and he had given his word not to tell Kolchinsky. At first he felt he had done the right thing. But the guilt had taken effect like a slow-acting poison and now it weighed heavily on his mind. He knew all he had to do was call Kolchinsky to clear his conscience. But he had given his word. No, he would stand by them, even if it went against him. He was still a field operative. He would only be transferred to the management side at the end of the year. His loyalty was still to Graham and Sabrina. It didn't ease his conscience, but at least he felt his actions were justified. But if they screwed up . . .

The telephone rang, interrupting his train of thought.

"C.W.?"

"Sergei?" Whitlock replied, immediately recognizing Kolchinsky's voice.

"How's the arm?"

Whitlock glanced toward the kitchen door. "It's OK, thanks. What's up? I'm sure you didn't call just to ask me about my arm."

"No," Kolchinsky agreed. "It's about your niece, Rosie."

"How do you know about Rosie?" Whitlock shot back in surprise.

"I'm not going to explain it over the phone. I've sent a car over for you. It should be there in about twenty minutes."

"Sergei, is she alright?" Whitlock demanded.

"I don't know," Kolchinsky replied.

"You don't know?" Whitlock retorted sharply. "Why are you being so damn evasive?"

Kolchinsky sighed deeply down the line. "A T-shirt with her name on it was found in a flat in the Murray Hill district. Three bodies were also found in the flat. Two of them were policemen. But Rosie wasn't there. That's all I know at the moment. I'm on my way down there now."

"Whose flat was it?"

"We don't know, not yet," Kolchinsky replied. "I'll see you there, C.W. And don't say anything to her parents until we've established what really happened."

"Sure," Whitlock muttered then replaced the receiver and looked up at Carmen who had been standing in the doorway for the duration of the call. "I've got to go out."

"It's Rosie, isn't it?"

Whitlock nodded then got to his feet.

"What's happened to her?"

"That's what I'm hoping to find out," Whitlock replied then squeezed her arm reassuringly before walking into the bedroom.

The whole street had been cordoned off by the police by the time Whitlock arrived. The driver pulled up next to Kolchinsky who was standing a few yards away from the growing crowd of onlookers struggling behind the police tape to get a better view of the entrance to the apartment block. Word had already spread among them of at least three murders inside the building, and all they wanted to see now were the bodies being brought out to the two ambulances parked close to the steps leading up into the foyer.

Kolchinsky opened the back door and Whitlock climbed out. The driver, who had already been told by Kolchinsky to wait for Whitlock, drove away in search of a parking space. Whitlock held his injured arm close to his chest as he followed Kolchinsky to the front of the crowd. A patrolman, who had already been told by a superior to give Kolchinsky authorized access to the area, immediately pulled up the tape to allow the two men through.

Whitlock grabbed Kolchinsky's arm once they were out of earshot of the crowd. "I want some answers before we go in there. Firstly, how did the police know to get in touch with you about Rosie?"

"We have files on the relatives of all UNACO personnel, both here and abroad. A list of those names is in the hands of Interpol, the FBI and the NYPD. We can't afford to take any chances, C.W."

"That's a violation of their civil rights," Whitlock shot back as they continued to walk toward the building.

"Spare the lecture, C.W. It's in their interests as much as ours. If they get into trouble with the law, we need to know about it to prevent the possibility of the organization being compromised in the ensuing investigation. And in certain cases, we can pull strings to have the charges dropped for the same reason."

"And who has access to these files?"

"Jacques Rust at our headquarters in Zurich, the Colonel and myself. They're completely confidential; that's why we've never told any of the staff about them. But you're an exception. You'll have access to them when you join the management team at the end of the year. You need to know about them."

"And what if I wasn't joining the management team at the end of the year?" Whitlock countered.

Kolchinsky smiled faintly. "Then you wouldn't be here, would you?"

"Are these relatives ever tailed?"

"If we feel it's necessary, yes."

"And Rosie?"

"No," Kolchinsky replied softly as they mounted the steps.

A policeman opened one of the glass doors for them and they stepped into the foyer.

Kolchinsky pressed the button for the lift. "In retrospect, I should have had her tailed. Who knows, perhaps this could have been averted. Truth is, I didn't even know she had violated her bail restrictions until tonight. I thought she was still in the custody of her parents."

They got into the lift and Kolchinsky pressed the button for the third floor.

"Did you know she was here?" Kolchinsky asked suddenly.

"No, but I knew she wasn't at home. She walked out the day she was released into her parents' custody. She had an argument with her father. He and I went looking for her in Times Square, that's where she usually hangs out, but we couldn't find her. If we'd called in the police she'd have been done for bail violation, and that would almost certainly have made the difference between a suspended sentence and a jail sentence."

"I'd already had a word with the commissioner. The charges were to have been dropped, even with a bail violation. But that was before this. It's out of my hands now, C.W. I'm sorry."

Whitlock nodded grimly but said nothing. The lift stopped at the third floor and Kolchinsky identified himself to a uniformed policeman who told him where the deputy police commissioner was waiting for them. Kolchinsky thanked him and led the way into the flat. Whitlock stopped in the entrance and looked down at the two dead policemen before following Kolchinsky into the lounge. The man seated in the armchair was in his early fifties with fine brown hair and a rugged, leathery face.

"Sergei, how are you?" the man asked in a surprisingly gentle voice.

Kolchinsky shook the extended hand. "C. W. Whitlock, Deputy Commissioner Sean Hagen. C.W. works for us. He's also Rosie's uncle."

"Pleased to meet you, sir," Whitlock said, also shaking the extended hand.

"Sit down, won't you?" Hagen said, indicating the sofa opposite him.

"What happened, Sean?" Kolchinsky asked, taking the proffered seat.

Hagen rubbed his hands over his face then explained about the note Doyle had left with his friend which had been forwarded on to the police after Doyle had failed to keep a rendezvous that afternoon.

"And the two patrolmen came here looking for Doyle?" Kolchinsky said.

Hagen nodded. "They were shot in cold blood, Sergei. Neither of them even had time to draw his weapon. Both were married with kids." His eyes instinctively flickered toward Whitlock. "I want their killer brought to book, and I'll leave no stone unturned in doing it."

"You think Rosie shot them?" Whitlock fired back in

amazement. "A sixteen-year-old kid? She's never picked up a gun in her life."

"C.W., that's enough," Kolchinsky said softly, but firmly, and put a hand lightly on Whitlock's arm.

"No, I don't think your niece shot them, Mr. Whitlock," Hagen said at length. "All three murders were professional hits."

"Who was the third victim?" Kolchinsky asked. "Doyle?"

"Yes. He was shot several hours before the two patrolmen. He was killed in the hall then taken into the bedroom and put under the bed. We found bloodstains on the carpet in the hall."

"What about fingerprints?" Whitlock asked.

"We've already lifted several sets. The only ones to be positively identified so far are your niece's. I've got a team working around the clock trying to match the other sets."

"If you need any help—"

"No," Hagen cut across Kolchinsky's words. He sighed deeply. "But thank you anyway. We'll trace them ourselves."

"And no other clues?" Whitlock asked.

"Only that a neighbour saw your niece leave here with a tall man about five o'clock this afternoon. She couldn't describe him because he was wearing dark glasses, a fedora and a leather jacket with the lapels up. But apart from that, nothing. Which only strengthens my belief that this was a professional job. It could have been the work of a hitman from one of the drug cartels, who knows? Your niece was mixed up in that scene, wasn't she?"

"She smoked a bit of pot, that's all. Christ, you make it sound as if she was a mule or a pusher for one of the cartels."

"Drugs are drugs," Hagen retorted.

"So ban nicotine and alcohol," Whitlock snapped then got to his feet and moved to the window.

Hagen stood up. "Well, if you'll excuse me, Sergei, I've got a press conference in twenty minutes."

Kolchinsky walked with Hagen to the door. "I'm sorry about C.W., Sean. He's upset, naturally. He and Rosie have always been close. She's probably closer to him than she is to her own father."

"I'll call you if anything comes up," Hagen said then shook Kolchinsky's hand and walked into the kitchen to consult with his detectives.

"We might as well go," Whitlock said behind Kolchinsky. "There isn't anything we can do here anyway."

"You're right; you've done enough already," Kolchinsky retorted angrily. "What got into you speaking to the deputy police commissioner like that? You were well out of turn."

"I'll see you outside," Whitlock retorted and strode out of the apartment toward the lift.

"C.W., wait up," Kolchinsky called out then hurried after him.

Whitlock held the lift and they descended to the foyer in silence.

"Hagen and I have different values, Sergei," Whitlock said as they walked toward the entrance. "He wants to find a cop's killer. I want to find Rosie. She's out there somewhere and you can be sure she's scared as hell. Whoever killed Doyle and those cops isn't going to just let her go, is he? She's a witness. It had crossed my mind that she might already be dead but I don't really think that's very likely now. Why take her away and kill her when he could have done the job here? No, I think he needs her for something. Why else take her with him? I'm scared for her, Sergei, really scared."

Kolchinsky put a consoling hand on Whitlock's arm then led the way down the steps into the street. He gave a curt "No comment," to a news reporter who was hovering hopefully for a story then ducked underneath the police tape and forced a path through the crowd to where the driver was waiting for them. Kolchinsky sent him off to fetch the car.

"I'll keep you posted on any new developments, C.W.," Kolchinsky assured him, "but there really isn't much else either of us can do tonight. And you need to rest that arm."

"It's OK," Whitlock replied.

"Then why were you cursing every time someone touched it when we were making our way through the crowd?" Kolchinsky smiled gently. "Of course it hurts. You need to rest it. Let Rogers handle the security tomorrow. It's the President's last engagement before he flies out and the Trade Center has to be one of the most security-conscious buildings in the state of New York."

"I want to be there," Whitlock said stubbornly.

"You've already prepared a schedule for the security team. You don't need to be there."

"I'm in charge of Mobuto's security until he flies out of JFK tomorrow night. End of story."

Kolchinsky shrugged helplessly. "I'm not going to argue with you. Ah, here comes your driver."

Whitlock slipped his hand into his inside jacket pocket and withdrew a newspaper. "Ask the lab boys to dust it for prints."

"What?" Kolchinsky replied in surprise.

"It was down the side of the sofa in the flat. I lifted it when you walked Hagen to the door. Some of the prints will be smudged from its being in my pocket but they're sure to pick up something, even if it's only Rosie's prints."

Kolchinsky took the paper carefully from Whitlock. "This is against the law, you know."

"So is keeping files on the relatives of UNACO personnel," Whitlock replied poker-faced. "Have you got a copy of Rosie's prints?"

"No, but it won't be difficult to get them. Now go on home."

"Call me tonight if the lab boys come up with something," Whitlock said then climbed into the back of the car.

Kolchinsky closed the door behind him then slapped the roof. The driver pulled away and moments later the Mercedes was swallowed up in the evening traffic. Kolchinsky looked back as the first of the bodies was loaded into one of the ambulances then turned away and walked toward his car.

Rosie woke with a splitting headache. She was lying on a single bed in a small room with a chest of drawers, an armchair and a small basin by the window. The curtains were drawn. She swung her legs slowly off the bed then sat forward, her face in her hands. It was then that she smelled the chloroform on her clothes. Then it all came back to her, a terrifying flashback: the two policemen; Kenny; then the blow on the back of the head.

When she had come round in the flat the man she knew as Marc had finished packing his belongings and the holdall and attaché case stood by the front door. He had been sitting against the wall, his knees drawn up in front of him, watching her. The automatic hung loosely in his right hand. He had told her that they were going to walk down to the street together where a car would be waiting for them. Any attempt to draw attention to themselves and he would kill her. After all, he had nothing to lose.

He had draped the jacket over his gun hand and carried the attaché case in the other. She had to carry the holdall. He had kept the barrel of the gun pressed firmly against her ribs until they reached the car parked in front of the building. The driver was a black man she had never seen before. The two men had spoken a language she didn't understand, then she was bundled into the back of the car and a chloroform-soaked cloth had been clamped over her face. That was the last thing she remembered. Until now. She didn't know where she was or how long she had been there. She rubbed her temples gingerly, trying to massage away the pain. What she would give for a headache tablet. She switched on the bedside lamp then got to her feet and moved to the door. It was locked. Then she went to the window. She drew back the curtains. A pair of shutters had been secured over the window. She tried to open the window. It was stuck. She tried again. It wouldn't budge. She looked about for something to break the glass. There wasn't anything. She checked the chest of drawers—empty. She slumped dejectedly on the bed and struggled to hold back the tears. Suddenly there was the sound of a key being inserted in the door. It was unlocked and opened. Bernard entered the room and sat down in the armchair.

"Where am I?" Rosie demanded.

"Safe," Bernard replied with a smile then glanced across at the chest of drawers. "That was good thinking, looking for something to break the window, but it wouldn't have done you any good anyway. It's reinforced glass."

"How did . . ." she trailed off and looked about the room before glaring at Bernard. "Where's the camera?"

"Behind the mirror," Bernard said, gesturing toward it.

"You're sick," she snapped then winced as a sharp pain shot through her head.

Bernard held up two aspirin. "You look like you need these."

"Go to hell!"

Bernard chuckled. "I admire your spirit, Rosie. You're quite a kid, you know that?"

"Why are you holding me here?"

Bernard put the tablets on the chest of drawers then got to his feet. "You're my insurance policy."

"What are you talking about? Insurance against what?"

"What you don't know won't hurt you. Let's keep it that way. I'd hate to see you end up like your friend Kenny. Strange as it may seem, I like you. You're a good kid. Mixed up, but still a good kid. Take those tablets and come on through to the lounge when you feel better." Bernard paused in the doorway and looked back at her. "You remind me a lot of myself when I was your age." He smiled thoughtfully then disappeared out into the hall.

She moved to the open door but the black man who had driven the car suddenly appeared in the doorway, his arms folded across his chest. He ran his eyes the length of her body then grinned to himself. She stepped away from the door then went to the chest of drawers and picked up the tablets. She poured some water into the plastic mug on the basin and washed down the aspirin.

Bernard called out to the man. When Rosie looked round he had disappeared from the doorway. She peered cautiously out into the hall. It was deserted. Then she noticed the door at the end of the hall. It had to be the front door. But was it locked? There was only one way of finding out. She could hardly contain her excitement as she hurried toward it. It was only on a Yale lock but when she unlocked it, it only opened a couple of inches. Damn, it was on a chain as well. She hadn't seen that.

"Rosie!" Bernard shouted from the doorway of the lounge.

She didn't look round. She fumbled desperately with the chain, half expecting to be ripped away from the door at any moment. She managed to unhook the chain and waited until he had almost reached her then, side-stepping his outstretched hand, she jerked the door back as hard as she could. The edge caught him in the face and he stumbled back against the wall, blood pouring from a gash above his right eye. She darted out and slammed the door behind her. She found herself on a porch. A wood surrounded the house as far as the eye could see but there was a two-hundred yard clearing before she reached the first of the trees. She bounded down the stairs, ran down the narrow path, and wrenched open the gate before sprinting across the clearing toward the trees.

Bernard pulled open the door and emerged onto the porch. The front of his shirt was already streaked with blood and his sleeve was stained from where he had used it to wipe the blood from his face. The second man appeared behind him and aimed his Walther P38 at Rosie.

Bernard pushed the man's arm down angrily. "Put the gun away, Elias!" He hurried to the gate and cupped his hands around his mouth. "Rosie, listen to me. Don't go into the woods. They're full of animal traps."

She kept running.

"Rosie, don't go in there!"

Elias came up behind Bernard and handed him a torch. "Animal traps?" he said in hesitant English then closed his hands together to represent the jaws of a trap snapping shut.

"Yes. The wood's full of them. If she stands on one of those it could take her foot off."

"What can we do?" Elias asked, switching to Arabic.

"We go after her," Bernard retorted then sprinted toward the section of the woods where he had seen Rosie disappear seconds earlier.

Elias stared after Bernard, reluctant to go near the trees.

Bernard stopped and looked round angrily at Elias. "Go round the side, cut her off," he shouted breathlessly then continued to run toward the trees.

Elias swallowed nervously. What was worse, the animal traps or Bernard's wrath if he refused to obey him? It wasn't a difficult choice. He moved toward the trees.

◆ ◆ ◆

Rosie paused for breath when she reached the edge of the trees. The wood looked dark and forbidding by the light of the moon. She had heard Bernard's warning but had it been a bluff? Or was he telling the truth? She had once seen a television documentary on the appalling injuries incurred by animals who had been caught in these traps. It had left her in tears. She looked back at the approaching silhouette of Bernard. She had to make a decision—and quickly. She had to go on. She picked up a branch then began to move further into the wood, using the branch to prod the ground in front of her. One mistake and she could be crippled for life. If, in fact, there were traps. But she couldn't afford to take the chance. She ducked behind a tree and listened carefully for the sound of Bernard behind her. It was silent. Not that she was surprised. He was obviously a professional. If only she could find somewhere to hide until daybreak. Then she could make her way safely through the wood. She was about to move further in the wood when she saw a light cut through the darkness to her left. She pressed herself against the tree, not daring to even wipe the sweat from her face. She tried to blink it away as it stung her eyes. The beam scythed across the darkness then went out as suddenly as it had come on.

"Rosie?" Bernard called out.

The voice came from behind her. The torch light had come from a different direction. Were they trying to close in on her from different directions? She wiped her forearm across her face then moved tentatively to her right, the branch still scraping the ground in front of her. It was noisy, but there was nothing she could do about it. She heard a rustle in front of her and ducked behind a tree a split-second before the torch beam sliced through the darkness again, panning the trees around her. Elias shouted something in Swahili and she heard him approaching the tree. Had he seen her? Or was he trying to force her to break cover? The footsteps came closer then stopped and the torch went out. Where was he? She swallowed nervously and ran her tongue across her dry lips. The silence was agonizing. Where the hell was he? Keeping her back pressed firmly against the tree, she turned her head slightly and peered cautiously into the darkness behind her. Nothing. At least he wasn't on the other side of the tree. Then she heard another noise, this time to her right. It had to be Bernard. But did they know where she was? She forced herself to control her ragged breathing. She had to keep silent. It was her only chance. Then a torch beam shone onto a cluster of trees thirty yards away from her. They didn't know where she was! She felt a surge of relief flow through her. Bernard called out her name again. It came from the direction of the torch beam. The light became fainter as he moved further into the wood.

She screamed in terror as someone grabbed her arm from behind and yanked her away from the tree. Elias switched on his torch then shouted to Bernard that he'd caught her. His voice seemed to bring her out of her shock. She lashed out with the branch, catching him on the side of the face. The Walther fell to the ground as he clutched his face in agony. She turned to run but he grabbed her roughly round the neck and threw her to the ground, winding her. He kept the torch beam trained on her as he felt in the darkness for the Walther. There was a sickening crunch of bone as the jaws of a trap, hidden under a pile of leaves, snapped over his wrist. He screamed in agony and the torch fell from his grasp as he slumped to his knees where he clawed desperately at the serrated edges of the trap in a frantic attempt to release his mangled wrist. Bernard reached them and shone his torch onto the trap. Rosie turned away sharply and clutched her stomach as she vomited against the tree.

"Help me!" Elias screamed at Bernard in Arabic.

"Why? You're no use to me now," Bernard said disdainfully and shot him through the head.

Rosie huddled against the tree as the gunshot echoed across the silent wood. Bernard grabbed her arm roughly and hauled her to her feet. She purposely averted her eyes from the body at her feet.

"Have you finished playing games now?" Bernard snapped, holstering his automatic.

She could only nod mutely.

"Then let's get out of here before we have another accident," he said then tightened his grip on her arm and marched her back to the house.

"That's better," Bernard said after he had handcuffed her to the radiator in the bedroom.

She tugged angrily at the handcuffs then slumped back against the wall. He left the room, closing the door behind him, and went to the main bathroom to attend to the cut above his eye. The bleeding had stopped and the area around the eye was already swollen and puffy. It would be closed by morning. He wet a cloth and dabbed it gingerly against his eyebrow. The wound turned out to be deeper than he had originally thought. He washed his hands and face then found some disinfectant and cotton wool in the wall cabinet above the basin. He sprinkled some of the disinfectant onto the cotton wool then pressed it against his eyebrow. His face remained expressionless as the disinfectant seeped agonizingly into the wound. He discarded the swab then went to his bedroom and changed into a clean shirt.

Sitting on the edge of the bed, he picked up the telephone and dialed an unlisted number then propped a pillow against the headboard and sat back against it, waiting for the call to be answered. When it was, there was only silence on the other end of the line.

"It's Columbus," Bernard said.

"This is Seabird. I've been trying to contact you for hours. Where the hell are you?"

"At the safe house off the Garden State Parkway."

"What?" came the incredulous reply. "You weren't cleared to stay there."

"I didn't exactly have much time to pick and choose, did I? Or haven't you heard about what happened at the apartment?"

"Of course I heard," Seabird retorted angrily. "That was one of our best safe houses in the city. And thanks to you it's been blown. Three bodies, two of them cops—what the hell happened there? And what's this about Whitlock's niece being involved?"

Bernard explained briefly about Rosie, her connection with Doyle and the reason the police had come to the apartment.

"And why wasn't I informed that you're holding Whitlock's niece?" Seabird said once Bernard had finished speaking. "You could blow the whole operation."

"You weren't informed because it doesn't concern you. She's my insurance in case something should go wrong tomorrow."

"Insurance against what? Do you honestly think UNACO will just let you walk away because you've got Whitlock's niece? Credit them with some professionalism."

"Of course they won't. But I can use her to buy time." Bernard swung his legs off the bed. "But we're speculating here. Nothing will go wrong, I guarantee that."

"Why don't I feel reassured?"

"I need a favour, that's why I called," Bernard said, then went on to explain what had happened earlier at the house. "I need another babysitter for the girl."

"Do you, now?" came the sarcastic riposte. "And who the hell was this Elias anyway?"

"The fifth member of the Zimbalan team."

"Fifth? I was told there were only four."

"I included a fifth man as backup. It seemed the sensible thing to do in case one of the others was killed or arrested before the operation began."

"*You* included him? This whole operation was devised after months of detailed planning. But that doesn't seem to bother you, does it? You just do what the hell you want, don't you? You work for us, in case you'd forgotten. And we tell you what to do. Is that understood?"

"Sure," Bernard replied disinterestedly. "What about that babysitter?"

"You're not getting one!"

"Then find yourself another assassin," Bernard replied and slammed the receiver back into the cradle.

The telephone rang moments later.

Bernard picked it up. "Yes?"

"Columbus?"

"Yes."

"Don't you ever do that to me again!"

"Then we'd better come to an arrangement about a babysitter," Bernard said matter-of-factly.

"Very well," came the bitter reply. "You'll have one in the morning. That's the best I can do."

"That's fine. I only need him to watch the girl while I'm at the Trade Center."

The line went dead.

Bailey sat thoughtfully in his study after he had replaced the receiver then reached for the bourbon beside him and took a sip. It was just as well he had already arranged to have Bernard eliminated after Mobuto's death. A babysitter indeed! He glanced at his watch. Seven forty-five. Brett would already be at the hotel, having relieved Rogers at six that evening. He found the number of the United Nations Plaza and, when he got through, asked the switchboard operator to connect him to the room which had been specially set aside for the presidential bodyguards. It was answered by Brett.

"It's Bailey, can you talk?"

"No," came the quick reply.

"Can you get to another phone and call me back?"

"Sure," Brett replied.

"I'll be waiting," Bailey said then replaced the receiver and drank down the remainder of the Scotch.

Brett called back five minutes later.

"What time does Rogers relieve you?" Bailey asked.

"Eight tomorrow morning," Brett answered.

"Right. When he gets there I want you to go straight from the hotel to the safe house off the Garden State Parkway. You know the one I mean?"

"I should do, sir; I helped to lay the traps."

"Bernard's there."

"But I thought he was staying at the apartment in Murray Hill?" Brett replied.

"He was until he shot two policemen there."

"Sweet Jesus, how did that happen?"

"I'll brief you tomorrow. All you have to worry about at the moment is getting to the safe house in the morning."

"I'll be there, sir."

"He's holding Whitlock's niece as a form of insurance in case anything should go wrong at the Trade Center tomorrow. He wants you there to keep an eye on her while he's away."

"Insurance? It sounds like he's cracking, sir."

"No, he's just being shrewd, like he always is. Do as he says then kill him when he returns to the house, irrespective of what's happened at the Trade Center. We won't be able to use him again after tomorrow anyway. But be careful. He's smart. He's sure to suspect we'll go after him once this is over."

"And the girl?"

"She's a witness, isn't she? But she mustn't be harmed until you've killed him. As I said, he's smart. He's quite likely to have devised a method of approaching the house unseen. And if he sees she's dead, he'll pull out. Then we'll have lost him."

"I understand, sir."

"Good. How's my favorite President?"

"He's in a meeting with his colleagues from the embassy. They've been locked away in his suite for the last three hours. God knows what they're discussing."

"It doesn't really matter, does it? By this time tomorrow he'll be dead."

Brett chuckled. "Yes, sir, he will."

Bailey smiled to himself then replaced the receiver. He left the study, secured the door behind him, then went downstairs to join his wife and children in the lounge.

Kolchinsky rubbed his eyes wearily then opened another of the files that had been left on Philpott's desk for him. It was one of half a dozen in front of him, each containing an update on one of the UNACO Strike Force teams currently on assignment. They were compiled by duty analysts in the Command Center. He read the first two paragraphs of the report then stifled a yawn and got to his feet. He wasn't taking any of it in. He needed a break. Pouring himself a coffee from the dispenser behind him, he moved to the nearest of the black sofas and sat down. He lit a cigarette and was about to reach for his coffee when the interleading door between the office and the Command Center slid open and an analyst entered carrying a folder.

"Not another update, Hans?" Kolchinsky said with a resigned sigh.

"No, we've matched the prints taken from the newspaper you brought in earlier." Hans held the folder out toward Kolchinsky. "I think you'd better take a look for yourself, sir."

Kolchinsky took the folder and opened it. Inside was a print-out of the computer file corresponding to the prints. The name was typed in capital letters across the top of the page: JEAN-JACQUES BERNARD. He closed the folder and placed it on the table.

"Is there anything else, sir?"

"No, thank you, Hans," Kolchinsky replied.

Hans returned to the Command Center, activating the door behind him. Kolchinsky looked at the folder again. He knew he should be surprised but he wasn't. He couldn't explain the feeling. It was almost as if he had expected something like this, sub-consciously. Had he? He glanced across at the telephone on Philpott's desk. Whitlock had asked him to call with any news on the fingerprints. But what good would it do waking Whitlock with that kind of news? He wouldn't get to sleep again. And it wasn't as if either of them could do anything about it. No, he'd tell Whitlock about it in the morning. He reached for the folder and inadvertently knocked the cup off the table, spilling coffee onto the carpet. He cursed angrily but when he bent down to retrieve the cup he noticed something attached to the underside of the table. At first he thought it was a spider or even a piece of gum but when he got closer he realized it was a microphone no bigger than a man's coat button. It had two prongs on the back which had been used to secure it to the wood. He made no attempt to remove it. No, that would only alert the person who had planted it there. And there was only one man who could have done it, Dave Forsythe, whose job it had been for the last year to check the Command Center, Philpott's office and Sarah's office for bugs when he came on duty every morning. He was one of the senior electronic experts in the organization.

Kolchinsky could hardly believe it, but the proof was there. And how long had it been there? How long had the organization been compromised? He got to his feet and picked up the folders. He'd read the rest of them at home. At least there he wouldn't feel betrayed. He used the sonic transmitter to activate the door, switched off the light in Philpott's office, then closed the door behind him.

◆ CHAPTER

TEN

Tambese's arms ached and he was sweating profusely. But at least the goggles stopped the sweat from seeping into his eyes. That would have made the situation even more unbearable. Apart from the goggles, he was also wearing a pair of thick, insulated gloves and the blow-pipe in his right hand was attached to the two oxyacetylene tanks strapped to his back. He was anchored to the wall-mounted ladder underneath the manhole cover by the rope which had been looped through his belt and secured to the sides of the ladder. Although uncomfortable, it left his hands free, and that was essential for the job he was doing.

Using the blueprint taken from the city hall, it had taken them almost seventy minutes to negotiate their way through the labyrinth of sewer tunnels to finally reach the manhole that led up directly into the prison grounds. They had decided to go in around two thirty that morning. That had left them a good two hours to devise the best method of cutting through the cover without alerting either the guards manning the watch-towers or their colleagues sleeping in the building which stood only a few yards away from the manhole.

They had found out from the blueprint that the manhole cover was protected by a time lock which they had to assume was regulated from the control room inside the prison compound so that it would be impossible to cut through it without triggering some sort of alarm. That meant they would have to cut a section from within the framework of the cover itself. They knew the guards couldn't see the manhole from the watchtower. Furthermore, it faced onto a windowless wall so the flame wouldn't be the problem. It would be the noise. That had narrowed their options considerably.

It was Graham who had come up with the most viable solution. The cover would have to be removed in segments. That way it would only need one person on the ladder. Tambese had insisted on doing the job. If, by chance, the flame was seen, he would be challenged, giving them time to flee. It was, after all, his friend they were going to spring from jail. Graham had suggested they take it in turns on the ladder but Tambese had refused to back down. They had done more than enough already to help him. He would do it alone.

Tambese shook the sweat from his face and glanced down at Graham and Sabrina who were sitting on the ledge with their backs to him to protect their eyes from the brilliant flame. They each had their Uzis in their laps. He had been tempted to take up Graham's offer of help several times in the past twenty-five minutes but now that he was on the last of the six sections he was just glad it was nearly over. He used his free hand to hold the metal as he cut through the last few inches, then, as it came away in his hand, he reached through the opening and placed the segment with the others that lay in a circle around the manhole.

He switched off the blowpipe then called out softly to Graham who immediately got to his feet and untied the rope from the ladder. Tambese climbed down to the ledge and gratefully unloaded the tanks from his back.

He put the apparatus in the holdall and tossed the goggles and gloves in after it. Graham used the canister of carbon dioxide to cool the rim of the cover then replaced it in the holdall. He waited until Tambese and Sabrina had climbed out of the sewer before passing the holdall up to them. He climbed up the ladder then hauled himself through the opening and joined the others who were standing with their backs to the wall. Tambese peered cautiously around the side of the building at the two tall, forbidding watchtowers on either side of the main gate two hundred yards away from the barracks. He could make out the silhouettes of the two armed guards in the reflection of the spotlight mounted above the gate. He dropped to his haunches and took the De Lisle carbine from the holdall.

"Give me the rifle," Sabrina whispered.

"No, I'll do it. I have done this kind of thing before, you know."

"Let Sabrina do it," Graham said softly behind Tambese. "She's the best sniper I've ever seen. And that's not something I'd say lightly."

"This is my operation," Tambese retorted. "I call the shots."

"It might be your operation, but it's my ass on the line," Graham hissed. "Let Sabrina do it."

"I wouldn't have offered to do it if I thought I'd screw up," Sabrina said to Tambese, trying to diffuse the sudden tension between the two men. "Trust me, David."

Tambese was caught off guard by her use of his first name. He sighed deeply then stood up and shrugged helplessly. "It seems I'm outvoted here."

Sabrina took the rifle from Tambese, attached the suppressor to the end of the barrel, then moved to the edge of the building and looked up at the watchtowers. It was a heavy responsibility on her shoulders but she was confident she could take them out silently. She wrapped the strap tightly around her arm then raised the butt to her shoulder and trained the barrel on the guard furthest away from her. She curled her finger around the trigger. The guard suddenly turned away from the railing and walked to the front of the watchtower. Now he was partially hidden behind one of the wooden struts. She couldn't risk the shot. She lowered the rifle fractionally and eased her finger off the trigger. Tambese noticed the gesture but Graham grabbed his arm and shook his head before Tambese could say anything.

Her eyes flickered to the second guard. He was still leaning on the railing, with his back to her. She willed him to stay where he was. Then the other guard suddenly turned around and walked to a chair in the corner of the watchtower. He took a pack of cigarettes from his pocket, lit one, then sat down and propped his AK-47 against the side of the chair. Sabrina immediately tightened her grip on the rifle then lined up the side of the guard's head in the sights. She squeezed the trigger. The bullet took the guard through the side of the head, punching him off the chair. Sabrina had already fed another bullet into the chamber by the time the second guard turned toward his fallen colleague. He had no chance to raise the alarm before she shot him through the head. The force of impact knocked him backwards and she bit her lip anxiously as he teetered precariously close to the railing. If he fell the sound of his body hitting the ground could wake a light sleeper. After what seemed like an eternity the guard fell face forward onto the floor. The AK-47 skidded across the floor and tumbled off the watchtower. She winced as it hit the ground with a muffled thud. Then there was only silence. She exhaled deeply and slumped back against the wall.

"Where did you learn to shoot like that?" Tambese asked in amazement.

She shrugged modestly as she replaced the rifle and

suppressor in the holdall. "You'd better lead the way to the cell block," she said to Tambese.

He nodded and looked around the side of the building at the cell block three hundred yards away. A single light shone above the main entrance, otherwise it looked deserted. At least, it did from the outside. Tambese disappeared around the side of the building. Sabrina followed. Graham picked up the holdall and went after them. They ducked low as they passed the windows of the barracks and only straightened up when they were clear of the building.

When Tambese reached the cell block he ignored the double doors and went directly to a window at the side of the building. He wasn't surprised to find it ajar, not on such a humid night. He pressed himself against the wall and peered cautiously into the room. There was a guard on duty. He sat with his back to the window, his feet propped up on a table, reading a newspaper. A radio was playing in the corner of the room. But there was no way of getting in without first cutting through the bars that protected the window. Tambese unslung his Uzi then dropped to one knee and eased the barrel through the opening, lining up the back of the guard's head in the sights. Sabrina looked away as he pulled the trigger. The guard was punched forward by the momentum of the bullet but as he landed heavily on the floor his foot caught the chair leg, knocking it over. Graham and Sabrina immediately took up positions on either side of the window. Tambese remained on one knee, his Uzi trained on the corridor which led off from the reception area. He doubted the noise would have carried above the music on the radio but they couldn't afford to take any chances, not when they were so close to their objective.

He waited a couple of minutes then, satisfied the noise hadn't alerted any of the other guards in the building, he propped his Uzi against the wall and removed the oxyacetylene equipment from the holdall.

Graham and Sabrina took up positions on opposite sides of the cell block as Tambese went to work, cutting through the iron bars across the window. It only took him a few minutes to complete the job then, after replacing the equipment in the holdall, he recalled the others to the window. He clambered through the opening first then took the holdall from Graham and dumped it on the floor. Graham and Sabrina climbed in after him and as they hid the body under the reception desk Tambese righted the chair and used a cloth he found under the desk to mop up the bloodstains. At least it wouldn't look suspicious if anyone happened to pass. They would just assume the guard had left the room.

After pulling the blind down over the window, Tambese led the way to a flight of stairs at the end of the corridor. He gestured for them to wait then tiptoed silently to the foot of the stairs and peered cautiously around the side of the wall. The corridor was lined with rows of cell doors. He could see the table and two chairs at the end of the corridor where the guards would have sat. But there were no guards on duty, which he automatically assumed meant there were no prisoners being held on that floor. He beckoned Graham and Sabrina toward him and told them to cover him while he checked the cells. He moved quickly and silently down the corridor, looking into every cell. He was right. They were all empty. He returned to the others and pointed to a second flight of stairs leading down to another floor.

"How many floors in all?" Graham whispered.

Tambese held up three fingers then moved stealthily down the stairs, pausing again at the bottom to peer carefully into the corridor. It, too, was deserted. He gestured for Graham and Sabrina to follow him then descended the third flight of stairs and held up a hand as he reached the bottom. He wiped his sweating forehead then pressed himself against the wall, his Uzi held upwards inches from his face, and looked warily round the side of the wall. The two guards sitting at the end of the corridor were engrossed in a game of cards. Tambese glanced at Graham and Sabrina and gave them a thumbs-up sign. They tiptoed down to where he was standing, waiting for his signal. The signal never came. Tambese suddenly stepped out into the corridor and opened fire. Neither guard had a chance to reach for the AK-47s against the wall before the fusillade of bullets cut them down where they sat. Tambese ejected the empty clip and slotted a new one into place before sprinting down the corridor to where the guards lay sprawled beside the overturned table and chairs. Both of them were dead.

"David, over here," said Graham.

Tambese hurried across to where Graham was shining the torch into one of the cells. Remy Mobuto lay motionless on a palliasse in the corner of the cell.

"Remy?" Tambese called through the bars. "Remy, it's David. David Tambese." He glanced anxiously at Graham when Mobuto remained silent. "Remy, can you hear me?"

Silence.

Sabrina appeared behind them. "All the other cells are empty." Then she noticed the concern on their faces. "What is it?"

"He's been drugged," Graham said grimly, strapping the oxyacetylene tanks onto his back.

"You say there are no prisoners in any of the other cells?" Tambese asked, turning to Sabrina.

She nodded.

"Which means they're moving out," Tambese concluded. "It looks like we got here just in time."

Graham switched on the blowpipe then dropped to one knee and began cutting through the lock.

"Moving out?" Sabrina repeated. "You mean they're preparing to march on Habane?"

"That's how I'd interpret it," Tambese answered.

"Why else would they clear the cell block? We had it on good authority that they were holding at least twenty prisoners here yesterday morning."

"Where will they have been taken? The garrison you spoke about earlier?"

"They won't have been taken anywhere," Tambese said, shaking his head.

"You mean they've been executed?"

"More than likely," Tambese replied matter-of-factly. "The Security Police will only spare your life if they think you'll be of some use to them. And when you've outlived that usefulness, then they'll kill you. That's the way they've worked for the last forty-five years, why change now?"

"I've got the lock," Graham called out before Sabrina could reply.

Tambese hurried into the cell and checked Mobuto's pulse.

"Well?" Graham asked behind him.

"It's steady," Tambese replied. "I'll carry him. Mike, you take my Uzi."

Graham shouldered Tambese's Uzi. Sabrina replaced the oxyacetylene equipment in the holdall then picked it up and moved back toward the stairs. Graham helped to get Mobuto to his feet then Tambese bent down and draped him over his shoulders. He nodded to Graham then emerged from the cell and followed Sabrina to the stairs. Graham brought up the rear, his Uzi at the ready. When they reached the reception area Tambese gratefully off-loaded Mobuto and eased him carefully onto the floor.

"I'll take him for a bit," Graham offered.

"No," Tambese retorted sharply. He smiled quickly to atone for his outburst. "Thanks anyway, Mike, but Remy's my friend. If anything does happen out there, I'll be responsible for his safety. I'm sure you understand."

"Yeah, sure," Graham replied then gestured toward the double doors. "Can we get through there?"

"I certainly hope so," Tambese replied. "It'll save a lot of time if we can avoid using the window. Getting him down the manhole is going to be hard enough."

Sabrina tried the door. It was locked. Graham searched in vain through the dead guard's pockets for the key. Then he looked through the drawers under the counter. It wasn't there either. He sighed deeply and shook his head.

"We'll have to use the window," Sabrina said. "We can't risk shooting off the lock. Even with a silenced weapon, it would still make a lot of noise."

"I'll go out first then you can—" Graham stopped abruptly when someone rapped sharply on the door.

They exchanged anxious glances then Sabrina stepped back and trained her Uzi on the door. Graham took up a position by the window. A voice called out through the door. Graham and Sabrina looked to Tambese for an interpretation.

"They were names," Tambese whispered. "Whoever it is probably saw that the two guards weren't in the watchtower and thinks they might be in here with the guard."

"I'm going outside," Graham said softly, placing Tambese's Uzi on the table. "We'll be trapped in here if he raises the alarm."

Both Tambese and Sabrina nodded their agreement. Graham pulled the blind up carefully then eased himself gingerly through the window and landed silently on the ground outside. His breathing was shallow and ragged as he moved cautiously toward the edge of the building. There was another knock at the door, this time louder, and the voice called out again in Swahili. He wiped his sweating face as he reached the end of the wall. He gripped the Uzi tightly in his hands then swiveled round to challenge the guard. The man, who was dressed in a pair of shorts and a vest, looked round sharply at Graham, his eyes narrowed in surprise and amazement. He held an AK-47 at his side. Graham indicated for him to drop it. The man swallowed nervously then jerked the barrel up toward Graham who shot him in the chest with a burst from his silenced Uzi. The man stumbled backwards, lost his footing on the steps, and as he fell his finger squeezed the trigger and a row of bullets ripped into the wall several feet above Graham's head. The noise echoed around the delicate silence. Graham cursed loudly. It would only be a matter of seconds before the whole compound converged on them. He shot off the lock and kicked the door in. Tambese, who already had Mobuto in a fireman's lift on his shoulders, hurried down the stairs and lumbered laboriously toward the manhole. He could already see several lights on in the barracks.

Sabrina threw Tambese's Uzi to Graham and they ran ahead, waiting for the first of the rebels to appear. They were still a good sixty yards away from the manhole. A window pane was smashed in the barracks and the barrel of an AK-47 pushed through the aperture. Graham, holding an Uzi in each hand, raked all four of the windows facing out toward them, spraying glass across the floor of the barracks. The AK-47 disappeared. The door was flung open and a rebel darted through but was cut down by Graham before he could fire. The momentum of his body cartwheeled him across the ground and he came to rest in a crumpled heap several yards from where he had been shot. Graham and Sabrina stood their ground and raked the windows and door of the barracks, giving Tambese precious seconds to get closer to the manhole. Graham tossed one of the Uzis away when the magazine was spent then snapped a fresh clip into the other Uzi and shouted to Sabrina to keep up with Tambese in case any of the rebels were waiting behind the building for them. She nodded then sprinted after Tambese as Graham raked the side of the barracks again.

He continued until the clip was finished. He ejected it, pushed his last clip into place, then ran toward the manhole. The clip ran out as he reached the end of the building. He darted round the side and stopped abruptly as he found himself facing half-a-dozen rebels, all armed with AK-47's. He could see two of their dead colleagues sprawled close to the manhole. And there was no sign of the others. He grinned. They'd made it. A man who had been standing beside the manhole turned round and looked at Graham. He was dressed in a grey tracksuit. Graham immediately recognized him as Tito Ngune. His face still bore the bruises from the beating he'd received several days earlier in Habane.

"That was quite a show, Mr. Graham," Ngune said. "Don't worry, though, we'll catch your companions before very long. They can't travel very fast under those conditions."

"You speak good English for a barbarian," Graham retorted, eyeing Ngune contemptuously.

Ngune smiled. "Drop the gun, please."

Graham tossed it onto the ground. He heard the footsteps behind him and was still turning when the butt of an AK-47 crashed against the back of his head. He was unconscious before he hit the ground.

"We can't leave Mike back there," Sabrina snapped.

"We'll have to, at least for the moment," Tambese replied through gritted teeth as he struggled to get a better grip on Mobuto.

Sabrina felt gutted. What would happen to Graham? She refused to even think about it. But she knew Tambese was right. There was nothing they could do for him, not without getting caught themselves. They had only managed to get out with seconds to spare before the rebels had descended on the manhole like a plague of rats. She knew she had shot three of them from inside the sewer. One had fallen through the opening and landed in the water. She also knew it would only be a matter of time before a team would be sent after them.

"There's a cover about five hundred yards from here. We can get out there."

"That's crazy," Sabrina shot back. "The rebels will have found the holdall by now. And that means they'll have the blueprint. They're sure to have men waiting at all the manholes by now."

"Trust me, Sabrina."

She didn't pursue the matter. It could wait. She had to concentrate fully on keeping them alive until they reached safety, wherever that may be. After all, she was the only one who was armed. Then she heard it—footsteps. It couldn't have been an echo of their own footsteps. They were both wearing rubber-soled shoes. These were boots. And there were more than one pair. She peered into the gloom behind them, not that she could see much further than a few yards in front of her. The lights, which were mounted on the opposite wall at intervals of forty yards, were weak and several of them had fused and never been replaced. If her friends could see her now. The thought brought a faint smile to her lips and helped to calm the sudden burst of anxiety that had swept over her. Had Tambese heard the footsteps as well? If he had, he wasn't saying anything. Then she saw a movement in the shadows thirty yards behind them. She was about to fire then she eased her finger off the trigger. Conserve your ammo, girl, she said to herself. She was down to her last clip and she didn't know how many bullets were left in it. She flicked the fire selector from automatic to single fire. Another silhouette flitted across the shadows. Again she held back. But why hadn't they opened fire? Unless they had instructions to bring them back alive? Possibly. The thought was still lingering when a figure appeared momentarily in a shaft of light behind her. She fired. There was an anguished cry followed a moment later by a loud splash.

"What was that?" Tambese called out over his shoulder.

"That *was* one of the rebels," Sabrina replied.

"Why didn't you say we were being followed?"

"I thought you'd have heard the footsteps."

"No, I didn't hear anything," Tambese replied guiltily.

"Don't worry about it, you just keep moving. How far's this manhole now?"

"A hundred yards or so," Tambese replied.

"Thank God for that," she muttered.

A bullet cracked against the roof of the sewer above them. Sabrina cursed under her breath. If only she had the torch. Then she saw another movement and she fired again. But there wasn't any anguished cry this time. This time she cursed herself for firing blindly. The footsteps suddenly grew louder. Bullets began chipping against the walls around them, but they were still only warning shots. Even so, Sabrina found herself doubled over as she moved backwards, her eyes continually darting behind her to make sure she didn't get too close to the edge of the path. Then they came into view. She counted at least seven of them, and they were closing in fast, their AK-47s held in front of them.

"How far to the manhole?" she shouted.

"Thirty yards," Tambese called back.

To hell with it, she thought, and flicked the Uzi back onto automatic fire. She fired a burst at the approaching men. Two fell and a third tripped over one of them and tumbled headlong into the water. Still they came. They had to be a suicide squad. There were probably another eight men behind them waiting to take over from their fallen colleagues. And all because Ngune wanted them alive. They would continue coming until she ran out of bullets. That had to be their strategy otherwise the three of them would be dead by now. How many bullets left? She fired again. Another man stumbled and fell.

"We're almost there," Tambese shouted to her.

She fired again. Another fell. Two left. She pulled the trigger. Click. The magazine was empty. And they were closing in fast. Were there others behind them? She couldn't see any. She was confident she could disarm them when they came into range. She discarded the Uzi and stood her ground, her hands held up protectively in front of her. A sudden burst of gunfire behind her scythed over her head, cutting them down when they were less than fifteen yards away from her. She dropped to the ground and looked round in horror at how close the bullets had passed over her head. Tambese stood on the ladder leading up to the manhole, an Uzi in his hand.

"Are you OK?" he asked.

"Just. Where did you get that from?" she asked incredulously, gesturing to the Uzi.

"Come up, I'll show you."

She pulled the woollen hat from her head and followed him up the ladder. A hand was held out toward her but after a sharp word from Tambese it was quickly withdrawn. She climbed out of the manhole and looked around her slowly, her eyes narrowed in uncertainty. The man standing next to Tambese was dressed in army fatigues and wore the rank of captain. An army jeep was parked at the side of the road behind them. Another eight soldiers stood beside the giant Challenger tank which was guarding the end of the street. The hatch was open and she could see the tank commander, his arms resting on the turret, goggles pulled up onto his forehead. He was smoking a cigarette.

"What's going on?" she finally asked, looking round at Tambese. "And where's Remy Mobuto?"

"I've had him taken to hospital. These are some of my men. The others have been deployed throughout the city. Kondese is no longer in the hands of the rebels. It's all gone according to plan—"

"What plan?" she demanded. "Why weren't we told about it?"

"It was top security. Jamel and I were the only two who knew about it. We couldn't afford to take any chances, not with so much at stake. There's a lot of sympathy for Ngune within the army. That's why I had to handpick these men personally for the operation. And they were only given their orders before I left the house." Tambese held up his hand before she could speak. "I know, I owe you an explanation. Later. First we've got to get Mike out of Branco."

"How?"

"You'll see." Tambese smiled at her bewildered expression. "It'll be quite a show, that I can promise you."

When Graham came round he found himself lying on a carpeted floor. He rubbed the back of his head gingerly then, after struggling to sit up, he looked slowly around him. It was an office. Then he saw the portrait of Alphonse Mobuto on the wall. Beside it was a framed photograph of Mobuto and Ngune shaking hands at some formal function. Both men were wearing tuxedos. There was also a picture of Ngune on the desk. It wasn't difficult to work out where he was. Then he noticed the armed guard standing by the door. The AK-47 was pointing straight at him. Graham continued to massage his neck until he heard the sound of approaching footsteps. The door opened and Ngune entered, still dressed in the gray tracksuit. He nodded to the guard who had snapped to attention then told him to stand easy and keep the AK-47 on Graham.

"Please, take a seat," Ngune said, indicating the armchair in front of the desk. He stepped behind the desk and eased himself onto his padded leather chair.

Graham pulled himself to his feet and slumped into the chair, his hand still rubbing the nape of his neck.

"Cigarette?" Ngune said, extending the silver box toward Graham.

Graham glared back at Ngune.

"As you wish," Ngune said then took one out for himself and lit it. He exhaled the smoke then sat back and studied Graham before smiling faintly at him. "As I said earlier, you certainly put on quite a show here tonight. Eight dead at the last count. There may be more."

"I certainly hope so," Graham retorted.

"They can be replaced," Ngune replied with a dismissive shrug, "unlike a wife and son."

"You son-of-a-bitch," Graham screamed and lunged at Ngune.

The guard slammed the AK-47's butt down onto Graham's shoulder, knocking him to the floor. Graham swung round on the guard but he was already out of striking range. The AK-47 was again aimed at his head. He pulled himself to his feet, ignoring the pain in his shoulder. His breathing was shallow and ragged as he glared down the barrel of the Walther P5 Ngune had taken from one of the desk drawers.

"Sit down, Mr. Graham, before you do yourself an injury."

The intercom buzzed on the desk. Ngune waited until Graham had sat down again before answering it.

"It's the control room here, sir," an anxious voice said in Swahili. "We can't get through to any of the patrols. They're not answering their radios."

Ngune wiped away a drop of sweat that trickled down his forehead. "Send out a patrol to reconnoitre the area. And keep trying to contact the other patrols."

"That's not all, sir. We can't get through to garrison either."

"Have you checked that there isn't something wrong with our radio?"

"Yes, sir. It's working."

"Keep trying. And keep me advised."

"Yes, sir."

Ngune switched off the intercom and looked across at Graham. "We know you were working with your partner tonight. Who was the third member of your team?"

"Mickey Mouse," Graham replied contemptuously.

"Who was it?" Ngune shouted, aiming the Walther at Graham's head.

"Got some trouble, have we?" Graham said, glancing at the intercom.

Ngune lowered the gun. "Killing you would be stupid. Either you answer my questions here in the comfort of my office or I will have you taken down to one of the interrogation rooms and tortured until you tell me what I want to know. The choice is yours, Graham."

"A choice?" Graham said in mock surprise. "And I thought you abhorred democracy. Perhaps I've been underestimating you all along."

"I will ask you for the last time. Who was the third member of your team?"

"I told you, Mickey Mouse."

Ngune sat back and stared at Graham. "I have come across your kind before. You think you can unnerve me by pretending to show no fear at the thought of being tortured, but it never works. I have never failed to get the answers I want from a prisoner, never. You will not be the exception, Graham, no matter what you may think. I will break you."

"Torture me as much as you want," Graham replied, holding Ngune's stare. "But you tell me this, how can you break a man who's already immune to pain?"

Ngune's eyes narrowed fractionally as he waited for Graham to continue.

"Do you honestly believe that whatever machinery you've got waiting for me down in your interrogation room can possibly match the pain I went through when I lost my family?" Graham shook his head. "Hell, you do what you want, Ngune. You can't hurt me, not any more."

"We will see," Ngune replied, but the intercom buzzed again before he could arrange to have Graham taken down to one of the interrogation rooms. He activated the switch. "Yes?"

"It's the control room here again, sir."

"Have you managed to reestablish contact with the outside yet?"

"No, sir." There was a nervous pause. "We've just picked up two aircraft on the radar scanner. They're headed this way. And judging by their speed, they have to be fighter jets."

"That doesn't make any sense," Ngune said suspiciously. "I haven't authorized the scrambling of any of our jets from the airbase in Chad. And we'd have been told by one of our informers if the air force had scrambled any of their jets from Habane."

"They don't originate from Habane, sir. They've come from one of the neighboring states in the south."

"Chad?"

"I can't say, sir."

"Have you tried to establish radio contact with them?"

"Yes, sir, but so far they're both maintaining complete radio silence."

"Range?"

"Forty miles, sir, and closing fast."

"Put out an alert but tell the men to hold their fire until we know the identity of the planes. They could be ours. And keep trying to get them on the radio."

"Yes, sir."

Ngune switched off the intercom and sat back in the chair. What was going on? First they lose contact with the patrols, then they lose contact with the garrison, and now two unidentified fighter jets were closing in on them. It had already crossed his mind that the government forces could have already recaptured Kondese. But there had been no gunfire. Well, no more than usual. And if the city had been taken, surely at least one patrol would have contacted the base? Then there was the mystery of the garrison on the Chad-Zimbalan border. If they had come under attack from government troops, they too, would have radioed through to the base. But nothing. Absolute silence. It was as if they had been isolated. The thought lingered in his mind. But how?

He pushed the thought from his mind and ordered the guard to take Graham to one of the interrogation rooms. He would join them presently. The guard prodded Graham in the back with the AK-47 and indicated for him to walk to the door. Ngune waited until the two men had left the room then removed a pair of powerful nightvision binoculars from the desk and moved to the window. He raised the binoculars to his eyes and scanned the horizon. Nothing. Then, a moment later, he saw the lights. At first they were hazy and distorted in the distance but as they grew nearer he could make out the silhouettes of two jets. He immediately recognized them as Dornier Alpha jets but he couldn't see the markings. Then the lead jet peeled away to the right and Ngune was able to see the markings of the Zimbalan Air Force on the underside of the wings. He lowered the binoculars and wiped his hand across his clammy forehead. It was impossible. How could two fighter planes have been smuggled off the airbase in Habane without at least one of his informers knowing about it? Dammit, they lived on the airbase. How could it have happened? He switched on the intercom and gave the order to open fire as soon as the jets came into range.

He returned to the window and instinctively ducked as one of the jets buzzed overhead. The first missile exploded several yards short of the fence but the men still had to take cover as a shower of rocks and stones rained down onto the yard. The second missile ripped through the fence and detonated underneath one of the watchtowers. Ngune stared, transfixed, as the watchtower buckled under the impact of the explosion before toppling over and crashing down onto the barracks where many of his men had taken cover seconds earlier. A handful of men tried to break cover from behind the barracks but were cut down by the concentrated gunfire that strafed across the yard. The third missile hit the main gate, ripping it off its hinges as though it were made of papier mâché.

Then the first of the army's Challenger tanks rumbled into the compound, its barrel already trained on the barracks where a handful of his men were making one last, determined stand. Machine-pistols against tanks, but he knew they would fight to the last man. It was a question of honor. Now suddenly it all made sense. They hadn't been able to get through to the garrison because it had already been destroyed by the jets. The garrison had no radar so the jets could have approached completely unnoticed. He had always anticipated an attack from Habane. And to get to the garrison from Habane, the air force would have had to bypass Kondese. But the whole plan had backfired. Badly. He had been outmanoeuvred by Jamel Mobuto, the man he had despised for so many years. And without men he couldn't mount a challenge on Habane. The dream was finally over. Now all that concerned him was staying alive, self-preservation. And the longer his men held out, the better his chances were of escaping. He opened the wall safe and stuffed his pockets full of bank notes. Then, unlocking the bottom drawer, he removed a miniature transmitter but the door burst open before he could use it to make good his escape. He put the transmitter down on the desk.

Graham entered and levelled the AK-47 at Ngune's chest. "You should have trained your men to expect the unexpected. It wasn't very difficult to disarm him."

Ngune swallowed nervously. "We can make a deal, Graham. Take the money from the safe. Take it."

"In return for letting you go?"

"Yes." Ngune gestured toward the safe. "It's all in pounds and dollars. Take it, all of it."

"Oh, I intend to—all of it—and I'll hand it over to the authorities when I hand you over." Graham moved forward and peered into the safe. He whistled softly. "Christ, there's enough in there to wipe out the trade deficit back home. You'll be crucified when you go on trial, Ngune. I only wish I could stay around to watch it."

Ngune's eyes flickered toward the Walther on the desk. Could he reach it before Graham shot him? He doubted it. But what other option did he have? He would be crucified at his trial. He had to take the chance and go for the gun. Then the moment was gone. Graham stepped forward and picked up the Walther. He ejected the clip and tossed the gun back onto the table.

"Empty your pockets," Graham snapped.

Ngune pulled the bundles of bank notes from his pockets and tossed them reluctantly onto the desk.

"All of it!" Graham said, pointing to the breast pocket on Ngune's tracksuit top.

Ngune pulled another bundle of notes from his breast pocket and dropped them onto the table.

"Let's go," Graham said, indicating the door.

Ngune had already moved round from behind the desk when the shell hit the side of the building. The window shattered and plaster showered the room. Ngune lashed out with his fist, catching Graham on the side of the head. Graham fell back heavily against the wall and the AK-47 slipped from his hands.

Ngune kicked Graham viciously in the stomach then grabbed the transmitter and used it to activate the door behind the desk. A panel, hidden in the wall, slid back, revealing a set of concrete steps leading down to a tunnel. Ngune darted through the opening and immediately activated the panel behind him. Graham hauled himself to his feet and lunged at the door, hooking his fingers around it when it was only inches away from resealing itself. He gritted his teeth as he began to slowly, painfully ease it open again. After what seemed an age he managed to open it enough to be able to slip through. The panel immediately closed behind him.

The tunnel was over three hundred yards in length, and Ngune had already covered half the distance. Graham bounded down the stairs and sprinted after him. He was surprised by Ngune's pace. He was certainly fit for a man of his age. Although Graham was able to close the gap considerably he still couldn't catch up with Ngune before he reached another flight of steps at the other end of the tunnel. Ngune paused at the foot of the steps, his face now bathed in sweat, and ripped the chain off from around his neck. From it hung a key. He scrambled to the top of the steps and unlocked the door. He pulled it open but made no attempt to retrieve the key from the lock. That would just waste valuable time—and yardage. He disappeared through the doorway.

Graham reached the foot of the steps a few seconds later. He took them two at a time but paused at the door and peered cautiously into the room which was lit by a single naked bulb hanging from a frayed length of flex in the center of the roof. It was a lock-up garage. Ngune had ignored the battered green Ford station wagon and continued instead on foot. The side door was ajar. Graham pulled open the door and cursed angrily to himself. It led out onto a street where a group of locals were dancing and singing to celebrate the liberation of their city. If Ngune could blend in with the locals Graham knew he would never find him. He looked the length of the street but couldn't see any sign of him. He couldn't have gone far, Graham said to himself, not after that run. Even he felt exhausted.

Then he noticed a movement in a doorway on the opposite side of the street. He waited until the locals had passed then ran across the road and moved slowly toward the doorway. A stray light swept across the street and for a split second Ngune's face was illuminated in the darkness. Graham broke into a run.

Then Ngune saw him. He darted out of the doorway but his legs wouldn't carry him any further and Graham was quick to grab him from behind and slam him up against the wall. Ngune's body sagged and Graham made the mistake of loosening his grip on the front of the tracksuit. Ngune caught Graham with a hammering punch to the side of the face then hit him again as he stumbled off balance. The second punch dropped Graham to the pavement. Ngune ran toward the end of the street. Graham scrambled to his feet and sprinted after him. He was quick to close the gap and felled Ngune with a bruising football tackle. Both men landed heavily on the pavement but Graham was the first to react and brought his elbow up sharply into Ngune's midriff. Ngune slumped back against the wall, temporarily winded. Graham stood up then hauled Ngune to his feet and shoved him face first against the wall.

It was then he noticed the mob standing on the corner of the street. He counted about a dozen of them, mostly men. And they were armed with sticks and chains. One had a machete. Ngune also saw them and started shouting to them in Swahili as he struggled to break free of Graham's vise-like grip.

The mob moved toward them. Graham was caught in a dilemma. He may need to defend himself, but that would mean releasing Ngune. One of the men suddenly broke free from the others and ran toward the two men. He caught Graham painfully on the shoulder with his stick. Graham stumbled back and Ngune began gesticulating wildly in his direction while continuing to incite the mob in Swahili. The men moved toward Graham. Ngune sensed his chance and began to move away from the mob. They had now surrounded Graham and were shouting at him in Swahili. Another blow was aimed at him but this time he was able to block it with his forearm. He couldn't hold out like this for long. But what could he do? He couldn't communicate with them. But you don't need to speak Swahili, he suddenly chided himself. Of course not.

"Tito Ngune!" Graham shouted and pointed an accusing finger toward the retreating figure. "Tito Ngune. Tito Ngune."

The name caused an immediate response. All heads turned toward Ngune who immediately tried to bluff his way out of trouble. A fat woman grabbed his arm and pulled him round to face her. She stared at his bowed head for several seconds then looked across at Graham and nodded in agreement. She pushed Ngune toward the men who shoved him roughly to the ground before beating him with their sticks.

Graham was about to try and intervene when an army jeep appeared at the end of the street. It pulled up beside the men and two soldiers jumped out and forced their way through to where Ngune lay huddled against the wall, his arms wrapped over his head. An officer, wearing the rank of lieutenant, climbed out of the passenger seat and stopped in front of Graham who estimated him to be no more than twenty-five.

Graham asked him if he could speak English. The lieutenant said nothing then turned and walked over to where Ngune was slumped against the wall, his tracksuit now matted with blood. The fat woman pushed through the crowd and spoke to the lieutenant. Graham thought he heard Ngune's name mentioned. The lieutenant barked out an order and the two soldiers hauled Ngune to his feet. The lieutenant looked carefully at Ngune's bloodied face then took a pair of handcuffs from his belt and manacled Ngune's hands behind his back. The two soldiers pushed Ngune to his knees then stepped back to allow the lieutenant to approach him.

Graham watched, unsure what was going to happen next. Ngune had been handcuffed. That implied arrest. But why hadn't he been taken to the jeep? Then the lieutenant took his RF83 revolver from the holster on his belt and pressed it against the back of Ngune's head.

Graham stepped forward, horrified at what he was witnessing. It was barbaric. Ngune's guilt wasn't in doubt. But he still had the right of a fair trial. That was the law, a universal law.

The lieutenant looked across at Graham and said something to him in Swahili. Graham shrugged helplessly but when he tried to get closer his path was blocked by the two soldiers, their M16 rifles aimed at his stomach. The lieutenant looked down at Ngune who was babbling incoherently as he pleaded pitifully for his life. Once the second-most powerful man in the country, Ngune was now nothing more than a sad, pathetic old man on the brink of death. The lieutenant pulled the trigger. Ngune's body jerked grotesquely as the back of his head disintegrated in a spray of blood and bone.

The mob cheered triumphantly when he slumped forward onto the pavement. The lieutenant holstered his revolver then snapped an order at the two soldiers who quickly shouldered their rifles and returned to the jeep. This time the lieutenant ignored Graham as he walked back to the jeep. The driver started the engine and drove away. Graham stared at the body, still struggling to come to terms with the savage justice that had been meted out seconds earlier. But then this was Africa, a continent where mercy was so often regarded as a sign of weakness and where brutality and violent death had become just another acceptable everyday occurrence.

He shook his head sadly as he watched the mob singing and dancing only a few feet away from Ngune's crumpled body then turned away and walked off slowly down the street.

♦ CHAPTER ELEVEN

Sabrina sat forward in the chair, her hands cupped over her face, her eyes riveted on the telephone. It had been over two hours since she had returned to the farm and there was still no news of Graham. She knew from Tambese that he hadn't been one of the casualties at Branco so where was he? And how had he managed to get out of the prison before it was bombed? The questions seemed irrelevant as she willed the telephone to ring.

Moredi and Laidlaw sat in the lounge with her. Neither of them had spoken for over thirty minutes, each engrossed in their own thoughts. She slumped back in her chair and banged the arm with her fist. Laidlaw glanced at her. She looked pale and drawn and he could see the anxiety mirrored in her eyes. She looked from Laidlaw to Moredi. He had been playing patience on the coffee table when she had arrived back at the farm. That had been an hour ago. He was still playing. He sensed she was watching him and looked up at her. He smiled fleetingly. She didn't respond. He was about to resume the game when the telephone rang. She was on her feet before she could check herself. She bit her lip nervously as Moredi lifted the receiver to his ear. He listened momentarily then extended the receiver toward her.

"Is it about Mike?" she asked anxiously.

"It is Mike," Moredi replied with a reassuring smile.

She took the receiver from him. "Mike?"

"Yeah," Graham replied.

"Nice of you to call," she said. "Where are you? And where have you been for the past two hours?"

"I'm OK, Sabrina. Thanks for asking," came the sharp reply.

She sighed deeply then rubbed her eyes wearily. "I'm sorry, Mike. it's been a long night."

"Tell me about it."

"Where are you calling from?"

"The hospital."

"Are you hurt?"

"No, nothing a few hours' sleep won't heal. You OK?"

"I'm fine. What happened? How did you get out of Branco?"

"It's a long story. I'll tell you about it when I see you. Tambese's also here. He's just finished questioning Mobuto. We should be with you soon."

"Sure. And Mike, it's good to hear your voice."

"Hey, don't get sentimental on me now."

She grinned sheepishly. "See you later."

"Yeah," Graham replied and hung up.

She replaced the receiver and looked round at Laidlaw and Moredi. "He's OK. He'll be coming back with David."

Moredi put a hand lightly on her shoulder. "Now you know he's OK why don't you put your head down for a couple of hours? You looked exhausted."

"I couldn't sleep even if I wanted to. There are too many unanswered questions up here," she replied, tapping her head.

"Then how about a coffee while you wait for them to get back from the hospital?"

"I'd love one, thanks," she replied then pointed to the door. "I'll be outside."

Moredi nodded and left the room. She pushed open the door and walked out onto the porch. The sun was just beginning to creep over the horizon which was bathed in a mirage of orange and gold—the unparalleled beauty of an African sunrise.

"Exquisite, isn't it?"

She looked round sharply at Laidlaw who had emerged silently onto the porch, a mug of coffee in each hand.

"Sorry, I didn't mean to startle you," he said, handing one of the mugs to her.

"Thanks," she said then moved to the edge of the porch and sat down on the top step.

"Do you mind if I sit down?"

"It's a free country now," she replied without looking round.

Laidlaw sat in the wicker chair by the door. "Can we talk?"

She put the mug down and glanced round at him, a look of irritation on her face. "Talk? What about?"

"Look, I know we haven't exactly hit it off these last few days. And a lot of it's been my fault, I realize that now. I'm sure I'm not the first guy to have doubted your ability because you're a woman."

"And you won't be the last either," she replied then sat back against the railing and drew her knees up to her chest. "But I've come to expect it now. It's all part of being a woman in a male-orientated profession. Not that it bothers me. I've got a job to do and I'll do it to the best of my ability. And if you guys can't accept that, that's your problem not mine."

"Well, you can count me as one of the converted after tonight."

"Hallelujah!" she retorted.

"I should have known better than to try and talk to you," he snapped, getting to his feet.

"Then talk to me, don't patronize me," she said, glaring up at him.

He sighed deeply then moved to the railing. "I didn't mean to sound patronizing. I'm sorry. Like you said, you're a woman in a male-orientated profession. I guess I'm just not used to dealing with that."

"At least you're honest. Most of my colleagues wouldn't have admitted to that."

"You and Mike seem to get along," he said.

"We do, up to a point." She smiled thoughtfully. "But it wasn't always this amicable. We've been partners for two years now, and it's only been in the last few months that we've started to get along. The first year was a nightmare, an absolute nightmare. All we seemed to do was argue and bicker about every little thing. It got to the point where it was starting to affect our work. That's when it came to a head. We had to decide whether we could continue working together or whether we'd be better off with different partners. I don't think the outcome was ever in doubt. We work well as a team. We always have. So we decided to bury the hatchet and get on with the job. We still have our differences, mainly because we're both very independent. But we've learned to live with that."

"You care a lot about him, don't you?"

"I guess," she replied with a nonchalant shrug. "He is my partner."

The evasive answer wasn't lost on Laidlaw. He decided against pursuing the matter. He leaned back against the railing and folded his arms across his chest. "I can't believe how much he's changed. It's hard to believe it's the same Mike Graham I knew at Delta. You mentioned how independent he is. If I hadn't seen it with my own eyes, I'd never have believed you."

She shifted round until she was facing him. It was the first time she had ever heard anyone talk about the

Mike Graham she had never known, and it fascinated her. "What do you mean?" she prompted, desperately trying to keep the conversation alive.

"Mike always encouraged a team spirit at Delta. We'd go places as a unit, not as individuals. And he was the worst practical joker I've ever come across. You always had to be on your guard when Mike was about. You never knew what to expect."

"Yeah?" Sabrina said with a grin.

Laidlaw shook his head slowly. "It's hard to believe it's the same man, it really is."

"It's understandable under the circumstances," she said, her face serious again. "From what he's told me about them, I get the impression he doted on Carrie and Mikey."

"Yeah, he did," Laidlaw replied then lapsed into silence.

A jeep appeared on the approach road to the farmhouse. She scrambled to her feet as it turned into the driveway. She could make out two occupants sitting up front but it was only when it reached the courtyard that she realized it was Graham and Tambese. The jeep came to a stop in front of the porch and Tambese killed the engine. Graham was the first to get out.

"Like the outfit," Sabrina said with a grin, indicating the white tunic and trousers Graham had borrowed from the hospital.

"Very chic, isn't it?" he replied, mounting the steps onto the porch.

"You've got a couple of nasty bruises there, buddy," Laidlaw said, pointing to Graham's face.

"Ngune caught me with a couple of good punches."

"Did you get him?" Sabrina asked.

"Not personally. He's under the tarpaulin in the back of the jeep. The army's going to put the body on public display in Habane." He moved to the door. "I'm going to change. I'll be down in a minute."

Sabrina watched Graham disappear into the house

then looked round at Tambese. "What happened to Ngune?"

"I'll explain everything inside," Tambese replied, opening the door for them.

Moredi and Okoye were waiting in the lounge for Tambese. They shook hands and the three of them spoke amongst themselves until Graham returned to the lounge, dressed now in a pair of faded jeans and a black T-shirt.

"Please, won't you all sit down?" Okoye said.

Graham and Sabrina sat on the sofa, Okoye, Laidlaw and Moredi in the armchairs close by. Laidlaw reached down to put his mug on the floor and his hand brushed against Sabrina's Uzi which was propped up against the wall. He immediately picked up the mug again and put it on the other side of his chair. It made him feel better.

"How is Mr. Mobuto?" Sabrina asked, looking up at Tambese who had decided to remain standing.

"Drowsy, but otherwise he's fine. The doctor who examined him said there would be no side-effects from the drugs. He'll be discharged tomorrow morning."

"I still don't understand why Ngune didn't kill him if he was such a threat," Laidlaw said.

"Ngune needed him alive in case his *coup* failed. Then he could have used him as a hostage to get out of the country. Jamel and Remy have always been close. It's a bond that's developed over the years through their mutual abhorrence of their father's regime. Jamel refused to contemplate any military action against Ngune until he knew Remy was safe."

"Why was he kidnapped?" Moredi asked. "What did he have on Ngune?"

"Plenty. His mysterious informer was Ngune's personal secretary."

Moredi whistled softly. "No wonder Remy was so secretive about him. He must have been a mine of information."

"Oh, he was. He knew about the *coup;* he also knew about the plot to assassinate Jamel; and he passed all this information on to Remy. When Ngune found out what had happened he had to stop Remy from printing the story, so he had him kidnapped."

"Did Ngune's secretary identify the third man?" Sabrina asked.

"It is Bernard," Tambese replied. "But what really interested me was the fact that the actual plot to assassinate Jamel didn't originate here in Zimbala, as our intelligence sources have been led to believe. It's been a CIA operation all along. Ngune was their man. He's been working for the CIA for the past twenty-four years."

"Ngune, CIA?" Moredi said in amazement. "Why would he work for them?"

Tambese shrugged. "I couldn't tell you. All I know is that it's been one of the CIA's best-kept secrets for all those years. His secretary only found out by chance."

"Did he know who was behind the operation at Langley?" Sabrina asked.

"No."

"It could be Bailey," Sabrina said, looking at Graham.

"Could be," Graham agreed. "But right now we've got more important things to worry about."

"What do you mean?" she asked suspiciously.

Graham looked at Tambese. "Tell her."

"You know that Jamel will be attending a trade fair in New York later this afternoon. It'll be his last public engagement before he flies out tonight."

"Yes," she replied hesitantly.

"Bernard will be there as well, armed with a high-powered sniper rifle. Ngune was told that a final attempt would be made to assassinate Jamel at the Trade Center if he was still alive on the last day of his trip to America."

Sabrina looked at her watch. "New York's seven hours behind Zimbalan time. That means it'll be almost eleven thirty at night back home." She turned to Graham. "I'll call Sergei and tell him about Bernard."

"What can he do without alerting the CIA?" Graham asked, holding her stare. "He'd have to tell the NYPD if he wanted to carry out a search of the building. And they're sure to have CIA moles at the highest level. It wouldn't take long for word to reach Langley that Bernard had been compromised, and he'd be told to pull out. Then we'd be back to square one again."

"Surely the CIA will abort the operation anyway when they find out the *coup* has failed and that Ngune is dead?" Okoye said, looking from Graham to Sabrina.

"But they don't know that," Tambese told him. "All they'll know at the moment is that Branco and the rebel garrison have been destroyed by troops loyal to the government. We haven't released any casualty figures yet. What Mike suggested we do is put out some disinformation that Ngune and about two hundred of his men have amassed on the Chadian border to try and retake Kondese within the next twelve hours—so the CIA will still believe that they can overthrow Jamel and the government."

"I'd like a word in private," Sabrina said to Graham then looked round at the others. "Would you excuse us for a moment, please?"

Graham followed her out onto the porch.

"You suggested that they should spread some disinformation about Ngune? Why, Mike?" She held up her hand before he could answer. "No, let me guess. So that it would give you enough time to get back to New York and deal with Bernard yourself."

"Not me, us," he retorted.

"This has become an obsession, hasn't it? You'll go to any lengths to confront Bernard yourself. Even to the point of deliberately putting an innocent man's life in danger. It doesn't bother you, does it?"

Graham rested his arms on the railing and nodded his head slowly to himself. "I admit I was wrong going after Bernard like I did. At the time it was an obsession. But not any more. I've seen what Mobuto means to this country. The people need him." He glanced round at her. "Don't get me wrong, I still want to see Bernard brought to justice. But right now it's more important to stop him before he can get to Mobuto."

She sat down slowly on the wicker chair by the door. Her emotions had ranged from anger to guilt in the space of a few seconds. And it wasn't the first time it had happened either. She knew she was vulnerable to this quiet, softly spoken side of him that rarely showed itself. But he was the one who had given her an ultimatum in Beirut to work with, or without, him to find Bernard, irrespective of the danger to Jamel Mobuto. How was she to know he'd had a change of heart? She wasn't a mind-reader. So why the hell was she feeling guilty?

"I know we should tell Sergei what's happening, but what could he do? Never mind the NYPD; that was just a smokescreen I put up in there. What about the CIA men working with C.W.? They're Bailey's men. And if he is behind this whole operation, which I'm certain he is, he'd be the first to know if Bernard was compromised. How could Sergei have a description of Bernard circulated amongst the security staff at the Trade Fair without Bailey's men finding out? He couldn't, could he? That's why we have to stop Bernard ourselves. It has to be done in complete secrecy so that by the time we get there it'll be too late for Bernard to pull out. He'll be trapped. Then we can take him and bust this whole case wide open."

She gave him a resigned nod. "How are we going to get back to New York in time?"

"Tambese's arranged for one of the presidential planes to be put on standby for us in Habane. The Cessna's already been refuelled. All we're waiting for now is a pilot. Tambese would have flown us to Habane himself but he's still got a lot of loose ends to tie up down here. He said we should reach New York with a couple of hours to spare.''

"And if we don't make it?"

"Then we'll have to radio through to Sergei and explain the situation to him. He could still prevent Mobuto from attending the Trade Fair but then Bernard would almost certainly get away. But it shouldn't come to that. We do have time on our side."

"God, I hope so," she replied, rubbing her hands over her face. "If something does happen to Mobuto, C.W. will be breaking in two new partners. We'll be out so fast our feet won't touch the ground."

"Nothing's going to happen to Mobuto," Graham replied.

The door opened and Tambese looked out. "Sorry to disturb you, but I thought you'd like to know that the pilot's on his way. He should be here in about ten minutes."

"Great," Graham said then looked around him slowly. "I'll be sad to leave this place. It seems so tranquil."

Tambese stepped out onto the porch. "It is, believe me. I've been coming down here with my wife for the last ten years. It's the perfect tonic when you want to get away from the hustle and bustle of Habane."

"I didn't know you were married," Sabrina said.

"Twelve years now. Matthew Okoye's my brother-in-law. That's why we come down here so often. We've always been close. After all, there weren't many of us who could stand up to Alphonse Mobuto and get away with it. Jamel, Remy and Matthew were his staunchest critics, Joseph Moredi and I to a lesser degree because we didn't have the same clout that they did. That's what brought us all together in the first place: our revulsion at Alphonse Mobuto and his puppets like Ngune and his deputy, Thomas Massenga. We were determined to bring peace to Zimbala in our lifetime."

"And you have," Graham said.

"I certainly hope so," Tambese replied thoughtfully.

"Any news of Massenga?" Graham asked.

"Nothing yet. There's a reward out for his capture. It shouldn't be long before he's apprehended."

"You still haven't told me what happened after you got caught in Branco," Sabrina said to Graham.

Graham recounted the events up to the time Ngune was executed in the street.

"Have you found the officer who shot him?" she asked, looking at Tambese.

"I'm not looking for him," Tambese replied. "I know who it was but I'm not taking any further action. These things happen in the heat of the moment."

"So you're condoning murder?" she shot back. "That's lowering yourself to Ngune's level."

"I'd have to sink a lot lower to reach Ngune's level." Tambese moved to the railing and looked down at the outline of the body underneath the tarpaulin. He turned back to her. "Ngune's dead; the *coup d'état* failed. For the first time in forty-five years there's peace in Zimbala. The officer concerned only did what twelve million other Zimbalans would have done in the same situation. The country would be up in arms if I persecuted him for that. Don't get me wrong. I'm not condoning what happened, but at the same time I'm not prepared to jeopardize this newfound peace just to see that Ngune's death is avenged. This is Africa, Sabrina, not America. It's a continent in turmoil. *Coup d'états* are a regular occurrence. One corrupt government replaces another. And it's always the people who suffer. If it's not the adults being massacred because they happen to belong to a different tribe to the one in power, or to the one seeking power, then it's the children dying of malnutrition because their parents can't cultivate barren fields. The African has come to accept death as part of his everyday life. We put different values on life to, say, the Americans or the Europeans. In Europe and America, you'd say life is for living. In Africa, we say life is for surviving. And if the death of a butcher like Ngune means the chances of survival are increased, then the people will welcome it. I know it sounds cynical, but that's become the way of life in Africa."

"I guess values are different," she replied, glancing across at the tarpaulin. "But I take your point anyway."

"You still haven't told how you masterminded the attack on Kondese," Graham said. "How did your troops manage to neutralize all those patrols without any gunfire?"

"There was gunfire, but it was minimal. We didn't hear it because we were down in the sewer at the time. All the government troops were armed with silenced weapons. They used a pincer movement to close in on the city and all had orders to shoot to kill. The radio frequencies were jammed just before the troops moved in and opened again when they had recaptured the city. That way the troops in Branco couldn't be contacted and warned of the attack. Had they known Ngune may have fled. That was our main worry. Ngune was their mastermind and with him on the loose the threat of another *coup d'état* could never have been ruled out. We had to get him, dead or alive."

"And the garrison?" Sabrina asked.

"Ngune had a radar scanner installed at Branco but not one at the garrison. That was his mistake. He reasoned that any air attack would have to be launched from Habane and his spies would tell him as soon as the jets were scrambled, then they could counter the attack with the jets they had in Chad. But what he couldn't know was that Jamel had come to an agreement with the Niger government while he was in New York. They agreed to let us use two of their jets on the condition that we put our own markings on them before they left Niger. They didn't want to be seen to be involved if we failed to stop Ngune from seizing power. They've always had close links with Zimbala and they wanted to keep it that way, irrespective of who came to power. Again we jammed the radio frequencies just before the jets were scrambled and the garrison was levelled to the ground within a matter of minutes. We had a division on standby to go in afterwards and capture any surviving rebels. Then, when the garrison was destroyed, we opened the radio frequencies again."

"How many rebels survived?" Sabrina asked.

"Seventeen out of a squad of nearly four hundred. They'll be put on trial when they've recovered from their injuries." Tambese looked at Sabrina. "They'll be given a fair trial, that I assure you. And if found guilty, they'll be locked up for the rest of their lives. And I mean that quite literally. We're determined to stamp out the past. The dictatorship is dead. It must never be allowed to return."

"When exactly was this plan agreed?" Graham asked.

"Jamel thrashed it out with his entourage in New York and we finalized the details over the phone two days ago."

"Were we part of the plan?" Sabrina asked.

Tambese smiled. "Only when we knew you were coming to Zimbala. That's why I had Joseph tail you from the airport. We needed to make contact, only we didn't know how you'd react. It's just as well he did tail you, otherwise you wouldn't be here now. Massenga doesn't miss from that distance."

"So he wasn't following Massenga. He was following me."

"We'd been watching Massenga ever since he arrived in Habane. No, Joseph was at the airport waiting for you. We just didn't know when you'd arrive."

"How did you know we were coming to Zimbala?" Graham asked suspiciously.

"We have our sources."

"Meaning?" Graham pressed.

"We've been monitoring all communications

between Ngune and the outside since he retook Branco.
The two of you were a regular topic of conversation
when Massenga contacted him. You see, Massenga was
Ngune's link to Bernard, so everything Bernard said
to Massenga was passed on to Ngune. Bernard holds
you in great esteem, Mike. It's almost a grudging
admiration."

"I'm not flattered," Graham retorted.

"You've used us from the start," Sabrina said, shaking her head.

"No," Tambese shot back, the anger evident in his
voice. "I respect you both too much for that. We've
been working on the same case only from different
angles. That's why I thought we could achieve a lot
more by putting our heads together. And I was right. I
know I held out on you, and for that I'm sorry. I wanted
to tell you what was going on but Jamel wouldn't hear
of it. What could I do? I know I could have trusted you
but I would never do anything behind Jamel's back.
We've been friends for too long. I suppose it's a bit like
the two of you working together. You keep each other
informed and don't do anything without letting the
other one know."

"You must be joking," Sabrina replied then looked
across at Graham who was trying to hide the smile that
was threatening the corners of his mouth. She grinned
and wagged an accusing finger at him.

Tambese looked from Sabrina to Graham and
smiled. "OK, I get the point. But you still make a damn
good team."

"We have our moments," Graham replied with a
half-smile.

Tambese returned inside.

Sabrina paused at the door and looked round at
Graham. "Are you coming in?"

Graham nodded then followed her inside, closing
the door behind him.

◆ ◆ ◆

Thomas Massenga, who was crouched behind a tree two hundred yards away from the house, waited until Graham had closed the door before getting to his feet. He propped the AK-47 against the trunk and wiped the back of his hand across his sweating forehead. He had arrived in Kondese minutes before the government forces launched their attack to recapture the city. There was nothing he could do against such odds. He and his driver Gubene had abandoned the car and gone on foot to a safe house in the city.

Although the gunfire had been minimal it had quickly become obvious from the activity in and around the surrounding streets that the city had fallen to government troops. Then the jets had come, sleek, fast and deadly. He had watched from a second-floor window as they destroyed Branco within a matter of minutes. Then the tanks had rolled into the compound to crush the last of the brave resistance.

It had left him stunned. He had tried to call up the garrison on a radio in the loft. Silence. He could only assume that it, too, had fallen. Then came word that Ngune was dead, executed in the street by a young army lieutenant. And that automatically put Massenga in charge. But in charge of what? He had neither the men nor the hardware to mount a counter-attack, which meant he only had one option open to him: revenge. And as the head of the government forces, Tambese would be his first victim.

They had commandeered an army jeep and found out from its two occupants, an officer and his driver, that Tambese was questioning Remy Mobuto at the city hospital. After killing the soldiers, they had changed into their uniforms and drove over to the hospital only to discover that Tambese had left minutes earlier. He had told the duty nurse that he would be at the Okoye farm in case she needed to contact him.

They went to the farm, parking a hundred yards away from the main driveway. Massenga had left Gubene in the jeep and approached the farm on foot. He had been challenged by two soldiers in the grounds but had dispatched them both with a hunting knife when they had made the mistake of coming to attention to salute him. He had reached the tree moments before Graham and Sabrina appeared on the porch. Then Tambese had joined them. He didn't have a clear shot at Tambese and although he could have sprayed the porch with gunfire there was no guarantee he would have killed him. And Tambese had to die . . .

He picked up the AK-47 and moved cautiously toward the house, ever vigilant for any other soldiers who may be patroling the grounds. He ducked down behind the jeep and gripped the side as he slowly raised his head to get a better look at the position of the steps in relation to the single window that looked out onto the porch. He immediately felt something sticky on his fingers. He peered into the jeep but when he eased back the corner of the tarpaulin he found himself looking into Ngune's wide, sightless eyes. He dropped the tarpaulin as if it had stung him then sunk to his haunches and clasped his hands over his face. It took him a few seconds to regain his composure.

He took several deep breaths then moved out from behind the jeep and ran, doubled over, to the steps and silently crossed the porch to the window. He pressed himself against the wall and peered cautiously through the lace curtain into the room. Okoye and Moredi were sitting on the sofa, Laidlaw and Graham in the armchairs opposite and Sabrina and Tambese were standing in front of the mantelpiece. And none of them were armed. He would have a clear shot at Tambese. But to hell with that. He could take them all out with one magazine. And he still had two spare clips in his pocket in case he encountered any resistance on the way back to the jeep.

He kept close to the wall as he covered the few feet from the window to the door then, tightening his grip on the AK 47, he reached out for the handle. He took a deep breath then, pushing down the handle, thrust open the door and swiveled round to fire into the room. Tambese knocked Sabrina to the ground a split-second before a row of bullets peppered the wall above them.

It was sheer instinct that made Laidlaw grab the Uzi from beside his chair and as he dived low onto the carpet he raked the doorway with a fusillade of bullets. Massenga was hit several times in the chest and he fired wildly into the air as he stumbled back against the railing. He could feel the blood bubbling in his throat and a trickle seeped from his mouth and ran down his chin. He grimaced in agony as the pain tore through his body. He knew he was dying, but he was still determined to take as many of them with him as possible. He moved unsteadily toward the door and was raising the AK-47 when Laidlaw fired again. The bullets ripped into Massenga's body and the AK-47 spun from his hand as he crashed through the railing and landed heavily on the ground in front of the porch. Laidlaw ran down the steps and checked for a pulse. There was none.

Only then did he look down at the Uzi in his hand. It was almost as if he were awakening from a dream. He looked up slowly at the others who had congregated on the porch and his eyes finally settled on Graham's face.

"I can't believe I did it," Laidlaw said, shaking his head slowly to himself.

Graham smiled. "You did it, buddy. There's the proof."

Four soldiers, alerted by the gunfire, appeared from behind the house, M16s at the ready. Tambese told them to check the area for any other rebels. They divided into pairs and hurried away.

"We owe you our lives, Mr. Laidlaw," Moredi said, breaking the silence. "Thank you."

"Any time," Laidlaw replied, giving Graham a knowing smile. "Who was he anyway?"

"Massenga, Ngune's right-hand man," Tambese replied then pointed to the door. "We'd better go back inside until the area's been declared safe."

Graham and Sabrina went upstairs to get their holdalls and when they returned they found Tambese talking to a man by the door. Tambese introduced him as the pilot.

"He doesn't speak any English," he added with an apologetic smile.

"Who cares, as long as he can fly us to Habane," Graham replied.

Tambese translated Graham's words and the pilot gave him a thumbs-up sign. A jeep turned into the courtyard and pulled up in front of the porch. A sergeant climbed out and hurried up the steps. Tambese returned his salute and indicated that he should enter the room. They spoke briefly then the sergeant saluted again before returning to the jeep. The driver did a U-turn and drove off.

"The area's been secured," Tambese said, turning to Graham and Sabrina. "The bodies of two of our soldiers were found in the grounds. Massenga must have killed them when he approached the house. His driver's been arrested. He was still waiting for Massenga in an army jeep about five hundred yards from here."

"So we can leave?" Graham asked.

Tambese nodded then asked Okoye to take the pilot to the Cessna on the runway. Moredi took up the offer of a walk and left the room with the two men.

"I've got to get back to the city," Tambese said. "There's a press conference scheduled for later this morning. I need to consult with my officers before I say anything. I'll put out that story about Ngune's still being alive. You just make sure you get to Jamel before Bernard does. If Jamel were to die now, it could throw the country back into turmoil. Mike, I know how much you want Bernard—"

"The President's safety comes first," Graham cut in, putting a reassuring hand on Tambese's arm. "You have my word on that."

"Thank you." Tambese shook hands with both of them then left the house.

"So what are you going to do now?" Graham asked Laidlaw.

Laidlaw shrugged. "I guess I'll go back to Beirut and take stock of the situation. After that, who knows? I might go back to the States again."

Sabrina held out a hand toward him. "Good luck, Russell, whatever you decide to do."

"Thanks," Laidlaw replied, shaking her hand.

"Mike, I'll see you at the plane," she said then picked up her holdall and left the room.

"She's a good kid, Mike," Laidlaw said, staring at the door.

"Kid? She's twenty-eight, Russ."

"You know what I mean." Laidlaw's face became serious. "I'd still be feeling sorry for myself in some Beirut bar if you hadn't brought me out here. You gave me back my dignity, Mike. I can never repay you for that."

"You can cut the schmaltz for a start," Graham replied. "I didn't do anything. You pulled the trigger, not me. And just as well you did."

Laidlaw shook Graham's hand. "You take care of yourself, buddy."

"And you. I got to go, Russ."

Laidlaw watched Graham leave and smiled sadly to himself. He knew he'd never see Graham again. He represented the past that Graham so desperately wanted to forget. But he had the memories, and that was enough.

♦ CHAPTER

TWELVE

Whitlock pressed the combination into the bellpush then opened the door and entered. He was surprised to find Kolchinsky sitting behind Sarah's desk. Kolchinsky indicated that he should close the door behind him.

"What's this all about, Sergei?" Whitlock asked, stifling a yawn. "It's seven thirty in the morning."

"Sit down, C.W.," Kolchinsky said, gesturing to the burgundy-colored couch against the wall.

"Why here? What's wrong with the office?"

"It's bugged," Kolchinsky replied.

"Bugged?" Whitlock said in amazement. "But that's impossible. Dave Forsythe checks these rooms every morning for bugs."

"Which means he's the only person who could have planted it."

"Dave? Come on, Sergei, he's one of the most senior technicians in the command center."

"I read through his personnel file before you got here." Kolchinsky held up a sheet of computer paper.

"This is the printout. You probably know we recruited him from the CIA."

"Yes, I know he came over from Langley," Whitlock replied.

"Do you know who he was working for when he resigned?"

Whitlock's eyes narrowed suspiciously. "I've got a horrible feeling you're going to say Robert Bailey."

"The same. He'd been Bailey's electronic guru for seven years."

Whitlock slumped back on the couch. "So Bailey's known everything that's been said in the office. Did you find any other bugs?"

"No, I personally checked all the rooms this morning. They're clean."

"I'm surprised he didn't bug the telephones as well."

"Too dangerous," Kolchinsky replied. "He knows the Colonel and I regularly check the phones ourselves. And anyway, if Sabrina called me I always briefed you on what she said."

"Where is the bug?"

"Under the coffee table."

"What are you going to do?" Whitlock asked.

"Nothing, yet. I don't want to alert Bailey. Let's get the President safely on his plane first. I'll confront Dave in the morning. But until then act as if nothing's wrong."

Whitlock nodded. "This certainly supports the theory that Bailey's behind this whole operation. Why else would he want the office bugged? This way he could pass everything on to Bernard to ensure he's always kept one step ahead of Mike."

"Yes, Bailey has to be behind it," Kolchinsky replied. "But how to prove it is going to be another matter altogether. We're talking about the Deputy Director of the CIA. He's already being tipped as a future American President. And that means he's got a lot of influential friends across the board. We can't make any accusations without the proof to back them up. And right now we don't have that proof. Even if Dave Forsythe confesses to bugging the office for Bailey, it's not enough to prove involvement in a conspiracy to kill a foreign head of state."

"Whatever happens, we're going to be left with egg on our faces," Whitlock said grimly. "It's been a serious breach of security for an organization that supposedly doesn't exist."

"What if the bug has been planted for a newspaper?"

"Then you'll be spending Christmas standing in a food queue in some Moscow street and I'll be on the first plane back to Kenya." Whitlock got to his feet and winced as he tried to adjust the sling supporting his injured arm. "It's not a newspaper. It has to be Bailey. It's too much of a coincidence for it not to be."

Kolchinsky sighed deeply then pointed to Whitlock's arm. "How is it?"

"A bit stiff," Whitlock replied with a dismissive shrug.

"I assume you haven't heard anything from Sabrina in the last twenty-four hours?"

The question caught Whitlock by surprise but he was quick to regain his composure. "No," he lied, shaking his head. "Nothing at all. Hasn't she contacted you?"

"The last time I spoke to her was yesterday morning after the attempt on her life. She was thinking then about going down to Kondese to spring Remy Mobuto from jail. I told her to get on the next flight back here. The last thing we need is for UNACO to get involved in a civil war. Since then nothing. I'm worried about her, C.W. It's not like her to disobey an order. I've made enquiries through the American embassy but she hasn't been admitted to any hospitals out there. She just seems to have disappeared."

"She's probably on her way back now," Whitlock replied, hating himself for his deceit. But he had given her his word to keep silent.

"I hope so," Kolchinsky said then got to his feet and moved round to the front of the desk.

"She can look after herself, Sergei," Whitlock said, noticing the concern on Kolchinsky's face.

"It's not that," Kolchinsky replied, shaking his head. "The lab boys came back with positive ID on a set of prints from that newspaper you lifted from the flat last night."

"And?" Whitlock asked, his voice suddenly anxious.

"They're Bernard's."

"Oh, my God," Whitlock said despairingly. "When did you find this out?"

"Last night."

"Why didn't you call me?" Whitlock demanded.

"It wouldn't have done any good. You'd have just lain awake all night worrying about it."

"I was awake most of the night with this arm anyway. You're right, though, there's nothing I could have done." Whitlock sat down again then looked up at Kolchinsky. "Bailey must have tipped Bernard off about Rosie. How else could Bernard have found out who Rosie was and where to find her?"

"I think it would be better if you stayed away from the Trade Center today, C.W. I don't want any confrontations with Bailey until the President's out of American airspace."

"Bailey's going to be at the Trade Center this afternoon?"

"Yes, he arrived in New York last night."

"There won't be any confrontations, that I promise you. I'm not Mike. I can keep my emotions in check."

"I still don't see why you want to be there. You've already made the security arrangements with the NYPD. Let them handle it. And I'll be there to keep an eye on things."

"So will I," Whitlock said. "Mobuto may be a pain in the arse at times but I'm still in charge of his security.

I'd never forgive myself if anything were to happen to him while I was swanning about at home."

"OK," Kolchinsky replied.

"Is there anything we can do to try and find Rosie before Mobuto leaves for the Trade Center?"

"I had Strike Force Nine check out all known CIA safe houses in and around the New York area. They didn't come up with anything. But those were only the ones we knew about. There are sure to be others. Bernard might not even be at a safe house. All we can do now is wait for him to make the first move."

"And you think he'll try something at the Trade Center?"

"It's possible, if Sabrina's theory's right about him being the third man." Kolchinsky shrugged. "There are so many unanswered questions at the moment. But we have to take every precaution. I had a photofit made up of Bernard and sent over to the NYPD. It'll be circulated to all the officers on duty at the Trade Center today. There are already metal detectors positioned at all public entrances and all other doors will be guarded by uniformed officers. It's not foolproof by any means, but it'll make it that bit harder for him if he does intend to try and hit the President this afternoon."

"You know something, Sergei, I'll be glad to see the back of him tonight."

"You're not the only one," Kolchinsky replied with a weak smile. "Have you eaten this morning?"

"I had a coffee while I was getting dressed."

"Fancy some breakfast at the Plaza? We'll chalk it up to expenses."

"I wouldn't say no," Whitlock said. "I've got a feeling this is just the start of a very long day."

"My thoughts exactly. Come on, let's go."

Bernard was watching the morning news when the doorbell rang. He picked up his Desert Eagle automatic from the table and went to the door. He peered through the spyhole. It was Brett. He unlocked the door.

"Jesus, what happened to your face?" Brett asked, staring at Bernard's half-closed eye.

"The girl tried to escape."

"And she did that to you?" Brett said, unable to keep the smile from his face. "A sixteen-year-old kid?"

"She caught me with the door," Bernard replied sullenly.

"You're going to stand out like a sore thumb at the Trade Center."

"You let me worry about that."

"Hey, it's not just your ass on the line."

"I don't need a lecture from one of Bailey's flunkeys," Bernard snarled.

Brett glared at Bernard then brushed past him into the hall. "Where's the girl now?"

"In the bedroom," Bernard replied, closing the front door. "She won't give you any trouble, she's handcuffed to the radiator."

"Which door?"

"First on the right."

Brett opened the door and entered the room.

"A visitor?" Rosie said facetiously then looked across at Bernard who was standing in the doorway. "You should have told me your boyfriend was coming over."

"You can cut the cute remarks," Brett snapped then left the room and closed the door behind him. "When are you leaving?"

"Now. And don't bother making her anything to eat; she won't touch it. She hasn't eaten since I brought her here yesterday."

"What if she wants to go to the toilet?"

"Then let her go. There aren't any windows in the bathroom if that's what you're worried about." Bernard took the key for the handcuffs from his pocket and gave it to Brett. "You've been up all night, haven't you?"

"Yeah, I came straight over here from the hotel."

"Put your head down for a few hours, you'll feel better for it." Bernard noticed Brett's frown. "You don't think I stayed up all night, do you? She's not going anywhere."

"Is there an alarm?"

"It's by the front door. But there's no need to activate it. Like I said, she's not going anywhere."

"I'd feel better if it were on."

"Suit yourself," Bernard replied then picked up the holdall and walked to the front door.

"What time will you be back?" Brett asked as Bernard opened the door.

"When the job's done," Bernard replied. "Don't wait up," he added with a faint smile then left, closing the door behind him.

"I'll be waiting," Brett said softly then unholstered his Smith & Wesson 645 and aimed it at the door. "You can count on it, my friend."

"Why weren't we told about this?" Kolchinsky demanded, dropping a folder onto the table.

"And good morning to you, too," Mobuto replied with a hint of sarcasm as he looked up at Kolchinsky who had brushed past Masala moments earlier when he answered the door. He leaned forward in his chair and opened the folder. Inside were several sheets of computer paper. He scanned the first paragraph of the top page then sat back and folded his arms across his chest. "It's a résumé of the offensive we launched against Ngune last night. Forgive me if I'm a little slow on the uptake this morning, Mr. Kolchinsky, but why should I have told you about this?"

"Because two of our operatives could still be out there," Kolchinsky shot back.

"They were, up until a few hours ago," Mobuto replied. "They're now on their way back to New York. Surely you knew that?"

"How did you know their movements?" Kolchinsky asked, ignoring Mobuto's question.

"Colonel Tambese told me."

"Who?"

"David Tambese, the man I've appointed as the new head of the armed forces."

"Has he had them under surveillance?"

"Surveillance?" Mobuto replied with a look of puzzlement. "They were working together. Your operatives, Mike and Sabrina, helped David get my brother out of Branco. He told me he couldn't have done it without their help."

Kolchinsky sat down slowly, his eyes never leaving Mobuto's face. "Michael and Sabrina were working together?"

Mobuto nodded. "With David Tambese. I purposely kept the plans of the offensive a secret because I couldn't risk Ngune finding out beforehand. Only David and I knew about them. Mike and Sabrina were as much in the dark as you were."

"No, I don't believe they were," Kolchinsky said after a thoughtful pause, barely able to contain his anger. "How long have you known that Michael and Sabrina were working as a team?"

"Yesterday, when David told me that he'd intercepted Mike and his friend Laidlaw near the airport. Ngune had been tipped off that they would be going to the airport and he'd dispatched a suicide squad to deal with them."

"Did he say why they were going to the airport?"

"Sabrina had left a message at the airport to tell them where she was staying."

"Which means she was already working with Michael in Beirut," Kolchinsky said softly to himself.

"Pardon?"

"Nothing, I was just thinking out loud."

Mobuto leaned forward, his arms resting on his knees. "Didn't you know they were working with David?"

"I've never even heard of David Tambese!" Kolchinsky snapped then held up a hand in apology. "I'm sorry, it's not your fault. I'm grateful you brought this to my attention."

"I hope I haven't put them in any trouble," Mobuto said with genuine concern. "They saved my brother's life, and that's something I'll never forget."

Kolchinsky sat back in the chair and stared at the folder on the table. There were so many questions that needed to be answered. But the one that stood out above all others was how long Sabrina had been lying to him. When did she and Graham first make contact in Beirut? He knew she must have had her reasons for holding out on him. She and Whitlock had always been the two operatives he had trusted implicitly. But he wouldn't pass judgment on her, not yet. She had the right to answer for her actions in person. He could wait. Tambese? The name suddenly entered his mind. He had never heard of him until Mobuto mentioned the name. So it was fair to assume that Sabrina wouldn't have heard of him either before she arrived in Zimbala, and she would never work that closely with someone unless she had first had him vetted. All vetting procedures went through the command center. But that could have been risky. What if word had got back to him? No, she would have had to confide in someone close, someone she knew she could trust. And he knew exactly who that was.

"Would you excuse me?" Kolchinsky said, getting to his feet.

"Of course," Mobuto replied then closed the folder and offered it to Kolchinsky. "I'm sorry I didn't give UNACO prior warning about the offensive last night, but I had to take every precaution in case of a leak. I'm sure you understand."

"Yes, of course," Kolchinsky replied, almost absently, then took the folder from Mobuto and moved to the door.

"Where can I reach you if any more news comes through from Zimbala?" Mobuto called out after him.

"I'll be at the Trade Center," Kolchinsky said. "I've got a few things to discuss with C.W."

"I gave her my word."

"And I thought the only conspiracy around here was against the President," Kolchinsky retorted angrily. "Now I find there's been another one, against me. Not only that, it involved the two people I trusted above all others at UNACO. You've disappointed me, C.W., you really have."

Whitlock remained silent. What could he say—he had no defense. He had known it would have to come out. If only it had remained under wraps until Mobuto had left the country. Then the assignment would have been deemed a success and the damage would have been minimal. Well, so he had thought until now. Had it been Philpott he would have been reprimanded and that would have been the end of the matter. Philpott encouraged initiative in the field. But he should have known better with Kolchinsky. Everything had to be done by the book. His years in the KGB had taught him that, and nothing would change those views. He was too damn pedantic! But Whitlock wisely chose not to voice his thoughts. He was in enough trouble as it was. He only hoped Philpott would see the situation in a different light, but that would mean undermining Kolchinsky, and Philpott respected Kolchinsky too much to do that. The outlook was bleak, whatever way he looked at it. Yet, given the same circumstances, he would have done it again. Sabrina was his partner, and he had too much respect for her to go back on his word.

"Don't you have anything to say?" Kolchinsky asked, breaking the lingering silence.

"What do you want me to say, Sergei? I admit I've been helping Mike and Sabrina without your authorization. But I still believe I did the right thing."

"What if they had been caught? UNACO personnel involved in a civil war? We'd have been crucified by the UN. We're an anti-crime organization. The Charter states quite clearly that UNACO is not to involve itself in the politics of any country. I'm sure you're familiar with the section in question."

"Then why are we guarding Mobuto?" That's political."

"His life is threatened. It makes no difference that he's a politician. It's still a criminal offense."

"Remy Mobuto was kidnapped against his will," Whitlock retorted. "That's a criminal offense."

"Of course it is," Kolchinsky replied, "but his release was linked directly to the government offensive against the rebels. That's what makes it political. And Michael and Sabrina were in the thick of it."

"They didn't know about the offensive when they went into Branco to free Mobuto's brother, he told you that himself."

"And a lot of good that would have done them if the offensive had failed and they had fallen into rebel hands."

"Their actions weren't political, Sergei, you know that. They were told that Remy Mobuto had information that could be vital to the case. What were they supposed to do, pass up the chance to get that information?"

"They were supposed to have gone through the proper channels for a start."

"Would you have sanctioned the break-in at Branco?"

"I would have told them to hold back and let Tambese and his men go into Branco. Then they could have questioned Remy Mobuto once he was out. That way it couldn't have been misconstrued as a political move." Kolchinsky rubbed his hands over his face. "But it's too late for that now. The Secretary-General's going to kick up a stink when he finds out what's happened."

"Will we be suspended?" Whitlock asked.

"That will be up to the Secretary-General. But if we can see the President off safely tonight that will certainly count in your favor. When did you last speak to Sabrina?"

"When she asked me to check on Tambese."

"So we don't know whether they found out anything from Remy Mobuto," Kolchinsky said.

"Didn't Mobuto say anything when you spoke to him?"

"I didn't ask him. I was hoping you would have heard from Sabrina in the last few hours. I'm going back to the hotel now to speak to him again." Kolchinsky closed the folder in front of him then picked it up and got to his feet. "I'm especially disappointed in you, C.W. This is hardly the sort of behavior I'd expect from the next Deputy Director of UNACO."

"I'm still a field operative, Sergei. My loyalties lie with Mike and Sabrina. I'm sorry if you can't see that."

Kolchinsky walked to the door then looked back at Whitlock. "I only hope this doesn't affect your promotion."

"You'll have my letter of resignation if it does," Whitlock replied matter-of-factly.

Kolchinsky held Whitlock's unyielding stare for several seconds then turned and left the room without another word.

The Trade Center had been built off the Shore Parkway in Brooklyn; it had cost nearly one-and-a-half-million dollars at a time when New York was crippled by mounting debts which had given rise to the theory that it had been financed largely by mob money. The mayor at the time had been quick to denounce these rumors, too quick, according to most New Yorkers. Then, when a local tabloid ran an article about it under the headline "Mafia House", the name had stuck. It had become an expensive white elephant over the years, despite its location overlooking Jamaica Bay and its proximity to John F. Kennedy International Airport.

The visit of Jamel Mobuto had brought with it an unexpected publicity boost for the building. The two attempts on his life had made him one of the most newsworthy faces in the country and although he was not due to arrive at the Trade Center for another forty minutes, the front lawn was already seething with reporters and cameramen jostling for positions, all hoping for a third attempt on his life that could be captured on film for their newspapers and television news-bulletins. And they all had the same thought in the back of their minds. Third time lucky . . .

Had they known the purpose of the rider on the red and white Honda 500cc that pulled up at the boom gate a hundred yards away from where they were encamped, they would have felt that their prayers had been answered.

An armed guard stepped out of the hut and approached the motorbike. "Can I help you?" he asked brusquely.

Bernard lifted the front of his visor fractionally, careful to ensure that the guard couldn't see the bruise around his eye. "I'm from Harris Bond Couriers. I have a letter here for a Robert Bailey. He is expecting it."

"Is he attending the conference?" the guard asked.

"Hey, I'm just the dispatch rider. I was told to bring the letter here to 'Mafia House'."

The guard returned to the hut and picked up a clipboard off the desk. He paged through it until he found Bailey's name. An extension number was written beside it. He rang the number. It was answered by Rogers who told him that Bailey hadn't yet arrived but that he was expecting a letter from Washington. The guard replaced the receiver and activated the boom gate.

"Leave the letter with the guard at the entrance, he'll see that Mr. Bailey gets it."

Bernard gave the guard a thumbs-up sign and drove off. He pulled up in front of the entrance and left the motorbike idling as he hurried across to the nearest guard and handed the envelope to him. The guard checked the name against the print-out on his clipboard then nodded and disappeared into the building. Bernard mounted the motorbike and headed back toward the boom gate. He turned off into a narrow alley at the side of the building and pulled up in front of an adjacent door. He climbed off the motorbike then unfastened the helmet and placed it on the seat. He also removed the leather jacket he was wearing and was about to drape it over the seat as well when the door was pushed open and a man emerged.

Bernard had never seen him before. He was the same height and build as himself and was wearing a pale blue shirt, navy trousers and a pair of black shoes—the same outfit as Bernard. He nodded in greeting to Bernard then pulled on the leather jacket and zipped it up. Then, after slipping the helmet over his head, he climbed onto the motorbike and headed off toward the boom gate.

"Any problems?"

Bernard looked round sharply at Rogers who had appeared silently at the door behind him, the envelope in his hand.

"No," Bernard replied.

"Jesus, what happened to your eye?"

"An accident," Bernard answered sharply.

"Come inside."

Bernard stepped past Rogers who immediately closed the door behind him and bolted it again. He found himself in a narrow corridor with several white-painted doors leading off from it. Rogers led the way to one of them then took a key from his pocket and opened it. Bernard went inside. It was a small room with a wooden chair and a battered locker in the corner.

"Your clothes are in there," Rogers said, indicating the locker.

"What is this place?"

"These used to be storerooms up until a few months ago. Then all the stock was moved to bigger rooms closer to the conference center. They're all empty now. The cops have already checked them so you won't have to worry about being disturbed." Rogers gave the key to Bernard. "Just make sure you lock the door behind me."

"Is Mobuto's address still scheduled for two o'clock?"

Rogers nodded then looked at his watch. "It's now twelve fourteen. You want to be in position no later than one forty."

"I'll be there."

"You'll have to hide that bruise. It'll only draw attention to yourself. I'll get you a pair of sunglasses."

"No need," Bernard said, taking a pair of sunglasses from his pocket.

"OK," Rogers replied then moved to the door. "Good luck."

"Luck's for amateurs," Bernard answered then pointed to the envelope Rogers was holding. "What's in there?"

"Nothing," Rogers replied with a grin then left the room and closed the door behind him.

Bernard locked the door then moved to the chair and sat down. All he had to do now was wait.

It had been Whitlock's idea to have Mobuto brought to the Trade Center in a police helicopter. That way he would not only avoid the posse of journalists expecting him to arrive by car, but it would also thwart any planned hit from one of the adjacent buildings. SWAT snipers had been in position on the surrounding roof-tops since daybreak and the helipad itself, situated on the roof of the Trade Center, had been under armed guard for the past twenty-four hours. He had deployed armed officers at all the strategic points inside the building and, with no reported sightings of Bernard, he was quietly confident that he had the situation under control.

Whitlock shielded his face with his hand as the heli-copter pilot executed a perfect landing on the helipad. Rogers hurried forward, his face screwed up against the swirling wind whipped up by the rotors, and opened the passenger door. Masala was the first out. He looked round slowly. Whitlock and Kolchinsky were standing by the door and four SWAT snipers were positioned at each corner of the roof. Satisfied, he nodded to Mobuto who clambered out of the helicopter and hurried, doubled over, toward Kolchinsky and Whitlock. Kolchinsky opened the door and Mobuto stepped inside, grateful to be out of the choppy wind. Whitlock and Masala followed him through the door. Kolchinsky gave the pilot a thumbs-up sign and the helicopter immediately rose off the helipad and mo-ments later peeled away to the right, heading back to-ward Manhattan. He closed the door behind him and crossed to the four men at the end of the corridor.

"Are you alright, sir?"

"A little windswept, but otherwise I'm fine, thank you," Mobuto replied to Kolchinsky's question. "What is the agenda for this afternoon? Is my speech still scheduled for two o'clock?"

"Yes," Kolchinsky said, brushing down his double-breasted jacket. "And the cocktail party will be held immediately after your speech."

"Excellent. I look forward to hearing what the country's leading financiers think of my proposed economic changes for Zimbala." Mobuto smiled to himself. "I hope they approve enough to give their backing to the investment program I have in mind. Well, we'll just have to wait and see, won't we?"

"The complex manager is waiting for us downstairs," Whitlock said to Mobuto. "He's offered to give you a tour of the building if you're interested."

Mobuto looked at his watch. "I've got fifty minutes to kill before I'm due to make my speech. Yes, I'd be delighted to see the building."

They took the lift down to the fourth floor where the manager and his senior aides had their offices. The manager, a short, dapper man in his late forties, was waiting in his office for them. The nameplate on his desk identified him as Anthony Lieberwitz.

"Would you care for something to drink, sir?" Lieberwitz asked after shaking Mobuto's hand.

"No, thank you. I had a coffee before I left the hotel."

There was a knock at the door and the receptionist who had ushered them in moments earlier appeared again and announced that there was a Mr. Bailey in her office. Lieberwitz told her to show him in.

Bailey forced a quick smile for the receptionist as he entered the room and the door was closed behind him. He nodded in greeting to Lieberwitz then turned to Mobuto and extended a hand in greeting. "Nice to see you again, Mr. President."

"Glad you could come," Mobuto said, shaking Bailey's hand.

"I wouldn't have missed it for the world." Bailey replied. He shook Kolchinsky's hand then sat down in one of the vacant armchairs.

"This came for you, sir," Rogers said, handing the envelope to Bailey.

"Ah, thank you," Bailey said, taking the envelope from Rogers. "I was worried it might not turn up."

"It got here in good time, sir," Rogers replied.

Lieberwitz got up from behind his desk. "Mr. President, would you care to see the rest of the building? We have a telescope on the top floor. The view of the city is quite breathtaking."

"I look forward to seeing it," Mobuto replied, getting to his feet.

The telephone rang.

"Excuse me," Lieberwitz said then answered it. He put his hand over the mouthpiece. "It's for you, Mr. Kolchinsky."

Kolchinsky took the receiver from Lieberwitz. "Hello."

"Mr. Kolchinsky?"

"Speaking. Is that you, Sarah?"

"Yes," she replied. "I've just spoken to Mike Graham. He's with Sabrina at JFK. They touched down about ten minutes ago. It seems there's been an accident near the airport which has completely blocked off the carriageway into the city. He's asked for a helicopter to pick them up from the airport and take them to the Trade Center. He says it's an emergency."

"Have one of our helicopters scrambled immediately and sent over to the airport."

"Who should I speak to about having it cleared for landing at JFK?" she asked.

"I'll see to that, don't worry. You just make sure the helicopter gets over there as soon as possible."

"Yes, sir."

"Did he say anything else?"

"No," Sarah replied.

"Thanks, Sarah." Kolchinsky replaced the receiver then looked round at Mobuto. "You'll have to excuse C.W. and me. We won't be joining you on the tour of the building. Something's come up."

"Nothing serious, I hope?" Mobuto said.

"Nothing for you to worry about, Mr. President," Kolchinsky replied with a reassuring smile.

Lieberwitz opened the door and Mobuto, Masala

and Rogers went into the outer office. Bailey remained in his seat. Lieberwitz looked from Bailey to Kolchinsky then withdrew discreetly, closing the door behind him.

"You're missing the tour," Kolchinsky said, eyeing Bailey coldly.

"Scramble one of your helicopters immediately and have it sent over to the airport? Why?"

"That doesn't concern you," Kolchinsky shot back.

"If it concerns this case, it does."

"C.W., show Mr. Bailey to the door."

"No need, I'm going," Bailey said, getting to his feet. "You'd better not be holding out on me, Kolchinsky. Because if you are you can be sure that will go in my report to the White House. And UNACO's in enough trouble as it is without my adding to your problems."

Whitlock closed the door behind Bailey. "Who was that on the phone?"

"Sarah," Kolchinsky replied. "Michael and Sabrina have just got back from Zimbala. Michael wants a helicopter to fly them over here. He says it's an emergency."

"An emergency? That has to mean Bernard's already here. Did Mike say where Bernard intends to make the hit?"

Kolchinsky shook his head. "But they should be here before the President starts his speech."

"And if they're not?"

"We could stall for time, but we don't even know if there is an assassin, whether it be Bernard or not, let alone where and when the hit's going to be made."

"The security's already been tightened in and around the main hall. I don't know what else we can do."

"Nothing, for the moment." Kolchinsky banged his fist angrily on the desk. "Why couldn't he have called us? He must know we're here. Our hands are tied until they get here."

"He must have had his reasons," Whitlock replied.

"Especially if it involves Bernard," Kolchinsky snapped. "I'll see you down at the hall. I've got to call the airport to get the necessary clearance for our helicopter to land there."

Whitlock left the room. Kolchinsky ran his hands over his face then sat down behind the desk and picked up the receiver.

Bernard finished applying the foundation and powder to the scar on his cheek then studied his reflection carefully in the cracked, full-length mirror attached to the inside of the open locker door. He smiled to himself. The scar was gone. Then, taking the cap from the bottom shelf of the locker, he placed it carefully on his head. Now the disguise was complete. He was just another New York cop. He picked up the identity tag that had been left in the locker for him and clipped it onto his jacket. He unlocked the door then opened it fractionally and peered out into the corridor. It was deserted. He left the room, locking it again behind him, then slipped on his sunglasses before walking to the stairs at the end of the corridor.

He glanced at his watch. One twenty-five. He climbed the stairs and found himself in another corridor. He knew where he was from the plans he had studied in Beirut. He made his way to a door further down the corridor which led onto another set of stairs. He descended them to the next level. There, as in the plans, were a men's and a ladies' room, and they had been specially set aside for the police for the day. He entered the men's room and smiled at the policeman standing in front of the urinal. He nodded in greeting. Bernard went to the nearest sink and washed his hands.

The policeman crossed to the row of sinks. He looked at Bernard's reflection in the mirror that ran the length of the wall in front of them. "Hey, that's some bruise you've got there."

"Happened last night," Bernard replied, affecting a New York accent. "Guy caught me by surprise with a baseball bat. But it's nothing compared to what I did to his face."

The policeman chuckled then wiped his hands on the roller towel. "I'm Hank Medford. Eighteenth Precinct."

"José Mendoza, Twenty-sixth." Bernard shook Medford's hand. "So where have they got you working today?"

"I'm up on the roof," Medford replied as they walked to the door.

"It's alright for some," Bernard said, holding the door open for Medford. "You've got the perfect weather to be outside."

"And you?"

"Good question," Bernard muttered. "I'm helping out wherever they need an extra pair of hands. At least I get to see round the building."

"Big deal," Medford said facetiously.

"Yeah," Bernard replied with a twisted grin. "I've just been told to get my ass over to the hall where Mobuto's making his speech at two."

"I'll walk with you. It's on my way back to the roof anyway."

"Great," Bernard said, patting Medford on the back. Two cops together were far less likely to draw attention to themselves than a single cop would by himself, especially one wearing dark glasses to help conceal a badly bruised eye. And by pretending to know Medford, it would add further credibility to his deception, especially when they reached the hall.

They walked to the lift and, once inside, Bernard pushed the button for the sixth floor. He touched his cap to the two receptionists already in the lift but ignored their inquisitive eyes as he talked to Medford. The receptionists got off on the fifth floor and both looked back at Bernard as the door closed over again behind them.

"I'd say you made quite an impression," Medford said with a salacious grin.

"So did the baseball bat. And that's all they were interested in—how I got the bruise—nothing more."

"How can you be so sure?"

"It was in their eyes." Bernard smiled at Medford's puzzled frown. "You have a lot to learn about women, my friend."

"Not much chance of that. I'm married."

The lift stopped again and the door opened onto the sixth-floor corridor.

Bernard stepped out of the lift then looked round at Medford. "See you around, Hank."

"Sure thing," Medford replied. "And keep away from baseball bats."

Bernard waited until the doors had closed before turning to the policeman who had approached him. "I'm looking for Captain D'Arcy."

"He's in the hall. If you've got a message for him, I'll see that he gets it."

"I've been sent here as an extra pair of eyes on the catwalk. Mr. Whitlock's orders." Bernard took a sheet of paper from his pocket. "That's his authorization."

The policeman opened the letter and read it quickly. "OK. I'll let Captain D'Arcy know you're here. You'd better get up there. The President's due here any time now."

"How do I get up there?" Bernard replied, feigning ignorance.

"Use that door over there," the policeman said, pointing further down the corridor. "Report to Sergeant Mason. He's up there already."

"How many men have we got up there?"

"Three."

Bernard thanked the policeman and smiled to himself as he walked to the door. Everything was going according to plan. The door was unlocked. He went inside and locked it behind him with a key Rogers had given him. He found himself in a room behind two lengths of heavy gray curtain that hung at the back of the stage. The irritating sound of bland muzak came from inside the hall. He moved to the metal ladder mounted against the wall and climbed effortlessly to the catwalk situated fifty feet above the stage. A tall, blond-haired policeman challenged him as soon as he reached the catwalk. Bernard recognized him from the dossier Bailey had prepared for him at the outset of the operation.

"Sergeant Mason?" Bernard said as a matter of formality.

"Yes," came the terse reply.

"I'm Columbus," Bernard said, taking off his sunglasses.

"What happened to your eye?"

"An accident," Bernard replied dismissively. "What about the other two policemen who're supposed to be up here with you?"

"Unconscious."

"I'm impressed," Bernard said absently, his eyes already scanning the catwalk for the best angle for the shot.

"They'll be out for another couple of hours. Those were the instructions—"

"Where's the rifle?" Bernard cut in.

"It was brought up earlier. I'll get it for you."

Bernard waited until Mason had left then looked round him slowly. Everything was just as he had visualized it when he had studied the plans back in Beirut. The catwalk was hidden from the main body of the hall by the heavy gray curtains that hung from the ceiling to the floor on the sides of the room. He found the break in the curtains behind the stage and tweaked one of them aside so that he could look out over the hall. The first of the businessmen had already taken their seats close to the stage and were talking amongst themselves as they waited for their colleagues to arrive.

Bernard looked down onto the stage. The lectern was centrally positioned at the front, perfectly placed for a head shot. But he didn't intend to wait until Mobuto reached the stage. He would pick him off as he entered the hall through the doors at the back of the room. That way all eyes would be on Mobuto and nobody would notice the slight movement in the curtains high above the stage. He let the curtain fall back into place then looked at his watch. One thirty-three. Bailey had already told him that Mobuto would reach the hall around one forty-five. Plenty of time. Mason returned with the black attaché case and gave it to Bernard.

"OK. Keep an eye on the door," Bernard said.

As Mason turned away Bernard clasped his hands on either side of the man's head and jerked it savagely to one side, breaking his neck. He grabbed Mason under the arms as his body went limp and eased him down noiselessly onto the catwalk. He was only carrying out Bailey's orders—no witnesses. He unlocked the case and opened it. Inside were the sections of the Galil sniper rifle. After he had put the rifle together, he connected the Nimrod X6 telescopic-sight-attachment and screwed the silencer onto the end of the barrel. He picked up the magazine, containing twenty rounds of subsonic ammunition, and carefully clipped it into place. He peered through the curtain again. More of the businessmen had filed into the hall but there was still no sign of Mobuto.

He carefully adjusted the telescopic sight until he had a perfect image of the doors. It would be a simple shot, one bullet through the head. That's all it would take. But he couldn't escape. He knew that. It would only take the authorities a few seconds to realize the bullet had come from the catwalk. And there was only one way to get off the catwalk, and that was down the ladder. He would never make it. But he had known that even before he accepted the assignment. So, once he had killed Mobuto, he would put the rifle down and wait for the police to arrest him. Not that he would be in custody for very long. Bailey had already paid off several senior policemen to arrange for Bernard to "escape" later that night. He would then be driven to an abandoned airstrip where a plane would be waiting to take him back to Beirut.

It wouldn't be in Bailey's interests to double-cross him. He had only gone along with Bailey's plan after he had written down a detailed account of all the CIA operations he had been involved in over the years which he had then passed onto a lawyer with instructions that it be forwarded on to the *New York Times* if anything were to happen to him before he made contact with the lawyer again. And Bailey had been made aware of the document's existence. He knew he was safe as long as the document remained in the lawyer's possession. And he would be in no rush to collect the document, no rush at all.

He looked at his watch. One forty. Mobuto could appear any time now. He picked up the rifle, wrapped the strap tightly around his arm, then rested the barrel lightly on the top railing, the telescopic sight trained on the doors. Now all he had to do was wait.

Kolchinsky and Whitlock were already waiting on the helipad as the UNACO helicopter came in to land. The cabin door was thrown open before the pads touched the ground and Graham jumped nimbly onto the helipad and ran, doubled over, to where they stood.

"What the hell is going on?" Kolchinsky demanded.

"Bernard's here. And he's got a sniper rifle with him," Graham shouted above the noise of the rotors.

"Mobuto's due at the hall in a couple of minutes," Whitlock said, glancing at his watch. "We have to warn him."

Kolchinsky opened his mouth to speak but Graham and Whitlock had already disappeared through the door behind him. Whitlock grabbed Graham's arm and pointed to the fire escape. Graham pushed it open and they bounded down the stairs, two at a time, and arrived breathlessly at the sixth floor less than a minute later. Whitlock's arm was throbbing from where it had banged against his chest but he ignored the pain as he emerged into the corridor. Mobuto was talking to Bailey at the door. Bailey looked up sharply at Whitlock then his eyes narrowed with uncertainty when he saw Graham appear behind him. Bailey knew something was wrong. He had to get Mobuto into the hall. Fast. He was still opening the door when Graham slammed it shut with his palm.

"What are you doing?" Bailey snarled.

"What's going on, Clarence?" Mobuto demanded, looking from Whitlock to Graham. "And who is this man?"

"Mike Graham," Whitlock replied with evident satisfaction.

"Mike Graham?" Mobuto said in a startled voice. He held out his hand. "It's a pleasure finally to meet you."

"Likewise," Graham said, shaking Mobuto's hand quickly. He noticed D'Arcy standing beside Whitlock. "Are you the senior officer here?"

D'Arcy nodded.

"Then arrest this son-of-a-bitch," Graham said, pointing to Bailey.

Rogers reached for his holstered Smith & Wesson but his hand froze on the butt when he saw the Browning in Whitlock's hand. He slowly withdrew his hand.

"You touch me and you'll be walking the beat for the rest of your days," Bailey snapped, glaring at D'Arcy.

"Clarence, what is going on?" Mobuto said in desperation.

"Robert Bailey was the mastermind behind the plot

to assassinate you, sir," Graham said. "Ngune and Bernard work for him."

"Is this true?" Mobuto said, staring at Bailey.

"Of course not," Bailey retorted angrily.

"Are you calling the President's brother a liar?" Graham said, his eyes never leaving Bailey's face.

"Remy told you that?" Mobuto asked Graham.

"He told Tambese, and Tambese told us. Who do you believe? Bailey or your brother?"

"There must be some—"

"Arrest him!" Mobuto said contemptuously, cutting across Bailey's outburst.

Whitlock nodded to D'Arcy. "And take him while you're at it," he said, indicating Rogers.

D'Arcy had the two men handcuffed. Whitlock gave instructions for them to be taken to a lounge further down the corridor then turned to D'Arcy and explained that Bernard was already in the building.

"I think it would be unwise of you to go ahead with your address until we've rechecked the hall, sir," Graham said to Mobuto.

"There's only one area a sniper could use in the hall, and that's the catwalk," D'Arcy said behind Graham. "And we've got that covered." He looked at Whitlock. "It seems that extra man you sent could come in useful after all."

"What extra man?" Whitlock replied suspiciously.

"The policeman you sent over ten minutes ago. He had a letter of authorization signed by you."

"I never sent a man over," Whitlock shot back.

"Bernard," Graham hissed. "I'm going up there, C.W. Give me your Browning. And that two-way radio on your belt."

"Take Captain D'Arcy and some of his men as backup," Whitlock said, handing the Browning and the radio to Graham.

"No," Graham replied quickly then put a hand on

Whitlock's arm. "If he is there, I want to take him myself."

"Alive, preferably," Whitlock said.

Graham moved to the door. "It's locked," he called out.

"It shouldn't be," D'Arcy said, approaching the door.

"You got a key?"

D'Arcy took a set of keys from his pocket. "I don't know which one it is."

Graham tried several of the keys before he found the right one. He unlocked the door then handed the keys back to D'Arcy.

"Are you sure you don't want any backup?" D'Arcy asked.

Graham shook his head then eased the door open and slipped into the room, closing it again behind him. He looked up at the catwalk but couldn't see anything, or anyone, from where he stood. He moved silently to the metal ladder and, tucking the Browning firmly into his belt, began to climb, slowly and carefully, toward the catwalk. He paused three-quarters of the way up the ladder and pulled the Browning from his belt. When he reached the top he raised his head fractionally above the level of the catwalk floor. Bernard was kneeling on his right knee with the rifle resting lightly on the railing for added stability. His body was at a forty-five-degree angle to the ladder and his head bent low over the top of the rifle. Graham was on his blind side. Graham kept the Browning trained on him as he climbed the last few rungs before he reached the catwalk. What if Bernard turned and fired when challenged? Graham knew it was a possibility. Could he afford to take that chance? He could kill Bernard with one shot. That's all it would take. Then his revenge would be complete. His finger tightened on the trigger as he aimed the Browning at Bernard's head. One shot. He thought of Carrie and Mikey. They deserved justice. Then he thought of

Ngune's execution in Kondese and how much it had appalled him. Shot in cold blood. It would be the same if he shot Bernard without giving him the chance to surrender. Could he live with that on his conscience? He eased the pressure on the trigger.

"Drop the gun, Bernard," Graham said softly but firmly, his body tensed in anticipation of Bernard's reaction.

Bernard raised his head and looked round slowly. He wasn't surprised that it was Graham. It was almost as if he had expected it to be him, the face that had haunted him ever since the incident in Libya. He had lost count of the times he had woken in the night, his body soaked with sweat, Graham's face still fresh in his mind. But it wasn't a nightmare any more. Now it was real. He knew Graham wouldn't kill him, not unless in self-defense. That much was obvious. He had already discounted any thoughts of trying to fire on the turn—not against someone of Graham's calibre. He would be dead before he even had a chance to move the rifle. And with Graham there, it meant Mobuto would already have been warned not to enter the hall, certainly not until the situation had been resolved one way or the other. And he still had the escape plan as backup. Bailey couldn't afford not to fulfill his side of the bargain, even if Mobuto were still alive. He unwound the strap from around his arm and laid the rifle carefully at his feet.

"Put your hands on your head and step away from the railing," Graham ordered.

Bernard did as he was told. Graham unclipped the two-way radio with his left hand and told Whitlock to have a couple of policemen waiting for Bernard at the foot of the ladder. He clipped the radio back onto his belt then gestured toward the ladder. His finger tightened on the trigger as Bernard passed him.

"Bernard?" Graham called out as Bernard reached the top of the ladder. He waited until Bernard had looked round before speaking again. "Was it a clean kill?"

"Yes, I believe it was," Bernard replied then began to slowly descend the ladder toward the waiting policemen. He was handcuffed when he reached the ground before being led away, flanked by two policemen.

Graham climbed down the ladder again. "The rifle's still up there," he said to D'Arcy who immediately dispatched one of his men to fetch it.

Sabrina hurried over to where Graham was standing. "Mike, are you OK?" she asked softly.

"Yeah, sure," he replied quickly then looked past her as Kolchinsky entered the room. "Here comes trouble."

"With a capital T," she said, glancing round as Kolchinsky approached them.

"I want to see you both in my office in an hour," Kolchinsky said sharply.

"We'll be there," Sabrina assured him.

Kolchinsky's eyes flickered from Sabrina to Graham. "Why didn't you kill him when you had the chance? It's what you set out to do."

"It's what I set out to do," Graham agreed. "But Sabrina talked me out of it when we were in Zimbala."

"Well, that's something in your favor," Kolchinsky said to her then walked back toward the door.

"I never talked you out of it," she said once Kolchinsky was out of earshot. "I tried, but you wouldn't listen."

"Maybe I did," Graham replied. "But that's not the point. I called the plays in Beirut and now I've got to deal with the consequences. I'm not going to let you be dragged down with me."

"We work as a team, Mike. And that means we face the ups and downs of the partnership together."

"No, not this time, Sabrina," he replied then crossed to the door and disappeared back out into the corridor.

◆　◆　◆

"Hi," Sarah said as Sabrina entered the office. "Welcome back."

"Thanks," Sabrina said with a grin. "Is Sergei in?"

Sarah nodded then flicked the intercom button on her desk. "Sabrina here, Mr. Kolchinsky."

"Send her in," came the terse reply.

Kolchinsky activated the door for Sabrina and closed it again behind her.

"Isn't Mike here yet?" she asked, glancing at her watch.

"He's been and gone," Kolchinsky replied.

"But I thought you wanted to see us together," Sabrina said, frowning.

"That was what I had in mind." Kolchinsky indicated the nearest of the two black couches. "Sit down."

She sat down slowly, her eyes never leaving Kolchinsky's face. "Something's wrong, Sergei. What is it?"

Kolchinsky shifted uncomfortably in his chair then reached for his cigarettes on the desk and lit one. "Michael handed in his resignation this afternoon."

She clasped her hands over her face and shook her head slowly to herself.

"I said he handed it in. I didn't say I accepted it."

She sat back and looked across at him. "Will you accept it?"

"That will all depend on the findings of the internal investigation the Secretary-General's asked me to set up to look into the way the three of you conducted yourselves during the operation."

"How long will that take?"

"A couple of days." Kolchinsky tapped a folder on his desk. "Michael's already given me a detailed account of what happened in both Beirut and Zimbala. I want your report on my desk by tomorrow afternoon at the latest."

"You'll have it."

"The investigation team will want to question you

personally after you've submitted your report to make sure your account tallies with those forwarded by Michael and C.W." He opened the folder, removed several sheets of paper which were stapled together in the top left-hand corner and held them out toward her. "This is a photocopy of Michael's report. Make sure your account tallies with his. It's your one chance of getting out of this with your job and your credibility intact."

She took the report hesitantly from him. "Why are you doing this, Sergei? If anyone finds out you've given this to me you'd be in a lot of trouble."

"Michael told me you'd try and cover for him. I can believe that. At least if you stick to the same story you'll minimalize the damage not only for yourself, but for Michael as well. I've already spoken to C.W. and he suggested the two of you work together on your reports tonight. I think it's a good idea." He pointed to the copy of Graham's report in her hand. "You and C.W. will have to share that one. And make sure you shred it when you've finished using it. As you said, I'd be in a lot of trouble if that were to fall into the wrong hands."

"Does the Colonel know about this?" she asked, holding up the report.

"No, and let's keep it that way."

"Thanks, Sergei," she said with a smile.

"This doesn't mean I'm any less angry at the way in which the three of you conducted this whole operation, especially you and C.W. I'm very disappointed in both of you."

"There wasn't any other way, Sergei."

"So Michael kept saying. It's not a very convincing excuse, is it?"

"I guess not," she replied glumly.

"We'll discuss it at length once all your reports are on my desk."

She got to her feet. "Where are Mike and C.W. now?"

"C.W.''s with the President at his hotel. I don't know where Michael is. He said he wanted some time on his own, which is understandable under the circumstances."

"What about Bailey, Bernard and Rogers? Anything from them yet?"

"Still nothing. It's obvious that Bailey and Rogers won't say a thing until they've been fully briefed on their rights by top Agency lawyers. Bernard's already been charged with the double murder of the two policemen in Murray Hill but he's taken his lawyer's advice and hasn't said a word since being taken into custody. C.W.''s out of his mind with worry about Rosie. I presume he's told you about her?"

She nodded. "Isn't there anything we can do to find her?"

"We've checked all the known CIA safe houses in and around the New York area. She isn't at any of them. I spoke to the CIA Director earlier and he's promised to fax us the list he has at Langley. We'll check them out as well but we could still come up with a blank. All senior Agency officials have a number of safe houses that only they know about. If Rosie is being held at one of Bailey's safe houses then we won't be able to find her without his co-operation."

"Which could mean some kind of deal?" Sabrina said bitterly.

Kolchinsky shrugged. "I don't know. The Colonel's on his way to Washington now to meet with the CIA Director."

"I didn't know the Colonel was back at work," she said in surprise.

"He left hospital last night. He was supposed to be resting at home but with all this going on he's decided to come back to work."

"What did his doctor say?"

"I don't think his doctor knows. Well, not yet. But

you know the Colonel, once he decides to do something, nothing will stop him."

"Until he has another heart attack."

"It's his choice, Sabrina."

"I guess so," she said tight-lipped. "Is there anything else?"

"Not for the moment," Kolchinsky replied. "Meet me in the foyer of the Plaza at seven. President Mobuto asked if he could see you and Michael before he flies out later tonight. Michael's already asked to be excused. That's why it's important that you make an appearance."

"I'll be there," she said then paused at the door and looked round at Kolchinsky. "By the way, what was this about Dave Forsythe? C.W. said something about his working for Bailey?"

"That's right. He obviously bugged the office so that Bailey could keep Bernard informed on the latest developments in Zimbala."

"What will happen to him?"

"He's already been dismissed."

"Will he be prosecuted?"

"And cause us further embarrassment? No, but he's finished anyway. None of the top intelligence agencies will take him on after what happened here. He can't be trusted. He'll end up running an electrical store in some backwater. That will be punishment enough."

"I guess so," she said thoughtfully then left the room.

Kolchinsky closed the door behind her then lit another cigarette and returned to his paperwork.

A light drizzle had set in over the city by the time Sabrina reached the hotel. She parked her champagne-colored Mercedes Benz 500 SEC close to the hotel and as she strode briskly toward the entrance, her stiletto heels clicking noisily on the sidewalk, she knew she was attracting the appreciative glances of the men on both sides of the street. Not that she gave them the satisfaction of looking back. That would only encourage them. It would also be a sign of vanity, and she despised vanity in any form.

She was relieved finally to reach the hotel and as she entered the foyer she looked around slowly, hoping to see Kolchinsky. He was sitting with Whitlock close to the lift. Whitlock immediately got to his feet and waved to catch her attention. She smiled back at him then crossed to where he was standing and kissed him lightly on the cheek. Kolchinsky nodded to her in greeting then looked at his watch. She was fifteen minutes early. He knew that was for his benefit. Good. Keep her on her toes. He took another sip of coffee.

"You look lovely," Whitlock said, appraising her dark beige suit and eye-catching jungle-print blouse.

"Thanks," she said. "How's the arm?"

"Still a bit sensitive, but it's on the mend."

"Have you heard anything from Mike?" she asked, looking from Whitlock to Kolchinsky.

Kolchinsky shook his head. "He said he'd call me in the morning, but he wanted to be alone tonight. I can understand that. Coming face to face with Bernard as he did this afternoon must have brought all the memories of Carrie and Mikey flooding back again."

"He'll be OK," Whitlock said with a reassuring smile when he noticed the look of uncertainty on her face.

"I know," she replied softly.

Kolchinsky finished his coffee then got to his feet. "I'll ring the President's room and find out if he's ready to see us yet."

Sabrina watched Kolchinsky cross to the reception desk then turned back to Whitlock. "Any news of Rosie?"

"No," Whitlock said grimly. "Bernard and Bailey are still refusing to cooperate with the authorities, and they're the only ones who know where Rosie's being held."

"I'm sorry, C.W. I only wish there were something I could do to help. I know how much Rosie means to you."

"She's the daughter I never had," Whitlock said with a sad smile. "Well, that's what Carmen says. Rosie and I have always been close. Eddie's never been much of a father to her. That's why she turns to me if she needs to talk to someone. Not that she bares her soul very often. She's like Mike—the maverick."

Kolchinsky returned and pressed the button for the lift. "The President's waiting for us."

They rode the lift to the thirtieth floor. Masala was waiting in the corridor for them. He ushered them into the lounge where Mobuto was seated, an open folder on the coffee table in front of him. Mobuto looked up and dismissed Masala with a flick of his hand.

"Good evening," Mobuto said, getting to his feet. "Is Mike Graham not with you?"

"Mike couldn't make it, I'm afraid," Sabrina replied. "He sends his apologies."

"You must be Sabrina Carver. I'm sorry I didn't get to meet you at the Trade Center this afternoon." Mobuto's eyes never left her face as he shook her hand. "David Tambese was right. You are beautiful."

"Thank you," she said, easing her hand gently from his lingering grip.

"How's your brother?" Kolchinsky asked, breaking the sudden silence.

"He left hospital this morning. He should be back at work in the next couple of days." Mobuto gestured toward the chairs. "Please, won't you sit down? Would anyone like a drink?"

They sat down but declined his offer.

"Do you mind if I smoke?" Kolchinsky asked.

"Not at all," Mobuto replied then crossed to the drinks cabinet and poured himself a small Scotch. "The reason I asked to see you tonight was so that I could thank you personally for all you've done for me, and my country, in these last three days. I thought it would be better if we met here rather than at the airport. It's sure to be teeming with reporters. And I know how much UNACO values its secrecy."

"We appreciate your discretion," Kolchinsky replied, reaching for an ashtray.

"I actually had a speech prepared for this moment but the more I thought about it, the more I realized just how pretentious that would have been." Mobuto looked at Whitlock. "You saved my life on more than one occasion. And that bullet could just as easily have killed you as winged you." He turned to Sabrina. "You and Mike pushed aside all thoughts of personal safety to help David get Remy out of Branco. You didn't have to do it, but you did. I owe the three of you a debt of gratitude that can never be repaid. Words seem very hollow at a time like this, but I can assure you that I shall be eternally grateful for what you did and for the professional way in which you did it. Thank you." He took two small red boxes, each no bigger than a compact case, from his pocket and handed them to Whitlock and Sabrina. Their names were written in gold lettering across the lids. They exchanged glances then carefully opened the boxes. Both contained a gold medallion with a portrait of Mobuto's face on one side and, on the reverse, an inscription bearing their names and the date of issue. "The Zimbalan Medal," he told them, "for outstanding bravery in the face of adversity. It's only ever been awarded half-a-dozen times in the last forty years. Those are the first to be issued bearing my face as the new President of Zimbala. And it's the first time the Zimbalan Medal has ever been awarded to a foreigner. I would be honored if you would accept them on behalf of my government and my people."

The UNACO Charter stipulated that no operative could accept any form of payment or gratuity from an individual, or from a government, which could be used to discredit the operative, or the organization, at a later date. But did a medal constitute such a gratuity? Whitlock and Sabrina looked at Kolchinsky, waiting for his reaction. He knew that if the medals were sold they could, theoretically, lead a trail back to UNACO. But these were two of his most dependable operatives, despite their deception of the past few days. They were hardly likely to pawn the medals. And he was also well aware that if he did have the medals returned, it would not only embarrass Mobuto in front of them, but also in front of his own government who had obviously agreed to let him present the medals in the first place. Although it was a delicate situation, he was satisfied that no part of the Charter would be breached under the circumstances. He nodded his consent. Both then thanked Mobuto for the honor that he, and his government, had bestowed upon them.

Mobuto removed a third box from his pocket and handed it to Sabrina. "That's for Mike Graham. Will you see that he gets it?"

"Of course," she replied, pocketing the box.

The telephone rang.

"Excuse me," Mobuto said, picking up the receiver. He spoke briefly in Swahili then replaced the receiver again. "The Zimbalan ambassador and his delegation have just arrived. You'll have to excuse me. I'm only sorry we didn't have more time to talk."

"I'll wait here and see the President to the airport," Kolchinsky said to Whitlock. "You and Sabrina can get started on your reports."

Whitlock looked at his watch. It was only another hour before Mobuto would be leaving for the airport. "If you're sure that's OK?"

"I wouldn't have offered if it wasn't," Kolchinsky shot back. "Now go on, you've got a long night ahead of you."

"It's been a pleasure to finally meet you, sir," Sabrina said, shaking Mobuto's hand.

"The pleasure's been all mine. And again, thank you." Mobuto turned to Whitlock. "I owe you my life, Clarence. And to a Zimbalan, that means I will be for ever in your debt. If there is ever anything I can do for you—"

"There is," Whitlock cut in.

"Name it," Mobuto replied, holding Whitlock's stare.

"Stop calling me Clarence!"

Mobuto chuckled and patted Whitlock on the back. "I'm sorry, it's just that I always knew you as Clarence when we were at Oxford together."

"We've both changed since then, but you more than me. And for the better, I might add."

"Insolent to the last," Mobuto said with a smile. "Goodbye, C.W."

"Goodbye, Mr. President," Whitlock replied then followed Sabrina to the door.

"Where do you want to work on the reports?" Sabrina asked, closing the door behind them.

"Eddie and Rachel are probably with Carmen at our apartment right now," Whitlock said as they walked to the lift. "It would save a lot of hassle if we could go to your place."

"Sure, as long as we can stop off for a take-out on the way over. I haven't eaten since I got off the plane this afternoon and I'm starving."

"I'm also a bit peckish now that you mention it," Whitlock said, stepping into the lift after her. "And as Sergei said, it's going to be a long night."

"Don't remind me," she said as the doors closed.

Kolchinsky arrived back at his apartment in the Bronx just before midnight. He switched on his answering machine then went through to the kitchen to make himself a coffee. There was only one message on the tape. He was to call Philpott as soon as he got home. He finished making the coffee then unhooked the receiver from his wallphone in the kitchen and rang Philpott's home number. Philpott answered it immediately.

"Malcolm, it's Sergei. I got your message. What's wrong?"

"I got a call from the police commissioner half an hour ago," Philpott told him. "Bailey, Bernard and Rogers were released without charge earlier this evening."

"On whose authority?" Kolchinsky asked, pulling up a stool and sitting down.

"It seems that Morgan Chilvers, the CIA Director, got on to the White House after I'd finished talking to him this afternoon. He spoke directly to the President who was adamant that he wanted to avoid a scandal at all costs, especially one involving a senior Agency figure like Bailey. But Bailey couldn't be released without the other two being released as well. So that's what happened."

"What about the murder charges against Bernard?"

"Overruled. The commissioner kicked up a big stink but as Chilvers pointed out, none of this was ever released to the press. They could afford a cover-up," Philpott replied angrily.

"Where is Bernard now?"

"I've no idea. I was only given the news after they were released. So there was no chance to put a tail on him."

Kolchinsky shook his head in frustration. "This is the sort of thing that used to happen in Russia twenty years ago."

"There is a slim chance of us picking up Bernard's trail again. We've got Rogers under surveillance at his house in Yorkville. It's my guess that Bailey will want Bernard out of the way as soon as possible before we can get to him. And he's sure to use Rogers or Brett to do the job."

"Where's Brett?"

"That's the problem. He's not at home. As I said, it's a slim chance. But I still think Rogers will come into it one way or the other. All we can do now is wait."

"What should I tell C.W.?"

"Nothing yet. Let's give Rogers some slack and see what he does with it. I'll call you if Rogers does make a move. Well, goodnight, Sergei."

"Night, Malcolm," Kolchinsky said softly and replaced the receiver.

THIRTEEN

Bernard parked the car out of sight of the house then, taking the Desert Eagle automatic from the glove compartment, he climbed out and, keeping to the dirt road, moved cautiously toward the house.

His clothes still stank from the stench of the cell where he had spent part of his eight hours in custody. It had felt like an eternity. He had always known that the CIA would have him released, even after he had been officially charged with the murders of the two policemen at the flat in Murray Hill. Not only could they not afford to let him go on trial for fear of what he would say, they also couldn't afford to let the detailed account of his CIA activities reach the *New York Times*. Either way they would have been crucified publicly. And he would have had no qualms about shooting his mouth off if they had left him to the mercy of the courts. A lawyer had been sent down from Washington to brief him on his rights while in custody. And to tell him to keep his mouth shut. He was to refuse to answer any questions, no matter how much the police provoked him. And they certainly tried, but to no avail. He had taken his lawyer's advice and remained silent.

He had been in his cell when the lawyer brought the news that he was free to go. An unconditional release, or so the lawyer had called it. He was just glad to get out. He had seen Bailey outside the precinct house, but both had wisely ignored each other. Bailey had disappeared into the back of a black limousine which had been sent to take him directly to La Guardia Airport where a chartered plane had been waiting to fly him back to Washington. Rogers had also ignored Bernard and caught a taxi at the end of the street. Bernard had ducked through several back alleys then, satisfied he had shaken off any tail, hailed a taxi which took him to Grand Central Station. He had picked up a key from the information desk, which he had left there on the day he arrived in New York, and gone directly to the corresponding locker. Inside was a black holdall containing a change of clothing, a Desert Eagle automatic and a set of keys for a hired Ford which was parked in a garage close to the station, an emergency backup for just such a situation. Again, he had made sure he wasn't being followed, then gone to the garage and driven to the safe house.

He reached the edge of the clearing and crouched down behind a tree. The hall light was on in the house. Not that it surprised him: Brett would already have been briefed, probably by Rogers, about their release from custody. But what else had he been told? Bernard knew he was probably overreacting. Why would Bailey have him killed, knowing that the lawyer would then hand the document over to the *New York Times?* It made no sense. But he still felt uneasy. He couldn't put his finger on the reason, and that's what worried him.

He kept close to the trees as he made his way round to the back of the house. He paused in the shadows to wipe his sweating forehead. The house was two hundred yards away and he would have to break cover to get to it. He could see a light on in the kitchen but the curtains were drawn. He inched his way round the perimeter of the wood until he was able to see the flight of steps that led down to the cellar at the side of the house. But he couldn't see the window beside the wooden door at the foot of the steps. He had left the window off the latch, and if Brett had primed the alarm system, it would be his only way into the house—unless Brett had latched it after he had left for the Trade Center. There was only one way of finding out.

He broke cover and sprinted toward the house. The automatic sensing security floodlight above the kitchen door detected his movement and bathed the area in bright, piercing light. He was still ten yards away from the steps when the back door was flung open and he hurled himself to the ground as Brett sprayed the clearing with a fusillade from his silenced Uzi. He got off a couple of shots, forcing Brett to take cover, and used those precious seconds to reach the steps where he paused, gasping for breath. He made his way to the bottom of the steps, continually glancing over his shoulder for any sign of Brett. He tugged at the window. It was locked! Then he saw the shadow fall across the steps above him. Brett had him cornered. And he didn't have time to turn and fire. He launched himself at the door, hitting it squarely with his shoulder. The lock buckled under the impact of the blow and the door flew open. He tumbled headlong into the darkened room as Brett raked the steps with another burst of gunfire. He fell heavily on his shoulder and the automatic clattered noisily to the floor.

Brett, hearing the noise, hurried down the steps and swiveled round, the Uzi clenched tightly in both hands. He saw the movement out of the corner of his eye and was still turning when Bernard brought the side of the spade down onto his head. Brett cried out in pain as he as slammed against the wall. The Uzi fell to the floor. Bernard kicked it away then picked up his automatic and trained it on Brett who was on his knees, his hand clenched over his ear. The blood seeped through his fingers and ran down the side of his face, soaking the collar of his light blue shirt.

"Did Bailey tell you to kill me?"

Brett looked up slowly, his face twisted in pain. "You were expendable, didn't you realize that?"

"Yes, that's why I covered myself by writing a detailed account of my CIA activities—"

"Which Bailey got from your lawyer friend a few days ago," Brett cut in, allowing himself a faint smile of satisfaction. "So when you didn't have a hold on the company any more, you became expendable."

"How did he know who I'd given it to?" Bernard demanded.

"We're a big organization, Bernard. We have moles everywhere. We managed to track down your friend to Cairo after you'd told Bailey about the document. I believe he put up quite a struggle before he died."

Brett made a desperate grab for the gun in Bernard's hand but Bernard sidestepped his clumsy lunge and shot him through the head. He closed the door, then propped the body against it to keep it shut.

He found a set of keys for the house in Brett's pocket then made his way across to a door that opened onto a flight of stairs which led up to the kitchen. The door at the top of the stairs was unlocked. He eased it open and stepped carefully into the kitchen. It was empty. He checked the rooms, apart from the bedroom where Rosie was being held. They, too, were empty. He moved to the bedroom and tried the handle. The door was locked. He cursed under his breath. He took the keys from his pocket, selected the one for the bedroom, then pressed himself against the wall as he unlocked the door. If Brett did have an accomplice in the bedroom, which he doubted, they would be sure to fire when the door was opened.

He pushed open the door and dived low through the

doorway, fanning the room with the automatic. Rosie was slumped in the corner of the room, her hand still manacled to the radiator. He scrambled to his feet and hurried over to where she lay, genuine concern in his eyes. He checked her pulse. It was steady. An over-turned mug lay on the floor beside her, the remains of the coffee having already formed a dark stain on the carpet. He lifted one of her eyelids. She had been drugged. He eased her onto her back, ensuring that she had some slack on her manacled wrist, then slipped a pillow under her head.

He looked at his watch. Twelve twenty A.M. How long before Brett's silence aroused suspicion? A couple of hours at the most. The chartered flight he'd arranged the previous day to take him to Cuba, where he would catch a connecting flight to the Lebanon, was only due to leave New York at five that morning. That left him with four-and-a-half hours to kill. He looked down at Rosie. She would be going with him, certainly as far as Cuba. Then she would be released, unharmed. He had no intention of killing her unless the authorities forced his hand. He doubted it would come to that. They would have to find him first. But for the moment she was exactly as he wanted her—unconscious. He still had some unfinished business to attend to before he left New York. That would take about an hour. Then he would come back for her and drive out to the field on the outskirts of the city to wait for the plane—and freedom. He smiled to himself then locked the bedroom door behind him and left the house. Brett's Audi Avant was parked in the driveway. He was momentarily tempted to use it then dismissed the thought and ran the three hundred yards to where the Ford was parked at the side of the dirt road. He started the engine, turned the car round, and headed back toward the highway.

◆　　◆　　◆

It took Bernard twenty minutes to reach his destination. He parked the car in a sidestreet. Then, after slipping the automatic into the back of his trousers, he walked the short distance to the main street. He looked around slowly. It was almost deserted—a couple returning from a late show, a drunk slumped against a wall. He waited until a car had driven past before crossing to the row of shops on the other side of the street. The windows were all protected by wire mesh and each building had a powerful alarm system in operation. He made his way to a shop near the end of the block, a firm of estate agents. It was actually a dubok—a company fronting for an intelligence agency, in this case, UNACO. And he had a duplicate set of keys for the reinforced back door. He had got them from Dave Forsythe. They had known each other since Forsythe's days as Bailey's electronic expert, and it was his knowledge from that time that had prompted them to put their heads together and come up with a way of making them both a lot of money. But Bernard's intentions were a lot more sinister than the merely financial, and Forsythe had no inkling of those intentions . . .

Bernard ducked up a narrow alley that ran parallel to the building and came out at the back of the shop. Although a security light illuminated the small courtyard, he knew there was nobody in the building. It was classified as a low-security risk. He took the two keys from his pocket and inserted them into the two locks, one at the top and one at the foot, of the metal door. An electronic circuit had been built into the two locks that would set off the alarm, both at the shop and at the command center, if the keys weren't turned simultaneously. He wiped his hands on his shirt then positioned himself in such a way as to be able to turn the keys together. He counted to three then turned the keys. The alarm remained silent. He exhaled deeply then removed the keys and entered the shop, closing the door behind him. Forsythe had told him that the computer suite was in a soundproofed room underneath the building. And the only means of access was through the manager's office. Bernard moved along the corridor and paused in front of a frosted glass door. He unlocked it with the third key Forsythe had duplicated for him.

Once inside, he went straight to the manager's safe and opened it using the combination that Forsythe had given him the previous day. He removed the sonic transmitter from the safe and activated the door built into the wall behind the desk. As it slid open, a light came on revealing a flight of stairs. He made his way to the foot of the stairs and used the sonic transmitter to open a second door.

The small room was dominated by a row of computers that ran the length of the far wall. He crossed to one of the terminals, sat down, and accessed the system. Then, using the Modem telephone link, he dialed out a number that Forsythe had given to him. He replaced the receiver in its special cradle on the VDU and tapped his fingers impatiently on the table as he waited for the program he'd dialed to appear on the screen. It came up moments later. He had hacked into Bailey's home computer. Forsythe had set up the whole system in Bailey's study, including all the access codes. But, for security reasons, Bailey had changed all the codes as soon as he took charge of the system. All the codes, that is, except for the one Forsythe had programmed in for himself. It bypassed all existing codes and went to the very heart of the program, showing all the new access codes. Forsythe, who had set up several sensitive systems for the CIA over the years, had a secret code for each one of them. And none could be detected. Bailey had several sensitive files in his system, files that even Morgan Chilvers knew nothing about. And now Bernard could access all those files, copy them onto another disc, and sell them to the highest bidder. The CIA and the KGB would be the obvious customers, but he didn't care whom he sold them to, as long as the price was right. He would split the money fifty-fifty with Forsythe. Had he known that Forsythe had been sacked from his position at UNACO, he could have negotiated a new deal. But that wasn't his style. Jean-Jacques Bernard wasn't a greedy man. He only needed the money to start a new life away from Beirut—a new face, a new identity. That was the deal he had made with Forsythe. But there was more to it than that, especially now that Bailey had sent his hatchet men after him.

Yes, there was certainly more to it than that. It was time for revenge.

Frances Bailey's eyes were red and puffy from hours of crying. But she had made sure she had sent her two teenage daughters over to her parents' house in Alexandria before she had shed the first of those tears. She had always been the perfect mother, and the perfect wife. Her friends had said that she would make an ideal First Lady when her husband was elected President of the United States of America. Their confidence in Robert Bailey, like her own, had never wavered. Now, within the space of a few hours, his career, and his future, lay in ruins. She was shattered. She was also bloody angry. It wasn't just his future that lay in ruins. What about their daughters? They would have to carry the stigma of their father's deceit with them for the rest of their lives. What right had he to blight their lives with his devious schemes? She knew Morgan Chilvers would do his utmost to keep her husband's arrest out of the papers, but it would already have circulated around Capitol Hill. And that's where it mattered as far as she was concerned. Samantha, the elder daughter, was already engaged to the son of a prominent Republican senator. What chance did they have now? And Kathleen had always wanted to become a political journalist on leaving school. And that meant mixing with politicians who would be the first to snigger behind her back at her father's misfortune. She had always idolized her husband. Now she hated him . . .

"Why?" she asked, looking up at her husband who stood by the window behind her.

"You wouldn't understand, Frances," he replied softly.

"Try me!" she snapped, jerking her head round to look at him.

"Zimbala's in a strategic position in the center of Africa. There are civil wars raging in all the neighboring states. If we could have put our own man in power, we could have fed weapons into Zimbala which, in turn, could have been distributed amongst the anti-Communist forces in those neighboring states. If we'd given them enough arms, it could have swung the wars in favor of those antiCommunist forces. We could have hammered another nail into the coffin of world Communism."

"Why couldn't you have tried to negotiate with Jamel Mobuto? He's a man of reason, a man of intelligence. That much was obvious from the way he came across on his visit to America."

"Jamel Mobuto's loyalty is to Zimbala. He'll do deals with whoever's prepared to help him, and that includes Russia and China."

"In other words, his loyalty is to his people, unlike your puppet Ngune. He was an animal, Robert. How many people were killed while he ran the Security Police?"

"Between them, Alphonse Mobuto and Tito Ngune kept Communism at bay in Zimbala for forty-five years. That's quite an achievement for a small African country."

"They kept it at bay with torture and murder. How could you have stood by a man like that?"

"Because he stood by me," Bailey replied, turning

away from the window. "Tito Ngune was one of the most loyal CIA operatives I've ever known."

"Well, I hope you were proud of *your* man, Robert. And I always thought you were a person who believed in the ideology of democracy. It shows just how much I really knew you." She got to her feet. "I've already packed a suitcase. It's in the car. I'll be at my parents until I've found my feet. We're finished, Robert."

Bailey didn't argue with her. He knew how futile that would be in her mood. He would call her in a few days, give her time to calm down.

"Aren't you even going to say anything?" she snapped scathingly.

"What's there to say? I said you wouldn't understand."

"No, I guess I didn't." She walked to the door then turned back to look at him. "I feel sorry for you, Robert. You're a pathetic, bigoted little man. God help this country if you'd ever reached the White House. Well, at least something good's come out of this, hasn't it?"

Bailey winced as she slammed the door behind her. The front door closed, followed moments later by the sound of an engine revving into life. The tires screeched as she spun the car round and headed toward the gate. He waited until the sound of the engine had faded into the distance then poured himself another bourbon before walking out into the corridor. His bodyguard, who was sitting discreetly at the end of the corridor, got to his feet. Bailey waved him away then climbed the stairs and crossed to the study door. He punched a code into the bellpush and the door slid open. He closed it behind him and sat down in front of the screen.

Bailey thought about the meeting he had had with Morgan Chilvers in the morning. He would be asked to resign. Failing that, he'd be fired. Chilvers had always been good to him. He was a naive man when it came to some of the more clandestine operations carried out by CIA personnel in both Africa and Central America and

Bailey was determined to destroy all those incriminating files before the auditors were sent in to analyze his system.

He switched on the computer and fed in his personal code. The words ACCESS DENIED flashed across the screen. He ran his hand through his hair and scratched the back of his head. Access denied? He stifled a yawn then shook his head. You're tired, Robert. Now concentrate this time. Feed in the right code this time. His fingers froze over the keyboard. He'd never made a mistake like that before. For a moment he wondered if somehow the access code had been tampered with by a professional hacker. He dismissed the thought. Why change the code? A hacker would be too busy reading the files. And even if the code had been altered, he could press the "9" button which would automatically cancel the whole program. That had been programmed into the system by Dave Forsythe. The man was an expert when it came to computers. He cursed himself for his suspicion. You pressed a wrong key, for God sake. Try again, slowly this time.

He pressed each key carefully then immediately put his finger lightly on the "9," just in case he did need to use it. ACCESS DENIED. He pressed the "9" button. Nothing happened. The door sealed behind him and the ten-second countdown began flashing on the screen. He pressed the "9" frantically. Someone had overridden it. He kicked over the chair and ran to the door, banging furiously on it. But the whole room was soundproofed. Nobody could hear him. He looked round at the screen again, knowing he was going to die. The countdown finished and the word ACTIVATE began flashing across the screen.

A jet of nerve gas streamed from the nozzle of the canister built into the wall directly above the door. He stumbled away and fell to the floor. Saliva bubbled on his lips and he clawed desperately at his throat as he struggled to breathe. It felt as if his chest were about to burst. His breathing became increasingly ragged as his body twisted uncontrollably on the floor. The spasms ended with a final shudder then his head lolled to the side. His breathing stopped.

The message, which had appeared on the screen as Bailey lay dying on the floor, was still there the following morning when the body was discovered: TO BE TERMINATED AFTER THE ASSASSINATION OF JAMEL MOBUTO.

FOURTEEN

Jack Rogers sat in his favorite armchair by the window, his hand resting lightly on the telephone. His mind was in turmoil. He'd lost count of the number of times he'd called the safe house in the last hour. And always the same. He picked up the receiver and dialed the number again. Still no reply. He looked at his watch. It was already one fifteen in the morning. Where was Brett? Why hadn't he called? Had Bernard got to him?

Rogers slipped on his shoulder holster then pulled on his jacket over it. He checked his Smith & Wesson then holstered it. He picked up the car keys off the hall table and left the house, closing the door silently behind him. He shivered as he walked down the footpath to the gate. But it wasn't cold—an omen? He dismissed the idea. He didn't believe in that nonsense. He got into his Fiat and started the engine. Then, after checking the side mirror, he pulled out into the road.

Dave Swain, a former presidential bodyguard, had been with UNACO for five years. He was the leader of

Strike Force Seven. He sat behind the wheel of a Mazda which was parked fifty yards away from the Rogers's house. He'd been there since ten thirty the previous evening. Philpott's orders. An empty coffee carton lay beside the half-eaten hamburger on the dashboard. The radio was on and he was tapping his fingers on the wheel to the beat of the music when Rogers emerged from the house. He immediately radioed in to the command center to let them know that Rogers was on the move. He switched off the radio and activated the tracking device on the seat beside him. It would pick up the signal from the homer he had attached to the underside of the Fiat. He gave Rogers a thirty-second start then followed him at a discreet distance.

The man in the black Sedan, which was parked at the end of the street, stubbed out his cigarette then started up the engine and followed the Mazda.

The telephone rang.

Kolchinsky rolled over in bed and patted the bedside table with his hand until he found the receiver.

"Sergei?"

"Yes," Kolchinsky replied sleepily. "Malcolm, is that you?"

"Yes," Philpott replied. "I've just had a call from the duty officer at the command center. Dave Swain followed Rogers to a house off the Garden State Parkway. Rogers parked out of sight of the house and approached it on foot. Then Dave heard a burst of gunfire. When he went to investigate he saw Rogers lying in a clearing close to the house."

"Where's David now?"

"He's got the house under surveillance. I don't want him to do anything until we get reinforcements to the area."

"Who are you bringing in? Strike Force Seven?"

"No, Strike Force Three. It's their operation. I've already told the duty officer to call C.W., Mike and Sabrina. They're meeting you outside the UN in twenty minutes. I'm going on ahead to talk to Dave."

"I'm on my way," Kolchinsky said, pulling the duvet to one side.

"I've sent a car over to pick you up," Philpott told him. "It should be with you in a few minutes."

"Thanks, Malcolm."

"See you at the house," Philpott replied then the line went dead.

Kolchinsky replaced the receiver, stifled a yawn, then hauled himself to his feet. He took a cigarette from the packet on the bedside table, lit it, then got dressed and went outside to wait for the car.

"What the hell are they doing here?" Graham demanded angrily, pointing to the row of police cars parked at the entrance to the approach road that led to the safe house.

"We're about to find out," Sabrina replied, braking gently as a policeman stepped out into the road and waved down the car. She stopped beside him and opened her window. "What's going on?"

"Who are you?" the policeman demanded.

Kolchinsky, who was sitting in the passenger seat, reached across to show his ID card. The policeman checked it then looked at Graham and Whitlock, who were sitting in the back of the car, before handing the card back to Kolchinsky.

"You can go through," the policeman said to Sabrina.

"You still haven't told us what the hell's going on?" Graham snapped. "What are you guys doing here?"

"There's a senior SWAT officer down there," the policeman replied, pointing to the approach road. "He'll brief you."

"There's a SWAT team here?" Kolchinsky said incredulously. "That's all we need."

Sabrina engaged the gears and turned down the approach road.

"There's the Colonel," Kolchinsky said, pointing to Philpott who was standing with Swain beside a SWAT van.

Sabrina pulled up behind the van then climbed out of her car and smiled at Philpott. "It's good to see you back on your feet, sir. How are you feeling?"

"I was feeling fine until I got here." Philpott gestured around him. "It's like a bloody circus."

"What's going on, sir?" Graham asked, closing the back door behind him.

Philpott shot Swain a dirty look. "Dave was followed by one of the SWAT boys. That's why they're here. I'll see you in my office tomorrow morning, nine o'clock sharp."

Swain nodded sullenly then walked to his Mazda and got behind the wheel. He started the engine then turned the car round and drove back toward the highway.

Philpott turned to Whitlock. "I spoke to Bernard on the phone soon after I got here. He's got Rosie in there."

"Is she alright?" Whitlock asked anxiously.

"Yes. He let me speak briefly to her. She's fine, considering the circumstances. She's a remarkable girl, C.W. You should be very proud of her."

"She's a great kid," Whitlock replied. "Has Bernard made any demands yet?"

"Not yet."

"What about Rogers?" Kolchinsky asked.

"Dead. Bernard let the SWAT team take the body away . . ." Philpott trailed off as an unmarked police car turned into the approach road. "Well, this is a surprise."

"Who is it, sir?" Sabrina asked.

"Sean Hagen, Deputy Commissioner of the NYPD. What brings him out at this ungodly hour?"

Hagen waited until the driver opened the door for him then climbed out. He was wearing a grey overcoat over his suit and had a trilby tucked firmly over his head.

"I didn't realize you had such little confidence in your men, Sean," Philpott said as Hagen approached him.

"The SWAT unit falls directly under my command," Hagen replied, digging his hands into his pockets. "Who do you think ordered the tail on your man? It's the only way we could find Bernard again. Like you, we lost him when he was released from custody."

"And now you've come to supervise his execution, is that it?" Philpott said coldly.

"I'm here to liaise with my men," Hagen shot back angrily. "What's UNACO doing here?"

"This is still a UNACO operation, Sean. And that puts me in overall command. I want your SWAT team out of here. Their presence is putting Rosie Kruger's life in danger."

"I can't do that, Malcolm. Rosie Kruger was kidnapped here in New York. This is our jurisdiction. I've already spoken to Lieutenant Stephens, the officer in charge of the SWAT team, and he's indicated that, because of the situation, he's prepared to work with UNACO to help secure the release of Miss Kruger. But that's as far as it goes. They won't be pulled out until this situation's been resolved."

"This has got nothing to do with jurisdictions, has it, Sean?" Kolchinsky said, struggling to contain his anger. "You don't give a damn about Rosie, do you? All you're interested in is avenging the death of the two officers Bernard shot at the apartment. You're still smarting from what happened tonight. And now that you know he'll never be allowed to stand trial, it only leaves you with one alternative. You'll have to kill him."

"That may be the way they do it in Russia, Sergei, but not in this country," Hagen said after a moment's silence. "I want to see Miss Kruger released, unharmed, just as much as you do. And with that in mind, I'm prepared to go in there and negotiate with Bernard on a one-to-one basis. I'm sure we can resolve this situation without bloodshed."

"Who's to say that Bernard will even want to talk to you?" Philpott countered.

"There's only one way to find out," Hagen replied then rapped on the back of the van. The door was opened from the inside and he gave the order to get Bernard on the line. He waited until the communications officer had got through before climbing into the back of the van and taking the receiver from him. "Bernard?"

"Yes. Who's that?"

"My name's Hagen. I'm the Deputy Commissioner of the New York Police Department."

"Sean Hagen. I am honored."

"You know me?" Hagen retorted.

"Of you," Bernard replied. "What do you want?"

"To talk. In person."

"Why?"

"I would have thought that was obvious," Hagen said, glancing at Philpott. "I want to resolve this without bloodshed."

"That makes two of us," There was a lengthy pause. "Come in alone. Unarmed. The door will be unlocked. But I warn you, Hagen, any attempt by your SWAT team to storm the house and Rosie dies. I don't have anything to lose, not any more."

"No attempt will be made to storm the house, you have my word on that."

The line went dead.

Hagen replaced the receiver and climbed out of the

van. "He's agreed to see me. At least it's a start. Do you know where I can find Lieutenant Stephens? I want to have a word with him before I go in."

"He's with his men on the edge of the clearing," Philpott answered.

"Thank you," Hagen said.

"Excuse me, sir," the communications officer called out after Hagen. "Do you want me to make up a wire for you?"

"Yes, good idea," Hagen replied then walked toward the wood.

Philpott was about to shout a warning about the animal traps when Hagen stopped abruptly as he neared the edge of the wood. He nodded to himself, then turned away and continued walking down the road.

Kolchinsky noticed the frown crease Philpott's brow. "What is it, Malcolm?"

"Nothing," Philpott replied with a dismissive shrug.

Philpott watched Hagen until he disappeared from sight around a bend in the road. Why had he suddenly changed his mind about entering the wood? Why would he purposely take the long way round to reach the clearing? Did he already know about the animal traps? It seemed unlikely as Stephens had only been told about them when one of his men had almost stood on one. And Philpott only knew about them through Stephens. He knew there was probably a logical explanation for Hagen's actions but he still felt uneasy. It was a feeling he couldn't seem to shake off.

"The only way Bernard leaves that house is in a body bag. Understood?"

No, Mark Stephens didn't understand. And what the hell was Hagen doing there anyway? Stephens, who was in his early thirties, had been with the NYPD's SWAT unit for five years, the last eighteen months of those as a lieutenant. He had been trained to deal with hostage situations. It was his job. And now his authority was being undermined by Hagen's interference. But what could he do? Hagen was officially the commander-in-chief of the NYPD's SWAT unit. And that meant his word was law. He knew the men, himself included, held Hagen in contempt—a desk man who only ever showed his solidarity with them when they were being praised for a successful operation.

"I asked you a question, Lieutenant," Hagen said sharply.

Stephens removed his black peaked cap and ran his hand over his short blond hair. "That depends on the circumstances, sir."

"What circumstances?"

"If we can get a clear shot at him. There's a sixteen-year-old kid in there as well. Her safety is my main concern."

"Your main concern is preventing Bernard from leaving the house alive."

"Sir, he has hostage—"

"I don't give a damn about his hostage," Hagen cut in, his eyes blazing. "She's a drug addict, for Christ's sake. What's her life compared to the lives of the two officers that son-of-a-bitch gunned down in cold blood? I had to break the news to their wives. Spare a thought for them, Lieutenant. And spare a thought for those kids who'll never see their fathers again."

Stephens had never seen Hagen so agitated. It was unnerving. What the hell had got into him? He knew the rules. And now he was willing to bend and twist them in some warped pursuit of revenge. Stephens wanted nothing to do with it, even if it meant losing his command. He wouldn't be party to killing an innocent teenager.

"Think about it, Lieutenant. Your future in this unit may depend on it. I'll try and talk Bernard into releasing the girl, but if he refuses, then the order will be given to storm the house. And if you won't give it, I will. Now give me that bullhorn.''

Stephens bit back his fury and handed Hagen the bullhorn he was holding. He looked around. At least his men were out of earshot. He certainly wouldn't give the order to storm the house, not without first hearing Bernard's demands. But would his men stand by him? Hagen could have them all suspended for insubordination. Was it worth putting his men's careers at risk? He suddenly found himself caught in two minds, and he hated himself for it.

"Bernard, I'm coming in," Hagen shouted through the bullhorn. "I'll be unarmed. And alone." He handed the bullhorn back to Stephens. "Think about your future, Lieutenant. Who knows, there could even be a promotion in it for you."

Stephens bit his lip to prevent himself from telling Hagen where to shove his promotion. Instead he unclipped his two-way radio from his belt and told his men that Hagen was about to approach the house, adding that if any of them got a clear shot of Bernard they were to take him out. He knew it was wishful thinking. The man was very professional. And professionals rarely make mistakes. Hagen removed his overcoat and hat then stepped out into the clearing and walked slowly toward the house.

Stephens looked round as Philpott and Whitlock appeared behind them. Philpott nodded in greeting then introduced Whitlock as Rosie's uncle. Stephens wondered how they would have reacted if he told them what Hagen had in mind if he failed to persuade Bernard to surrender. Some chance of that happening anyway! How he hoped he was wrong . . .

Hagen reached the gate and paused to look at the house. It was in complete darkness, as it had been ever since the SWAT team took up their positions on the edge of the clearing. The gate squeaked as he opened it. Well, now Bernard would definitely know he was there. He walked up the path and was about to mount the steps to the porch when the outside light came on. He froze mid-step, his eyes riveted on the closed door, waiting. He remained like that for several seconds, almost as if in a trance, then climbed the steps and moved slowly to the door. He was about to try the handle then thought he'd better warn Bernard that it was him, and not one of the SWAT team. He knocked on the door.

"Bernard, it's Hagen."

"It's open," came the reply from inside the house.

Hagen pushed the handle down and opened the door. The light from the porch illuminated the hallway. He stepped inside, almost reluctant to close the door behind him. The light was his sanctuary.

"Close the door," Bernard called out from the lounge at the end of the hallway.

Hagen closed the door, severing the light. He had lost his sanctuary.

"I've got the girl with me, Hagen," Bernard said. "Any tricks and she's dead. Now switch on the hall light and step away from the door."

Hagen did as he was told.

Bernard emerged from the lounge alone, the Desert Eagle in his hand. It was aimed at Hagen's stomach.

"Where's the girl?" Hagen demanded.

"Safe," Bernard replied, moving toward Hagen. He locked the door then frisked Hagen quickly and professionally.

"I told you I was unarmed," Hagen said once Bernard had finished.

"So you did," Bernard replied with a sneer.

"I want to see the girl."

"She's in there," Bernard replied, pointing to the bedroom. "And don't switch on the light."

Hagen opened the bedroom door. Rosie, who had regained consciousness less than an hour earlier, was still manacled to the radiator. She had been gagged. She stared at Hagen, her eyes wide and questioning.

"I'm Deputy Commissioner Hagen, Rosie. We're doing everything in our power to try and secure your release. Don't worry, we won't let anything happen to you."

"How touching. Now close the door."

"Hold in there, Rosie," Hagen said with a reassuring smile then closed the door again. "Let's talk in the lounge, shall we?"

"Sure," Bernard replied with a shrug. "But no lights. We'll manage with the reflection from the hall light. After you, Hagen."

Hagen glanced at the automatic in Bernard's hand then reluctantly turned his back on him and entered the lounge. He made for the armchair by the window and sat down.

"I assume you're carrying a mike of some sort," Bernard said from the doorway. "The tie-pin?"

"No."

"No, you're not wired, or no it's not the tie-pin?"

"Both."

"Why don't I believe you?" Bernard said then shrugged. "But then it doesn't bother me whether you're wired or not. It might just backfire on you, though."

"What?" Hagen said with a frown.

"Drink?" Bernard said, indicating the drinks cabinet against the far wall.

"Yes," Hagen said, nodding slowly. "Bourbon, if you have one."

"Of course," Bernard replied, crossing the room to the drinks cabinet.

"What did you mean just now about its backfiring on me if I were wired?" Hagen asked.

Bernard used his free hand to pour the drink then placed it on the table beside Hagen's chair. He crossed to the door then turned his back momentarily on Hagen and looked out into the hallway. When he swung round Hagen was clawing desperately at the underside of the chair.

"Looking for this?" Bernard said, taking a Smith & Wesson from his pocket. "Good place to hide a gun for an emergency, but I found it when I first got here. Question is, how did you know there was supposed to be a gun holstered under that particular chair? A chair that you made for as soon as you entered the room. Now, if you are wired, which I'm sure you are, your colleagues are no doubt waiting for you to clear up this obvious misunderstanding. Well?"

"I don't know what you're talking about," Hagen said, fidgeting nervously with his tie-pin.

"So I was right, it is the tie-pin," Bernard said with a knowing smile. "I'd say you were in a catch-twenty-two situation right now. If you discard the mike, it's obviously a sign of guilt. But if you leave it on, your colleagues are going to find out how you knew the location of the gun. It's your choice, Hagen. Or should I call you Seabird?"

The blood drained from Hagen's face and his hand was trembling when he picked up the glass from the table. He drank it down in one gulp.

"Lost for words?" Bernard said, sitting down on the sofa. "I can understand that. You certainly had me fooled. I thought Bailey was Seabird. I guess it was a natural assumption to make under the circumstances. But there it was when I hacked into Bailey's personal computer earlier tonight: a whole file about Seabird. None other than the Deputy Commissioner of the New York Police Department, Sean Matthew Hagen. It certainly surprised me. But it makes sense when you think about it. Bailey's inside man at the NYPD, a future police commissioner. Quite a *coup* for him. You were the one who had Forsythe bug UNACO headquarters, weren't you? Not Bailey. And you would have arranged my escape had I been arrested after I'd killed

Mobuto. You recruited Mason to help me at the Trade Center. Who would have questioned your decision to put Mason in charge of the police support-team on the catwalk? Clever, Hagen. Very clever. And you'd have got away with it as well if I hadn't managed to access those files that Bailey had hidden away in the depths of his home computer. Fascinating reading. I've got it all on disc in case you're still thinking of trying to bluff your way out of this. Call it an insurance policy—a very expensive insurance policy." He shook his head slowly. "Seabird. Who would have guessed?"

Hagen swallowed nervously and wiped the back of his hand across his clammy forehead. He tired to speak but his mouth was dry. He got to his feet and moved slowly, pathetically, to the drinks cabinet. His shoulders were hunched, his head drooping. He poured himself a stiff bourbon and gulped it down.

"You came here tonight to kill me, didn't you? Brett failed, so did Rogers. So it was left to you. What were you going to do? Make out that you managed to disarm me then shoot me with the Smith & Wesson? Then, by pocketing the Desert Eagle, you could have made out that I had the Smith & Wesson all along? Am I right?"

"You're a dead man, Bernard. Even if you do manage to get away from here, they'll find you. They won't stop looking for you."

'They' being the CIA?"

'They' being the CIA's top assassins. You're good, Bernard, but you're not in their league."

"No, probably not. But I've made plans to cover for that eventuality." Bernard got to his feet. "Well, I think you've outstayed your welcome, Hagen. I'm sure there are some people out there who'll want some answers, starting with UNACO. I bet they're pretty pissed off with you right now."

Hagen hurled the empty glass at Bernard. It missed him by inches and smashed against the wall. Hagen then grabbed the bottle of bourbon and lunged at

Bernard. Bernard ducked as Hagen lashed out wildly with the bottle and caught him with a vicious punch to the kidney. Hagen stumbled back against the door and the bottle fell to the floor.

Bernard levelled the automatic at Hagen. "Come to think of it, there would just be another cover-up, wouldn't there? Like there was today. You'd be pensioned off quietly and that would be the end of it. No, you're not going to get off that lightly. See you in hell, Hagen."

Bernard shot Hagen through the chest. The force of the bullet slammed him back against the wall. The blood bubbled in his mouth and ran down his chin as he slid slowly to the floor, leaving a streak on the wall above him.

Bernard dialed the number of the telephone in the SWAT van. "Let me speak to Colonel Philpott," he said when it was answered.

"This is Philpott," came the response seconds later.

"I take it you heard our little conversation, Colonel?"

"Is Hagen dead?" Philpott demanded.

Bernard looked down at the crumpled figure by the door. "It certainly looks that way. But I wouldn't lose any sleep over it. He would have been immune from prosecution, just like me. Don't even think of doing anything silly now, Colonel, like sending in the stormtroopers. Rosie would be the first to die. Do I make myself clear?"

"Perfectly," Philpott hissed.

Bernard looked at his watch. Two seventeen A.M. Still two-and-a-half hours before he was due to leave for Cuba. It would only be a matter of time before the SWAT team discovered the broken cellar door. And the door connecting the cellar and the kitchen was only protected by a flimsy bolt. No, it wasn't safe here any more. He would have to rethink his strategy. "Stay by the phone, Philpott. I'll call you again in a few minutes."

"Is Rosie—"

Bernard cut the connection before Philpott had time to finish. He left the receiver off the hook then crossed to the sideboard and opened the bottom drawer. Inside was a second telephone, a scrambled line. He placed it on the sideboard then sat down and dialed a number he had already committed to memory. It was answered immediately.

"It's Columbus," Bernard said.

"What is it?" came the suspicious reply.

"The plans have been changed. Is the plane refuelled and ready for take-off?"

"It's been ready since yesterday. What's happened?"

Bernard explained the situation briefly. "You told me you can fly anything, right?"

"Yeah," came the hesitant reply.

"Helicopter?"

"Sure. I flew them in 'Nam."

"I want you to get over here as fast as you can. I'll arrange to have a helicopter on standby. You can fly us to the plane then we can get out of here."

"Come over there? Are you crazy?"

"Listen, Demerest, you've been well paid for your troubles—if anything, overpaid. But believe me, if I go down you're coming with me. You'll be inside for a long stretch."

"I want a Huey," Demerest said after a lengthy pause. "It's the chopper I know best."

"I'll arrange it," Bernard replied.

"You said there were cops there. How the hell am I supposed to get past them?"

"What car will you be driving?"

"A Datsun."

"Color?"

"Light blue."

"I'll see to it that you aren't stopped. When you get

here, drive round to the back of the house. Park as close to the back door as you can, understood?"

"Understood," Demerest replied. "If this back-fires . . ."

"It won't, as long as you play by my rules," Bernard said then dropped the receiver back into its cradle.

Philpott hung up after he'd finished talking to Bernard then looked at the others who had congregated outside the van. "He's threatened to kill Rosie unless we get him a helicopter by three o'clock. It has to be a Huey. He was very insistent on that."

"We've got a Huey at Newark Airport," Kolchinsky said.

"Can you fly it?"

Kolchinsky nodded. He'd flown almost every heli-copter imaginable since he'd got his license when he was still with the KGB.

Philpott looked at Stephens. "We could have it here by three."

"Yeah, sure," Stephens replied absently. He was still stunned by what he'd heard minutes earlier over the loudspeaker in the back of the van. Hagen worked for Bailey—a CIA stooge. Much as he had disliked the man, he wouldn't have believed it unless he'd heard it with his own ears. The son-of-a-bitch!

"I'll get over to the airport straight away," Kolchinsky said. "Will you clear everything with the necessary people?"

"Yes, don't worry about that," Philpott replied. "Sabrina, take Sergei in your car."

"I'll get one of the police cars to take me," Kolchinsky said. "With the siren on, it won't take us long to reach the airport."

"It'll be even quicker in Sabrina's car. It's fast and she knows how to handle it. I'll see to it that you're given a free passage to the airport."

Sabrina held up the keys and grinned at Kolchinsky. "Well, what are we waiting for?"

Kolchinsky shot Philpott a despairing look then hurried after her.

"I have some calls to make," Philpott said then indicated the telephone in front of him. "May I use it?"

"Yes, of course," Stephens replied.

"They are private calls," Philpott said to the communications officer who was hovering behind him.

Stephens nodded to the communications officer who climbed down the metal steps and closed the door behind him. He waited until the man was out of earshot then told Whitlock what Hagen had said before he went into the house.

"It makes sense," Whitlock said thoughtfully. "But I doubt he cared any more about those two officers than he did about Rosie. He'd obviously been sent here by Bailey to kill Bernard. That's why he was so insistent that Bernard leaves the house in a body bag. Bernard knows too much about the CIA and their operations."

"Hagen was right about the CIA sending an assassination squad after Bernard, especially now that he's got the disc," Stephens said. "That would be sure to blow the lid off some of the CIA's most covert operations if it were ever made public."

"Which is exactly why I think he'll be given a wide berth from now on, at least until the disc's been recovered," Whitlock replied. "Bernard's nobody's fool. He'll have stashed the disc away somewhere safe so that if the CIA do hit him, it'll be made public. And that's the last thing Bailey would want to happen."

"I'd have to go along with C.W. on that," Graham said. "Bailey can't afford to have those files made public, even if he has left the CIA by then. The whole point of their release tonight was to cover up a potential scandal. But if this is made public, he won't be able to hide behind the cover-up any more. There would be a public outcry if those responsible weren't brought to trail, starting with Bailey."

"You're forgetting one thing. He still has to leave the house to get to the helicopter," Stephens said, looking at each of them in turn. "If any of my men gets a clear shot, they'll take him out. Those are their orders. Then let's see what happens to Mr. Bailey and his precious files."

"If anything happens to Rosie as a direct result of your team you can be sure I'll come after you," Whitlock said in a soft, menacing voice. "You bear that in mind, Lieutenant."

"These men are highly trained, Mr. Whitlock," Stephens shot back defensively. "They'll only fire if they're one hundred percent sure of hitting their target."

"For your sake, I hope you're right," Whitlock said then walked back toward the van.

It was a side of Whitlock that Graham had never seen before—cold, cynical, threatening. He hadn't realized until then just how close Whitlock was to Rosie. Had he not known better, he would have sworn that Whitlock was her father, not just her uncle. He smiled sadly to himself. Whitlock would make a great father. Well, perhaps one day. Hell, he was only in his mid-forties. Yeah, a great father . . .

Philpott removed a pair of headphones and placed them on the table in front of him. "Sergei's on his way. He should get here within the next ten minutes."

Whitlock looked at his watch. Two forty-six A.M. "Is Sabrina with him?"

"No, she driving back. If she were to suddenly emerge from the helicopter after it landed, Bernard might think it was some sort of trap. I don't care how much of a professional he is, right now he'll be on edge. It's only natural with a dozen highly trained snipers just waiting for him to make a mistake. So there's no use in adding to the tension."

Whitlock sat down next to Philpott and looked across at Graham who was sitting on the top step, his back against the open door, sipping hot coffee from a plastic cup.

Graham sensed he was being watched and glanced round at Whitlock. "You should try the coffee sometime. In fact, have this one."

Whitlock smiled as Graham extended the plastic cup toward him. "That good, huh?"

"Hell, no," Graham retorted then tossed the remainder of the coffee into the bushes behind the van. "Why is bad coffee always associated with cops? Making a drinkable cup of coffee should be part of their basics."

Philpott smiled faintly then picked up the receiver and dialed the house. Bernard answered. "You told me to let you know when the helicopter was on its way."

"Is it a Huey?" Bernard demanded.

"Yes. Where do you want it to land?"

"As close to the house as possible. Then your pilot's to shut down the engine, switch off all lights, and withdraw. I'm using my own pilot. He's on his way over here now. He'll be driving a light blue Datsun. He's not to be stopped. Is that clear?"

"Quite clear," Philpott replied contemptuously. "When will Rosie be released?"

"When I'm satisfied I haven't been tricked by either you or the CIA. Strange as it may seem, Colonel, I don't want to see her hurt any more than you do. She's a great kid. Don't make me do something we'll all regret."

"How will I know when you've released her?"

"You'll be the first to know, Colonel, you can be sure of that."

Then the line went dead.

◆   ◆   ◆

Bernard glanced at his watch as he heard the sound of the helicopter in the distance. Two fifty-seven A.M. Good timing. He switched off the hall light then went into the front bedroom and, pressing himself against the wall, tweaked back the curtain and peered cautiously out across the clearing. Although it was in darkness he knew the SWAT team would be positioned on the edge of the wood, their sniper rifles fitted with the latest in high-tech infra-red sights. He couldn't afford to make the slightest mistake or they'd cut him down without a moment's hesitation. It seemed to give him added confidence. No cop was going to kill him.

The helicopter suddenly appeared from behind the wood and came to within a few feet of the front gate before descending carefully to the ground. Kolchinsky cut the engine, switched off the lights, then unstrapped himself and got out. He looked toward the house then turned away and strode briskly to where Philpott was waiting for him at the edge of the clearing. Bernard let the curtain fall back into place then left the room. Philpott had kept his side of the bargain, so where the hell was Demerest?

Warren Demerest touched the brakes when he saw the row of police cars in the distance, their lights flashing menacingly in the semidarkness. He took the balaclava off the dashboard and pulled it over his head then continued for another hundred yards to where a policeman stood in the middle of the road, a flashlight in his hand. He shone the flashlight into the car. The beam lingered on the balaclava. Demerest swallowed nervously. What if Bernard had already been caught or killed? Jesus, he'd never thought of that. Another conviction and they'd throw away the key. Well, that's what the governor had told him when he'd been released from San Quentin at the beginning of the year. The policeman, who had been instructed by Stephens to let the car through, stepped back and pointed to the approach road. Demerest put the car into gear and headed down it. He passed the van and several members of the SWAT team in their black uniforms. They were all armed. What the hell had Bernard got him into here? Well, it was too late to turn back now. He turned up the narrow driveway at the side of the house, just as Bernard had instructed, and drove round the back, pulling up within a foot of the back door. What the hell was he supposed to do now? Stay in the car? Go into the house? Where was Bernard?

The door opened fractionally. "Kill the lights," Bernard hissed from inside.

Demerest switched off the lights.

"Get in here!" Bernard snapped.

Demerest climbed out of the car and slipped into the kitchen. Bernard had handcuffed himself to Rosie. He held the automatic in his free hand.

"Hey, man, careful with that thing," Demerest said nervously, indicating the automatic which was pointed at his midriff.

"Take off the balaclava," Bernard said softly.

Demerest pulled it off to reveal his face. He was in his late thirties with cropped brown hair and a gold sleeper in his left ear. "Satisfied?" he said sharply.

"Get that blanket," Bernard said pointing to the blanket on the table. "Drape it over Rosie and me then lead us out to the car. "We'll ride in the back. They won't risk a shot if they can't see me."

Demerest tugged the balaclava back over his face then, glancing quickly at Rosie, unfolded the blanket and covered them with it. Bernard pulled Rosie to him and pressed the automatic into her ribs. She winced as the barrel dug into her but said nothing. She wouldn't give Bernard the satisfaction of knowing he was hurting her.

"Let's go," Bernard snapped from under the blanket.

Demerest wiped the sweat from his face. He knew

there would be rifles trained on the back door. What if they opened fire when he opened it?

"Demerest, what the hell's going on?" Bernard snarled. "I said, let's go."

"OK," Demerest replied irritably.

He eased the door open and held his breath as he stepped outside. No gunfire. So far, so good. He grabbed Bernard's arm through the blanket and led them to the car. He opened the back door. Bernard kept Rosie close to him as he ducked into the back seat, making it impossible for the snipers to distinguish between the shapes under the blanket. Demerest slammed the door shut behind them. He got in behind the wheel and looked in the rear-view mirror. Bernard and Rosie were lying on the back seat, the blanket over them. No sniper would risk a shot. Demerest still felt vulnerable. They could take him out at any time—one bullet, that's all it would take.

"Start the car, dammit!" Bernard shouted. "And no lights."

Demerest muttered an apology as he grated the gears. His hands were shaking. He tried again. This time he found first gear. He turned the car round and headed back down the driveway but instead of branching off onto the approach road he headed toward the silhouette of the Huey on the edge of the clearing.

"Park as close as you can to the helicopter," Bernard told him.

Demerest pulled up beside the cabin door and killed the engine. He climbed out of the car and glanced toward the wood. He could see some figures standing in the shadows. Obviously not from the SWAT team. They would be invisible in their black uniforms. That only unnerved him even more. How many unseen guns were aimed at him at that very moment? He pushed the thought from his mind. He was scared enough as it was. He pulled open the cabin door and peered inside. There was a small set of metal steps close to the door.

He unhooked them from the wall and placed them in front of the door.

"Ready," he told Bernard through the open driver's window.

"Open the back door."

Demerest did so and Bernard wriggled backwards, taking Rosie with him. A hand pushed her head down as she felt her foot touch the ground. The hand remained on her head until she was out of the car.

"There's some steps in front—"

A bullet ricocheted off the side of the helicopter, inches above Demerest's head. Bernard froze as he forced himself not to pull the trigger. He felt Rosie's body stiffen against his. She closed her eyes, waiting for him to kill her. Demerest was down on one knee, his eyes wide with fear. They heard the shouted order from the direction of the wood. Then silence.

"Bernard?" Stephens yelled through the bullhorn. "Don't harm the girl. It was an accident. There'll be no more shooting."

Bernard winced as the sweat seeped into his eyes. He eased his finger off the trigger but kept the automatic pressed into her ribs. He heard himself sigh. It had been that close. He'd so nearly lost his ace.

"Demerest?" he hissed. "Demerest?"

"I'm here," Demerest said, straightening up.

"Lead us to the steps," Bernard ordered.

Demerest took Bernard's arm through the blanket and talked them up the steps into the back of the helicopter. He kicked the steps away, slammed the door shut then scrambled into the cockpit and started up the engine.

Bernard discarded the blanket and, careful to remain flat on the cabin floor, he unlocked the handcuff from his wrist and secured it around a metal pipe that ran the length of the wall. He wiped the sweat from his face and inhaled sharply as his thumb brushed against the wound above his eye. "How long before we can take off?" he called out to Demerest.

"Almost ready," came the reply.

Bernard allowed himself a faint smile of satisfaction. He looked across at Rosie. She stared back at him, her face expressionless.

Then the helicopter began to rise.

Graham and Whitlock had used the cover of darkness to slip away unnoticed from the others but by the time they had reached the back of the house the car was already heading away down the driveway. They waited until it had turned off into the clearing before breaking cover and sprinting to the steps at the side of the house. It was then that Whitlock had discovered the body of Brett slumped against the half-open cellar door. Graham had remained crouched at the top of the steps, out of sight of the car which had by then pulled up next to the helicopter.

Although armed, he knew the Beretta would be of little use from that range. There were snipers all around the house who would take Bernard out if he did make a mistake. *If.* But Graham knew Bernard better than any of them. Bernard wouldn't make a mistake. Which was why he and Whitlock had come up with an alternative plan. Whitlock, because of his injured arm, could only be a bystander. It simply added to his frustration. But he wanted to be with Graham when they put their plan into operation. They had a bond, an alliance. Bernard had escaped after Carrie and Mikey had gone missing. And now he was threatening to do the same again. Only this time he was using Rosie. And they knew her life would be worthless if he did manage to flee the country and start up a new life somewhere else. He had to be stopped.

Whitlock put a hand lightly on Graham's shoulder. Graham gave him a thumbs-up then broke cover and sprinted toward the helicopter as it began to slowly lift off the ground.

Demerest only saw Graham out of the corner of his eye when he was within ten yards of the helicopter. He instinctively applied more pressure on the collective-lever pitch to force the helicopter to climb further away from the ground. Graham, realizing he wouldn't reach the nearest landing pad from the ground, scrambled onto the Datsun's hood, then onto its roof, before launching himself at the pad. The fingers of his right hand touched the cold steel. He clamped his hand in a vice-like grip around the pad as the helicopter continued to rise further away from the ground. His arm felt as if it were going to be pulled out of its socket. Slowly, carefully, he brought up his left hand and his fingers curled around the pad, easing the pressure off his right arm. He began swaying from side to side then, when he felt he had enough momentum, he heaved himself upwards and managed to hook his right leg around the pad. Then he looked down. The helicopter was already a hundred feet above the ground and still climbing.

Demerest continued to glance anxiously out of the side window at Graham, mesmerized by the agility he'd used to haul himself up onto the landing pad. Bernard, who had already been alerted by Demerest, had his automatic at the ready, waiting. He knew instinctively it was Graham. It was exactly the sort of stunt he would pull. The man had a death wish. But he couldn't do anything until the helicopter was clear of the wood—and the snipers. And that was giving Graham valuable seconds to stabilize himself on the landing pad. Bernard knew what he had to do when he pulled open the door. His fingers tightened around the automatic.

Demerest had initially wanted to drag the pads

through the tops of the trees to try and dislodge Graham from the helicopter. Bernard had quickly ruled the idea out as too dangerous. What if one of the pads snagged on a thick branch? It could result in the helicopter losing altitude and ploughing into the trees. Demerest see-sawed the helicopter from side to side, desperately trying to pitch Graham off the pad—to no avail. Graham clung resolutely on, waiting, almost cat-like, for the moment when Bernard would open the door. The trees ended abruptly at the edge of the freeway. Demerest called out to Bernard that they were clear of the wood.

Bernard reached out a hand then yanked open the door. He was still raising the automatic to fire when Rosie slammed the sole of her boot against the side of his face, ripping open the bruise above his eye. He screamed in agony and the automatic fell from his grasp as he stumbled backwards, his hand clasped over his eye. The blood poured down through his fingers onto his shirt. He caught her with a vicious backhand slap which slammed her against the side of the cabin, knocking a wooden box off the wall above her.

He was still reaching for the fallen automatic when Graham launched himself through the doorway and felled him with a low football tackle. Bernard landed heavily on the floor and the automatic skidded toward the open door. It came to rest a foot away from the door. Graham pulled his Beretta from his shoulder holster but Bernard managed to grab his wrist and force the barrel up toward the ceiling. He slammed the back of Graham's hand against the side of the cabin and the Beretta fell from his fingers. He caught Graham with a hammering jab to the side of the face, rocking his head back against the floor. Graham lashed out with his elbow, catching Bernard squarely on his gashed eyebrow. Bernard recoiled in agony but was quick to react when Graham reached for the fallen Beretta.

They grappled for possession of the automatic but as

Bernard tore it from Graham's hand, Graham butted him viciously in the face, again catching him on the eyebrow. Bernard stumbled and as he fell the Beretta spun from his hands and disappeared through the open doorway. He brought his foot up sharply into Graham's stomach and as Graham buckled forward he caught him with a hammering punch to the face. Graham fell to his knees, his eyes watering from the force of the punch. Bernard dived for the Desert Eagle. Graham knew he could never reach Bernard before he recovered the automatic.

"Hey, catch," Rosie shouted to Graham.

Graham turned to Rosie. She was holding the Very pistol which had fallen out of the box when it landed on the floor. She threw it to him. He didn't even know if it was loaded, but there wasn't time to find out. Bernard was already turning, the automatic in his hand. Graham aimed the Very pistol at him and pulled the trigger. The aluminum-cased cartridge slammed into Bernard's chest with the force of a hammer. He was rocked back on his heels and lost his balance as he stepped out of the doorway. He clawed frantically at the side of the cabin but his bloodied fingers couldn't get a grip on the smooth surface and his eyes widened in horror as he fell backwards. The wind tore the scream from his lips as he plunged to his death.

Graham picked up the Desert Eagle which had slipped out of Bernard's hand as he fell and pressed it into the back of Demerest's neck. "Go back to the house."

"Sure thing, man," Demerest said nervously. "I don't want any trouble."

"Give me your piece," Graham demanded.

"I ain't carrying," Demerest replied, shaking his head vigorously. "I never carry. I'm just a flier, man."

Graham was convinced Demerest was telling the truth. "Give me the radio."

Demerest unhooked the radio and handed it to

Graham who called Philpott to let him know that they were returning to the safe house. He closed the cabin door then sat down beside Rosie and tilted her head gently as he looked at the discolored bruise that was already beginning to form on her left cheek.

"I'm OK," she said softly.

"Did you load it?" Graham asked, gesturing to the Very pistol on the floor in front of them.

She nodded. "I wanted to shoot him myself but I couldn't bring myself to pull the trigger. I'm sorry."

Graham smiled gently at her. "What are you apologizing for? You saved my life, Rosie. Thanks."

"Who are you?"

"My name's Mike."

"Mike Graham?"

"Yeah, how did you know?"

She took a cassette from her pocket and handed it to him. "Bernard—that is his name, isn't it?" Graham nodded. "Well, he gave it to me before we left the house. He said I was to give it to my uncle when I saw him again. He was to give it to you."

"Did he say what was on the tape?"

She shook her head.

Graham sat back against the side of the cabin and turned the cassette around slowly in his fingers. His name had been printed in capital letters on both sides in black pen. It had to contain something about Carrie and Mikey. But it didn't make any sense. Bernard wasn't the sort of man to gloat. It wasn't in his nature. So why had he made the cassette for him? The question lingered in his mind for the rest of the journey back to the safe house.

The helicopter was surrounded by members of the SWAT team when it landed in the clearing. Demerest closed down the engine then unbuckled his safety belt and clambered out of the cockpit. He was immediately handcuffed and led away toward a police car.

The door was pulled open from the outside and Whitlock peered anxiously into the cabin. Rosie smiled at him then bit her lip as a tear trickled down her face. Graham helped Whitlock into the cabin then went off to find something to use to cut Rosie free.

"Thank God you're safe," Whitlock said, hurrying over to her.

She hugged him and suddenly the tears began to spill down her face. Whitlock took a handkerchief from his pocket and gave it to her. She smiled self-consciously as she wiped her eyes.

"Who hit you?" he asked, a sudden anger entering his voice. "Bernard?"

She nodded. "I'm OK. What happened to your arm?"

"It's nothing," he replied with a dismissive shrug. "Your parents are going to be over the moon when they find out you're safe. So will Carmen. We've all been out of our minds with worry."

"Is it still alright if I come and stay with you and Carmen for a few days? Just until I feel strong enough to face my parents again."

"The spare bed's already made up," Whitlock replied. "You can stay as long as you want, you know that."

"Knock, knock," Graham said, peering into the cabin.

"Come in, Mike," Whitlock said, looking round at Graham.

Graham climbed back into the helicopter, a small hacksaw in his hand. "We'll have you out of here in no time, Rosie."

"How come you two know each other?" Rosie asked as Graham crouched down beside her.

Graham glanced at Whitlock, waiting for him to answer. It was up to him to decide whether he was going to tell her about UNACO. In some ways Graham felt she deserved an explanation but he wouldn't say anything, not without Whitlock's lead.

Whitlock gave her a knowing smile. "You get to meet a lot of different people in the diplomatic corps. I first met Mike at a reception at the UN. We've bumped into each other a few times since then. Mike called me when they'd found out where Bernard was holding you. I got over here as quick as I could."

"Are you a cop?" she asked Graham.

Graham stopped cutting to look up at her. "Yeah, a sort of a cop."

"A sort of a cop?" she queried. "What kind of an answer's that?"

"The only one you're getting," Graham replied then went back to cutting through the handcuff around her wrist.

"I can take a hint," she said.

It took Graham another minute to cut through the handcuff. He plied apart the two halves and she pulled her wrist free.

"Well, are you ready for a hot bath, a good meal and a long sleep in a warm bed?" Whitlock asked her.

"You bet," she replied, rubbing her chafed wrist.

"Come on then," Whitlock said, helping her to her feet.

"Thanks, Mike," she said softly then kissed him lightly on the cheek.

"Get out of here," he said good-humouredly.

She followed Whitlock to the door then looked back at Graham. "Are you an undercover cop?"

"Yeah, a sort of an undercover cop," Graham replied poker-faced.

She smiled. "Bye, Mike."

"See you, Rosie," Graham replied with a smile.

Sabrina waited until Whitlock and Rosie had been helped out of the helicopter before looking in at Graham. "You're crazy, do you know that?"

"Sure, I know that," Graham replied, nodding his head. "How come it's taken you so long to realize it?"

"Why didn't either of you say anything before you went off like that?"

"I'm sure the Colonel would have sanctioned what we had in mind, aren't you? I take it he's pretty pissed off about what we did."

"He's only pissed off that neither of you told him what you were going to do. He actually seems quite pleased with the outcome. He wants to see you. Now."

Graham moved to the door and was about to jump to the ground when something caught his eye on the floor in the corner of the cabin. He went over for a closer look.

"What is it?" Sabrina asked.

"It's a computer disc," he replied then picked it up and looked round at her. "Are you thinking what I'm thinking?"

"Aha," she said, slowly nodding her head. "Bernard's insurance policy."

"It must have fallen out of his pocket when we were fighting. This is quite a coup for UNACO."

"Especially as the CIA don't even know we've got it," Sabrina added.

"And knowing the antagonism that exists between the Colonel and Langley, you can bet your life he's going to keep it that way."

"We'll have to return it to them, of course," Philpott said, taking the disc from Graham.

"Return it to them?" Graham said in disbelief. "I don't understand, sir. We could monitor all the operations on this disc for years to come without Langley's ever knowing about it."

"We will," Philpott replied. "These covert operations are obviously very important to the company so it's highly unlikely that they'll be terminated after

Bailey's gone. They'll just be assigned to a new controller, possibly Bailey's successor. But if Langley know we're monitoring these operations, they'll want to make sure that none of their agents are compromised. And that's where we can turn it to our advantage. Our silence will have a price. I think you'll find that they'll be a lot more co-operative in the future. And let's face it, that can't be a bad thing, can it?''

"No, sir," Graham replied with a knowing smile.

Philpott slipped the disc into his pocket. "Now, about this little escapade of yours."

"It was my idea, sir," Graham said.

"Strange, those were C.W.''s exact words as well. Whose idea it was is irrelevant. What does bother me is that neither of you said anything before you sloped off. I thought you'd have both learned your lesson by now about keeping things from Sergei and me. Obviously you haven't."

"You wouldn't have sanctioned it anyway, sir."

"That's not the point, Michael," Kolchinsky said sharply. "We're your superiors. Not that that seems to have made much impression on any of you these past few days, especially you. It's because of your maverick tendencies that Strike Force Three is the subject of this internal investigation."

"Bernard killed my family, Sergei—my wife and my five-year-old son. What the hell was I supposed to do when I heard he'd been seen in Beirut?" Graham held up his hand before Kolchinsky could answer. "Yeah, I know, tell you. Then you could have made the necessary arrangements to have him taken into custody. Then what? Would they have extradited him to face charges over here? You know they wouldn't. He'd probably have been put on a plane bound for Libya and been given a hero's welcome when he got there. I don't expect you to understand the torment I've been through these last two years.

"Hell, I'm not going to stand here and explain myself

to you, Sergei. I did what I thought was right not only for the memory of my family but also for my own piece of mind. My only regret is that I had to drag Sabrina and C.W. into it as well. That's why I resigned—to spare them any further trouble. And if you've got any sense you'll accept my resignation and put an end to the matter."

"Your resignation is on my desk," Philpott said, holding Graham's stare. "And it'll be considered more carefully when the results of the investigations are known. Until then, you're still part of this organization. And that means co-operating fully with the investigation. You'll each be interviewed individually this afternoon. The panel will use my office as a base. So be there at two o'clock sharp."

"When will the results be known?" Sabrina asked.

"Late this afternoon. I'm dining with the Secretary-General tonight. We'll discuss the findings then."

Sabrina glanced at her watch. Three forty-seven A.M. She stifled a yawn. "Can we get some sleep now, sir?"

"Yes, go on. I won't see you this afternoon. I'll be in Washington talking to Morgan Chilvers, the CIA Director. But Sergei will be at the UN. We'll all meet again in my office at nine o'clock tomorrow morning to discuss the implications of the findings. By then I'll also know how the Secretary-General stands on the issue. Sabrina, will you give Mike a lift back to his hotel?"

"Sure," she replied. "Does C.W. know about the meeting tomorrow morning?"

"Yes, I told him before he took Rosie home." Philpott's eyes flickered toward Graham. "You did well tonight, Mike."

"Rosie's safe, that's all that matters now," Graham looked at Sabrina. "Ready?"

She nodded then said good night to Philpott and Kolchinsky before hurrying after him.

"You got a tape deck in your car?" Graham asked.

"No, only a CD player. Why?"

He took the cassette from his pocket and showed it to her. "Bernard gave this to Rosie before they left the house. It's for me. It has to be something about Carrie and Mikey."

"I've got a tape deck at the apartment. You can listen to it there."

He looked at his watch. "You sure you don't mind?"

"Don't be silly," she replied, unlocking the driver's door.

"Thanks, I appreciate it."

She climbed into the car and opened the passenger door for him. He slipped the cassette back into his shirt pocket then got in beside her. She drove back up the approach road and rejoined the highway. "Thanks," Graham said, taking the cup of hot chocolate from Sabrina and placing it on the table beside him. "It's a nice place you've got here."

"Liar," she said with a grin.

"Sure, it's a bit arty for my taste but it's still a lot better than I thought it would be—seriously. I'll tell what does impress me, though: your CD collection. You've got some good jazz there."

"You know how much I love jazz music," she said, glancing down at the row of compact discs on the shelf beside the player. Her eyes shot to the cassette on the table. "I'll leave you alone to listen to the tape. I'll be in the kitchen when you're through."

"Yeah, thanks," he replied then waited until she had left the room before pressing the "play" button. He sat down, his arms resting on his knees, his eyes riveted on the cassette as it turned slowly on the spools.

"When you receive this tape, Graham, I'll have already left the country with the intention of starting up a new life in some distant corner of the world. I know you'll never stop looking for me and, frankly, I can't say I blame you. I know you've always held me personally responsible for what happened to your wife, Carol, and your son, Michael. This tape isn't an attempt to try and exonerate myself. I can't. I'll always be partly responsible for their deaths, I know that. But you have the right to know what really happened that afternoon outside your apartment in New York.

"I was in Libya at the time on the orders of the CIA—or Robert Bailey, to be more specific. As you no doubt know by now, he's been my handler ever since I first started working for the company. The reason I was there was because Salim Al-Makesh, who was then a senior advisor in Abu Nidal's Black June movement, had come up with a plan to mount a bombing operation across the United States. The idea was to hit, amongst others, shopping malls, sports stadiums and school buildings—in other words, a soft target campaign. The CIA found out about it through a mole they had in the Black June movement but he was killed under mysterious circumstances before he could pass on all the information to them. Whether he was murdered, or whether he died accidently, was never established. But the CIA were worried because they still didn't know exactly where and when the bombs were due to go off. That's why I was sent to meet with Al-Makesh—to fill in the missing dates so that the bombers could be arrested when they arrived in the United States.

"We'd been talking for about forty minutes, without much success I might add, when we first heard that you, and your men, had surrounded the base camp. But at the time we had no idea who you were or where you'd come from. So I called Bailey in Washington and told him what was happening. He knew that if Al-Makesh were killed, the CIA would have lost their last chance to prevent the bombing campaign. I don't know how he found out but it wasn't five minutes later when he rang back to say that it was a unit of the US anti-terrorist squad, Delta. Then I knew we were in trouble. Apart from the two of us, there were another eight men at the base—no match for a crack Delta unit. Bailey said he would 'arrange something'. Those were his exact words. He called back a few minutes later to say that the Delta unit would be pulled out. That was great news—until you attacked. Al-Makesh ordered his men to stand and fight then he took me to an underground tunnel and we managed to get out only minutes before your unit overran the camp.

"I called Bailey that night to find out what had gone wrong. That's when he told me what had really happened. He had found out that a Delta unit was in the area, under your command, but he couldn't risk telling your commanding officer that I was a CIA asset without compromising my position. He knew it was your first operation as a unit leader and, understandably, he thought you might crack, given the right pressure. Your wife and son were kidnapped on his orders to force you to give the order to pull back. I know several eyewitnesses claimed that three Arabs, all wearing balaclavas, were involved in the kidnapping because they were sure the men had been speaking a language similar to Arabic. It was Arabic but they weren't Arabs. They were Americans speaking Arabic: Bailey's men—Paul Brett, Jack Rogers and a third man called Kennedy, Rick Kennedy. He was killed in a light plane crash a few months ago.

"Your wife and son were brought here, to this safe house. That's why I came here after I was forced to leave the apartment in Murray Hill. It's the only other CIA safe house that I know of in the United States. I don't know whether Bailey ever intended to let them go but it seems your wife went for one of the men after he'd manhandled your son and in the ensuing struggle she managed to unmask him. They couldn't let either of them go after that. Both were shot that same day and their bodies buried at the back of the house. I don't know exactly where but it was somewhere close to the house. That's what happened, Graham. I don't expect you to take my word for it. There's a file in Bailey's computer entitled 'Operation Delta'. It's all there. I'm sure your Colonel Philpott will be given access to it by the CIA.

"You must be wondering right now why I made this tape for you. Well, I can answer that in one word— respect. Like me, you're a field man, and one of the best by all accounts. Bailey's a desk man who manipulates the lives of the people around him. He may have been my controller, but that didn't mean I had to respect him. How could I? You, though, gained my respect the moment you gave the order to attack. You believed in your principles enough to sacrifice your own family for them. That's the mark of a true soldier.

"But having said that, the past can never be undone. We both have to live with what happened that day. Each of us has our own guilt to bear. And no matter what happens, we'll have to carry that guilt to our graves. *Assalam alaikum.*"

Graham sat back in the chair and rubbed his hands slowly over his face. He knew the anger would come, in time. But at that moment all he felt was relief, relief that the last pieces of the jigsaw had finally slotted into place. At last, he knew the truth. The pain and the anguish of the past two years were at an end. But most importantly of all, Carrie and Mikey could now be laid to rest in sacred ground. Carrie had always been the religious one of the family, and he knew she would have wanted it, not only for herself, but for Mikey as well—together, side by side for ever.

He switched off the tape deck, pocketed the cassette, then picked up his cup and went through to the kitchen. Sabrina was sitting at the pine table.

"Are you OK?" she asked softly.

"Yeah," he replied then went on to quickly outline the gist of what Bernard had said on the cassette.

"I'm sorry, Mike," she said softly when he'd finished speaking.

"I always knew they were dead. I can't explain why, though. I guess it's just a feeling you have when you're as close as I was to them. What's always preyed on my mind these last couple of years was the fact that they'd never had a proper burial. But now I can rectify that. Then I can visit the graves every week and be with them again." He shrugged uncomfortably. "I know that sounds kind of corny . . ."

"Only to you. You've never allowed your feelings to surface since they disappeared, have you? You've always made yourself out to be the hard, uncaring maverick. Well, that's the image you wanted to portray, and it's worked with most people. It even worked with me, at first. But not now. I've seen the other side of Mike Graham. And he's not as hard as he likes the world to believe."

"Yeah?" he said then put the cup down on the table. "It's late. I'd better be going."

"There's a spare room. It's only ever used when my parents come up from Miami."

"No, I want to get back to the hotel. But thanks anyway."

"OK. I'll get my keys."

"I'll get a cab. You need your beauty sleep."

"Don't be silly—"

"I'm taking a cab." Graham indicated the cup on the table. "Thanks for the hot chocolate."

She nodded then got up and walked him to the front door. "Are you sure I can't give you a lift? It's no trouble."

"I'm sure." He opened the door then looked back at her. "See you this afternoon."

She kissed him lightly on the cheek. "Night, Mike."

"Yeah," he muttered and closed the door behind him.

EPILOGUE

"Hello, Mike," Sarah said as Graham entered the room.

"Hi," he replied, closing the door behind him. "Are C.W. and Sabrina here yet?"

"They've already gone through," Sarah replied then switched on the intercom and announced Graham's arrival.

"Send him in, Sarah," Philpott replied.

The door slid open and Graham walked into Philpott's office. He greeted Philpott then nodded to Sabrina and Whitlock who were sitting on one of the black sofas.

"I'm not late, am I, sir?" Graham said, looking at his watch. "You did say nine."

"You're not late. Sit down."

Graham sat on the second sofa. "Is there any news from the safe house yet?"

"Yes, word came through about an hour ago. The police have found something. Sergei's over there now. I'm waiting for his call."

"Something, sir?"

Philpott turned his empty pipe around slowly in his fingers then pushed it away from him. "Human remains. I've arranged to have you driven out there as soon as we're through here."

"Thank you, sir."

Philpott tapped the folder in front of him. "These are the findings of the internal investigation. It's highly critical of C.W. and Sabrina for withholding information from Sergei during the course of the assignment, especially you, Sabrina. You became involved in the politics of a foreign power, a point the Secretary-General raised on several occasions. I know it's easy to fall into that trap when an assignment verges on the political, but you have to know where to draw the line. That's what the Charter's there for, to clarify those boundaries. And if you're still not sure, you ask. We have enough enemies at the UN as it is without further aggravating the situation by blatantly taking sides as you did in Zimbala. What if it hadn't turned out the way it did? What if Ngune had seized power? We would have been branded mercenaries. There are already whispers to that effect amongst some of the more radical African and Asian countries as it is. Why give them the ammunition they want to shoot us down? You're here because you're regarded as the best in the business. Let's act that way, shall we?"

"Yes, sir," Sabrina muttered guiltily.

Philpott's eyes shifted to Graham and he shook he head slowly. "I don't even know where to start with you. I'm not going to go through all the rules you've broken in these past few days, you know what they are already. And that's what makes it all the more serious—your blatant disregard for your colleagues and for UNACO in general. And even when Sabrina went out to Beirut to bring you back you gave her an ultimatum that put her in an impossible position. She had no option but to go along with your plan. And that's what got her into trouble in the first place."

"It was my decision, sir," Sabrina said. "I could have reported Mike when I spoke to Sergei but I thought it best to work with him rather than against him. And I doubt Sergei would have understood that, do you?"

"Your loyalty's touching, Sabrina," Philpott said. "But the fact remains that Mike disobeyed a directive to return home with you."

"And can you blame him?" she shot back. "What would have happened if he had come back with me? Bernard would probably have succeeded in killing President Mobuto. It was only Mike's determination that eventually led us to Remy Mobuto and to ultimately preventing a serious embarrassment to the White House."

"But those weren't Mike's intentions when he went after Bernard, were they?" Philpott said, glancing from Sabrina to Graham. "Your sole intention was to put a bullet in him, wasn't it?"

"Initially," Graham replied. "But when Sabrina agreed to work with me, my first duty was to prevent Mobuto's being assassinated, not to put a bullet in Bernard. I've already explained all this at the hearing yesterday."

"Which brings me to another point. You were even abusive to the panel of investigators. Why?"

"Four desk men: two ex-CIA, two ex-Feds. What the hell do they know about field work? All they've done is push pens all their lives. Their questions were loaded and misleading and my answers were twisted when I did try to explain myself. What was I expected to do, sir? Thank them?"

Philpott shook his head in dismay. "The Secretary-General wants you thrown out, do you know that?"

"You have my resignation, sir."

"Yes, I do. But that doesn't mean I'm going to accept it. I'm the Director of UNACO. You're my operatives and I have the final say on whether anyone is to be dismissed from this organization. And the Secretary-

General knows that." Philpott removed the letter from the folder and tossed it onto the desk. "Get rid of it before it falls into the wrong hands."

Graham got up and took it off the desk.

"That doesn't mean I condone your actions for one moment, Mike. I had to do a lot of hard talking to convince the Secretary-General that you were worth a second chance."

"I appreciate it, sir."

"I should hope so," Philpott shot back. "I realize this was a one-time situation. And now that Bernard and Bailey are dead, perhaps we can expect a little more co-operation from you in the future. Believe me, Mike, you screw up again and you will be out. That goes without saying. There's a black mark against your name right now and it's up to you to prove to UNACO, and the Secretary-General, that you're worthy of another chance."

"I won't let you down, sir."

"No, you won't, because I won't be here."

"I don't understand, sir." Graham said, frowning.

"My doctor nearly had a heart attack of his own when he found out I was back at work. He thought I was resting at home. He's told me that the next attack could be the big one. That's why I submitted my resignation to the Secretary-General last night. I'll be leaving as soon as I've handed over properly to Sergei. He'll be taking over as the new Director."

"And who's taking his place?" Sabrina asked.

Philpott gestured toward Whitlock. "I know all the Strike Force teams will give him their full support."

Sabrina was the first to congratulate him, kissing him lightly on the cheek. Graham pumped his hand firmly.

"I know C.W. still has some reservations about the job, because, like you, Mike, he's not a great admirer of the desk man. But let's face it, C.W., you're not getting any younger, you know."

"So Carmen keeps reminding me," Whitlock said.

"How long have you known about this?" Sabrina asked Whitlock.

"A couple of months now. Look, I would have told you guys before but I was sworn to silence."

"Has anyone been pencilled in to take C.W.'s place yet?" Graham asked.

Philpott nodded. "We've been grooming his successor for the last six weeks. You worked with him on your last assignment when he was still with the Italian antiterrorist squad, the NOCS."

"Fabio Paluzzi?" Sabrina said.

"Yes. As you know he's been with Strike Force Nine since he joined us from the NOCS. But that was just to let him get the feel of the organization. He'll be taking over from C.W. in the next couple of weeks."

"That's great," Sabrina said with a grin then quickly patted Whitlock on the arm. "Don't take that the wrong way, C.W."

"I would if I didn't know you better."

"I'll be briefing Fabio this afternoon, so if you do happen to see him before that, don't say anything."

"Drinks at my apartment tonight," Whitlock said. "I'll invite Fabio after the Colonel's had a word with him. Mike, I hope you can make it but I'd fully understand if you wanted to be by yourself tonight."

"I'll be there, buddy," Graham said, wagging a finger at him. "You just make sure the Perrier's cold."

"It's already in the fridge," Whitlock replied with a smile.

"C.W., Sabrina, I'd like a few words with Mike. I'll see you both at the flat tonight."

Sabrina paused in front of Graham and put a hand lightly on his shoulder. "If you want to talk, you know where to find me."

"I might take you up on that," Graham replied. "It just depends what time I get away from the safe house."

"See you, Mike," Whitlock said then followed Sabrina from the room.

Philpott activated the door behind them. "I spoke to Sergei and C.W. after I'd seen the Secretary-General last night. They're both behind you one hundred percent. Don't let them down."

"Sergei? He's been on my back ever since I got back from Zimbala."

"Quite right, too. You screwed up, Mike. Badly. But he also knows how valuable you are to the organization. We all do, that's why you're still here. I doubt any other operative would have been given another chance if they'd flouted the rules as you've done. You've got the potential to be the best operative UNACO's ever had, but you've got to work on this maverick streak that seems to come out at the worst possible times. I know a lot of it has to do with what happened to your family. You always felt that someone at Delta had let slip your position to Bernard and Al-Makesh. Trust suddenly became a dirty word in your book. But now you know the truth. It had nothing to do with any of your men. Use that knowledge to channel your resources positively back into Strike Force Three from now on.

"I don't have to tell you how lucky you are to have Sabrina as a partner. There isn't a field operative here who wouldn't give his right arm to trade places with you. Not only that, she also thinks the world of you. That's a great compliment from a fellow professional. And now Fabio's coming in. He'll need to draw off both of you until he's found his feet. And that means supporting him. What use will you be to him if you're going to continue with these maverick tendencies? Now that C.W."'s coming onto the management side, you'll be the most experienced field operative not only in Strike Force Three but in the whole of UNACO. That's quite a responsibility, Mike. Added to which you'll be officially promoted to team leader when Fabio joins you. And a good leader always leads by example, doesn't he? You of all people should know that."

"Yes, sir, I do."

"There's a car waiting outside to take you over to the safe house."

"Thank you, sir."

Philpott activated the door then closed it again behind Graham. Sarah looked up from her typing as Graham approached her desk.

"Excuse me," he said then leaned across the desk and dropped the letter into the shredding machine beside her. 'Things that are done, it is needless to speak about. Things that are past, it is needless to blame.' "

She frowned.

"Confucius," he added.

She watched him leave the office then, shrugging her shoulders, went back to her typing.

ALISTAIR MACLEAN, who died in 1987, was the best-selling author of thirty books, including world famous novels such as *The Guns of Navarone* and *Where Eagles Dare*.

ALASTAIR MACNEILL was born in Scotland in 1960. His family moved to South Africa when he was six years old, where he showed a growing interest in writing, winning several school competitions. He returned to Britain in 1985 to pursue a full-time writing career.

CAMPBELL ARMSTRONG

Agents of Darkness

Suspended from the LAPD, Charlie Galloway decides his life has no meaning. But when his Filipino housekeeper is murdered, Charlie finds a new purpose in tracking the killer. He never expects, though, to be drawn into a conspiracy that reaches from the Filipino jungles to the White House.

Mazurka

For Frank Pagan of Scotland Yard, it begins with the murder of a Russian at crowded Waverly Station, Edinburgh. From that moment on, Pagan's life becomes an ever-darkening nightmare as he finds himself trapped in a complex web of intrigue, treachery, and murder.

Mambo

Super-terrorist Gunther Ruhr has been captured. Scotland Yard's Frank Pagan must escort him to a maximum security prison, but with blinding swiftness and brutality, Ruhr escapes. Once again, Pagan must stalk Ruhr, this time into an earth-shattering secret conspiracy.

Brainfire

American John Rayner is a man on fire with grief and anger over the death of his powerful brother. Some say it was suicide, but Rayner suspects something more sinister. His suspicions prove correct as he becomes trapped in a Soviet-made maze of betrayal and terror.

Asterisk Destiny

Asterisk is America's most fragile and chilling secret. It waits somewhere in the Arizona desert to pave the way to world domination...or damnation. Two men, White House aide John Thorne and CIA agent Ted Hollander, race to crack the wall of silence surrounding Asterisk and tell the world of their terrifying discovery.